COURTSIDE

TAYLOR E WESTON

This one is for the sports girls.

PREFACE

This book contains sexually explicit content and explicit language. Additionally, there are references to the following content that may be triggering to some readers: past grooming behavior*, past adult/minor relationship*, and confronting a past abuser*.

None of the mentioned content occurs between the two main characters.

CHAPTER 1
A GIRL WALKS INTO A BAR
SAGE

Late summer 2016

Sage Fogerty should be unpacking.

The responsible thing would be to cook dinner, open a bottle of the peach wine that everyone told her tasted like garbage but that she loved anyway, and tackle the pile of boxes that sat in the middle of her new apartment.

But instead she walked down the sidewalk, the late-summer night still hot enough that it left her not quite sweating but not entirely comfortable either. Jeans probably hadn't been the best choice, but they were the first thing she'd found rifling through her packed clothes. At least the white camisole she'd stolen from her older sister Brinley didn't require a bra.

Sage loved Charleston at night — the lingering warmth from the day punctuated by the occasional breeze curling up from the water had captured her from the very first time she'd come to visit Brinley at Southeastern University. Brinley had fallen in love with South Carolina, undergoing — in their mother's words — a "Southern belle awakening." She'd joined a sorority, learned how to straighten her hair, wear eye cream, and perfectly color-match her foundation. It was jarring at first when Brinley had come home from college with a Vera Bradley bag and wearing a full face of makeup, but honestly, the transformation suited her.

Eight years later, when it was Sage's turn to pick a college, she ended up following in her sister's footsteps, leaving Santa Barbara, the only home she'd ever known, and catching a one-way flight across the country.

Now, after finishing four years of undergrad, Sage was back in Charleston to complete her fifth year master's in Sports Management.

She was back, and very fucking alone. She could have tried to find new roommates, but the thought of living with strangers as a grad student was, quite frankly, nauseating.

She'd lucked out with her three roommates from freshman year, and it'd been easy for them to stick together. Danika was a soccer player, Mary had shared Sage's love of Western romance novels, and Cori had been the life of the party. While they didn't share *everything* in common, they'd gotten along well enough that they'd lived together through all four years of undergrad.

Just that morning, Mary had texted their group chat a photo of herself wearing a felt cowboy hat. *"Texas, y'all,"* she'd said. Dannika had responded with a picture of the Chicago skyline from her high-rise apartment's balcony, and then Cori had almost immediately replied with a photo of textbooks piled high on a table next to a picturesque latte and croissant.

What was Sage supposed to respond with? *Hey, here's my apartment in the same city you all just moved away from?* Instead she'd sent a picture of one of her spider plants that had just grown about five new runners all at the same time. *Babies!* she'd texted.

She checked her phone, finding no new messages. Straightening her shoulders, she looked up at the intentionally weathered wooden sign with dark letters spelling out: The Grove.

She and Cori had been to The Grove many times over the years. It was one of their favorite spots, for multiple reasons. Firstly, it catered to young professionals, meaning the crowd was generally older and more into beer and live music than jello shots and DJs. Secondly, they had the best jalapeño margarita in Charleston. Spicy and sweet? Fucking transcendent. And thirdly, their food was greasy and delicious in the best way possible. While Sage tended to eat veggies when she cooked for herself, she was a big believer in variety and moderation.

She flashed her ID at the bouncer who stood by the tall fence that bordered the bar. A wrought-iron gate served as the entrance, and inside a large courtyard was filled with picnic tables under the shade of wide-reaching live oak trees. There was a small stage tucked into one corner of the space with a dance floor cleared out in front of it, and along the opposite side was a brightly polished wooden bar lined with tall bar stools.

It was already crowded, even though daylight was only just beginning to fade. Strings of Christmas lights draped from the branches lit up the space, and Sage had to duck under a few of the strands as she made her way over to the bar.

Sliding onto an open stool, she made eye contact with the bartender. She'd seen the purple-haired woman a few times, although if she remembered correctly, her hair had been black the last time she was there.

"What can I get ya?" The woman slapped a square napkin down on the bar and grinned at Sage, revealing slightly crooked front teeth.

"Jalapeño margarita, please," Sage replied, raising her voice so she could be heard over the din of laughter and conversation.

Purple-hair gave her a nod as she began to assemble the drink. "Good choice. I like a woman who likes it spicy."

Sage couldn't help the snorted laugh, tossing her blonde hair back behind her shoulder. It had gotten long, down past the middle of her back, and if she didn't spend most of the time with it braided or in a ponytail she would probably consider cutting it short. "What can I say? I like a little pain with my pleasure."

The bartender let out a cackle that was loud, even with the background buzz. "I like you, blondie. You from 'round here?"

Sage shook her head. "California. I've been here for school."

"Ooooh, a smartie pants, are ya?" She wiggled heavily drawn brows. "What are you studyin'?"

"Sports management," Sage said. "Oh, and no straw," she added, stopping the woman before she grabbed one of the clear cocktail straws. Ever since she'd read about plastic straws being found up the noses of dead sea turtles, she swore them off. She had no idea if it was actually making a difference, but fuck it — she could try.

"I like you and I've decided that we're gonna be friends." The bartender set the drink down on the napkin before extending a hand. "I'm Maggie."

Sage blinked once before reaching out and shaking her hand. "Sage." She let go and reached for the drink. "Are you always like this?"

Maggie cackled again. She looked to be a few years older than Sage, maybe in her late 20's, and she wore a black band tee with cut off sleeves and jean shorts.

"Life's too short to pretend that some people aren't really fuckin' awesome, and others aren't really fuckin' terrible." Maggie shrugged, stepping away toward the other end of the bar. "And I have a feelin' that you're pretty fuckin' awesome."

Sage couldn't help but grin at that, watching as Maggie turned to take orders at the other end of the bar. Grabbing her margarita, Sage swiveled on her stool until she was facing the rest of the courtyard, crossed one knee over the other, and settled in to watch.

Like many college students, Sage had spent most of the past four years going out on the weekends. The first two years had mostly been frat parties or other house parties, with the occasional club trip facilitated by a *very* questionable fake ID that said she was a thirty year old woman named Dorthea Wiggenshoe. Once she and her roommates had moved to their house off campus, they gladly gave up the frat parties in favor of bars and clubs.

In that time, Sage had gotten very good at reading a room.

More specifically, she'd gotten good at evaluating potential…suitors? No, that wasn't right. Fuck buddies?

Sure.

Sage was *very* good at scoping out potential fuck buddies, and tonight, all that she wanted was to get tipsy and find someone to go home with. She wanted to get lost in the high of initial attraction, and ride the wave until she was in the bed of a man with facial hair and a big body who'd do deliciously wicked things to her until she'd had enough and decided to go home.

She was self-aware enough to know that she didn't appeal to the entirety of the male population. Her height alone — six feet — was a non-starter for about seventy five percent of the men in Charleston. Then there was the fact that she had the body of someone who'd spent long hours in the gym. Even though she'd lost a lot of her muscle throughout college, she'd never been able to walk away from the routine of lifting and running.

Her body hadn't caught on to the fact that there was nothing to train for. Not anymore.

But it still showed. It showed in the definition of her shoulders, in the way her thighs filled the legs of her jeans and in the build of her arms. And in general, Sage fucking *loved* her powerful body, but she was a realist and knew that not all men would be into it.

It just meant that she looked carefully, searching for signs of potential compatibility before making a move. Sage's type, according to Cori, was "tall and ancient," to which Sage had argued that preferring men with adult jobs over college frat boys who all had navy blue sheets and smelled like Irish Spring was basic logic. Height was the one thing she most frequently had to compromise on, but she made sure to look for bulk and mass that wouldn't be intimidated by her strength.

And even though it was just a hookup — for her, it was *always* just a hookup — Sage couldn't help but look for a genuine smile, a wide-mouthed laugh, and kind eyes. There was something about the look in a man's eyes where she could *immediately* get a sense for what he was about.

She'd only been wrong once.

Tonight the crowd was definitely the after work crew: men still in slacks and button-downs with the sleeves rolled up, or in branded polo shirts with khakis. There were a few outliers — three bikers in leathers with bandanas wrapped around their long, graying hair, two skinny white guys in tight jeans and black t-shirts who were ogling Maggie like she was a free VIP pass to Lollapalooza, and a group of six men, all wearing some version of athletic gear.

Her eyes snagged on the last group. They were sitting around a table, but a few looked like they could have the height. The three whose faces she could see were...well, they were decent looking, but didn't do anything in particular for her. The other three were facing away from her — one with a shaved head, one with a back-wards cap, and the last one with reddish blonde curls. Two of them had broad backs — a good sign.

She'd keep an eye on them.

Taking a long drink of her margarita, she looked over at one of the business bros who looked somewhat promising. He was tall... ish. Maybe had an inch on her? He was the kind of generic, good looking guy who worked out, had a jawline, and wore his dirty blonde hair parted to one side. Decent, but unremarkable. Maybe he was one of those people who was better off once you talked to them?

Movement back at the athletic gear table caught her attention. The man in the backwards hat rose from the table, and *fuck* he was tall. Like, maybe even 6'5" tall. His back was wide, muscles stretching against the fabric of his white t-shirt, and the black athletic shorts he wore only reached about halfway down thick thighs that were covered in a smattering of dark hair.

When he turned around, her entire body stilled. Breathing, blinking, fidgeting — it all stopped with the exception of her heartbeat, which seemed to get louder and louder until it was pounding like a bass drum in her ears.

He was the kind of big that said that he used to be an athlete — maybe still was — but age had softened him slightly, leaving bulk in the place of lean, defined muscle. From the front, she could see the V of his quads above his knees that indicated that he probably hit the leg press when he worked out.

Fuck did she love some defined thighs.

And his *face*. She guessed he was somewhere between 30 and 40, based on the laugh lines etched into the corners of his dark eyes. Brown hair stuck out from under his hat, long enough that it was almost curling over his forehead and around the nape of his neck. His face was clean-shaven, although there was the hint of afternoon shadow gathering along his strong jaw. His mouth rested in an easy smile, and Sage couldn't take her eyes off of him, tracking him as he walked toward the bar.

He was the kind of good looking that she felt in her entire body. The fine blonde hairs on her arms pricked, and she shifted in her seat in a failed attempt to relieve the distinct heat between her legs.

She registered the exact moment when he noticed her stare. His eyes met hers and he came to a sudden stop, focusing on her with heavy, earnest attention. She felt his gaze like a physical touch against her skin.

Sage refused to look away. She knew that some people preferred to play coy, to pretend that they weren't interested, but in her mind, why lie? When a man looked like *that*, why the fuck would she pretend?

She knew what she wanted.

He looked at her, *really* looked at her, and when his eyes trailed down her body, she felt her skin heat under his attention.

The man looked back up into her eyes and smiled. It was a good smile, one that was almost nervous as it creased the skin around his dark eyes. Her gaze dropped to his mouth just in time to watch his tongue dart out and wet his upper lip as he walked toward her, his long legs and easy stride on full display.

She didn't take her eyes away as he approached, sliding onto the empty stool beside her. He shifted so that he faced her, his long legs bent and one of his thick forearms braced on the bar in front of him.

"Hey," he said, his voice graveled and warm in a way that reminded her of a country singer in a rural bar. He was the kind of man who belonged on the pages of one of her Western romances, all big and dark-eyed and messy-haired under his baseball cap.

"Hi," she replied. Up close she could see that his eyes were a rich brown, framed by feminine eyelashes, with unruly, expressive brows. His nose was prominent, but didn't look at all out of place with the rest of his features.

"I'm David," he said, extending a hand toward her.

"Sage," she replied, taking his large hand, which was just rough enough to not be considered soft. "You're beautiful."

David's brows shot up as a deep laugh burst from him. He shook his head at her, blinking like he couldn't quite figure out how to respond. "I...thank you?"

Sage drained the last of her margarita and grinned. "You're welcome." She'd obviously caught him off guard.

"I think that's the first time a woman's ever called me beautiful," he finally said, eyes dancing with amusement. "I mean, I was thinking of using that word to describe you, but now you've stolen it."

"You poor thing," Sage teased, feeling her cheeks warm at the compliment.

"Can I buy you another of whatever you're drinking?" David asked, pointing at her empty glass.

She nodded. "Jalapeño margarita."

He wrinkled his nose, an unexpectedly adorable look on such a large man. "I can't handle spicy."

"But it makes everything better!"

David shook his head. "No way. I like my flavors predictable; sweet and salty are more than enough for me."

She scoffed. "That sounds like a terribly boring way to live."

With a low chuckle, David turned to the bar, waving to try to catch Maggie's attention.

Sage hadn't even noticed that she'd turned in her seat to face him. His legs had somehow gotten on either side of hers, close enough that if she widened her thighs slightly they'd brush against his. There was something about him that pulled her in, drawing her into his orbit in a matter of minutes.

"What can I get you and my new best friend?" Sage heard Maggie ask as she stopped in front of them.

David glanced over at Sage before turning back to the bartender. "A jalapeño margarita, and a Corona, dressed."

Maggie shot a wink at Sage. "This one's beautiful," she said, nodding her chin in David's direction. "Go get 'em, girl."

Sage felt her cheeks heat again as she let out a loud snort.

David looked indignantly between them. "I mean, I'm obviously flattered, but this is twice in five minutes that I've been called beautiful."

Maggie gave him a sympathetic smile as she mixed Sage's margarita. "It's the lashes. Anyone with eyelashes like yours automatically gets categorized as beautiful."

David rolled his eyes, and Sage couldn't help but laugh at the expression. She poked him in the arm, leaning her head close. "Please tell me you aren't actually complaining about two women gushing over how attractive you are."

He turned back toward her, his head angling down and leaving barely any space between their faces. She looked up, meeting his brown eyes.

"Sorry," he said, his voice low, quiet enough that his words were contained between the two of them. "You honestly caught me off guard." His eyes dipped down to her mouth before he looked back up at her. "I came out tonight with the guys planning on having two beers, destroying a plate of nachos and some loaded tots, and then calling it a night."

Sage shrugged, her lips curving up in a smirk. "I like nachos and tots."

A low humming sound came from David's throat. "And how about after the nachos?"

"And the tots. Don't forget the tots," she whispered. She could see the clumps in his lashes, where they clung together and curled. He was just so fucking *lovely*, while still being an absolute bear of a man. She couldn't imagine a more perfect combination.

David chuckled. "Sorry. Wouldn't dream of forgetting the tots." She felt the warmth of his breath against her cheek, and felt a shiver spread down her arms. "Would you want to come home with me *after* the nachos and tots?"

Sage searched his eyes, looking for any warning signs that would indicate that he wasn't safe, that leaving with him could go badly. But she saw nothing there but the hungry, heady gaze of a man who wanted a woman, preferably naked and in his bed.

With a slow grin, Sage closed the minimal distance between them, her cheek grazing against his as she set her lips against his ear and whispered, "Yeah, David. I think I would want that."

She felt the brush of soft hair against her bare shoulder as he stretched his arm along the back of her barstool. His fingertips were gentle against her back as they trailed down over her shoulder blade. All of her focus was pulled to where his skin touched hers, little pin-pricks that made her feel alive.

The clink of glass on the bar broke through the moment, and Sage turned to find her straw-less margarita and a sweating Corona with coarse salt clinging to the neck of the bottle and a lime wedge shoved in the top.

Behind the bar, Maggie watched them with a grin, fanning herself with one hand. "Shit, you two are hot. Like, whew. Hot damn. Two tall Amazonians fucking is a great day for humanity. Make those strong babies. Sports babies. Warrior babies."

Sage glanced over at David, who was watching Maggie ramble on with his mouth open, eyebrows arched like he couldn't quite believe what he was hearing. He turned to Sage. "Is she always like this?" he asked, not even trying to lower his voice.

Shaking her head, Sage grabbed her drink. "I literally just met her. I have no context for her behavior beyond what I've seen tonight."

Maggie reached down behind the bar, and suddenly Sage was hit in the shoulder with something cold. Looking down, she saw the ice cube skid across the bar where it landed.

She looked over at the bartender, who grinned at her wickedly.. Sage set down her drink slowly, looking Maggie dead in the eye, and then flicked the cube back at her.

Maggie shrieked as the cube hit her perfectly in the patch of bare skin exposed on her stomach. Sage broke down laughing, barely noticing David looking between the two women with obvious confusion.

"I honestly have no idea what's happening right now," he muttered, shoving the lime down into his beer with a long finger.

Maggie joined in laughing with Sage, flipping her the bird with a wide smile before she moved down the bar to help someone else. Sage turned back to David, taking a long drink as she raised her brows in a silent question.

David shook his head. "Was that flirting? It looked like middle school flirting."

Sage just laughed. "I think I just made a new friend." Suddenly she felt the weight of eyes on her, and glancing over David's shoulder, she realized that a few of the guys from the table where he'd been sitting were watching them with expressions that ranged from curious to amused. She nudged David's thigh with her knee. "Your friends are watching us," she said. One of them, the one with the strawberry blonde curls, looked vaguely familiar, but she couldn't place where she recognized him from.

David turned, the movement flexing the muscles in his arms,

and Sage had to bite back a groan. "Ah shit," he said. He turned back to Sage, wincing. "Please ignore them. They're, ah, a bit much."

"Am I stealing you away from them?" she asked, sincerely concerned that she'd taken David away from his friends. She'd be disappointed if he left her at that point, but she also wasn't one to encroach on someone's plans.

David shook his head, setting down his beer and reaching down to rest his hand on her denim-covered thigh. "No. No no. They get enough of me as it is." He let out a quiet laugh. "Honestly, they're probably placing bets on how quickly I strike out." His eyes flashed to hers, wide with sudden panic. "Ah, shit. Not like that's what this is, I just —"

"David." Sage reached out and grabbed a handful of his t-shirt over his chest. "We both know what this is. No need to pretend it's anything else."

For a moment, something crossed his face, but within a second it was gone, replaced by that wide smile that made her bones melt. "You're very cool. You know that, right?"

Sage shrugged one shoulder. "So I've been told."

David leaned forward, his hand on her thigh tightening its grip. His eyes dropped to her mouth.

He was going to kiss her. She knew it, he knew it. Probably the whole bar knew it was about to happen.

Their foreheads connected first, and it felt like each second slowed to a crawl as David's nose dragged across her cheek as his lips positioned over hers. Sage inhaled at the soft brush of his mouth, and then suddenly he was gone.

She blinked her eyes open; she hadn't even realized they'd closed. David maintained his hold on her thigh, but glared at the strawberry-blonde from the table, who now stood next to them looking like he'd rather be anywhere else.

"What the hell, Chuck?" David growled at him.

"I'm so sorry," the man said, glancing back over his shoulder at the table. "It's Tommy. He's a mess, and we've got to get him out of here."

Sage watched David's eyes fall closed for a second. "I'm going to kill that goddamn idiot," he said through gritted teeth. She could feel the tension rolling off of him in waves. "It's like college all over again."

The other man, Chuck, shifted on his feet. "Dude, if any of us could drive, we'd do it." To his credit, he looked genuinely apologetic.

David shook his head before looking at Chuck. "To be clear, I hate you right now. So damn much."

With a wince, Chuck nodded. "I know, man. I'm the worst, and I know it." He looked over at Sage, giving her an apologetic smile. "Hi. You seem lovely. I'm really sorry."

Heaving a sigh, David pushed his beer away. It was still half full, and it left a wet trail on the surface of the bar. "I'll be right over," he said to Chuck. He waited until his friend walked away before turning to Sage with a pained look in his eyes. "I...I have to go. I have a friend who's going through a divorce and he can't keep his shit together right now, and I guess I'm the only one sober enough to get him home. The last time I called him a ride he spent an hour crying to the driver and she gave him a one star review, so now no one will pick him up." He still held her thigh, and he rubbed his thumb back and forth over the denim. "I'm so sorry."

Sage gave him a small smile, trying to hide her disappointment. "It's okay," she said, and it wasn't a lie. It was going to be okay. It wouldn't be as okay as it could have been if she'd completed her night with this beautiful man, but it would, ultimately, be okay.

Things always turned out okay.

"How are you getting home?" David asked, searching her face.

"I walked here," she said, taking a long drink of her margarita.

It was the point in the night where she had to decide whether to bail or redirect. There was still time if she wanted to find someone else, but there was a part of her that couldn't shake the feeling that anyone else would be a consolation prize after the potential of her chemistry with David. It seemed impossible that she'd find anyone who compared.

"Can I order you a ride?" David was asking, his concern clear in the furrow of his dark brows.

Sage tried for a reassuring smile. "I live really close by, and I think I might stay a while."

David opened and then closed his mouth, looking down between them at the place where his large hand spanned her thigh. "Please let me help you get you home safely," he whispered. "Please, Sage."

Sage opened her mouth to argue, to say with absolute certainty that she could take care of herself, when across the bar, a male voice shouted above the music and conversation.

"Courtney! I'm coming for you, Courtney! You're my sunshine, Courtney, and the sun never sets!"

"Damnit!" David withdrew his hand from her leg, and she immediately felt the absence of him. He looked at her, *really* looked at her, before shaking his head one last time. "You're really something," he said, rising to his feet. "And I'm so sorry. You have no idea how sorry I am." He pressed his lips to her cheek in a kiss that was over before it even began, and then he was gone, his massive form retreating from the bar in long strides, moving toward the exit. She watched him, let her eyes drift down his muscular legs before jumping up to the broad expanse of his back.

As he reached the gate, he turned, looking at her one last time. She was certain that she mirrored the sad smile on his face, like there was an understanding between them that *something* had been lost that could have been.

Even if it was just for one night, it would have been something.

His dark eyes seemed to send something across the distance between them, like a message or a promise. She wasn't sure. But she felt something in that final moment before he turned and disappeared, and she knew, without a single doubt, that if she wasn't going home with that big, beautiful, brown-eyed man after sharing nachos and tots, then she wasn't going home with anyone.

CHAPTER 2
IN SPITE OF CAREFUL PLANNING
SAGE

Sage woke up to her alarm shrieking — she could never be bothered to change it from the pre-programmed sound — and the sun just barely brightening the sky. She rolled out of bed quickly, pulling on a sports bra and running shorts before putting the t-shirt she'd slept in back on again. She found a pair of socks and slipped on her running shoes. She stopped briefly in the kitchen, filling up her water bottle from the jug she kept in her fridge, and then quietly left her apartment.

The gym was only a few buildings over, and Sage had already integrated the new facility into the rhythm of her days. She climbed onto an open treadmill, upping the speed until she broke into a run, feeling her lungs expand and contract with the pounding rhythm of her steps as she found her pace.

She had to start her days like this. Even when the requirement to maintain a certain fitness level was no longer the driving force in her life, Sage still found herself drawn to both the external routine and the internal grounding that habitual exercise brought her.

It helped her maintain a clear head, and honestly just felt fucking good.

After a run and a cooldown that she knew was too short, she

dismounted and went over to the free weights. She worked through a circuit of lunges, squats, arm presses and curls, lifting enough weight that her muscles shook with the effort by the time she reached her final reps.

Finally she dropped down to the wide mat set up in a corner, busting out twenty push-ups before pausing, leaning back on her knees as she watched sweat drip down to the mat below her. Her breaths were heavy, and she forced herself to fill her lungs to full capacity, overriding the burn in her core.

As she leaned forward again, she caught a glimpse of a man walking down the sidewalk. Tall, well built, and walking a tiny dog. *Adorable*, she thought as she watched the golden dog's short legs working overtime to keep up with the man's long stride. The guy's ass was something far less wholesome than adorable, and Sage caught herself licking her lips as he disappeared from view. *Damn* there were some good looking men in the area.

She shook her head.

Her workout finished with a series of crunches with her legs lifted in the air above her that made her abs practically scream in pain. She pushed herself off the floor, cleaned up her area with one of the provided wipes, and then proceeded to hobble back to her apartment.

Did she stretch? Nope.

Did she know that she was supposed to stretch? Yep.

After a quick shower, Sage stood in the kitchen dressed in cut off jean shorts and a faded Fleetwood Mac shirt that had been her mom's, tossing the chopped ingredients of her breakfast scramble into a cast iron pan and stirring them absently while she warmed tortillas on the open range.

It was the first day of classes, so she didn't entirely know what to expect now that she was a grad student. Would there be the same endless stream of articles to read and papers to write? She had no idea.

It was going to be a good year. She'd landed her dream internship with the Southeastern Women's Soccer team. They were dominant — they'd won their conference eight out of the last nine years — and Danika had introduced Sage to the coach at the end of last year. It was a requirement for the Sports Management graduate program that everyone needed to get a managerial internship with either a collegiate or professional team. While Southeastern was only a NCAA Division III school, they were still known for having strong sports programs.

Sage had put in hours of effort to earn the Women's Soccer Team Manager spot. Because they were so good, it was one of the most sought after positions, and even though Sage didn't have a soccer background, she'd studied her ass off to learn the game well enough to impress the coaches.

The team had already started practicing, but she hadn't heard yet when she'd officially start. She supposed they wouldn't need her until the games began.

She heated her copper kettle, making a to-go thermos of Earl Gray with milk and honey. She'd never been able to handle coffee, but the caffeine of black tea was the perfect balance for her.

Since she still had a little bit of time before she had to leave for her first class, Sage took her tea and breakfast tacos out to her small balcony. She'd set up a hammock chair and a small folding table, and along all of the edges she had potted plants in varying stages of growth. Some, like the hibiscus that was practically a tree, had been with her since her freshman year, while others, like the hanging fuschia and the window box of pansies, were new.

Done with her breakfast, she quickly hand-washed her dish and ducked into her bathroom, where she brushed her teeth and pulled her long hair back into a single braid that hung down her back. She ignored her makeup.

Moving through her apartment, she grabbed her backpack, refilled her water bottle, and then slipped her feet into the worn pair of Birkenstocks that sat beside the front door. Locking her door behind her, she ran down the stairs.

Sage jogged up the wide, stone steps toward the front entrance of the Robert D. Humphrey Athletic Center, pausing only to give a friendly slap to the tail feathers of Eckbert the Eagle, their rather unfortunately named mascot, who was captured in a ferocious bronze statue that greeted everyone who approached.

The massive, limestone building housed the natatorium, gym, and the shared basketball and volleyball practice courts, in addition to the typical things one would expect from a small college's athletic facility: racquetball and squash courts, a weight room and fitness room, and numerous classrooms.

It was where she'd spent the majority of her time at Southeastern University, as almost all of her Sports Management classes met in the mostly windowless classrooms tucked in the lower floors of the building.

The wall of freezing air hit her as soon as she walked into the high-ceilinged atrium. Mindlessly, she unzipped her backpack and grabbed the crewneck sweatshirt she carried with her everywhere. Sure, it was hot in Charleston, but did everyone have to have the air conditioning so fucking cold?

She barely took in the trophy cases and dark green and gold accents that covered the walls around her, and resolutely ignored the wide bank of doors that led into the gymnasium, instead turning to the staircase that led to the lower floors of the building. She went down two flights, before following a hallway that led to one of the many classrooms tucked away into a corner.

The class, Sports Revenue Strategies and Analysis, was taught by the assistant athletic director, an ex-baseball player who'd spent some years in pro sports. He went by Coach Smith, even though Sage wasn't sure he'd ever actually been a coach in all of his professional years. He was well-liked by the students in the program, as he walked the fine line between being casual and easy-going while still commanding the respect of those in his classroom. He also happened to be Sage's advisor.

The class passed by quickly, with Coach Smith moving through slide after slide giving an overview of the course and the content they'd be covering. It was genuinely interesting, but was definitely geared toward those who were looking to pursue a career in sports marketing. Sage wasn't entirely sure what she was going to do with her degree yet, but was pretty certain that marketing wasn't where she wanted to end up.

"Sage, hang back a minute," Coach Smith called as everyone was packing up to leave.

Shoving her laptop into her bag, she walked over to the front of the classroom. Once they were alone, Coach Smith rubbed a hand over his thinning hair.

"Well, I've got some bad news," he started, not looking directly at her. "I just got a call from Coach Rivera, and they've decided to go with someone else for the Team Manager spot."

Sage stilled. Coach Rivera was the head coach of the Women's soccer team. "What?"

"I'm sorry," Coach Smith said, finally looking her in the eye. "She said that one of their seniors had a season-ending injury during pre-season, and since she's also in the Sports Management program, Rivera is doing her a solid and letting her complete her internship requirement a year early." He gave her a sad smile. "She said to offer her apologies to you."

Sage couldn't believe what she was hearing. "But I need the internship to graduate!"

Coach Smith held up a hand. "I know, Sage. And I've already got another team lined up."

"Who?"

"Men's basketball."

Sage froze. "No."

Fuck no.

"No?" Coach Smith raised his brows at her, shaking his head. "Sage, you need this job. I know it's not what you want —"

"Coach, it's the worst program in the entire school." *Sure. Let him think that was why she couldn't work with the team.*

He at least had the decency to wince at that. "The new coach is good. He's an alum. Has real potential to turn it all around."

Panic clawed its way up her throat. *What was happening? It was all planned out. Everything was going to go according to plan.* "Isn't there someone else?" She was trying to keep her voice even. "Racquetball? Pickleball?"

"Not real teams and no," Coach Smith replied. "At this point there's no one else."

Fuck.

Sage took a slow, deep breath, her body completely still as her mind raced, running through every possible scenario, seeking any alternative solution to the problem currently facing her.

She had to graduate after this year. She needed the internship for that to happen, and couldn't put it off until later.

There was no other way.

"Okay," she finally said, trying to force a smile onto her face. "I guess I'm in, then."

She barely registered the goodbye she and Coach Smith exchanged, walking on autopilot out of the classroom. Rather than turning right, the direction she needed to go to get to her next class, her feet carried her left, winding down the carpeted hallway. She walked past the workout room that catered to the general student population and a few of the team locker rooms. She continued on, not really seeing what was in front of her, until she reached a set of wooden double doors at the end of a hallway. She pulled on the brushed metal handles, immediately hit with the familiar smell of industrial cleaners, a hint of sweat, and the faintest scent of leather. Four open courts stretched before her, the hoops lowered on two of them, while volleyball nets stretched across the other two.

The Southeastern practice gym was a beautiful space. A line of windows bathed the wooden floors with sunlight, while light stone pillars that stretched up to the high ceiling cast dramatic shadows against the walls.

She didn't normally see the practice gym bright with natural light that brought out the warm, golden streaks in the wooden floors. She couldn't normally tell that the lines that delineated the basketball court were painted burnt orange and not red, and that the volleyball lines that bisected the other court boundaries were dark navy rather than black.

She dropped down onto the bleachers that stood along the wall closest to the door. The cold metal bit against the bare skin on her thighs, but she barely noticed.

All of her attention was caught up in a silent storm in her head.

She'd had a plan. A *good* plan. She was going to work for the soccer team, learn from a coach with a winning pedigree, support *women* in sports, and somehow, through that, she was going to figure out how to turn her degree into a paying career.

But now?

Basketball.

She'd made such a conscious effort to put some distance between herself and the teams here. She'd avoided the games, the players, and even carefully navigated away from any news or articles about them.

She'd maintained her relationship with the sport. But that was personal. It was an agreement between herself, the ball, and the basket, and even then, she was only able to do it in the privacy provided by the silence of the night when the court around her was empty.

And now, in spite of years of running and careful planning, there she was: the new team manager for the Southeastern Men's Basketball team.

Her phone rang as she sat on her couch reading a handout for her Baseball Analytics class. While she didn't necessarily have a burning passion for the sport, it was an elective that worked with her schedule and, based on the first class, was going to be interesting enough.

She grabbed her phone and put it on speaker. "Hello?"

"Hey you."

Sage immediately relaxed at the sound of her sister's voice. "Hey Brin," she said, smiling. "What's up?"

Her older sister, Brinley, lived in Thousand Oaks, in the San Fernando Valley just north of Los Angeles, and about an hour drive from where their mom lived in Santa Barbara. Brinley worked as a lawyer in the entertainment industry, doing something relating to contract negotiations. It was fancy and paid a shit ton of money.

"Wanted to see how your first week is going and check in about Alumni Weekend." There was the sudden screech of brakes and the honking of a horn in the background. "I hate humans," she snapped. "Have I told you that recently?"

Sage laughed. "Only every time we talk." She got up from the couch, walking over to the kitchen to refill her water. "First week is fine. My internship got fucked up though."

"What? What happened?" Concern was evident in Brinley's tone.

"Soccer found someone else who actually knew the sport," Sage said, pausing to take a long drink from her bottle. "So now I'm stuck with Men's Basketball."

It was silent over the line for a long moment. "Are you okay?" Brinley finally asked.

"Fine," Sage said. She started walking through her apartment, her phone gripped in one hand while her toes brushed over the soft carpet. "I don't have a choice if I want to complete my program, Brin."

"I'm so sorry," Brinley's voice was soft. "We'll have to drink about it when I'm down there."

"Right!" Bless her sister for the seamless topic change. "You're still coming?"

Brinley laughed, her giggle light and feminine. "Like I'd miss the chance to see my friends from college and hang with my little sister?"

"What day do you get in?" Sage gently pressed her finger into the dirt in one of her bright ceramic pots that sat on the top of a bookshelf that she'd set up in her living room. When she couldn't feel any moisture, she went to the kitchen and grabbed the watering can she kept on her counter. Filling it, she moved methodically from plant to plant, checking each one before sprinkling the dirt with water.

"I fly in on Thursday around noon, and then leave late Sunday morning," Brinley was saying. "I'm going to stay with McKenna at her place, but you'll be around to hang, right?"

"Of course."

Sage missed her sister, and genuinely looked forward to hanging with her and her friends throughout the weekend. They were wild when they were together — something about the sorority bond that got them all worked up, even though Brinley and her friends were now in their early thirties.

"How's mom?"

Brinley hesitated before responding. "She's fine. I was home last weekend. The garden looks amazing, as usual. She was canning tomatoes and making pickled jalapeños. She'll probably send some with me when I come to visit." There was a slight pause. "She was going on about good marketing jobs in LA. She had a whole folder on her desktop of saved job postings with the Kings and Dodgers."

Sage let out a groan.

Cheryl Fogerty was, in most ways, a quintessential hippie: hated war, only ate real food that was either grown by herself or someone she knew, and was a feminist to her very core. However, after their dad left them for his secretary when Sage was a kid, their mom had gone from being an easy-going stay-at-home mom to suddenly being saddled with the full financial responsibility for two kids and their household. She'd had to take the first job she could find, which was a substitute teaching position at the local high school. Somehow, she'd juggled raising two kids on her own and getting a teaching certificate, and had worked hard ever since.

She was undeniably a badass. Sage was forever impressed by what she'd accomplished, infinitely grateful for what she'd sacrificed to give her and Brinley a comfortable life.

But a bitterness had gripped Cheryl Fogerty when her husband left. She told her daughters over and over again that their primary mission in life should be finding independence — financial and emotional — and that putting themselves in positions where men were in power over them was the ultimate act of betrayal to the women who'd fought for their rights.

Brinley, for her part, was crushing it. A female lawyer taking the world by storm, working at a firm where her boss was a woman. Her income was more than Sage could imagine, and in their mom's eyes, being in a position of never having to rely on a man was the definition of success.

Hence their mother's obsession with trying to figure out how to turn Sage's sports management degree into something lucrative. And the unfortunate reality was that, at the moment, the positions with the most potential upward mobility and earning potential in sports were in social media and marketing. Especially for women.

There was also the added piece that their mom assumed that Sage would be moving home to California after graduation. Brinley had, so of course it was presumed that Sage would follow.

But Sage didn't want to work in social media, and she definitely didn't want to move home to Santa Barbara.

"You there?" Brinley asked, and Sage realized she'd gone quiet, lost in her thoughts.

"Sorry. Yeah. Just trying to grapple with the existential dread that comes with thinking about what happens after graduation."

Another laugh from Brinley. "You'll be incredible no matter what you decide to do, Sage. And ignore Mom. Don't let her bullshit become yours. She loves us, but she's...well, she's Mom."

Sage felt a wave of gratitude for her sister. "Can't wait to see you," she said.

"You too," Brinley replied. "Okay, I've gotta run. Love you."

"Love you too."

Brinley hung up before Sage had a chance to end the call.

By 8:30pm, the practice gym was as she knew it: empty, and lit only by the harsh white overhead lights. Sage moved to the bleachers, opening her bag and pulling out her worn Hyper-dunks, the red and orange accents scuffed and the laces beginning to fray. She slid her feet into the shoes, kicking her heels back against the floor before tying the laces tight, just how she'd always liked it.

She reached into the bag, pulling out a basketball. The leather was a rusty orange, with only a few scuffs on the surface. Sage had had the same ball that she'd stolen from her high school gym since she'd left California.

With only the ball in her hand, she walked over to one of the baskets, craning her neck up to look at the orange of the rim and fresh white of the new net. Positioning herself only about a foot away, she held up the ball in one hand, and then shot.

The flick of her wrist was second nature. The slight bend in her knees before she shot. The ball rolling off of her middle finger, the angle of her head as she watched the ball barely brush the rim before falling through the net with a soft *swish*.

Her hands were ready when the ball bounced back to her. She repeated the shot, lifting just her left hand and shooting; this time the ball fell perfectly into the net, just missing the rim. A small smile twitched at her lips.

She repeated the same shot twenty times, before moving to the front of the basket, where she did the same thing. She moved from spot to spot, shooting again and again, and eventually her right hand came up to guide the ball from the side. Her movements sped up, more of her body getting involved as she deepened the bend in her knees to give more strength to her shot.

She made more than she missed. In the wake of a miss, she

made tiny adjustments, but for the most part her body fell into the routine of shooting, reuniting with each familiar spot within fifteen feet of the basket. It was a rhythm so familiar that her mind quieted until there was nothing but the squeak of her shoes on the wood, the swish of the net, and the almost metallic-sounding bounce of the ball.

An hour later, her back and face were drenched with sweat, and her lungs burned with each breath. She walked back to her little pile of stuff on the bleachers, nudging out of her shoes and sliding her now soaked socks into her Birks.

She should stretch. If she were more responsible, she would stretch.

But at that point she was so hungry that all she could think about was getting home to her stocked fridge. She packed her bag, already feeling stiffness settle into her hamstrings, and shuffled out of the gym, flipping the lights off behind her.

When she got back to her apartment she showered, but didn't bother with washing her hair. Once she had a big bowl of rice, beans, and sautéed veggies and chicken topped with hot sauce, she curled up on the couch with a novel; she probably had an hour and a half to read before she needed to go to bed.

Just as she was settling in, her phone pinged with an email notification.

Swiping it open, she read the message.

From: dhughes@southeastern.edu

Subject: Meeting

Miss Fogerty,

Please let me know if you'd be available to come by my office tomorrow afternoon. As I'm sure you are busy with classes, I can be flexible on the timing. Let me know when would work best for you.

Looking forward to meeting you,

Coach Hughes

Southeastern University Men's Basketball

Sage exhaled loudly, sinking her head back into the couch behind her. She gave herself a few seconds to think about just how *shitty* this was before she sat up and tapped out a response.

From: sfogerty@southeastern.edu
Subject: Meeting
Coach Hughes,
I am available tomorrow at 1pm.
Looking forward to it.
Sage Fogerty

CHAPTER 3
TWENTY-THREE POINTS PER GAME
SAGE

As she killed the engine of her ancient, beat-to-shit Corolla, Sage flipped down the visor and checked herself in the warped mirror. She only had about thirty seconds before the August heat reduced her to a gooey puddle on the seat.

Her eyes darted over her face, checking the minimal makeup she'd applied that morning. Concealer covered the zit on her left temple. Mascara somehow survived the malfunctioning AC and hadn't melted down her face. Her cheeks were doing that thing where they turned a vibrant fuchsia the second the temperature got over 85 degrees. The high ponytail she'd pulled her hair into was still resolutely in place, with only a few flyaway hairs fanning out around her head.

She glanced down, picking a piece of lint from the soft gray t-shirt she wore with a pair of tailored blue slacks. *Dusky blue,* Brinley had called the color when Sage had video-called her that morning for fashion advice.

Sage had no issue with her personal style — athletic gear and jeans with the exception of a few dresses she pulled out occasion-ally — but figured that Brinley, who dressed professionally on a daily basis, was a better judge of appropriate interview attire. Well, it wasn't exactly an *interview,* since she already had the internship, but she still thought she should put effort into the initial meeting with the coaches.

It was Brinley's idea to pair the blue slacks and blazer their mom had bought Sage for graduation with a nicer t-shirt, saying it was "more your vibe, Sage." She appreciated the consideration.

She reached over into the passenger seat, grabbing the matching blazer and a worn canvas bag that had served as her purse for the past eight years of her life. Stepping out, she squinted against the bright sun as she walked across the parking lot and into the Humphrey Center.

She gave Eckbert the customary pat, and then wriggled her long arms into her blazer as soon as she met the freezing air inside.

Her shoes made an obnoxious clicking sound against the brick floor as she walked down the long hallway that stretched the length of the building, and she scowled down at her feet. She honestly felt silly in the nude ballet flats, but her sister had *insisted* that Nikes were not appropriate for a job interview.

When she reached a pair of frosted glass doors she paused, reading the neatly stenciled letters: *Southeastern University Athletic Department.*

Exhaling loudly through her nose, Sage pulled the door open, making a conscious effort to project confidence in her movements and expression.

The girl sitting at the front desk beamed at her. "Hi there! How can I help you today?"

"I'm here for a meeting with Coach Hughes," Sage replied, trying to smile back.

"And you are?"

"Sage Fogerty."

"Right!" Picking up the corded office phone beside her, she dialed in a series of tonal beeps. "Hello sir. Yes, your one o'clock is here. Miss Fogerty." A pause. "Mmhm. I'll send her right back." She hung up the phone with a click, and pointed down a hallway behind her. "He's ready for you. He's in office 1113 down on the left."

Again, Sage tried to smile. "Thanks," she said, turning and walking in the direction the young woman had pointed in. She scanned the nameplates as she passed. Football, softball, soccer, swimming, tennis, volleyball...and basketball.

There it was. Room 1113. And in gold lettering:

David Hughes
Men's Basketball
Head Coach

She took a deep breath, straightened her shoulders, and knocked three times.

"Come in," a low voice called, muffled through the door.

Sage turned the handle, pushed the door open, and walked inside.

The first thing she noticed was that the walls were empty. Two generic, cushioned chairs sat in front of the wide, wooden desk that was covered with stacks of papers, boxes, at least one coaching board, and three different coffee mugs beside the open laptop computer.

An older man sat in a chair off to the side of the desk. He had a shaved head that looked like it concealed hair loss, white eyebrows furrowed to match a frown, and wiry arms crossed over his chest. Based on the team-branded polo, he was a member of the coaching staff.

And then, behind the desk there was —

What the actual fuck?

Standing there, looking down at her with his mouth open and eyes wide under thick brows, was the beautiful man from the bar.

There he was, in all his over-six-feet-tall glory, a green South-eastern hat pulled down over his dark hair, and...why was he also wearing a team-branded shirt? Why did it say *Eagles Basketball* right there on his chest?

Her eyes darted up to meet his.

It was definitely him, and based on the way he looked at her, he remembered her too.

A throat cleared. "So," a voice spoke, breaking the silence that had filled the room ever since she stepped inside. "You must be Miss Fogerty."

Sage blinked, tearing her eyes away from the man behind the desk and looking back at the older man, who stood there with his hand extended towards her. She didn't miss the unimpressed glance he sent to his counterpart, who was still frozen in place.

This was a shit show.

She shook her head and forced a smile. "Hi. Sorry." She took his hand, shaking it twice before letting go. "Please call me Sage."

The man gave her a nod. "Coach Dixon. Assistant. Thanks for coming in." He cleared his throat again, looking over at the desk. "Coach?" The question was forceful, and Sage tried to hide her wince.

The tall man seemed to come back into his body. "Right. Have a seat. Please." He gestured to one of the empty chairs. "I'm Coach Hughes. Or David. Whichever you want."

Sage sat down, dropping her bag on the floor next to the chair as the two men both returned to their seats.

David — no, *Coach Hughes* — looked even larger than she remembered, sitting in the chair with his long legs stretched out in front of him. She definitely didn't let her eyes linger on his exposed forearms and the way his shirt stretched indecently across his chest.

She swallowed against the dryness in her throat, realizing the room was waiting for her response. "Coach Hughes should be fine," she finally managed to croak out.

Get your shit together, Sage.

"Can I get you a water?" David was looking at her intently, and based on how his dark eyes flicked back and forth across her face, she suspected he was looking at her flushed cheeks.

She waved off the offer. "No, no thanks. I've got my own." She reached down in her bag, grateful for the distraction, and pulled out her water bottle.

"Good," he said, and it was like something loosened in his posture as he watched her unscrew the lid and take a long drink.

Willing her face to cool the fuck down, she screwed the lid back on, and returned the bottle to her bag.

"So," Coach Dixon said. "You're doing the five year Masters?"

Sage nodded. "Yes." It was challenging to focus on the actual purpose of their meeting and not the presence of the man she'd fully intended to fuck. Ideally more than once. *Focus, Sage.* "I considered a few other programs, but ultimately decided I wanted to finish up here."

"So what's the endgame? Professional sports? Marketing?" Coach Dixon adjusted the silver-framed glasses that were perched on his nose.

She couldn't help but wrinkle her nose at the last one. Why did everyone assume that a woman in sports was ultimately angling for a sales job? It brought her right back to her mom, who had taken to sending her at least one article a day about the incredible opportunities in social media marketing for sports. According to her — and the first two articles that Sage had read in an effort to be polite — there were plenty of jobs that not only paid well, but had almost endless upward mobility. And, most importantly to her mom, there were *lots* of jobs in California.

But she had absolutely no interest in being the one with the phone filming content and capturing the players in candid, potentially viral moments. She didn't want to be stuck in a press box or selling season tickets.

The terrifying truth was that she had absolutely no idea *what* she wanted to do with her degree yet. All she knew was that she'd spent her whole life in the world of sports and she couldn't imagine giving that up. How to make a career of it was what she was supposed to figure out this year.

"Still trying to figure that out," she finally replied.

"You were supposed to work with women's soccer, right?"

David's voice sent an actual shiver down her spine. That tiny hint of a drawl...*fuck.*

"I was, but I don't have an extensive background with the sport, and they were able to find someone who does." She shifted in her seat.

David leaned forward, elbows braced on the desk in front of him. "Well, our program is definitely at a different place than women's soccer," he began, "but I think that we're building something different this year."

There was a beat of silence. She looked between David and Coach Dixon, noticing that the older man looked nowhere near as confident as the new head coach.

Coach Dixon fixed his attention on her. "So, Miss Fogerty. What do you know about basketball?"

Her mouth opened before she had a chance to second guess herself. "More than I know about soccer."

"Are you a fan?" David asked, his eyes appraising her with something new, something different.

"Something like that."

"What kind of experience with the sport are we talking about?" Coach Dixon looked decidedly unimpressed by her so far.

"I played." She looked down, noticing her fingers picking at the seam on the side of her slacks. *She should have expected they'd ask this. Of course they would fucking ask her.*

Stop it. Her fingers stilled.

Coach Dixon made a quiet huffing sound. "Were you any good?"

Sage couldn't help but exhale a laugh at his question.

Had she been any good at the thing she'd devoted every waking moment of her life to? Had she been any good at the thing she sacrificed friendships and freedom for?

"I was decent," she said.

"Points per game?" David asked.

Sage exhaled slowly through her nose. "Twenty three."

His eyes widened. "Average?"

"Yep."

His eyes dipped down, surveying her body in a way that was calculating. She had to force herself to sit still. "Post?"

"Forward."

He nodded. Her eyes were drawn to the divot above his upper lip; it was pronounced, almost feminine, so at odds with the dark hair that grew on his face and his sheer mass.

"Rebounds?" He asked.

"Ten."

"Shooting percentage?"

"Fifty-six percent from the field."

His brows furrowed, lips pulled into a frown, and he leaned back in his chair, the motion shifting the energy in the small room.

Again, quiet settled over them.

It was Coach Dixon who finally spoke. Leaning forward, he looked at her with obvious confusion. "So why in Heaven's name didn't you play college ball?"

It felt like an invisible hand closed around her chest, squeezing and squeezing until her lungs could barely expand enough to take in the air that she needed. Her brain buzzed, a sound filling her ears like the hum of halogen lights, and she dug her fingers into her thighs.

She needed to say something. Hadn't she gotten good at that? Over and over again, she'd answered the exact same question, ignoring the confusion on people's faces when they asked her why such a promising athlete wasn't continuing their career.

But it had been so long, and the words just wouldn't come, no matter how hard she tried to force her mouth to open. In a moment of desperation, her eyes darted over to David, who watched her with earnest attention that made her feel like he could see right through her.

He obviously saw something in her eyes, because he spoke, his voice soft, possessing a gentleness that hadn't been there before. "You don't have to answer that if you don't want to," he said, reaching up and pushing a wayward piece of hair off of his fore-head before adjusting his hat. "But if playing in college was a choice that was taken away from you, then I'm sorry." He glanced over at Coach Dixon. "We understand the pain of having that dream stolen."

It took a monumental amount of self-control to blink away the tears that burned at the corners of her eyes. *You're a grown-ass woman about to cry in a job interview, Sage. Get your shit together.* She shoved the emotion down, schooling her expression and straight-ening her posture, hoping that she was projecting strength.

"Nothing like that," she finally said, offering a smile that she hoped was confident and reassuring. "I just decided to focus on my studies instead."

The lie tasted like chalk on her tongue, but it was necessary.

David's eyes narrowed slightly, like maybe he didn't believe her, but, with a small shake of his head, he moved on. "Because this job is a program requirement for you, you'll technically be reporting to your academic advisor. We," he pointed to Coach Dixon and himself, "will be more like supervisors, in the sense that we will work together on scheduling and your job duties. You'll officially start with the team once practices begin, but there will of course be travel scheduling, team community service to plan, and some other things that might come up in the preseason. Once things pick up, we'll be on from October to February. Does that sound alright?"

She nodded, relieved as the knot of tension in her chest loos-ened a fraction. "That all sounds fine. And will I be traveling with the team?"

"Yes," David said. "For away games you'll be taking on some of the equipment manager duties as well, in addition to keeping travel, food, and lodging organized and taking stats."

She gave another nod, confirming her understanding. She watched as David scratched his jaw, a layer of dark hair there that hadn't been there when they'd first met. The beard, though still obviously new, looked really fucking good.

Stop it.

"Do you have any questions for us?" David asked, gesturing between himself and Coach Dixon.

She shifted in her seat. She did, actually, have a question, but she wasn't entirely sure how it was going to be received. "What do you bring as a new coach that's going to turn this team around? Last year's record was 10 and 17, so you've got a lot of ground to make up."

"Ah," David began, once again messing with his hat. He almost looked nervous. "I'm good with players. That's the main thing I bring. As for the basketball, I've got years of experience coaching for different programs under my belt, and can draw from all of that as I get to know my personnel and their particular skill sets. I'd say that my philosophy is to work within a really clear structure, where everyone knows their role."

She nodded along as he spoke. While the words themselves were assured, she thought she could detect a bit of uncertainty in his tone as he described his plans for the team. Like maybe the ideas were locked in, but he wasn't sure he could execute them.

"Sounds like you'll be good for the team," she said, pushing aside her questions for the moment.

David gave her a small smile that looked like it was a touch forced, if not reluctant. His eyes were trained down on the desk, and she watched as he picked up a pen and began spinning it in his fingers. *He was a fidgeter.*

It was obvious from the quiet that settled in the room that the interview was done. Sage waited, realizing she was holding her breath.

Coach Dixon was the one who stood up, seeming to break David from whatever stupor had fallen over him. "Well thanks for coming in, Sage," the older man said, extending a hand for her to shake.

"I appreciate you both taking the time," she replied, completing the handshake and then turning to David.

"Right," he said, thrusting his arm out with a bit too much

gusto. He immediately winced, pulling back some and gripping her hand with just enough pressure.

She tried to ignore the tingling that ran up the inside of her arm as she looked up at him. She hoped it wasn't obvious that she wanted to nuzzle her face into the dip between his pecs, but wasn't sure she was doing a very convincing job.

"It was nice to meet you, Miss Fogerty," he said in his low, melodic voice.

"Likewise, Coach Hughes."

It was time to let go of his hand. She knew it, and there was no way that he didn't know it. But it was like she couldn't convince her fingers to let go, like her hand had found its home wrapped up in his warm, solid grasp. She watched as his eyes dropped to where they were connected, his brow slightly furrowed. She felt his fingers squeeze around hers once, and then he let go.

"We'll be in touch," Coach Dixon said, and once again Sage sensed that the older man was picking up on the invisible *something* that was obviously present in the room.

Sending a nod in Coach Dixon's direction, she picked up her bag, draped it over her shoulder, and walked out, refusing to look back as the door shut behind her.

CHAPTER 4
BRICK SHITHOUSE
DAVID

David sat back in his chair, the joints groaning under his weight. Somehow he'd managed to land himself right in the middle of a goddamn shit storm, and practices hadn't even started yet.

A tiny part of him had wondered when he saw the name *Sage* come across his inbox. But it would have been a laughable coincidence if it was the same woman, right?

Who's laughing now, David?

He closed his eyes, trying to call upon the part of himself that was good at showing up on the tough days and facing challenges with a cool, calm demeanor worthy of a man who was rapidly approaching middle aged.

But that part of himself was, unsurprisingly, nowhere to be found.

"Well that was something."

David glanced over at his assistant coach, whose glasses had slipped down his nose. When the older man peered at him over the silver frames, it made David feel like a kid in the principal's office — not the feeling he should have with the guy who was supposed to be taking direction *from* him.

He still didn't know what to think about Tim Dixon.

He definitely knew Tim Dixon didn't know what to think about him.

He suspected that Tim was still deciding whether or not David had what it took to lead the Southeastern team. Tim had been the assistant for Coach Reyes, the previous coach, and when the university hired David, it had been under the condition that he kept Tim as an assistant. They'd said something about *continuity for the players* and *offering valuable experience*, but all David heard was: *We don't believe in you...yet. So here's a safety net.*

Clearing his throat, he scratched his face, where the two-day beard was an almost constant distraction. He'd decided to grow it out to try something different — Chuck's suggestion, not his — but already regretted it. "Yeah, it was. She certainly knows basketball."

He couldn't tell Tim that after seeing Sage under the warm glow of string lights with her bare arms and the jeans that hugged her thighs he had no doubt in his mind that the woman could hold her own in any situation. It had been obvious from the first second that he saw her that her body was powerful, but her confidence...*goddamn* her confidence had turned him inside out. The way she'd looked at him, refusing to look away, practically dared him to refuse her. She could have eaten him alive, and he would have been absolutely thrilled to have been chosen. And, if that night had gone according to plan, he would have spent every second in her company proving just how much he had to offer her, with his voice or hands or tongue or whatever she asked of him.

Well now that possibility was about as laughable as David actually managing to pull off a winning season.

The beginnings of a headache throbbed behind his left eye.

He knew he was a good coach. That wasn't the issue. He'd had years of experience as an assistant at the college level, and knew that he was ready to take on a head coaching job. The X's and O's, the practice planning, the building of a team — that he could do. It was just the fact that the job was *here*, at Southeastern, the place where he'd captained the very same team thirteen years ago. It was a place that meant more to him than he knew how to express, and the idea that he might mess it up? Well, frankly, it terrified him.

He shook himself, realizing belatedly that Tim was talking to him. "Sorry, what was that?" David asked, cringing at his inability to focus today.

Tim looked unimpressed. "What's your plan for meeting the guys?"

David glanced down at the printed school calendar on his desk. "I want them to get through the first week of classes first." He glanced up at Tim. "I'm thinking team meeting Sunday afternoon."

"Hm." Tim remained expressionless. "That might work."

Might?

David took a deep breath and forced a smile onto his face. "So we're a go with Sage Fogerty?"

"Not like we have another choice," Tim replied, shrugging. "Well, I'm out," he continued, standing up and giving David a quick nod. "Enjoy your weekend."

"You too, Coach."

When the door shut behind him, David sighed and dropped his head down onto the desk.

Everything is going to be fine, he told himself. *Absolutely fine.*

"What'll it be?"

David slid onto the wooden barstool, dropping his phone, wallet, and keys onto the bar in front of him. "Corona dressed, please."

He immediately recognized Maggie, the bartender from the other night, and he guessed that she recognized him based on how she cocked a pierced brow at him as she sauntered up. "If it ain't the beautiful man himself," she said, grinning at him.

He hadn't been back to The Grove since that night when, once again, being a good friend had taken him away from what he knew would have been an incredible night with the tall, self-assured blonde.

Who just so happened to be his new team manager.

Goddamn poetic bad luck.

Something must have shown on his face, because Maggie asked, "Rough day?" as she slid the beer toward him.

"Nah." David accepted the drink, nodding in thanks. "Just adjusting to a new job." He reached into his wallet and pulled out a five and a one, tossing them down.

Maggie collected the cash and stuffed it into her apron pocket. "It isn't right for a man who looks like you to be drinkin' alone," she said, shaking her head at him. "What ever happened with you and my new best friend?" Her red-painted lips pulled down into a frown. "Speakin' of that feisty blonde, I haven't seen her since that night you were here. Have you been keepin' her busy?" She waggled her brows as her eyes widened. "Doin' some of the horizontal tango, if you know what I'm sayin'?"

David choked on his beer, sputtering as he tried to find his breath again. "Yeah…nope. None of the horizontal tango. Didn't work out, unfortunately."

"I mean, you did bail on her," Maggie muttered as she wiped down the bar.

It was early enough that David was the only one sitting at the bar, and only a few tables in the courtyard were occupied. He didn't make a habit of drinking while the sun was out — or really, drinking very much in general — but he felt like he needed a beer after the day he'd had.

Still, he wasn't in the mood to ignore what the woman was implying. "I had to get a friend home safely," he said, a bit of annoyance sneaking into his tone. "I don't mess around with letting my friends drink and drive."

Maggie's face softened. "I respect the hell out of that, Mr. Brick Shithouse."

Again, David sputtered around his beer. "Excuse me?"

"Where I come from, we say that a man like you is built like a brick shithouse," she said, eyes twinkling.

"Last time you called me beautiful, and now you're comparing me to an outhouse. Whatever the punchline is, I think I missed it."

Maggie let out a loud laugh. "Being built like a "brick shit-house" simply means that you're a big man with a big body."

David unconsciously ran his hand over his broad chest and down to his stomach that had gained a softness in recent years years that no number of push ups could get rid of.

"It's a good thing," Maggie added, her eyes watching him knowingly. "A very good thing."

Rolling his eyes, David waved off the compliment.

"But seriously," Maggie leaned forward onto the bar, long pink nails drumming on the polished wood surface. "Did you get her number? You two were all sorts of sparkly together."

"Ah...no. Didn't get her number." He took a long swig of his beer. "Wouldn't have worked out anyway."

Maggie scoffed. "We both know that's bullshit."

"She works for, well, sort of *with* me." David leveled his stare at the bartender, whose eyebrows had popped halfway up her forehead. "Walked right into my office this morning."

What he didn't tell her was that for the tiniest moment, David had thought that Sage had been there for him. That somehow she'd tracked him down and had shown up at his office to resume whatever they'd started that night at the bar.

David was fully aware that he was completely delusional, and an idiot.

Leaning back against the bar, Maggie shook her head, like she couldn't believe what she was hearing. "So you're her boss?"

"Technically, no." David drained the last of his beer, setting it down with a *thunk*. "She's a graduate student doing an internship for the team that I coach."

"I *knew* you were both jocks," Maggie said with a self-satisfied grin. "You looked at her like she was a basket you were trying to strike."

David laughed. "That's not a thing." When she pointed at his empty beer in a silent offering of another, he waved her off.

"Whatever. My point is that the two of you screamed sports with your height and muscles." Maggie took away the empty bottle. "So what are you gonna do about it?"

He scratched his jaw. "Nothing. I'm going to do nothing."

"Lame," Maggie said, her tone teasing.

Pocketing his phone, keys, and wallet, David rolled his eyes. "Smart," he retorted.

"See you later, beautiful!" Maggie called out, her laughter following him out of the bar and onto the sidewalk.

As he started walking in the direction of home, his thoughts turned to Sage.

The smart thing to do would be to send her a politely worded email to schedule a meeting so that they could clear the air before they actually started working together. But that would involve him figuring out what the hell he was supposed to say to her.

Oh yes, hi there. We met at a bar and had reached a verbal agreement that we'd be engaging in sexual behavior together. While that sexual behavior never happened, I've already imagined your naked body in technicolor and for some reason I think that you're a silent screamer when you come.

He audibly snorted, startling a grackle that had been on the sidewalk next to him. Of course, the grackle flew right at his face, leading David to jump to the side and frantically wave his arms about in an attempt to escape the bird.

Finally the bird found its way into the air above him, and David shook off a shudder. *Fucking birds who didn't know their place in the world.* Which, for clarity's sake, was up in the tops of trees or in the sky. Not on sidewalks or public beaches.

It was still hot, but the devilwood trees that lined the street provided some dappled shade. The Grove was situated on the outskirts of a shopping center that had a nice grocery store, a pet groomer, a bookstore, a coffee shop, at least one insurance agent, and some other businesses David hadn't taken the time to remember.

He liked this part of town; it was only a six minute drive to the university, so it had been an obvious choice for David to pick an apartment in one of the surrounding complexes. He'd chosen the complex he had for the pool, the larger than average gym, and the fenced, off-leash dog park.

When he reached the metal fence that surrounded his building, he typed in the code for the heavy gate. From there it was a short walk along a winding sidewalk to his building, which was right next to the central communal area that housed the pool and gym.

He jogged up the stairs to the second level, fiddling with his keys before finding the correct one and unlocking the door.

He liked his place. His apartment had an open floor plan, with a carpeted living room next to the tiled kitchen and dining area. There was a bar in the kitchen, and a wide window over the sink that looked out at the tall trees. To the right was a hallway that led to his bedroom and a spacious bathroom that he paid extra for, and to the left was a second bedroom that he currently used as a home office.

He'd sold most of the furniture from his apartment in Chicago before he left. He didn't have an emotional attachment to the generic couch, tables, chairs, and bed that he'd purchased as cheaply as possible when he'd moved out there six years ago.

What he had kept from his Chicago apartment were the little pieces of home that he'd gradually accumulated over the years. A large black-and-white photo of his friends huddled together on the dock at the house on Lake Murray was framed above the gray sectional along one wall. Three concert posters — Modest Mouse, Red Hot Chili Peppers, and George Strait — were framed along another wall. His mom had convinced him that the fake plant tucked next to the dark wood TV stand was a necessary decorative statement, but in David's eye he much preferred the bookshelf crammed with worn, paperback copies of police procedurals and detective novels, his preferred method of escapism.

An excited bark and the jingle of a collar had David dropping down to his knees just in time to catch the flash of golden fur that careened toward him.

"Hey, sweet girl," he crooned to the wriggling golden dachshund as he stood up, cradling the small dog in his arms. "How was your day?"

He got a high-pitched *yip* in response, and he wasted no time grabbing the leash and harness that hung beside his front door.

His days at the office weren't too long in the summer, and he made a point to come home at lunch to let Daisy out to do her business and run around. She was still a puppy, and even though her legs were comically short, she had a lot of energy.

Daisy stilled once she realized he was trying to put on her harness, and as soon as he clipped the leash into place and set her on the ground, she darted off toward the door.

"Whoa there," he said with a laugh, stashing a few dog bags in the pocket of his basketball shorts before following her out of his apartment. "Slow down, you crazy beast."

Daisy gave him a look that could only be described as annoyed before resuming her charge toward the stairs. David locked the door behind them and picked up the pace, jogging to keep up.

It was only a minute walk from his unit to the complex's dog park. It was empty at the moment, the air quiet and still around the wax myrtle trees that offered welcome shade.

As soon as they passed through the gate, he unclipped the leash and gave Daisy a scratch on the head before she darted off at a run, her long ears flopping behind her. There were park benches scattered around, but there was too much churning in David's head to make sitting an option. Instead he walked slowly, his footsteps crunching the gravel path that circled the perimeter of the park. Daisy trotted in and out of view as she sniffed and explored.

He hadn't initially wanted to come back to Charleston. His

college years had been both the happiest and most challenging of his life, and there was a part of him that would have been happy to leave South Carolina in the past.

After graduating college, he'd moved home to Atlanta, needing the support of his family after what had happened his senior year. *It's okay to take some time, honey,* his mom had told him over and over again. It had helped that he'd gotten an assistant coaching job at one of the larger local high schools with a dominant program. That job had been everything he'd ever wanted, and he'd been able to start to piece himself back together during the long hours spent under the harsh, white, fluorescent lights.

For six years he'd lived out of his childhood bedroom, eating dinner at the table with his parents like no time had passed since high school. But time had passed, and at some point he started scanning job postings for coaching positions at smaller colleges.

He'd moved to Chicago, fitting all of his belongings into the back of the '90 Bronco that he'd had since high school. The city was cold, the wind harsh, but he loved the pace of life there. While it never quite felt like home, he'd built a life there consisting of late night pizza, concerts, long lifting sessions at the Chicago Institute of Technology gym, and hours and hours spent building himself into the kind of coach he'd always dreamed of being.

But when Chuck, his best friend and college roommate, had sent him the posting for the head coaching position at Southeastern, he couldn't stay away. No, this was the chance he'd been searching for in every practice and every game he'd coached since graduating and moving away.

It was the chance to do it right. The chance to be a coach who made a true difference in the lives of young men. Who took the time to see them — truly see them — and listen when they needed to talk.

He could be the kind of leader who wouldn't miss the small stuff.

And it had always been a dream to coach at Southeastern. For years it was an idea that he nurtured in the quiet, late hours of the night, when he'd pull up the university website and check on how the team was doing. He wasn't sure how it was possible to want something with every part of himself while simultaneously feeling terrified of the possibility of it coming to pass.

But it was here now. The dream was at his feet, ready and waiting for him. Shit, it was already happening around him: preseason meetings with his assistant, watching game film, crafting a plan for how he was going to approach this team.

It was here, whether or not he was ready.

"Daisy," David called out, and his dog came trotting over. He quickly located where she'd done her business, picking up the small pile with the baggie and disposing of it in the provided trash can.

Only assholes didn't clean up after their dogs.

Clipping the leash back into place, David started back toward his building. The afternoon shadows were growing longer, the heat just beginning to fade as the sun dipped behind the tall trees.

As he passed another unit, he thought he saw the flash of a long blonde ponytail, but when he turned around, there was nothing but the green backdrop of the trees and an empty staircase.

Damn blonde team managers with their high ponytails and thighs, already haunting him.

CHAPTER 5
ROMANCING MISS FOGERTY
SAGE

The first month of school flew by.

While grad school was similar to undergrad in the overall quantity of essays and readings assigned each day, there was the additional expectation that not only did they need to be accurate and concise in their work, but they needed to demonstrate that they could apply what they were learning to case-studies based on real-world situations. It was engaging, and kept Sage actively reading ahead in her textbooks out of genuine interest.

Was she a little bit stressed that all of her classmates had very solidly committed to post-graduate plans and specific careers? Sure. Maybe a little bit.

But it would be fine.

The team manager job was actually helping keep the stress of her future at bay. Things wouldn't really pick up until the season officially started in mid-October, but there were still responsibilities to help with the season preparation. So far, she'd had meetings with the equipment manager, a stout and severe woman named Felicity Armison (fondly called "Armie" by everyone in the athletic department), who commanded a large crew of student workers to help with the less-glamorous parts of the job — namely, laundry.

Piles and piles of nasty, sweaty laundry.

But, for Sage's part, Armie was getting her up to speed on what she, as team manager, was responsible for, especially when they went on the road, where she would have to handle all of the equipment herself.

She felt a vague pang of jealousy at the little conveniences the college athletes had access to: laundry service, branded sweat-shirts and jackets, team t-shirts, and the new Nike team shoes, complete with green accents.

It looked pretty damn nice to be a college athlete.

She also was in email communications with the admin guy who handled the nuts and bolts of travel bookings. There were eight teams in their conference, and while three of them were reachable by bus, five required a flight. As a smaller, Division III school, they flew commercially, but bus rides were chartered for the team. Additionally, there were hotel rooms to book, food budgets to consider, and a whole slew of other things that she would be responsible for keeping track of. It all kept her busy, but it wasn't quite enough to completely dull the shadow of dread that hovered just out of reach.

It was the end of September, and she'd just finished her last class for the day in the Business and Marketing building. She rushed across campus toward the Humphry Center, where she was meeting the team for the first time.

She'd received an email from David — *fuck*, Coach Hughes — asking if she'd come to an open gym to meet the team. While the start of the season was still a week or two away, the team was going to be running an after-school basketball camp at a local recreation center. When she'd suggested the idea of the team doing community service there to Coach Hughes, he'd immedi-ately jumped at the idea.

She pulled on her hoodie as soon as she walked in the front doors, silently cursing the temperature swing from sweltering outside to freezing inside.

The team was playing in the practice gym. She could hear the bouncing balls and echoing shouts before she reached the wooden doors. Pausing for a moment with her hand on the handle, she took a practiced deep breath before pulling the doors open.

The scene before her was so achingly familiar that it felt like a blow to the stomach. For a second, she couldn't breathe. Tall, leanly-muscled bodies wearing team-issued shorts and practice jerseys ran up and down the court, while other players sat on the bleachers watching the game.

God, the sounds…the squeak of shoes, the heavy breathing, the shouts of "I'm open," and "ball" and "screen right" were the soundtrack of her life up until four and a half years ago.

She spotted David and Coach Dixon sitting apart from the players, heads bowed together in conversation.

Adjusting her bag on her shoulder, she walked toward the two men.

David looked up. She watched as his jaw tightened, and his gaze dipped down to her bare legs. *Why the fuck was she wearing running shorts?* For a moment, she stopped, unable to get her feet to keep moving.

You're a grown-ass woman Sage. You've kept your shit together around hot guys before. Even if they didn't have his arm hair or tree-trunk thighs or an almost shy smile that threatened to melt her.

Forcing a smile onto her own face, she walked toward him, raising her hand in a wave.

Coach Dixon must have noticed that David's attention was elsewhere, because he turned to look over his shoulder, giving Sage a nod when he saw her.

"Miss Fogerty," Coach Dixon said, adjusting in his seat so that he faced her. "Good to see you."

"Thanks, Coach," she replied, lowering down to the bleachers next to him. A few of the players had turned to watch them, obviously wondering who she was and why she was there.

"Hey." David gave her a tight smile, leaning forward to brace his forearms on his knees. She noticed that he'd kept the facial hair, although it was trimmed a bit closer to his face. His dark hair was still too long, even though she could tell he was trying to hide that fact by wearing a baseball cap.

"They've only got six points left to finish this one," he continued. "They're playing to twenty-one."

Sage nodded in understanding, turning her attention to watch the team play.

She'd done her research. There were fifteen guys on the team, which was pretty typical for a college roster. Four seniors, three juniors, four sophomores, and four freshmen.

Immediately, she picked up on a few players who were obviously freshmen, based on their hesitation on the court and their tendency to pass instead of looking for a shot. She also picked up on the guys who were shooting the ball way more than they should. There was one guy who looked to be almost 7 feet tall with the body of a true center, who, while he didn't seem to be the most skilled with the ball, played with a huge grin on his face and had an obvious knack for finding the open man on the court. Another player, with bleached twist-braids pulled up into a knot at the top of his head and legs so skinny that it looked like his ankles could snap at any moment, commanded the outside, showing speed and handles that identified him as a point guard.

One player took more shots than any of the others. He looked like a military kid: tall, muscle bound, with short blonde hair and the kind of rigid posture that looked like it'd been drilled into him from a young age. She could see the tension in his body from the sideline, and watched how he grew more and more stiff with every shot he missed.

That guy needed to meditate or *something*.

The game ended on a breakaway layup that had the other team groaning and cursing.

Sage watched David's face, noting the furrow in his brow as he watched the team in the first moments after gameplay. She bet that he was watching which players turned to each other, exchanging fist bumps and high fives as they talked through the game. There was also no way that he missed the ones who turned away, standing alone. The blonde kid was one of those, his practice jersey pulled up over his head as he walked, alone, to the wall.

"Alright, circle up," David's loud voice called out as he pushed to standing, walking onto the court. His physical presence, even among the young players, was commanding, and he had a few inches on most of the team.

The guys shuffled over, not seeming to be in a particular hurry. It struck Sage in that moment, watching how the players responded to their head coach, that David was still actively working to earn their respect. In their eyes, he was still the unproven new guy.

Once the group was assembled around him, David looked back over his shoulder and gestured for her to join them. The weight of his eyes on her was heavy, like his hand on her thigh at the bar.

She stood up, walking over to stand between David and Coach Dixon. The guys immediately zeroed in on her. She noticed a few of them looked her up and down, with one guy even biting his lip and raising his dark brows at her. She returned his stare with one of her own, doing her best to project an expression that said: *Not in your fucking dreams.*

David cleared his throat, the sound low and almost threatening. "This is Miss Fogerty, who'll be our team manager this year. This means she'll be keeping stats, traveling with us, and helping keep us organized and on schedule." He cast a quick glance in her direction before turning back to the team. "You'll treat her with respect and listen to what she has to say. Any questions?"

The guy who'd given her the flirty eyes earlier raised his hand. *Idiot,* Sage thought as she rolled her eyes.

David seemed to have a similar reaction, looking unimpressed as he said, "Yes, Chris?"

The player's wide, white grin contrasted with the deep mahogany of his skin. "Are there any rules about romancing Miss Fogerty, Coach?"

Most of the players laughed, although a number of them at least tried to hide it. Sage saw David start to open his mouth to respond, but she jumped in before he had a chance to speak.

"Chris Terrence, right?" She tried to make her voice as saccharine as possible. "While I don't doubt that you are a legendary romancer, I'd recommend re-focusing some of that energy toward your free throws." She shook her head. "Forty-five percent last season? That's bad, Terrence. That's really bad."

Once again, the entire team devolved into laughter and teasing, a few of them shoving at Chris' chest. To his credit, he took her ribbing as she'd hoped he would — clasping a hand over his heart and dramatically stumbling back as though she'd wounded him with his words.

She looked quickly between both coaches, gauging their reaction. Coach Dixon looked amused, a small smile playing on his normally downturned mouth. David, though — he looked between her and the rest of the team, and she couldn't quite read the expression on his face. Confusion, and maybe a bit impressed. When he looked back at her, she gave him a smile, needing in that moment to reassure him. Of what, she wasn't sure.

Something loosened in his shoulders when he saw her smile, and he shook his head as his own smile grew. Turning back to the guys, he held up his hands. "Alright alright, now that we've all learned a valuable lesson about what happens when you try to romance Miss Fogerty —" He had to pause as the team once again laughed, but didn't seem overly put out with their behavior. If anything, he looked relieved, like their laughter was something he'd been trying to find. "We've got some stuff coming up this week, so listen to Miss Fogerty and check your emails for the details."

"Right, so you've got a community service event next week on Wednesday. You're going to be putting on an after-school camp for kids at the local rec center. It's a free program, so a lot of these kids may not have access to sports camps. It might be their first experience playing basketball." She paused, tucked a stray hair back behind her ear. "I already checked everyone's schedule, so all of you need to be there. Wear your gray team shirts."

"And it's alumni weekend this weekend," Coach Dixon added. "So you boys need to be out and about before the football game, since we typically have a pretty big alumni turnout. What with this guy returning," he cocked his thumb toward David, "there's liable to be a bunch of guys coming in. So behave, and make the program look good."

The guys nodded, and Sage noticed that their response to Coach Dixon was different from how they responded to David. No, Coach Hughes.

Fuck.

"Alright guys, get out of here and remember to eat green stuff," Coach Hughes said, effectively dismissing the team.

Only one player — the skinny guard with the topknot — responded to his blatant attempt at humor. "I cook a damn good mac n' cheese with all the sneaky veggies in it, Coach," he said, grinning and revealing deep dimples and slightly crooked teeth. "Me and Erik are making dank meals over at our place."

"I'll take your word for it, Monty," Coach Hughes replied, a fond smile on his face as he watched Monty jog off to join the guys as slowly left the gym, undoubtedly going to the locker room.

Sage walked back over to the bleachers and sat down, waiting to give the players time to get out the door. While she was going to be around the team, she had no illusions that she was *part* of the team, and wanted to respect that boundary.

She watched Coach Dixon shake David's hand, the assistant coach's face once again stuck in a frown. They exchanged a few quiet words, and then the older man turned toward the door, following the players out of the gym. She watched as the heavy wooden door slid shut behind him, the click amplified in the suddenly silent space.

"Mind if I walk with you?"

She started at the sound of David's voice so close to her.

Getting up, she adjusted her bag over her shoulder, shrugging as she started toward the door. She felt him fall into step beside her, and she caught a whiff of him that she hadn't before — a clean, familiar smell that she couldn't place.

He reached out ahead of her, pushing open the door and stepping aside so that she could walk through first.

"Thanks," she said, chancing a glance up at him as she walked past.

He watched her with intense focus, like observing her was the only thing on his mind at that moment. It was an uncanny feeling, and she felt her cheeks warm in response.

She slowed, waiting for him to join her as the door shut behind them. She noted with a smile how well-matched their long legs were as they walked down the quiet, empty hallway that bordered the glass-walled racquetball courts.

"So," David said, breaking the silence between them. "I feel like we should probably talk about what almost happened between us."

"Probably a good idea," she said, bracing herself for what was inevitably going to be an uncomfortable, if not necessary, conversation. Sometimes, being an adult was a real fucking bummer.

"So," he said again, pausing to clear his throat. "We met at a bar, hit it off, and were planning on going home together."

She couldn't help but snort. "We were going to fuck, David."

Ah fuck.

"I mean —" She came to a sudden stop as she stumbled over her words, feeling her cheeks heat beyond what should be physically possible to endure without bursting into flames. "Coach Hughes. You're Coach Hughes." She shook her head. "Shit. I just mean, there's no reason to be vague. We both knew where that night was ending."

He reached a hand up to scratch his beard as he looked away from her, and she noticed his own face was flushed. "Yeah. We both knew, Sage." He exhaled loudly, turning back to look her directly in the eye. "What do you want to do about the fact that we have a history — even though it's very brief — of being interested in each other?"

Sage blinked up at him. She hadn't been expecting that question. Men like David Hughes were supposed to say *"So here's how this is going to go"* and lay down all the rules. But here he was asking what *she* wanted to do about it. It was an odd sense of power she'd never felt, like she held the future in the palm of her hand.

"I," she began, hesitating as she tried to organize her thoughts. "I would like for us to be however we want to be with each other." When David opened his mouth, his brow furrowing, she held up a hand to stop him. "Nothing physical. I'm not saying that," she rushed to explain, internally berating herself for her clumsy attempt to explain what was in her head. "If you feel friendly towards me, then act friendly. If you just want to keep a polite distance, then do that." She looked into his brown eyes, losing herself for a moment in their maple-syrup warmth. "If that's alright with you, then that's what I'd like to do."

He seemed to search her face, his expression unreadable, and then his mouth slowly curved up into a reluctant smile. "That works for me." He shook his head, and for a moment something that looked a lot like regret flashed in his eyes. Her face must have held a silent question, because he grimaced as he added, "I really did enjoy meeting you. Just so you know."

She felt her own lips quirk up, a pang of something constricting her chest. "Me too."

Again, quiet stretched between them, only this time it was obvious that they were both thinking about what *almost* was. It was a monumental task to take someone who you had very neatly grouped in your head and re-categorize them. In this case, it was changing: *David: hot, good chemistry, and very interested* to *Coach Hughes: colleague, kind, and off limits.*

"Are you one of those farmers market girls?" David's voice interrupted her thoughts.

"What?" She had no idea what he was...*oh*. She pointed at her canvas bag that touted the faded *Santa Barbara Farmers Market* logo. "This?"

He nodded, and then did a thing where he scrunched up his nose in an almost-grimace, like he'd just replayed his words in his head. "I like the farmers market. It's good." Again, that fucking *adorable* expression that was so at odds with the formidable bulk of him. "I mean, I was just trying to make conversation." He shook his head. "Shit."

Sage felt the laugh bubble up out of her throat. "Yeah, I guess you could say that I am one of those farmer's market girls."

"Nice." He looked relieved at her reaction, his smile widening as his eyes crinkled in the corners. "Let me guess: you've got a house full of plants and you eat granola for breakfast every morning."

She raised a brow at him. "Only one of those is accurate."

"My money's on the granola," he said, his tone teasing.

"Guess you'll have to wonder, then." She shrugged, a warmth under her skin at how *easy* it was to share air with this man.

He shoved his hands into his pockets, turning and beginning to walk slowly down the hallway. She fell into step beside him, unable to look away from the relaxed smile on his face.

"You have friends coming back this weekend?" he asked.

Sage shook her head. "None can make it this year," she admitted. She hated the fact that none of her roommates were going to be back in Charleston for their first weekend as official alumni. She understood that they were busy, but she still hated it. "My older sister is coming, though."

David looked surprised. "She went here?"

"Yep," she replied. She couldn't help but smile when she thought of her older sister. "She graduated in 2007, but she still has a ton of friends around here."

"Nice. I hope you have a good visit with her."

"Thanks."

They'd reached the top of the stairs. *When had they climbed the fucking stairs?*

Talking to David Hughes was easy and comfortable and weirdly normal, like for a few minutes she'd been able to forget all about the almost-sex and simply enjoy his company. Well, she hadn't completely forgotten about the almost-sex. How could she when he was all huge and *himself*?

"I guess I'll see you next week," David said, tipping his thumb over his shoulder in the direction of the athletic offices. "Have a nice weekend?"

Based on the pained expression on his face, she guessed that he hadn't intended for that to be a question. "You too." She gave him a quick nod, turning away quickly, not wanting to prolong the moment.

Only she *wanted* to prolong the moment, but she knew she shouldn't.

Couldn't.

Clinging to her sister's hand as they walked down the busy sidewalk on King Street, Sage thought about how much she hated heels. It was Saturday night, which meant that the streets were packed with bar and club patrons, bachelorette parties, and, on that particular weekend, crowds of Southeastern alumni.

Sage had spent as much time as possible with Brinley since she'd finished class on Friday, tagging along with whatever she and her friends were doing. They mostly sat around restaurant patios or went for long walks, both activities that she independently enjoyed. The laughter and stories were an added bonus.

Tonight, Brinley was vibrant as always, wearing an outfit that somehow walked the fine line between looking hot as fuck and sophisticated. Her group of five friends were all dressed similarly: floral sheath dresses or tight jeans with bright blouses. And of course, they were all wearing heels.

At Brinley's insistence, Sage was wearing a thin strapped, vibrant blue dress that brushed her mid-thigh, and she'd lost the argument about the brown leather pumps. Brinley had relented on leaving her hair unstyled, as long as Sage agreed to wear it down. She already regretted making that choice, as she felt her hair sticking to her neck.

The things she did for her sister.

Brinley and company stopped in front of a dark stoop with swooping letters in white neon above it that said *Verve*. Low, rhythmic music pulsed from inside, but it was decidedly more subdued than some of the other clubs they'd passed on King Street.

It took a moment for her eyes to adjust to the darkness inside. It was certainly an establishment that catered to an older clientele, what with the lack of flashing strobe lights and the music that was just quiet enough that you could hold a conversation without shouting. A long bar ran the entire length of one wall, and high cocktail tables filled the space between the far wall, which held secluded booths. There was minimal lighting, which only reinforced the feeling that you'd entered into another world and could forget about your troubles, at least for a little while.

Sage followed Brinley to the bar, where her sister immediately commanded the attention of one of the smartly dressed bartenders, ordering the group a round of tequila shots.

Brinley, while a consummate mature adult for the majority of the year, let loose every year with her old college friends. They always started with tequila shots, moved to frozen margaritas, and almost always concluded the night with fried chicken sandwiches from Ricky's, a 24 hour diner that looked like it was plucked straight from the fifties.

Nicole, one of Brinley's friends, led them to a corner booth, and the women all piled in together before shooting back the tequila.

Sage sucked on the provided lime as she settled back into the cushioned seat. While she had no claim to Brinley's friends, they were all so fucking nice to her that it made her painfully aware of the lack of friendship in her life this year.

They included her seamlessly in their conversations, asking about school, her new apartment, and if she was still exercising like a maniac. She rolled her eyes at the last one, but admitted that yes, she still started most mornings with a workout.

"Brinley said you're doing your grad school internship with the basketball team?" Anecia asked, tossing her long, carmel-colored braids over one shoulder. She glanced at the rest of the group. "Isn't David Hughes coaching the team this year?"

Sage nodded, watching with curiosity as the rest of the table reacted.

Everyone's eyebrows shot up.

"Oh my god," Nicole said, leaning forward toward Sage. "He's really back?"

She shrugged. "Yeah, he's the head coach this year."

Anecia groaned, throwing her head back. "That absolutely devastatingly hot man is back in town. How am I supposed to show up for work every day now that I know we are breathing the same air?"

The rest of the women laughed. Brinley shoved at Anecia's shoulder. "No chasing after men who don't know that you exist, Necie. It's not good for you."

Sticking her tongue out at Brinley, Anecia turned back to Sage. "David was a senior when we were freshmen. We were all obsessed."

"Not me," Brinley said, wrinkling her nose. "I was too busy with my upsettingly mediocre boyfriend."

Again, the women laughed, and then promptly launched into mercilessly teasing Brinley about Shipley, the guy who she'd dated for the first two years of college. Sage had met him only once, and he was just as terrible as they made him sound.

They ordered another round of shots. The bar was starting to fill up, and soon enough a group of men who knew Nicole came over. The group continued to fracture into smaller factions as more and more Southeastern alumni showed up.

Sage didn't see anyone she knew beyond recognition, so she

made her way back to the bar to order another drink. Just as she was leaning forward to catch the bartender's eye, she felt someone move in beside her.

She looked back over her shoulder, coming face to face with a wide torso covered in a gray button up. The man was handsome, probably a few years older than her, and looked like a Viking-lumberjack with his shoulder-length blonde hair and reddish beard.

He smiled at her. "Can I get you a drink?" He leaned in closer, bracing himself against the bar.

She searched his face for a moment. "Sure," she said, opening up her body to face him. She ignored the part of her that looked at his blue eyes and wished they were dark and shadowed by curling lashes.

"I'm Gus," he said, reaching out a hand that was covered in dark, geometric tattoos.

She slid her fingers between his. "Sage."

CHAPTER 6
IT WAS MEDIOCRE
DAVID

The minute David showed up back in Charleston, he'd been absorbed by the group of his college friends who'd stuck around after graduating. Chuck had been his roommate, and then Darius, Tommy, and Ford had all been on the basketball team with him. Additionally, there was Keaton, who'd been one of Chuck's teammates on the swimming team.

It was more than a homecoming to be coaching at Southeastern. It was a return to his community.

And, since the minute he'd locked up his office for the weekend, David hadn't stopped smiling.

They'd all gone to dinner together earlier: twelve men — the local guys and old teammates visiting from out of town — catching up on their families, spouses, and kids, and of course a healthy amount of reminiscing about the past.

Now they were heading into a dark bar where, according to the guys, the alumni from their time were gathering.

It was crowded, with a clinging heat hanging in the air from the bodies that filled every corner of the place. David was glad he'd gone with a short sleeved button up, as he was already sweating. Laughter and conversations almost entirely drowned out the music.

He followed the guys as they wove their way through the crowd toward the bar. David was always painfully aware of his size in environments like this; he tried to dodge as many people as he could, muttering a constant stream of apologies as he inevitably brushed against the bodies around him.

Finally, they made it to the bar.

He'd already had a beer with dinner, which meant whatever ordered would be his last drink of the night. Given that it sounded like the guys were planning to hang out for a while, he gambled and ordered a whiskey ginger, figuring he had enough time for the buzz to wear off before he needed to worry about making sure everyone made it home safely.

Once he had his drink, he almost immediately got sucked into a conversation with someone he vaguely recognized who wanted to congratulate him on his new job.

Time passed in a bit of a blur. It felt like he was having the same conversation over and over again: *Hey, it's so and so, remember me? What are you doing these days? You married? Got kids?*

Finally he extracted from a conversation with a woman who had been particularly interested in his lack of a wife, and, while she was attractive, there was something about how she looked at him that made his skin crawl.

He beelined for the bathroom, letting out a relieved sigh when he saw that the line was for the women's room. As he washed his hands, he glanced up at his reflection in the mirror.

He scowled at himself as he tugged his shirt down from where the fabric stuck to his stomach, silently cursing the extra layer of padding he couldn't get rid of.

Aging was a pain in the ass.

He walked back out into the crowd, eyes catching a familiar face sitting at one of the tables.

Changing his course, he made his way over to the table. "Gus," he called out as soon as he was within earshot, raising a hand in a wave. "Haven't seen you in years, man."

"Hughes!" Gus stood up, and David noticed then that he was

sitting with a blonde woman whose back was to him. The bearded man pulled him into a back-slapping hug that David returned before stepping back. "How the hell are you?"

"I'm -" David started, only to promptly lose all memory of what words were when the blonde turned around and revealed a face that he definitely hadn't been trying not to think about.

Goddamnit she looked beautiful. Her hair hung loose, waving around her shoulders like she was a mermaid or something. Her dress was low cut and there was so much of her skin exposed that he felt like his brain hit a speed bump. Glancing down, he actually had to stop himself from groaning at the sight of the short dress revealing miles of tan, bare thighs.

His hand had been on that thigh before, only there had been a thick layer of denim in the way. He wanted, no, *needed*, to feel the real thing.

Suddenly, his brain decided to come back online, and he was painfully aware of the fact that he had not-at-all subtly been staring.

At Sage Fogerty.

Who he wasn't allowed to stare at.

God *damn* it.

He turned back to Gus, who was looking at him with an expression that very clearly communicated *what the fuck are you doing?* Because Gus and Sage had obviously been having a moment together, and he'd interrupted. Clearing his throat, David tried to salvage the situation. "Sorry man," he mumbled, forcing a grin. "Had a few tonight."

Gus, ever the good-natured, easy-going guy, waved off the apology. "Congrats on the coaching gig."

"Thanks. It feels good to be back."

"You guys know each other?"

Both men looked at Sage, whose eyes darted back and forth between them.

It was Gus who answered her question. "We were in school together. He was a year ahead, but his roommate Chuck was on the swim team with me, so we hung out a lot." A curious look crossed his face. "Do you know each other?"

David opened his mouth, but Sage spoke first. "I'm the team manager for men's basketball for my master's program."

"Badass," Gus said, the word directed toward Sage like an affectionate nickname as his hand came down to rest on her back.

David watched with a small amount of satisfaction as she rolled her eyes, even as her cheeks gained a bit of that pink flush.

"Right," Gus turned back to him, all the while maintaining his hold on Sage, who had redirected her attention to her drink. "It was really good to see you, Hughes."

It was an obvious dismissal, and David couldn't figure out whether or not he wanted to stay or get as far away from them as possible.

"Good to see you too, Gus."

He turned, walking in the opposite direction without any clear sense of where he was going.

When he bumped into Chuck, who was sitting on his phone in an empty booth, David squeezed in beside him with a groan.

"What're you stressed about now?" Chuck asked, not even looking up from his phone.

Goddamned friends who knew him too well.

"Remember the girl from the bar?" David asked, knowing better than to try to lie to him.

Chuck looked up at that. "The blonde?"

David nodded. "She's my team manager."

"What?" Chuck blinked bright blue eyes at him, his reddish brows lowering like he was puzzling through a math problem. "How?"

"She's a grad student at Southeastern. Doing the Master's in sports management."

"Oh shit," Chuck shook his head. "But you guys didn't..."

"No!" David almost shouted the response. "But we were planning on it. There's no doubt that the plan was to... You know. Take her home."

Chuck scooted his chair closer. "Have you worked with her yet?"

Nodding as he scratched his cheek, David tried to figure out how to describe how things had been between himself and Sage so far.

He wasn't sure what he'd been expecting from the younger woman when they came face to face in his office, but she'd defied every assumption.

There was a youthful innocence to the way her round cheeks flushed bright pink, but then there was a steadiness and certainty about her that he could only dream of possessing. She handled herself around the team, easily slipping into humor while maintaining a toughness that made it very clear that she wouldn't tolerate being messed with.

And the way she'd addressed what had *almost* happened between them head on?

I want you to treat me however you want.

She was a force, and not a single day had passed without him thinking about her.

"We've worked together a few times," he said to Chuck. "She's professional. Basically said that we could be friendly and adults about it."

"Good on her." Chuck seemed impressed. "So why are you freaking out right now?"

"She's here." He didn't try to hide the frown on his face. "With Gus Brown."

At that, Chuck laughed. "Oh shit. That's rough."

"What do you mean?" *He* knew why it was rough. He just didn't understand why Chuck thought it was.

His friend gave him a look like he was a colossal idiot. "Gus gets the girl, and you have to sit back, behave, and watch it happen." A sympathetic smile played on his mouth. "Objectively, it sucks."

David pushed his empty tumbler away from himself. "It's fine."

"You know that it's okay if it's not fine, right?"

Damn Chuck and his damn friend telepathy.

All David could do was nod.

⊏━━━⊐

It was after midnight, and any hint of buzz he'd had had faded into a headache that concentrated right behind his left eye.

He'd wrangled all of his buddies into rideshares and cabs, confirming each address with the drivers before sending them off with the promise that they'd all text him when they got home safely. It didn't matter that they were all men in their thirties who had their shit together. He had to make sure they were safe.

The bar was still crowded, with the conversations and laughter growing increasingly louder as the booze caught up with everyone.

He'd barely been able to unclench his jaw in the past hour. He could finally go home, but for some reason his eyes kept going to where Gus and Sage still sat together. There was no space between them, and he knew, in his gut, that if he waited around, he'd watch Gus wrap an arm around her waist and take her home.

Was she there alone? Was there anyone who was looking out for her?

He let out a frustrated breath. She wasn't his problem. Not his responsibility. It wasn't his job to make sure that she made it home safely. He was being a goddamned idiot, and he needed to get out of there.

Without a backwards glance, he closed his tab and walked out of the bar, going down the block to where he'd parked his Bronco.

He drove home, his knee bouncing and veins buzzing. He expected the late hour to catch up with him, but he couldn't shake the energy in his body.

When he unlocked his apartment, he grabbed Daisy, not even bothering with a leash, carrying the wriggling, licking dog down to a little patch of grass, where she promptly did her business. He should be tired, but even after Daisy was curled in a ball in the little dog bed that sat next to his, he still couldn't settle.

Thank god for the twenty-four hour gym.

Three minutes later he was on the treadmill, feet pounding the belt as his attention sunk down into his body, finally replacing the noise of his head with pins and needles as his muscles woke up, responding to the exertion.

He pushed through twenty minutes of running, stepping off of the still-moving belt and moving to the mat, where he worked through another twenty minutes of deep stretching. He was too old to avoid it, and everything felt better after a deep stretch.

An hour later, he was finally exhausted. He lay back on the mat, muscles burning perfectly after lifting weights and then finishing with a short yoga flow. He rolled up to his feet, wiping down the wet spot where he'd been lying before moving to the door.

It was still hot even under the cover of midnight. Tall lamps lit the sidewalk that wound its way through the apartment complex, and he could smell the heavy fragrance of magnolia blossoms.

He started toward his building, only to stop short as he saw someone walking toward him. He would recognize those legs anywhere.

"Sage?"

She started, staggering a bit in the high heels that made her even taller than usual. He scanned her, subconsciously checking for injury or discomfort, but other than the slightly glazed look in her eyes she seemed fine.

Drunk and too damn beautiful for her own good, but fine.

"Are you alright?" He asked, walking toward her. He couldn't stop himself from reaching out to gently grip her elbow, and felt a profound sense of contentment when she leaned some of her weight into him.

"Totally fine." She smiled, and it was softer than he was used to seeing. "Sleepy, but fine." She then seemed to focus on his face, her expression fading to puzzlement. "What are you doing here?"

David had been so relieved to see her that he hadn't even gotten that far in his head. "I was about to ask you the same thing," he said, because of course that's what he should be worried about, not the fact that her hair was tangled in the back and dark makeup smudged under her eyes.

Sage looked around them, her lips turning down in a frown that looked more like a pout.

It was *adorable*.

"I live here." She turned to look behind her, before peering around David's shoulder. "Up there, I think."

Goddamnit.

"Oh," he managed to choke out. "I live here too. Over there." He released his hold on her arm to point toward his building, only to immediately grab her again when she swayed back in the absence of his touch. *Shit.* "Can I walk you home?"

"Nope."

He raised his brows at her. "Seriously?"

She scowled at him. "I don't want your help."

"Please, Sage." He wasn't above begging if meant getting her home safely.

She shook her head. "Nope. I got it."

"What if I told you that I'm actually your neighbor so I happen to be walking that way?"

"That's bullshit."

Annoyance and amusement warred within him. She was being frustratingly stubborn, but *damn* if a tiny part of him wasn't enjoying himself. "Or what if I need to run a set of stairs to finish off my workout?"

She looked down, as though she was just noticing his workout gear and the fact that he was drenched in sweat.

"You don't need the stairs," she said, waving a hand toward his lower body. "You've got the hottest thighs I've ever seen and a perfect, perfect butt." She twirled, ankles wobbling, but managed to regain her balance. "I'm going now."

"I'm coming with you."

He started walking beside her, a hand hovering behind her in case she stumbled.

She looked over at him. Again, there was that scowl. "Am I allowed to call you annoying?"

He snorted, amusement officially winning out. "I think in this situation, you can call me whatever you want."

They walked together in silence for a moment, before David couldn't hold back his question any longer.

"How'd you get home?"

Her steps faltered. His hand was on her back in an instant, supporting her until she regained her balance. "Fuck these shoes," she muttered, leaning down and pulling the heels off one at a time. Now barefoot, she resumed walking, and David reluctantly removed his hand.

"Gus," she finally answered.

David felt his jaw clench as the muscles in his shoulders tightened. He forced himself to take a deep breath. When he'd completely emptied his lungs, he responded. "Oh."

Quiet fell between them again. David's head spun, too many simultaneous things up there to pin down or name.

"It was mediocre."

"What?" He looked over at her. Her gaze was down on the ground as she walked. He noticed that her toenails were painted blue.

"The sex," she said, the words falling from her lips like she was commenting on the weather. "It was in the back of a car. Too crowded."

He choked on nothing, sputtering as he attempted to cover it up with a cough. *What in the ever-loving shit was he supposed to say to that?*

"Oh," he managed to croak out.

Sage made a soft humming noise. "You should line up Jordan's shot on the left."

His brain was breaking. Did she seriously just jump from commenting on how another man had been in bed to *basketball*?

"Oh?" Apparently his entire vocabulary had been reduced to a single word.

"He's right handed," she said, matter of fact, "but his shot improves by 25% when he's shooting on the left side."

Huh.

It was the kind of thing he was looking for when he watched game tape, but honestly he'd been so caught up in watching the team as a whole that he'd just only just started to scratch the surface of evaluating the individual players.

He looked over at Sage, curious. "Been watching them play?"

She shrugged. "I'm around. Sometimes we're in the gym at the same time, and the other night I rebounded for him."

"You still play?" Based on how she'd reacted to questions about her playing during their meeting, he'd assumed that she'd left the game behind.

"Of course I still play." She looked at him with a sad smile. "Well, I shoot. Alone." One of her hands reached up to tuck a strand of blonde hair behind her ear. "Do you?"

"Not as much as I want to," he admitted. "But yes, occasionally."

Sage moved toward a set of stairs that led to the second story apartments. He followed behind, never letting his eyes leave her. If she stumbled, he would be there.

"If you weren't you, I'd say we should play together," she said, glancing back over her shoulder at him. Her mouth curved up into a smirk. "I think I could probably beat you."

He chuckled, trying to imagine the woman in front of him on the court. He found that it wasn't such a reach to imagine her playing, her long body stretching toward the basket.

He definitely shouldn't find that image arousing.

What the hell was wrong with him?

When she stopped at a door and fumbled with a key ring, he looked down, reading the mat that said "Welcome-ish" in looping cursive. She opened the door, turning for a moment and locking eyes with him.

Why did she have to be so *lovely*?

She looked at him with a small, crooked smile as she leaned against the door jamb. "Night, Coach," she said softly.

"Goodnight, Sage." He dipped his chin, already starting to back away even though all he wanted to do was follow her.

CHAPTER 7
NO MORE BUTT TALK
SAGE

"Morning!"

Sage glared across the console as Brinley dropped into the front seat of her car, looking polished and refined as ever in black leggings and a matching quarter zip.

Stupid sisters who could drink stupid tequila and still look like that before noon.

Brinley gave her a knowing smile as she handed her a to-go cup. "I got you a tea."

The perfectly brewed Earl Gray with honey and milk was exactly how she liked it. It at least started to make up for the excruciating pain of taking her sister to the airport the morning after drinking way too much.

"So." Brinley looked her over, eyes lingering on the mascara Sage knew was smudged under her eyes and the bun she'd piled her hair into. "Have fun last night?"

"Eh," Sage said. She didn't hold back from Brinley. There was no point in trying to lie to her sister. "I hooked up with that guy Gus, who was fine."

"Fine?"

She rolled her eyes. "He tried hard and he had nice hands."

Brinley laughed. "Ah, how high the bar is for men."

"And he gave me a ride home, which was nice."

"Sage," her sister's expression grew more serious. "That's literally the bare minimum."

Sage waved off the comment, adding, "And then I ran into David Hughes at my apartment complex."

"What?" Brinley's dark brows practically reached her hairline. "Why?"

"Apparently he's my neighbor."

Brinley's responding laugh held absolutely no sympathy. "So you're telling me that your hot sort-of-boss is your neighbor, and you ran into him after doing the dirty deed with someone he went to school with?"

If only it were just that.

Sage wrinkled her nose. "Please don't say 'dirty deed,' Brin." She paused, rubbing at the leather of the steering wheel as she waited at a red light. "It's actually worse than that," Sage admitted. "Before I got the internship with the team, I may or may not have met David Hughes at a bar."

Brinley gasped. "No!"

"Nothing happened," Sage jumped in. "But it was going to. We had literally verbally confirmed that we were going to fuck."

"You're so fucking cool," Brinley said, looking at Sage like she'd just revealed a hidden superpower.

"And then," Sage continued, "last night I was all drunk and *stupid* and I ran into him and then I told him that he had a perfect butt and that I'd had *mediocre fucking sex with Gus.*"

Brinley was actually howling with laughter. "What is wrong with you?" she wheezed, rocking forward and back as much as the seat belt would allow.

"I don't know," Sage said with a groan. "It was like I couldn't stop talking. Like my brain rebelled and wanted to taunt him with the fact that I'd gotten laid, but even then I couldn't lie and pretend that it was a great time."

Her sister's laughter subsided a bit. "Are you okay with that?"

"What do you mean?"

"With the hooking up," Brinley continued, her voice softening to the tone she used when she was trying to be a good older sister. "I know it's worked for you in the past, but do you ever think about —"

"Nope." Sage shook her head vehemently, even as the movement triggered a throb in her head. "No relationships. None of that 'needing someone else to be happy' bullshit."

Brinley sighed. "You know it doesn't have to be like that, right?"

"Show me, then." Sage shook her head, an anger that was as familiar as breathing rising up in her chest. "Where are the people in relationships who can claim their own happiness? Who hold onto their independence?"

Again, Brinley sighed, only this time there was sadness there that hadn't been there before. Sage glanced over, trying to read her sister's face before turning back to the road. "What?" she asked.

"I've been dating someone," Brinley said. "And he's fucking *awesome*, Sage. Like, has his shit together financially, drives a Honda SUV even though he could afford something nicer, only wants to hang out a few times a week, and thinks that I am the greatest person ever." She paused, and a quick look over revealed the fond smile on her face. "Someday, someone is going to prove you wrong, Sage. And I can't wait to say 'I told you so.'"

"You're dating someone?" Sage asked, still not fully computing the news. "What does Mom think?"

Brinley snorted, the same indignant snort that their mom had passed down to both of her daughters. It was a Fogerty thing.

"Mom doesn't know. And she will continue to not know," she added, and Sage could feel her glare.

"I got you," she reassured her sister. "I just... I'm happy for you. Really."

"Then why are you being weird?"

Sage worried the inside of her cheek for a moment as she tried to figure out why there was a knot of anxiety in her stomach. "Aren't you afraid?"

Brinley reached across to lay a soft hand on Sage's arm. "Fucking terrified. But it's worth it. At least, in my mind, the possibility of a good outcome outweighs the fear of it all going to shit."

"Speaking of it all going to shit," Sage said, needing to change the subject. "You heard from Dad recently?"

"The customary birthday card and two hundred bucks," Brinley responded. "Mom got going about him the other day. I guess his wife posted a family photo from a resort in Mexico, which set her off. No matter how many times I tell her that she doesn't *have* to stalk his new family online, she still does it." She shook her head. "Do you think she's ever going to move on? I mean, it's been over ten years since he left."

"Honestly? I think that at this point the hate is so much a part of who she is that I can't really imagine her letting it go."

Brinley got quiet, seeming to soak in Sage's words. For a few minutes, it was just the sound of the tires against the pavement and the occasional distant siren or horn.

Finally, she spoke, just as they were pulling into the airport. "Don't let Mom get to you, Sage," she said softly. "I know you had the whole thing with Evan that didn't help, but you survived that. I mean, look at you. You're a badass. Don't let other people's bullshit steal your life."

Pulling up to the curb and throwing her car into park, Sage lunged across the console and pulled her sister into a hug. She tucked her face into the soft skin of her neck, deeply inhaling Brinley's comforting and familiar floral scent.

"Love you," she said, the words muffled against Brinley's skin.

Brinley returned the hug, holding Sage tightly against her. "Love you too." She gave one final squeeze and then pulled away. "Call me all the time."

"You too." Sage smiled, overwhelmed with fondness for her

sister. She was so fucking lucky to have someone like Brinley in her corner.

They exchanged a final hug, and Sage lingered at the curb long enough to watch Brinley's perfectly straightened hair swish through the automatic doors.

———

Back at her apartment, she tackled her normal workout, pushing through the hungover discomfort. By the end she was a sweaty mess, and her entire body had a distinctly tequila-ish scent. *Disgusting.*

She pushed the gym door open, relieved that at least her headache had faded. Now she just needed a shower.

"Sage!"

She turned at the sound of her name, and immediately froze.

David *fucking* Hughes, looking absolutely mouth-watering in basketball shorts and an old mesh jersey, was walking a tiny dog and waving at her.

Arms. Holy fucking *arms.* Shoulders and arms. His shoulders were broad, and rounded muscles tapered down to his defined biceps. And his forearms were ripped. *How were his forearms so ripped?*

She needed to say something. *Don't be weird, Sage.*

"You have a dog," she blurted out. Immediately, she felt her face heat.

David's face broke out into a fond smile as he looked down at the small, wriggling dog that pranced about on the sidewalk in front of him. He bent down, picking up the golden-colored creature and cradling it into his chest as he scratched the floppy ears, his hands appearing gigantic next to the small animal.

"This is Daisy," he said, walking up to Sage.

Sage wasn't someone who was easily moved by cute things. Tiny pigs in teacups didn't do it for her. But the sight of this massive, powerful man basically *nuzzling* at this dog had turned her bones to goo. Straight up *goo*.

"She's so cute," she said, her hand unconsciously reaching for the bundle of fur. She froze, glancing up at David, who was still smiling like a goon. "May I," she asked, nodding toward her hand.

He held the dog out to her.

She lightly scratched at the tiny head with her fingers. Daisy leaned into the touch, her little tongue hanging out one side of the wide grin that showed impossibly small teeth.

"Oh aren't you just perfect," Sage breathed, smiling at the dog. "You seriously couldn't be more cute."

"When I moved back my mom came to visit and, in her words, 'I needed to get a dog to make my life less sad,'" David said, and when Sage looked up at his face, she saw a softness in his eyes as he looked down at Daisy. "I had plans to adopt something big and burly but then Daisy looked at me with those big eyes and I was hopeless."

It was Sage's favorite trope to read: the big, gruff cowboy caring for a wounded pony or baking pies. Physical brawn offset by softness absolutely ruined her.

"Well good on your mom, then," Sage said, smoothing down the golden hair that she'd ruffled on Daisy's head. Stepping back, she steeled herself for what she knew she needed to say next.

She met David's eyes and held his gaze. "Last night," she started.

David shifted Daisy into the crook of one arm and held up another hand to stop her. "I'm just glad you made it home safely," he said. His expression was kind, his brown eyes watching her carefully.

"David. I complimented your butt," she argued, not sure why she was bringing up something that would be better forgotten.

He laughed, lifting his hand up to scratch at his jaw like he was trying to hide his smile. "Ah, yes you did." He cocked a dark brow at her. "Thanks for that, by the way."

She shook her head. "No more butt talk."

"You started it," he retorted, still grinning.

"Well thanks for being nice about it," she said, starting to back away from him. She needed space; it was like every second she let herself be around him made her feel farther away from their current reality, where they worked together and were going to spend hours and hours in each other's company.

He must have been able to read her body language, because he ducked his head and gave Daisy a gentle scratch before looking back at her. "See you later, Sage."

She gave him a wave. "See you around, Coach."

As she walked back up the stairs to her apartment, she could almost feel the ghost of a palm on her back, ready to catch her if she fell. She blinked, shaking away the image.

Sage showed up to the rec center about an hour before the Southeastern team was scheduled to arrive. The back seat and trunk of her Corolla were stuffed with the t-shirts and basketballs they were going to give to the kids who came to the after-school camp.

She'd dressed practically, as her job was going to be carrying boxes and running around making sure everyone was in the right place and doing what needed to be done. She wore navy blue leggings with a Southeastern t-shirt, and, of course, a big green hoodie with the Southeastern basketball team logo in the middle. She might or might not have found it in a corner of the equipment room. Of course, she washed it before wearing it.

The rec center had a big double court, which was nice for a facility that otherwise was pretty standard. She got everything set up on the metal bleachers that were tucked along one wall, and then settled in with her most recent Western romance.

She was completely lost in a scene where the male lead, a cowboy who had to step up to manage his family's ranch, was arguing over ranching practices with the female lead, the daughter of the ranch foreman, making her effectively *off limits*. Sage was about halfway through the book, which meant that at any moment things were going to escalate from snappy banter to making out against a barn.

It felt like only a few minutes had passed when the team showed up. Stashing her book in her bag, she got up and grabbed the clipboard where she'd divided the guys into smaller groups to run drills with the kids.

The players jumped to attention when she started directing them to set up cones and ladders, responding to her barked commands with a respectful earnestness that made her want to laugh.

She was vaguely aware of David showing up, wearing basketball shorts and a black polo that somehow made his upper body look even bigger than usual. She definitely wasn't watching him.

When the kids showed up, it was a madhouse. A perfect explosion of chaos trapped in an enclosed space full of one hundred and fifty kids shrieking and bouncing balls. As she ran from drill to drill to make sure the guys were instructing the kids somewhat effectively and not cursing, Sage felt a wave of emotion rise in her chest.

She'd forgotten about this part of basketball. The enthusiasm and messiness before the game became so skilled and calculated. Kids trying moves for the first time, and then ten reps later executing a layup with the correct footwork.

There was so much potential and optimism in the room that she thought she might choke on it.

An hour and a half flew by, and then they were handing out t-shirts and balls to all of the kids, some of whom were asking the guys on the team for autographs. It was adorable, and Sage watched as David gathered the guys together as the last of the kids left. She started to clean up, and was pleasantly surprised when the team and David joined her, collapsing the now-empty cardboard boxes, gathering the university's balls into the large mesh bags, and picking up any trash that was left in the bleachers.

"Alright guys," David called out, but his voice was so hoarse it came out like a harsh rasp. Sage wasn't the only one who couldn't hold back a laugh as David coughed and tried again. "We're all good here. See you boys at pick-up tomorrow."

Sage accepted a few fist bumps and high fives from the guys as they left, and then stopped to dig through her canvas bag. Finding what she was looking for, she called out to David as he walked toward the door. "Coach!"

He paused, and she ran to catch up with him. She held out the yellow and green wrappered lozenge to him, pressing it into his palm when he offered her his hand. His skin was warm to the touch. "Throat lozenge," she said, pulling her hand away from his.

He looked down at the lozenge and then up at her. "Ah, thank you." He smiled, almost hesitantly. "For this, and for today."

"Happy to help," she replied, adjusting her bag on her shoulder. "The guys were good today."

"They really were," David said with a smile that carried a hint of pride. "Now I've just got to figure out how to put them all together and make a winning basketball team."

"Isn't that your job?" Sage teased, falling into step beside him as they walked toward the front doors.

Rather than laugh at what she'd thought was an obvious joke, David's face fell into a frown. He looked blankly in front of him, his mind obviously a million miles away.

When she stopped at the front desk to wrap up with the staff, David seemed to shake out of whatever stupor had taken him. "Well thanks again for today, Sage."

She glanced back at him as she signed some paperwork. "You know it's my job, right?" She hoped that her smile would make it *crystal fucking clear* that she was messing around.

But David was looking at her hand, brown eyes staring

intently where she still gripped the provided pen. He cleared his throat. "You're left handed?"

"Yeah," she said, setting the pen down and thanking the front staff before turning back to join David where he waited for her. Because that's what he was doing — waiting, walking her out, and she'd be willing to bet that he was the kind of man who would walk her all the way to her car.

"Do you shoot left-handed?" He held open the door for her as they walked out into the late afternoon heat.

"Yes," she said. "Although, funny story, I actually shot right handed when I first started. Even though I wrote left-handed, my coaches told me it would be easier to shoot righty. So I played that way until I broke my arm in 7th grade." She couldn't help but smile; she remembered that time like it was yesterday. "Rather than sit out of practice for the three months it was going to take to heal, I decided to teach myself how to shoot left-handed. It totally changed my game. Being down low, being able to shoot with either hand was a huge advantage."

They stood beside her car. As she unlocked the door she looked up at David, finding him watching her, the expression on his face almost amused. "What," she asked, feeling suddenly defensive. Like maybe she'd said too much, or she'd been too real in sharing about herself.

"Nothing." He grinned as he started to back away. "Drive safe, Lefty," he called out as the distance between them grew.

Sage wasn't sure what to say, so she just waved before lowering herself down into her car. Once the engine groaned to life and she threw it into reverse, she let herself, for just one tiny moment, think about the name David had called her.

Lefty.

She didn't mind that at all. Not one little bit.

CHAPTER 8
DON'T FORGET THE GREEN STUFF
DAVID

David hit the spacebar on his laptop, freezing the tape from their intersquad scrimmage that he had up on the TV in his home office. The folding table in the middle of the room was strewn with bits of scrap paper, three different play boards, and two partially drunk cups of coffee.

He needed a shower, and based on how Daisy was looking at him, he needed to take her outside for a walk.

Standing up with a groan, he ran a hand through his dirty hair before scooping Daisy up, shoving a hat onto his head, and then stepping outside. He squinted against the bright sun, his eyes straining to adjust after hours spent inside in the blacked-out room.

He hadn't bothered with a leash, trusting that Daisy would stay close as he walked toward the dog park. His legs felt heavy, his body lethargic, and although he tried to find some enjoyment in the day around him, his mind was elsewhere.

The team was a mess. A real goddamn mess, and he had no idea what to do about it.

Well, he knew what to do about it, but the guys were slow on the uptake. On some level, he could understand: he was a new coach bringing in a new style and new systems, and it was bound to take a while for them to get on board.

But *damn*, he'd thought things would be better by now.

So he was pushing them harder, increasing their practice time from two hours to three, and, on his own, spending every waking hour watching game tape from the previous year, film from practices, and researching their opponents. He had three different offensive sets that he wanted to introduce in addition to the pages of set plays he'd drawn up to combat specific scenarios. He'd started keeping a legal pad on his bedside table so that when he woke up in the middle of the night with an idea for a new strategy he could write it down.

He'd largely given up on cooking, instead heating up frozen dinners that boasted low calories and reduced sodium. Apparently, they were healthy. They tasted like garbage, but they were doing the job of keeping his stomach full.

His apartment was also starting to descend into a level of disarray that wasn't like him. He usually took pride in keeping his space neat and tidy, even doing the little things like dusting the shelves and picture frames. But the countdown to their first game weighed on him in a way that left him feeling uncharacteristically exhausted at the end of every day.

This was his chance to be the kind of head coach he'd always dreamed of being. He wouldn't —no, *couldn't* let the opportunity go to waste.

His phone buzzed in his pocket. "Hello?" He answered without looking at the screen.

"Dude," Chuck's voice was almost painfully loud in his ear. "Where the hell have you been?"

"Busy," David replied, trying to ignore the sharp pang of regret in his chest. He'd been so focused on the team recently that he hadn't been keeping up with the guys like he typically did. David was usually the one who organized pick up games, dinners out, or Sundays at one of their places to watch football. As one of the only single guys still in an apartment, he almost never hosted, but he always showed up early and helped with the planning.

It was just what he always did.

Chuck snorted. "When was the last time you left your place?"

"I'm outside right now," David replied, squinting up at the sun, noticing that it was already late afternoon.

"Walking Daisy doesn't count."

David sighed. "Fine. I've been pretty holed up between the office and home."

"When's the first game?"

"Five days." David may have completely lost his sense of the passage of hours during the day, but he couldn't escape the looming, invisible clock counting down the hours until his first game as a head coach.

"Come over for dinner later, okay?" Chuck's tone made it very clear that it wasn't actually a question.

David considered saying no. There were hours of practice footage left to watch, but he couldn't say no to a friend. Especially not to Chuck. "Need me to bring anything?" He finally asked.

"Nah," Chuck replied. "I've got stuff for burgers ready to go."

Now David definitely couldn't say no. "Alright. Gotta run to the store, but I'll be over there after."

They hung up, and David scooped up Daisy and carried her back to his apartment. Once he made sure that her bowl was full of water, he grabbed his keys and a water bottle from the fridge. He paused at the mirror that hung by his front door, trying for a second to fix his hair where it stuck out around his ears and down his neck. He needed a haircut, but every time he went they made him either look like a child with a bowl cut or a teenager trying too hard with some sort of fashionable fade.

How hard could it be to cut a man's hair?

The grocery store was right across the street from his apartment, and because he was only grabbing a few things, he decided to walk. Once he was in the store, he immediately went for the basics that were sustaining him: bananas, protein bars, and frozen dinners.

He turned down the condiments aisle to grab some peanut butter when he noticed a pair of very bare, very golden, *very* beautiful long legs at the other end. The woman's back was to him, but the short jean shorts she wore left her tan and muscular thighs exposed and *goddamnit* was his mouth actually watering?

She was blonde, with a braid that ran down the middle of her back, and as he approached her he realized that she happened to be standing in front of the peanut butter.

He'd been considering dating recently. After the hiccup at the bar with another blonde, he'd been too busy and preoccupied to think about it. Maybe this was the universe telling him to live a little.

Hell, he knew how to flirt.

The wheels of his cart squeaked as he slowed down, and the woman turned to look at him.

Goddamn it.

Why did every beautiful woman in Charleston have to turn into Sage Fogerty? Obviously, the universe was fucking with him.

"Coach?"

He plastered a smile on his face and took another step toward Sage, who looked surprised to see him.

"Fancy seeing you here, neighbor," was what came out of his mouth. He immediately winced.

Sage, to her credit, laughed, her mouth tilting up in that crooked smile as she leaned on her own shopping cart. David glanced down, noticing how many green and leafy things she had selected.

"I take it you don't cook much?" Sage asked, and David followed her gaze to the contents of his cart, which were almost exclusively packaged in cardboard. *At least there were bananas,* he thought to himself.

"Yeah," David admitted. "I can cook, but I've been busy." He didn't say that his cooking was primarily grilling chicken breasts, making instant rice, and steaming frozen broccoli. And he did make a mean fried egg, which he had almost every morning on toast. He pointed at Sage's cart. "I honestly wouldn't even know what to do with all of that."

Sage looked down at her cart and shrugged. "I just like to eat good food," she said, and once again that crooked smile tugged at her lips. "My mom's always had a garden, so we ate a lot of veggies and made things from scratch." She reached down, shuffling through the produce until she produced a package of bacon. "And bacon. All veggies are better with bacon."

David couldn't help but laugh. "I'll have to take your word for it," he said.

"Are you okay?"

He started, confused, only then noticing that her smile had faded and she looked at him like she was concerned. "Am I okay?" he repeated, not entirely knowing how to respond.

"Yeah," she said. There was warmth in her voice as she continued to watch him. "I asked if you were okay."

"Totally fine," he replied, forcing out a laugh as he took off his hat with one hand and pushed his hair back with the other. Tugging the hat back down on his head, he gave her what he hoped was a reassuring smile. "All good."

"You getting ready for the first game?"

A nervous laugh bubbled up from his chest before he could stop it. *Get it together, David.* "Yeah. Totally ready." His voice was too high, and he felt sweat gathering on his palms.

Sage moved toward him, circling her own cart to stand right beside his. She was close enough that he caught a hint of her scent — flowers, maybe?

And then she reached out and gripped his wrist, her touch somehow both gentle and firm. Her skin was surprisingly cool against his. "You're allowed to be nervous, you know." Her voice was quiet, her words just for him.

In that moment, David could feel just how easy it would be to tell her everything. There was something about her steadiness that made him want to confess to her just how much the upcoming season was weighing on him. He wanted to tell her that he had five different half court traps that he couldn't choose between, and how he couldn't figure out how to get Jordan out of his own head. How he wanted Tim's respect more than almost anything, but all he got from his assistant coach were head shakes and frowns.

He couldn't explain how, but in that moment he knew, in his gut, that she would get it.

But he couldn't do that to her. He wouldn't burden her with his insecurities. They were his and his alone. It was his job to get his shit together and figure out how to lead the team. Sage was only there to satisfy a graduation requirement. That was all.

David took a step back, pulling away from Sage's touch. Her fingers brushed the inside of his wrist as he moved, and for a moment he considered chasing her hand down and asking her to do it again. To touch him like that again.

"It's all good," he said, breaking the quiet between them.

Sage returned to her own cart, giving him a sad smile before she started to push past him. "Well don't forget to take your own advice," she said, nodding toward his groceries.

"What's that?"

Her cheeks dimpled as she grinned at him, and it was such a bright expression that he could have sworn that it warmed the air surrounding her. She walked with the certainty of someone who knew where they were going, and just before she turned away at the end of the aisle, she glanced back. "Don't forget the green stuff," she called out, her voice teasing.

David laughed at that, and watching the space where she'd disappeared, he felt a brief stab of discomfort in his chest, knowing that there was probably some lucky guy out there who got to eat Sage Fogerty's cooking.

David parked at the curb in front of Chuck's house, grabbing an excitedly wriggling Daisy from her perch in the passenger seat and tucking her under one arm, while he reached down for the bag of groceries he'd brought with the other.

Sure, Chuck had said he didn't need to bring anything, but David knew better than that.

Chuck lived in West Ashley, in an old residential neighborhood with smaller family homes nestled under the tall, spreading oaks. While Chuck was still single, he'd made it clear that he was looking to settle down, and he'd bought the house as soon as he'd landed the head coaching job for Southeastern's swimming team.

David jogged up the paved steps and knocked on the door.

"Hughes!" Chuck opened the door wearing an old Southeastern t-shirt with the sleeves cut off and basketball shorts. "You look like absolute death, man."

David grunted, unamused, and pushed past his friend into the living room. He placed Daisy on the floor, watching fondly as she scampered off in search of one of Chuck's three cats. They tended to make themselves scarce whenever David brought Daisy over, but there had definitely been a few amusing games of chase when the dachshund managed to find them.

He went straight to the kitchen, placing the bag of groceries on the clean, white island. True to his word, Chuck had burger patties already made and had even taken the time to prepare toppings: lettuce, tomato, onion, and cheese were sliced and neatly plated.

Chuck had always been more put together than the rest of them, putting more thought into his wardrobe and surroundings than the other jocks David had come up with. As his roommate, David had been more than happy to let Chuck take the lead on what should go on the walls and which shirt he should wear when they'd gone out to parties in college.

Now, Chuck's home reflected that same attention to detail, with black and white framed photographs of Texas, his home state, artfully arranged on the dark blue walls. Even his furniture was nice, with matching pillows and throw blankets draped over the top.

He heard Chuck's bare feet on the wood floor behind him. "You okay?" his friend asked, stepping up behind David and clasping a hand on his shoulder.

David's palms gripped at the edge of the countertop, which was at the perfect height for him to lean his weight forward and let his head hang down. He sighed, trying to figure out exactly how to articulate what he was feeling at that moment.

Words definitely weren't his strong suit. He was more of a *doing* guy. But this was Chuck, so he had to at least try.

"I'm..." David began, pausing to swallow against the dryness of his mouth. "I'm worried."

That was a start, at least.

Chuck walked around to the other side of the island, leaning back against the stainless steel fridge. "Worried about the season?"

David nodded.

"Of course you are. It's your first year as a head coach, and you're back at Southeastern. It's a lot."

"How'd you do it?"

"Transition to being a head coach?" Chuck shifted away from the fridge, reaching in and grabbing a beer. He looked to David in a silent offering, but David shook his head.

Cracking open the can, Chuck seemed to think over the question for a minute before answering. "It was probably different for me because I stayed on after graduation, transitioning right into being a graduate assistant with the team. I learned how to coach here, got to know the staff, and so moving up to being an assistant was easier. I didn't have to adjust to a new system or culture."

It made sense. David could only imagine how it would have been different if he'd stayed at Southeastern to coach.

No. He couldn't have done it. He'd needed time to repair his relationship with the sport, to learn to love it again. He'd needed the space, and he liked to think that he was better for it.

"What about becoming head coach? What changed?" David asked Chuck.

Chuck shrugged. "Honestly, by that point I'd absorbed so much as an assistant that I was ready to put my ideas to the test. Fewer ideas about actually coaching the mechanics of swimming, but more about training and motivation and how to be on a team. *That* was what made me so hungry to lead."

"I get that," David said, thinking of the legal pads full of notes he'd taken on all of the motivational speeches he'd heard coaches deliver over the years. What'd worked, what hadn't. He finally had the chance to put it all to use. "How long did it take the new team to adapt to you and your style?"

"It was rocky at first, but by Christmas we'd found our stride," Chuck admitted. Swimming had a similar season to basketball, starting at the beginning of the school year and going through March. "It took a while for them to trust that my ideas worked. Once they made that connection, they were bought in."

David huffed, turning to the bag of groceries he'd brought over. He began to unload the things he'd picked up from the store that he knew Chuck used frequently. Why the man ate so many damn olives he'd never been able to understand.

Chuck looked down at the spread of food on the counter. "I really didn't need anything, you know," he said, but there was a fond smile on his face as he shook his head at David. "But thank you anyway."

He felt the back of his neck heat, self conscious at being thanked. It was just something that he did whenever he came over here, not wanting to come empty handed. It also felt like a way to gradually pay his friend back for all the years of putting up with him.

"Thanks for the advice," David said, balling up the bag and stuffing it into Chuck's trash. "Now how about those burgers?"

"Grill is already hot," Chuck replied, thankfully picking up on the change of topic. "Grab that spatula for me."

They spent the rest of the evening in the comfortable lounge chairs out on Chuck's back patio, catching up while they ate the homemade burgers with potato chips.

Chuck was busy coaching too, but his practices were typically in the early morning, leaving his afternoons free. They tried to hang out at least once a week. Their group of guy friends usually tried to go out to dinner or happy hour at The Grove one afternoon a week as well, but David could admit that he valued the time spent with Chuck differently than the hang outs with the rest of the men.

"Anything new on the dating front?"

David grimaced at the question. "Nope. You?"

"Nah. I kind of turn into a hermit during the season," Chuck replied. "I mean...I'll occasionally hook up, but nothing serious." He shifted in his seat, looking over at David with narrowed eyes. "When was the last time you dated someone?"

"Uh," he started, thinking back. It was definitely in Chicago. "I think it was Fatima, so maybe a year ago?"

"What ever happened with you two?"

David scratched at his beard, tilting his head back to look at the dark tree branches spreading overhead, the sky a dim blue behind them. "I...well she..." He sighed. "I like taking care of people. Especially whoever I'm with. She didn't like that."

Chuck frowned. "What do you mean?"

"I wanted to spend as much time with her as I could, and I think she thought it was excessive. I just...you know how I am about drinking, and she went out to bars with her friends a lot. I get that I can be too much, but I don't know how the hell I'm supposed to shut off the part of me that needs to make sure the people that I care about are okay."

"Caring about the person you're with isn't a bad thing," Chuck said, his voice kind, even patient. "But maybe give your partners some credit, Hughes. There's a difference between being caring and controlling. Most women probably like to know that their partner is looking out for them, but maybe it felt like you didn't trust her to take care of herself."

David considered Chuck's words. It made sense — he just couldn't figure out how to let those things go.

"Just don't give up on it all," Chuck added. "The dating thing. It can be really good to share your life with someone else."

David turned to stare at his friend, incredulous. "Like you're one to talk, *he who is serially single.*"

He could see Chuck's wide grin under the warm porch lights. "Hey, I'm a coach," he said, shrugging his skinny shoulders. "I'm really good at telling other people what to do. Doesn't mean I've got it all figured out for myself."

The conversation moved on from there to the topics they typically discussed: family, how strange college kids were these days, and their plans for their annual spring trip with their close group of friends out to the lakehouse on Lake Murray.

It was late when David bundled up a snoozing Daisy and made the short drive back to his apartment. As he crawled under his simple navy blue sheets, he couldn't stop thinking about what Chuck had said. That maybe his past girlfriends hadn't felt like he'd believed in them.

He'd always been drawn toward women who were capable and strong. Fatima had been a goddamn lawyer. He'd known she was able to take care of herself.

He'd believed in her.

Hadn't he?

CHAPTER 9
SO UTTERLY ALONE
SAGE

Sage walked down the wide hallway, following David and Coach Dixon, barely registering their urgent, hushed conversation as they walked to the locker room at half time.

The team's first preseason game was off to a rough start. It was typical for teams to play at least one game before the official start of the season. The games were viewed as a trial, and often featured a shifting roster that served to give players the chance to prove themselves before the launch of the regular season.

Sage was barely holding it together.

When she'd walked out of the players' entrance into the gymnasium before the game, there had been a sharp pinch in her chest and a heaviness that settled on her shoulders at the sight of the bleachers slowly filling with students, the gleaming wooden floors with the green eagle painted mid-flight in the center circle, and the new nets hanging from the baskets.

If she hadn't had a job to do, Sage would've gotten the fuck out of there. She would have turned right around and torn off her low heels, running and running and running until the bright lights faded and the burning in her lungs drowned out the *what-might-have-been*'s.

But there hadn't been time for that.

She'd needed to make sure the bench was stocked with the team water bottles and that the balls were in position for warm ups. She'd forced herself to breathe, trying to fill her lungs completely with every inhale, wiping her sweaty hands against her slacks and focusing only on what was in front of her.

And she had. As soon as the team started warming up, the pain faded to a dull ache that was easy enough to ignore. Her attention was pulled to making sure the players' names and numbers were accurately written in the official book, and then loading up the tablet where she would be taking in-game stats.

While the team warmed up, David paced in front of the bench, alternating between shoving his hands into the pockets of his navy slacks and snapping his fingers absently at his sides. If the guys on the court looked nervous, then David looked positively terrified.

But she hadn't had time to think about it, as the horn signaled the countdown to the start of the game.

As soon as the ref tossed the ball up and the game began, tracking stats required every bit of her attention. She made note of where on the court players were taking shots, and documented passing errors, rebounds, and assists.

It was a different side of the game than what she'd experienced as a player. As a player, her world had narrowed the second that she stepped onto the court. Instinct took over, and while she'd been trained to keep an ear out for her coach's voice, she would fall into the flow of the game like a fish swept along in a current.

But now, she watched the game from the outside, noticing patterns and missed opportunities. Her feet twitched in her heels as she felt her body react to an opening that she, were she on the court, would have immediately taken advantage of. It was excruciating to be on the sideline, but there was also a sense of appreciation for the beauty of the game that caught her off guard.

Southeastern, though, was playing horribly. Passes weren't

connecting, shots were rushed, and their defense fell apart the second the offense attacked the basket.

It wasn't like there was a lack of skill on the court. No, they were all undeniably talented. But it almost looked like each player was going at a different speed. Like they were going to the right places and making the right passes, but no matter what their timing was off.

They'd finished the half down 15 - 48 against a team who, on paper, they should have been evenly matched with.

As she slipped into the locker room behind David and Coach Dixon, she looked more closely at David. She'd heard his voice barking out plays throughout the first half, his efforts to sound encouraging quickly giving way to frustration as their play continued to decline.

Now, his shoulders drooped, his brows were knit low over his eyes, and his expression was tight as he stood at the edge of the locker room. The guys sat on the low benches, their jerseys drenched in sweat, and their gazes cast down onto the floor. Only Jenks and Monty looked up, and while they both were clearly frustrated, they looked directly at David.

Sage hung back as David and Coach Dixon both said their piece. Neither of them said anything surprising: it was a lot of *talk to your teammates, hustle back on defense,* and *you're a team, damnit.*

"How many turnovers do we have?"

David turned to look over his shoulder at where Sage stood leaning against a metal locker. She quickly navigated through the game software on the tablet. "Ten."

David shook his head, and a thick piece of hair flopped down into his eyes. He pushed it back with his hand, only for the hair to immediately fall back where it had been. He exhaled slowly, and then turned back to the guys.

"You've got to go out there and execute the plays. You've got to play together and trust the guys on the court with you. Take your time on your shots. Let's go."

The guys got up, heavy on their feet, but they dutifully put their hands together in the center of their huddled circle. Sage shifted away from them, hovering by the door.

It was Jenks who called out, "Let's go, boys. Battle on three!"

"One, two, three. Battle!"

The guys filed out of the room, Coach Dixon following behind them.

David paused at the doorway, and Sage watched as his eyes closed for a moment and his chest expanded and contracted in a deep breath. His hands were clenched into fists at his sides, a game board gripped tightly in one.

"They're going to get it," Sage said.

David unclenched his hands, reaching up to push his hair back from his face. It was futile, really, his hair too long and unkempt to stay back. He cleared his throat, turning to face her. "Sure."

She cocked a brow at him. "You know this is just the beginning, right?"

His mouth curved up into a strained smile. "Right," he said, but Sage could tell that he didn't believe it. She could already see the defeat in the heaviness of his posture.

Fuck. He'd never survive a whole season thinking like that.

"They need you, you know," she said, taking a half step closer to where David still hovered by the door.

He barked out a harsh laugh. "I'm not so sure about that."

She could tell that she wasn't getting through to him. Whatever it was that weighed on him felt greater than early season jitters. For whatever reason, the man who was supposed to model confidence and bring conviction to the team was floundering.

Sage brushed past him as she reached for the door handle. "Cut yourself come slack, Coach," she said, unable to think of anything else to say.

When the door shut behind her, she heard a loud crack that sounded distinctly like a board slammed against a wall.

By the end, any hope that Southeastern could have turned the game around was completely shattered. They lost 78 - 30, and the locker room was somber as Coach Dixon and David delivered their post-game speeches.

As the coaches were leaving, Sage approached David, slipping another honey lozenge into his hand with as much subtlety as she could manage. She didn't look at him, but she heard the low, hoarse "thank you" as he moved past her.

When the coaches cleared out of the locker room, Sage went back to the gymnasium, hanging around long enough to wrap up her duties and email the game stat reports off to the coaches. She and Sarah, one of the equipment interns, cleared away the cushioned bench chairs and got the bleachers rolled back into the walls. There was nothing left to do at that point but go home.

As Sage climbed into her car, she tossed her blazer and bag into the passenger seat, letting out a breath she hadn't realized she was holding. It was dark out, and as she drove the familiar streets she was suddenly overwhelmed, like everything she'd shoved away throughout the game came bubbling up simultaneously, demanding her attention.

She'd been in a gym today — not just a court with a hoop, but a true gymnasium where teams competed and played — for the first time in almost five years. She'd been close enough to a game ball that she could've jumped up from her seat and stolen it, moving through either teams' defense to score.

Now she felt emotion rise in her throat and her vision blurred. She blinked furiously against the burning in the corners of her eyes.

She would not cry. *No.* She wouldn't give another second of her life to mourning, not after all of those years had passed. Not after she'd rebuilt herself to stand strong on her own.

She wouldn't think about the man who'd once held her future in his hands.

But still, when she pulled into her parking spot and turned off the ignition, she pulled out her phone and opened Instagram, thumbs tapping on the screen, typing a name into the search bar that she hadn't let herself type in years.

Evan White.

His profile immediately popped up.

There he was. His smile was just as smooth, his teeth as vibrantly white as she remembered. His golden brown skin still looked like it had been sculpted by an artist, and his tight curls were still shaved close to his head.

He was still, objectively, the most handsome man she'd ever seen in her life.

She scrolled through his photos, noting that he was alone in every photo he chose to share. Many of them were selfies in a gym mirror, featuring a peek of toned abs or a flexed arm.

Sage looked up from her phone, staring out at the tall lamp that illuminated the sidewalk.

What the fuck was she doing?

Without looking down, she pressed the lock button on the side of her phone, shaking herself as if she could break out of the painful melancholy that settled over her.

But it only grew when she got back to her dark apartment, painfully aware in that moment of how *alone* she was.

She hated the fact that she was reduced to loneliness after years of building herself up to be fiercely independent. Sage took pride in the fact that she needed no one.

Her education was paid for with merit scholarships, and the rest of her living expenses came from the hotel job she worked over the summer. After growing up with the constant sense that there wasn't enough looming over her, it was the least she could do to free her mom and sister from the burden of supporting her.

It was why, even though the constant job postings drove her crazy, she couldn't tell her mom to stop sending them. Because she knew that whatever job she took coming out of college needed to be enough to support herself, and it was up to her to make that happen.

She felt her chest tightening, her eyes still threatening to spill tears, and so she did the only thing that she knew how to do when it all started to feel like too much. She quickly changed and then ran down the stairs from her apartment, her old tennis shoes squeaking against the cement steps.

She was barely aware of her surroundings as she entered the fitness center, blinking against the harsh white lights. It was quiet, save for the whirring of one of the treadmill belts and the harsh, heavy breathing of someone exercising.

She glanced up, surprised to see someone else there.

But her surprise faded when she recognized the looming body of David Hughes running at a punishing pace. His face was reflected in the tall windows, and she could see his mouth pulled down into a frown. The skin on his bare arms shone with sweat, and his shorts revealed his long, strong legs.

Sage hesitated.

She should go. She should let him have the space. Based on how he looked after the game, he needed the processing and release of a hard workout more than she did.

But then she thought about him in the locker room, in that moment of vulnerability where he too had been alone, facing the pressure and disappointment of a team that wasn't performing. It was obvious that he held himself, as their coach, responsible for their play.

Maybe, like Sage, he needed to not feel so utterly alone.

So she stepped up onto the treadmill directly beside him, even though they were the only two in the room. David glanced up, doing a double take when he noticed her. She thought he might say something, but he only gave her a silent nod before turning back to staring mindlessly out of the window in front of them.

Sage sped up to a run, subconsciously matching his pace, her long legs finding rhythm with his stride.

As her breaths lengthened and her lungs began to feel the familiar burn, she felt a quiet wave of relief in the simple fact that, in that moment, she wasn't alone.

CHAPTER 10
THERE WASN'T TIME
DAVID

David tugged his hat down over his hair, which was absolutely nuts that morning. He'd resorted to using some sort of pomade product that Chuck had lent him, but even that couldn't keep it pushed back.

He and Tim walked down the hall from their offices to the athletic director's office; Connie Brown, Southeastern's AD, had requested the conversation after their fifth loss of the season.

David could already feel himself sweating through his team branded polo, palms itching as he tried to keep himself from fidgeting. The four cups of coffee he'd powered through that morning probably weren't helping, but there was no undoing that now.

The door to Connie's office was propped open, and Tim stepped aside to let David walk in first. He shared a look with his assistant coach, wishing yet again that Tim would give him *something* other than distance and vague disapproval.

He could really use a sidekick right about now.

David rapped his knuckles on the door frame. "Good morning, Connie," he said, relieved that his voice was steady.

Connie Brown looked up from where she sat at her desk. She was a formidable woman, maybe in her mid-fifties, brown skin weathered from years spent coaching track, with short hair, wire framed glasses, and an old, green Southeastern windbreaker that she wore regardless of the weather.

She smiled at them, gesturing for them to sit in the two chairs in front of her desk. "Mornin', gentlemen," she said, her strong Southern accent shaping her words. "Come on in and have a seat."

Connie Brown scared the shit out of David. While she was undeniably nice, she was unrelenting in her desire to build a winning sports program, and from his first conversation with her it had been made abundantly clear that, if he wanted a lasting career at Southeastern, he needed to produce wins.

Once he and Tim sat down, Connie folded her hands under her chin and looked between the two of them. "It's not lookin' good," she stated.

David looked over at Tim, only to find him watching David with slightly raised brows. *Wonderful. He'd be no damn help.* Turning back to Connie, David straightened his shoulders and took a deep breath. "I know. We are doing what we can to turn it around — pushing the guys harder, adding practice time, working to find the plays that work within their skillset."

Connie's expression remained impassive. "David, we hired you because every single one of your references mentioned how good you were with player development. Not just skill development, but building trust and relationships with these kids." She grabbed a stack of papers from her desk, shaking them in their direction. "These stats? They're the result of a fractured team. Everyone can see it." Tossing the papers to the side, she looked David dead in the eye. "Do what you were hired to do. Build up these boys and you will build up your team."

He started to open his mouth to respond, but thought better of it.

Standing up, he extended a hand out to Connie. Her handshake was strong. As she shook Tim's hand, she added, "I'm rootin' for you both. Don't disappoint me."

The two men were quiet as they walked back to David's office. Tim followed him in, shutting the door behind them. David groaned as he collapsed into his chair, rubbing at his face with his hands before reaching for the cold cup of coffee on the corner of his desk.

"You don't need that, Coach," Tim commented.

David scowled at the older man, but took his advice and reached for the half-empty water bottle instead. He drained it all, and then tossed it at the trash can that stood by the door.

Of course he missed.

He got up, picked up the bottle and threw it into the trash with a bit more force than was necessary.

When he sat back down, Tim was looking at him, his expression more thoughtful than usual.

"What," David asked, uncaring in that moment if he came off as sharp. It was all feeling like a bit too much at the moment, and his give-a-shits had all abandoned him.

Tim shrugged, crossing his arms. "I'm just wondering what the plan is."

"The plan?" David barked out a pained laugh. "I don't know. I'm executing my plan, trying to get the guys to listen to me, but it's like they don't buy in. They don't trust me."

"Maybe they don't trust you because they don't know you," Tim offered.

"What do you mean they don't know me? I'm there with them. I talk. They get to see my ugly mug almost every day."

Tim shook his head. "But they don't know you." He went quiet for a moment, as though considering what to say next. David waited for him to continue, drumming his fingers against the desk. "You know, as an assistant, we spend a lot of time getting to know the guys. It's almost like it's in our job description. *Be approachable, be the good guy who they can talk to.* But they've got to have that with you, too. Of course it's your job to do all of the X's and O's, but they've got to respect you, and ultimately, that has to be earned."

David had never heard Tim talk so much in all the months they'd been working together. He couldn't quite figure out how to feel about the sudden onslaught of opinion from his otherwise tight-lipped assistant.

"So how am I supposed to earn their respect?" David asked, resigned to the fact that if he survived this day, he would probably come out of it without an ounce of his pride or dignity intact.

"I can't tell you that," Tim said. "But like Connie said, if it was what you were good at before, then figure it out. The guys need it. Hell, *we* need it."

And David didn't know what to say to that. He was the head coach. It was his job to make it happen: the wins, the player development, the team chemistry. It was on him, on his shoulders, and Tim couldn't possibly understand what that pressure was like. He was trying so goddamn hard to do it all, and it wasn't working.

If what they needed was more — more time, more energy, more attention, he would give it.

He'd find a way.

That evening's practice was a shit-show.

They were scrimmaging, with the current starters in white and the second five against them in black.

David was running them through a half court trap that focused on picking off the cross-court reversal pass, but Chris Terrence, who was playing the middle spot, wasn't fast enough to hover in the middle and then make it to steal the pass.

"It's not working, Coach." Jordan Peak, one of their captains, turned to David and Tim after yet another successful play from the offense broke through their trap.

Rather than responding to Jordan, David turned to Chris Terrence. "Terrence, you've got to stay on your toes there in the middle. You're letting the offense trick you with the pass fake, but you've got to stay steady in your position."

The tall forward heaved a sigh, obviously frustrated, but muttered a reluctant "Yes, Coach," before walking away.

At David's whistle, they ran through it again. This time, it was Monty who got pulled too far up the wing and left a man wide open in the corner.

"Damnit!" David slammed his board against his thigh, turning away from the guys as he tried to rein in his frustration. There was no reason why they shouldn't be able to execute this defense. He knew they were fast enough. He knew they were smart enough. But no matter how he drilled it, they just didn't click.

Shaking his head, he turned back to the court. The guys all watched him, wary expressions on their faces. A few of the freshmen even looked afraid. They were drenched in sweat, faces red with exertion as those on the court struggled to catch their breath.

The silence stretched out, the team obviously waiting for him to say something. But he wasn't sure where to start.

What could he say?

It was Jenks, their other captain, who spoke up. He was on the black squad, playing against the starters. "Want us to run it again, Coach?"

David shook his head. "Finish up with free throws, and then let's call it early."

A few of the guys looked surprised, but they all split into small groups at each of the baskets. The gym got quiet as they settled into shooting free throws.

Sighing, David took off his hat and raked his hand through his hair.

"You alright there, Coach?"

He glanced over at Tim, who watched him with a small frown.

"Fine," David responded.

He wasn't fine, but there wasn't time for him to take away from the work they were doing to figure out whatever he was going through. He'd get over it. The team needed him to be fine.

When Tim didn't respond, David felt some of the tightness in his shoulders loosen.

Practice wrapped up quietly. They huddled, as was customary, but it was obvious that they were floundering, both as individuals and as a group. David said something about bringing their best tomorrow, but the words obviously fell flat as the guys slouched off to the locker room.

David retreated to his office. He planned on watching tape for a few hours before going home, but after ten minutes of watching the same play over and over again and seeing nothing new, he decided to call it.

He drove home through the darkness, the familiar strains of *Stadium Arcadium* filling his car. He rolled the windows down, needing the wind on his face to clear his head. He hummed along as he drove across one of the many bridges in Charleston.

It was a takeout kind of night. He ran through the local restaurants in his head, deciding that a big caesar salad with chicken was probably his best bet after all of the crap he'd been eating.

He was slowing down at a red light when he saw a silver sedan pulled over on the side of the road. Smoke billowed out from under the popped hood, and he could see a figure bent over the engine. David immediately clicked on his turn signal, and as soon as the light changed he pulled over behind the car.

Climbing out of his Bronco, David walked over to the vehicle. "Hey," he called out, wanting to alert the driver to his presence before he snuck up on them in the dark. "You need some help?"

"Totally good!" A woman's voice called out, immediately followed by a muttered curse and a thud that didn't sound good at all.

"You sure?" David moved a bit closer, standing beside the driver's door. The car was a Corolla that had definitely seen better days.

"Yeah, totally good over here. I've got it handled, but thanks!" There was another thud and a snapping noise. "Fucking fuck!"

David rounded the car. "Ma'am, please let me —"

Sage Fogerty stared at him, her blonde hair wild around her face. There was a grease smudge streaking from the tip of her nose across her cheek, and David had to clench his hand into a fist to stop himself from reaching out to wipe it off of her skin.

She blinked, barely illuminated by the headlights. "You've got to be fucking kidding me."

CHAPTER 11
OF COURSE IT WAS
SAGE

Of all of the people in Charleston who could have happened upon her and her broken down car, it had to be David Hughes.

Oh, and Sage was *completely* fine.

She had a phone, and she was wearing perfectly suitable walking shoes. She was only a few miles from home, and it wouldn't be a big deal at all to walk back to her apartment.

She'd popped the hood because that's what she thought she was supposed to do, even though she had no fucking idea how to fix whatever was going on beneath it. If the smoke pouring out from what she guessed was the engine was any indication, it probably wasn't a simple "pour some more oil in the car" kind of problem. Pulling on some of the tubes that wound through the dark cavity probably wasn't her best move, but come on, she needed to at least *pretend* like she knew what she was doing.

But it was all fine, because she could handle a broken down car. She was independent. Competent.

This was no big deal.

"What happened?"

Shit. David was still there, now looming over her like some sort of stoic, stubborn bear in the night.

"The hood started smoking and I pulled over," Sage explained, wiping her grease-covered hands on her jeans. *Shit. Those were probably ruined.* She slammed the hood shut. "Well, thanks for stopping, but I've got it from here."

David blinked at her, his thick brows pulling down in confusion. "Have you called a tow truck?"

"Yeah. They'll be here in about an hour."

"How are you going to get home?" David's voice had dropped lower somehow, and she willed her body to cut the shit when her skin broke out in goosebumps.

"I'm going to walk."

David barked out a laugh. "Like hell you're going to walk."

Bristling, Sage turned to face him, hands planted on her hips. "What? Are you going to stop me?" She circled to the passenger side of the car, wrenching the door open and grabbing her bag before returning to the driver's side. She wrestled the key out of the ignition, manually locking the door before stashing the keys on the tire as instructed by the tow company. She left her gym bag, seeing as there weren't any valuables inside. "See you later, Coach."

There wasn't a sidewalk on this section of the road, so she started walking on the small strip of pavement before the road sloped down into what was probably wet marsh down below.

"Seriously, Sage?" David's voice called out from behind her. "Can I please give you a ride?"

"I'm fine!"

She heard what sounded like a low growling noise, but she kept going. She was perfectly fine, and she would show David *fucking* Hughes that she was more than capable of taking care of herself.

"I don't know what you're trying to prove," he shouted, and Sage found her feet coming to a stop. "And I honestly don't give a shit, because I *cannot*, in good conscience, leave you alone to walk home in the dark. So if you don't want to ride in my car, then fine. You've made it very clear that you have no interest in listening to me. But if you walk, I'm going to drive behind you with my goddamn blinkers on until you make it back to your apartment."

Sage turned around to look at him. She couldn't see his face in the darkness, but his body was impossibly big where he stood beside her car. She was torn between wanting to punch him in his beautiful face and, even more terrifying, the urge to run back to him.

"Why are you like this?" she asked, holding her ground.

"I could ask you the same thing, Lefty."

Sage sighed. "Fine." She started back toward the two cars. "You can give me a ride, but it's only because the thought of you driving behind me at two miles an hour is absolutely humiliating."

She could hear his chuckle as he held open the passenger door for her. She climbed up into the leather seat, and he firmly shut the door behind her. She shook her head — *of course*, he was also the kind of man who opened car doors for women.

When he got into the driver's seat, Sage shifted so that her shoulder leaned against the window. As the engine purred to life, loud music suddenly filled the car.

"Sorry," David said, fumbling with the volume dial and turning it down.

She recognized the song. "Chili Peppers?"

David nodded as he glanced back over his shoulder to check for oncoming traffic. It was excessive, since he'd be able to see anyone by their headlights in the rearview or side mirrors, but hey, she wasn't complaining if he wanted to take extra precautions to drive safely. They pulled out onto the quiet street.

"So," David started. She could see now, with the glow of the dash lights, that he wore a team polo and basketball shorts. Since the season began she'd rarely seen him in anything but team branded gear, with the exception of the games, where he showed up in well-tailored suits that looked so fucking good on his big body that Sage had gotten in the habit of visiting the bathroom to splash cold water on her cheeks at halftime.

As usual, a baseball cap was pulled tight over his dark hair, which had only grown longer and more untamed since she'd met him. Honestly, he looked exhausted, his eyes heavy and his face drawn.

It was obvious that the season was already wearing on him.

"Have you eaten?"

"No," she admitted.

David shifted his legs, his shorts drifting up his hairy thighs. Sage averted her eyes. "I was already planning on grabbing something on my way home. Do you mind if we stop? I'll get you something."

Sage was tempted to argue. Her instinct was to put up a fight. But she was starving, and she was already in the car, so what was she going to do? Pout while he grabbed food for himself?

"Food would be great," she said. "But I'm going to buy my own."

"Does Italian work for you?"

"Fuck yes. I mean, yes. Just yes." She turned her face to try to hide her hot cheeks.

A minute later, they were pulling into the drive through at Angelo's. David ordered a chicken caesar salad, while Sage got fettuccine alfredo. They only had to wait a few minutes until the food was ready.

They were mostly quiet as David drove them home. Sage expected it to be awkward, but instead it was surprisingly easy to relax back into the worn leather seat and let the quiet music fill the space between them. David, for his part, glared at the road like he was driving in a storm rather than a clear, moonlit night.

When they pulled into a spot a few buildings over from Sage's apartment, David was out of the car and around to her door before she had a chance to unbuckle her seatbelt. Grabbing her bag and her container of pasta, she climbed out.

"Thanks," she said, and she hesitated, waiting while David got his own backpack out of the back seat.

"Mind if I walk you up?" David asked, hovering a few feet

away from her as though he wasn't sure if she would mind if he got closer.

It was oddly sweet to see him so cautious around her. "Sure," she said, unable to justify fighting him on this one little thing.

They walked side by side with about a foot between them. It struck Sage how strange it was that she was here, in this moment, with this particular man who had become an unexpected fixture in her life. From a potential one-night stand to a sort of coworker and now a neighbor, David Hughes had somehow infiltrated all of her waking hours.

And her less-than-professional dreams, but she wasn't acknowledging that.

Sage dug through her bag as they reached the top of the stairs. Her stomach sank when she didn't hear the distinct jingle of the ring that held her keys.

"You've got to be fucking kidding me."

"Everything okay?" David moved closer to her, and she thought she might have felt the brush of his fingers on her back for a moment.

Sage searched again. Even though she knew, logically, that her keys were currently somewhere north of town at the mechanic, she searched again. And then she took every single item out of her bag, setting them down on the cement floor in front of her apartment door: water bottle, textbook, laptop, chamomile tea bag, chapstick, five wrapped lozenges, three tampons, and a rock that she'd picked up once because she thought it was pretty.

She buried her face into her hands and screamed, muffling the sound so that it probably sounded more like a strangled goose.

Fuck this day.

She looked up at David, who was standing there watching her with such obvious worry on his face that she couldn't help but laugh.

"My apartment key is with my car."

David seemed unphased. "Let's go to the office and get you a replacement."

Right. That made sense. Relief filled her. "Great. You don't have to come with me," she added as she shoved her things back into her bag. She felt her cheeks and the back of her neck heat — she hated the fact that someone was seeing her like this — disorganized and incapable.

But the look David gave her made it very clear that, like it or not, there was no way in hell that she was going to the office alone.

▭

Of course the office was already closed for the night. *Of course* it was.

Sage yanked on the locked door one more time before turning away.

David hovered beside her, tall and quiet. His hands were shoved deep in his pockets, and he rocked back on his heels.

She shifted so that she was facing away from him. She blinked against the burning in her eyes and she could feel the itching in her nose, clenching her jaw as she willed herself not to cry.

She had her phone. She could call a ride share and go…somewhere. She could find a hotel, probably, or even go to campus and curl up on one of the couches in the library. She would figure it out.

"Right," she said. There was a tremor in her voice, and she cleared her throat and straightened her shoulders. "Well, thanks for the help again. I'm going to get a ride and find somewhere to stay."

"Are you going to stay with friends?"

Sage felt her body stiffen. "No," she admitted, but didn't elaborate.

"Where are you going to go?"

Why couldn't he just let things be?

"Probably a hotel."

She heard his sharp inhale and turned to face him. His head

was tilted back like he was looking up at the stars, but when Sage followed his line of sight, all she saw was the dark web of oak branches stretching above them.

"You should stay with me." The words were soft, almost whispered. David still looked up, and her eyes dropped down to the shadow of stubble on his throat before she absorbed what he'd said.

"What?" *He couldn't have possibly...*

"It's after ten," David said, and there was a quiet defeat to his voice that made Sage pause. "It's late, and I have a really big couch that, if I'm honest, I end up falling asleep on most nights. You can take my bed. I'll even change the sheets." He rubbed his eyes. "Please, Sage."

Sage opened and closed her mouth.

This was a colossally bad idea. But the reality was that she didn't have a friend she could stay with, and while she could swing a hotel room, it was less than ideal for her budget.

And there was something about David in that moment, like he was hovering right on the edge of collapse, and a very, very small part of her had the feeling that maybe he wanted the company.

She let out a resigned sigh. "Yeah, okay," she said. She watched as his eyes dropped closed for just a second, some of the tension in his body easing. "And thank you," she added. "Really, I appreciate it."

The smile that curved David's mouth was genuine, and she was reminded of just how handsome he was. So fucking handsome, kind, and annoyingly concerned with her safety.

CHAPTER 12
BIG AND SOFT
DAVID

"This is me."

David fumbled with his key for a moment before successfully unlocking his apartment. Holding the door open, he gestured for Sage to walk inside first.

The jingle of Daisy's collar greeted them, and before David could react, Sage had reached down and scooped up his dog, who greeted her with licks against her cheek.

"Hi, sweet pup," Sage whispered softly, and David felt a wave of relief when he saw a hint of her crooked smirk. She still had the grease smudges on her face, and he hadn't been able to bring himself to tell her when it seemed like she was already on the verge of losing it.

She was so goddamn lovely, even if she was so unrelentingly stubborn that he wanted to tear his hair out.

"Nice spot," she said as she carried Daisy into his living room. She'd taken off her shoes by the door — Air Force 1's, he noticed, impressed — leaving her in colorful knit socks. Her jeans were faded, a little bit baggy, but he could still see her thighs stretching the material.

He wet his lower lip with his tongue before he could stop himself.

David followed her, suddenly self conscious of how dark, how *sterile* his space was. Now that Sage was in his home, something about her made it all seem lifeless in comparison.

"Ah, thanks," he replied, moving into the kitchen and stashing his bag of takeout on the counter. He grabbed a few discarded wrappers and empty water bottles that littered the counter, stuffing them into the trash can. "It's not much," he added. For some reason, he needed her to know that his apartment wasn't his best attempt at creating a home.

He watched as she walked slowly along the far wall of the room where his concert posters hung. She was turned away from him, and her long braid hung down her spine, almost reaching her waist.

"You like music," she said. It was a statement, not a question.

David shrugged, and then realized that she couldn't see his non-verbal response. "Yeah," he said, and his voice felt too loud for the enclosed space of his apartment.

Sage looked back over her shoulder, flashing him one of her crooked smiles. "You've got good taste," she commented, before turning back to her perusal.

"When I was up in Chicago there was tons of live music," David commented. "I got to see a lot of my favorites." He scratched at his beard. "Of course, having Lollapalooza every year was incredible."

"I wouldn't take you for a music festival guy," Sage said with a laugh, lowering a wriggling Daisy down to the couch before walking across the room toward him. She approached the high bar counter, bracing her elbows against it and looking up at him with those eyes that were just so damn pretty- *green*. He meant *green*.

"I mean, I was never riding the rail like a maniac," David said, "but I was known to bust out a tank top and tie a bandana around my head."

Sage tried to contain her laugh, but only lasted for a second before she completely cracked, eyes wide as huge, gasping laughs

shook her upper body. David felt her laughter loosen something
in his own chest, and next thing he knew his own laugh joined in
with hers.

This is what it could have been like.

The thought showed up suddenly, unexpected, but once it was
there it was all he could think about as their laughter faded, both
of them lapsing into silence.

He could have brought this vibrant woman home, and they
could have stood there, laughing together. He could have
rounded the counter and drawn her into his arms, backing her up
until his body pressed hers against the wall. He could have kissed
her — would have kissed her — until they had to break apart to
catch their breaths. But he wouldn't have let her go yet, instead
maintaining the connection between their bodies by resting his
forehead against hers.

David blinked away the achingly vivid image, finding Sage
watching him. Her lips were barely parted, and he knew without
a doubt that her bottom lip would feel perfect pillowed between
his teeth.

"Can I get you some water?" he asked, needing to bring some
space back between them.

Sage reached into her bag, pulling out the same hard plastic
bottle he'd noticed she always had with her. "Can I refill this?"

"Sure," David said, and he moved aside so that she could get
to the fridge door. Once she was done, David opened the door
and grabbed a bottle for himself. As he unscrewed the lid, Sage let
out a snort.

He raised his brows at her, unable to hide his amusement
when her round cheeks flushed pink. "What," he asked, taking
another sip.

"You realized that just about everyone has decided that single
use plastic water bottles are pretty bad for the planet, right?"

David paused, lowering the bottle from his lips. "I might have
heard that," he admitted.

"So why still buy them?" Sage looked at him with that defiant fire in her eyes, and *damn* if his body didn't like that a whole hell of a lot.

"Honestly, they're convenient," he responded. "It's a lame excuse, I know, but it's easy."

Sage shrugged at him. "This is pretty convenient, if you ask me," she said, swinging her plastic bottle from one long finger. "Do you mind if we eat? I'm starving."

"Yeah, of course," David said, kicking himself for not immediately setting up their meal. He grabbed silverware from a drawer and tore off a few paper towels from the roll that sat on the counter. Picking up his salad, he looked between his small dining table that was covered in paperwork and the wide sectional. "Do you mind if we eat on the couch?"

"Not at all." Sage followed him, choosing a spot on the far end, leaving about four feet between her and where David sat. It was a good distance, an *appropriate* distance, to have between them.

She tucked her feet up under herself as she started in on her pasta. She twirled the long noodles around her fork, before stabbing a piece of grilled chicken on the end. As she took her first bite, she hummed, obviously pleased with the food.

"Is it alright if I put on some game tape while we eat?"

Sage glanced over at him. "Not at all."

It only took him a second to set up his laptop and get the game up on his large TV. He kept the remote next to him, and grabbed one of the legal pads from the cluttered table.

They watched in silence for a few minutes. It was their third game of the season, and the other team had come out at the beginning with full court pressure. Monty was good with the ball, but he was getting pushed to the sideline where he couldn't complete the cross court pass. It was getting picked off almost every time.

After the fifth sloppy turnover, David couldn't keep the frustrated "dammit" in.

"What about trying a two man front?"

He looked over at Sage, who was fully focused on the game

playing out on the screen. "Who would you put up there with him?"

She frowned. "That's tough, because you definitely have a bigger team. You're much deeper in the center than you are outside." She chewed another bite, clearly thinking deeply about her response. "Honestly, I would say Jordan."

"Really?" Jordan was a great player, but he tended to hold onto the ball once it was in his hands. It was hard to imagine him giving up the ball, which was what they needed in this situation.

"He doesn't like to give up the ball, but his confidence will help when it comes to getting through the pressure up top."

She made a good point.

The game carried on. Occasionally David would pause the tape, scribbling notes for things to work on in practice.

"It just doesn't make sense." A play had just broken down when Jordan tried a no-look pass across the lane to Zephyr, their center. David looked over at Sage, who was shaking her head. She continued, pointing with her fork at the TV. "On half of the plays, Jordan is keeping the ball in his hands for too long and taking a bad shot, and then on this one, when he actually has the open lane, he tries to force the pass."

"Your guess is as good as mine," David sighed. He was still trying to figure out how to coach Jordan, who was the kind of kid who seemed to carry the weight of the whole team on his shoulders.

David knew something about that.

"Is he stat motivated? Win motivated?"

"It's mixed," David replied. "To be fair, I haven't seen him after a win. But when the team loses and he plays well, he seems just as disappointed as the other guys. When he does poorly, it's almost like he's both angry with himself and afraid." He shook his head. "Of what, I can't figure out."

Sage nodded just as her mouth opened wide into a yawn.

"Shit," David jumped up off the couch. "You're tired. Right. Sorry. Do you need anything? Give me a minute to change the sheets and you'll be all set." He took a few steps toward the bedroom before turning back around. "And I've got a spare tooth-brush, and soaps and stuff." *Shit.* "I...I also have tampons, if you need them."

Goddamn his stupid mouth.

Sage grinned around another yawn. "I think I'm all set on the menstrual products, but thank you." She wiped at her face as she unfolded from the couch and stood up. "Do you have a t-shirt I could borrow?"

You're goddamn right I've got a t-shirt for you to sleep in, Lefty.

"Yep. Yeah. I'll grab you one." He practically ran to his bedroom, vaguely aware of her soft footsteps on the carpet as she followed him. Moving to his dresser, he opened a drawer and began sifting through his t-shirts. "Big and soft," he muttered under his breath as his hands fingered at the folded cotton. *That's how women like their t-shirts.* He stopped at one of his old South-eastern basketball shirts from when he'd been a player. It was worn to the point that it was almost threadbare, but damn if it wasn't soft.

He turned, finding her leaning against his open bedroom door with a soft, sleepy expression on her face. He held out the shirt, and it took a monumental effort to not grab hold of her extended hand and tug her against his body.

God, he wanted her.

He stepped back, clearing his throat. "I'll get the sheets sorted for you if you need to use the bathroom," he said, pointing to the door across the hall. "Extra toothbrushes are in the top drawer."

She nodded, that soft smile still on her pink lips as she turned away from him. He watched her, frozen in place, until the bath-room door clicked shut behind her.

He crossed to the bedroom door and shut it, needing a moment to himself.

As he changed the navy sheets on his bed and replaced them with a gray set, he thought about the woman currently in his apartment. He thought about how quiet the anxiety of the day had been since he'd found her on the side of the road. He thought about her comments about the team, about how engaged she'd been watching game tape with him. How *alive* and beautiful she was.

He straightened his duvet and tried to tidy as much as he could. Quickly, he changed into a t-shirt and flannel pajama pants, accepting that he was probably going to have to take a shower in the morning. Grabbing his glasses and the police procedural he was currently reading, he opened his bedroom door and walked back to the living room.

"The room is —"

He swallowed the rest of his sentence. Sage had curled up in one corner of the couch against the cushions. David's t-shirt hung down, just barely covering her ass and the tops of thighs. Her eyes were shut and the soft sound of her breaths were barely audible from across the room.

David crept forward, careful to be as quiet as possible. While he knew she'd be more comfortable in his bed, he didn't want to wake her up. He grabbed a fleece blanket that he kept folded on top of the couch and draped it over her, gently smoothing the soft fabric and tucking it under her feet. She shifted slightly in her sleep, murmuring something unintelligible before burrowing down deeper into the cushions.

God, he wanted to… hug her? Cuddle with her? Kiss her nose?

He shook his head, stepping away from her and quietly making his way back to his room.

As he lay there in the darkness, he couldn't help but wonder what it would feel like to have Sage Fogerty in his bed, tucked against his body.

Would it be so wrong if she was?

CHAPTER 13
YOU DON'T LIKE SPICY
SAGE

Sage blinked awake slowly. She was warm, comfortable, and... *fuck*. She was definitely not in her bed.

Untangling her arms and legs from the soft blanket that covered her, she sat up, taking in her surroundings as she tried to get her brain functioning. Gray sectional couch, framed posters on the wall, a big TV on a dark wood shelf, a table covered in papers and game boards...Oh.

She was in David Hughes' apartment.

Her car, then the food, then the game tape, and then pulling his stupidly soft shirt on and not being able to keep her eyes open a moment longer.

She stood up slowly, wiggling her toes into the carpet. The living room and kitchen were empty, and based on the bright sun that shone in around the closed blinds, it was already later than she usually slept in.

Down the hall, she could make out the sounds of muted shouts and shoes squeaking on the court coming from behind a closed door. She glanced over at the time displayed on the microwave. *8:15am*. Was he seriously watching more game tape? On a Saturday morning?

Sage walked toward the closed door, pausing for a second to

look down at herself. David's t-shirt was big enough that it reached her mid-thigh — decent enough. She was braless, too, but having been born a member of the itty bitty titty committee made it a non-issue.

Thanks for that, Mom.

"David?" she called out as she knocked twice.

"Come in."

Sage opened the door, finding a home office. A futon couch was shoved up against one wall, a folding white table was covered in more papers, empty water bottles and mugs, and two white boards were mounted on the wall facing the couch. They were covered in David's neat, printed handwriting — numbers, names, and plays sketched in the margins.

David sat on the futon, with Daisy curled up on his lap. A legal pad balanced on one knee, and his laptop sat open on a chair in front of him. More gametape played: this time their match up with College of Newport from earlier that week.

For a moment, she just watched him. His dark brows were drawn down low over his eyes as he watched the game, and he worried his bottom lip with his teeth. Square, black-framed glasses were balanced on his prominent nose, and fuck if he didn't look good with those on. His beard was starting to tuft out unevenly along his jaw, like it might have been a few days since he last paid any attention to his reflection in a mirror.

He looked anxious and occupied, and Sage thought that if one more thing was added to the invisible weight he seemed to carry he might collapse.

"Morning," Sage said, unsure of how to approach him. There was something profoundly intimate about being in his home with him, leaving her with a feeling of uncertainty that she wasn't used to.

David blinked up at her, like he'd forgotten that he'd invited her in. "Sorry, did I wake you up?"

"No, you're fine." She moved to sit on the edge of the couch, and saw the exact moment when David noticed her bare legs. His brows shot up and she could feel his gaze tracing her exposed skin like a touch. Settling in on the couch, she tucked one of her legs up under her, very aware of the way he tracked every movement. "You're back at it early," she commented, pointing over at the laptop.

David shot her a pained smile as one of his hands started to absently scratch at Daisy's ears. "I have to figure this out. I've got to turn this around for them."

"What are your plans for today?"

"You're looking at it," he said with a low chuckle.

Sage should go home. It was the weekend, and she had stuff to do. She'd undoubtedly overstayed her welcome, and while David was being incredibly nice and gracious about her being there, it would be good to put some space between them. Wearing his clothes, sharing meals, and sleeping on his couch were not going to help her valiant attempts to shut down the way her body fucking *screamed* for him.

"Let's go for a walk." She stood up, and her movement woke Daisy, whose tail immediately started thumping against David's wide thigh.

"What?" The look David gave her was exasperated, like what she was suggesting was ridiculous.

"You need to go outside. Your dog needs to go outside. It's a Saturday, and there's nothing for you to do until practice on Monday."

There was a hint of a smile on David's lips. "You're very bossy, Lefty."

Sage snorted. "Come on. Get up and put on some clothes." She glanced down at her own attire. "Mind if I wear the t-shirt?" she asked, looking up at him.

"Not at all." David picked up a wriggling Daisy, setting her down on the floor. Immediately she raced for the door, her collar jingling and golden tail wagging behind her. "There's coffee in the pot in the kitchen if you want some," he said as he walked toward his bedroom.

"I don't drink coffee, but thank you."

David turned to face her fully, disbelief on his face. "What do you drink in the morning?" He frowned. "Are you a smoothie girl? I think I have some frozen strawberries…"

"Tea," Sage said with a quiet laugh. "Earl Gray with milk and honey."

"What kind of milk?"

"Whole."

David nodded, thoughtful, like he was carefully committing her response to memory before disappearing into his room. Sage went and brushed her teeth with the borrowed toothbrush again before pulling on her jeans and tucking the front of the t-shirt in. She took out her braid, running her fingers through the tangles before pulling it up into a ponytail. Daisy danced around her feet, yipping excitedly, sensing that the humans were about to go do something.

"Are you sure you have the time to do this?" David asked, emerging from his room dressed in a t-shirt and basketball shorts. It was a painfully normal outfit, and yet on him it looked almost obscene — his built, hairy legs, his wide arms and chest straining against the cotton of his shirt.

Sage shook her head. "I've got nothing planned today," she said. It wasn't entirely true, but delaying the start of her to-do list seemed like the most obvious thing in the world.

David got Daisy fastened in her harness and leash, and he held the door open for Sage as they walked outside.

It was a calm morning. The air was fresh and still, while still maintaining the slight coolness that held over from the night before. They walked side by side with Daisy prancing ahead of them, using every bit of the reach of the leash to sniff at the grass on either side of the sidewalk.

"Thanks for this," David said, his voice soft, almost hesitant.

Sage looked up at him. "It's a nice way to start a morning," she replied. "In California, my mom would get us up every morning before school with enough time to go for a walk. We don't have a lot of land around the house, but we would go and look at all of the plants, checking in on what was blooming or dying or changing color." She smiled, feeling a rare wave of missing home. "I still like to run outside when I can."

"Me too. A treadmill just isn't the same as running outside."

"And yet you still use plastic water bottles."

David huffed a laugh, shaking his head. Quiet settled between them. "This is weird."

"What do you mean?" She kept her voice carefully calm, even as her shoulders stiffened.

"This," he said, gesturing between the two of them. "Hanging out with you. It's —" He paused, obviously struggling to find the words to express himself. "It's nice, Sage. It's really damn nice."

"Oh," she said, something softening in her.

"But the team, and the work." He reached a hand up to scratch at his jaw. "It's just weird, because the more time that I spend with you the more I realize that I like you, and I actually want to hang out with you. And that's all fine, except for the fact that you're also beautiful and confident and my goddamn brain can't seem to get the memo that you're off limits." He shot her a pained glance. "You're a student, you're young, and I'm your superior in a professional environment, and that all matters, Sage. I won't be the guy who pretends like it means nothing."

Oh.

Sage opened and closed her mouth, but she couldn't find a single word to follow up what David had just said.

"Damnit, Sage." He scrubbed his hands over his face before dropping them down to his sides and letting out a strained laugh. "I'm sorry, I shouldn't have said anything."

Before she could stop herself, Sage reached out and grabbed David's forearm, pulling him to a stop. "Don't apologize," she said, wishing that her voice sounded stronger, more confident. But what he'd said had shaken her. She hadn't been expecting any of it. She'd known the attraction was there, sure, but the rest of it? "I appreciate the honesty," she added, and it was the truth. She'd asked for him to explain himself, and he had.

She just hadn't anticipated that response.

Gently, David pulled his arm out of her grip. For a moment, her fingers chased him, not yet ready to give up his touch. He shot a sad smile her way. "Want to head over to the office and grab your key? They should be open by now."

Sage could only nod, and fell into step with David as he wound his way through the shaded buildings to the front office. David waited outside with Daisy while she went in and got a new key.

"All set," she said, holding up the key as she rejoined them outside. She knelt down to scratch at Daisy's ears, glancing up at David. His hands were shoved into his pockets, his posture stiff as he watched her.

"I'll let you get on with your weekend, then." David tugged at Daisy's leash, starting to back away toward his apartment. "And…I'm sorry. What I said was out of line, and, well, yeah. I'm sorry."

For the second time that day, Sage found herself presented with a chance to walk away. Except now there was the added weight of David's words between them. She really should go.

But she had a feeling that if she left him now, whatever door he'd opened with his honesty would be shut. And while she hadn't quite figured out how to respond, she knew with absolute certainty that she wanted to say something.

"Want to come up to my place for breakfast?"

What the fuck, Sage?

David looked as surprised as she felt. "Are you sure?" he asked, caution in his voice.

Sage nodded, warming up to the idea. She had plenty of groceries, and cooking was something she did well. It would be a good way to even the playing field between them after all of David's generosity.

Sure. That was why she wanted to cook for him.

"For sure." She turned in the direction of her apartment, hearing the crunch of David's shoes against the sidewalk as he followed her. "And Daisy is invited too," she said, grinning back over her shoulder.

"I...okay," she heard David say as he followed her.

She still wasn't entirely sure what she was doing, but something about the idea of the sad, subdued David that she'd seen in the last twelve hours sitting alone in his apartment didn't feel right to her.

"Come on in," she said as she pushed open the door. Her blinds were all open, and the white walls practically glowed in the sunlight. Her plants had taken well to the new environment, many of them sporting new growth — vines or leaves that stretched out toward the windows.

Daisy pranced about once she was off of her leash, and Sage went right to the kitchen to fill up a bowl of water for her. David followed quietly behind her, and when he saw what she was doing he thanked her.

"No problem," Sage said. Opening her fridge, she called out behind her, "Any food allergies or things you don't like? Other than spicy. I know you don't like spicy."

"You remember that?"

Sage turned around, finding David watching her carefully. "Yes, David. Of course I remember the conversation with the hot man at the bar who is now standing in my kitchen."

David let out a huff of a laugh. "No allergies and I'll eat whatever." After a moment, he added: "Can I help?"

Sage got David set up with a cutting board, and within ten minutes a big pan of scrambled eggs, bacon, and veggies was sizzling on her stove. He was a bit awkward with a knife and the pieces he cut were anything but uniform in size, but he got the job done.

"So that's a no on the granola," he said, eyeing the scramble as he stirred it.

Sage let out a loud laugh. "There's nothing wrong with granola, but I'm worthless without meat in the morning."

He nodded in response, eyes darting over to where she warmed the tortillas on the stove, flipping them after a few seconds on the open range.

"Impressive," David commented as she quickly flipped another tortilla from the stove to a plate.

"It's really not." Sage had grown up cooking with her mom, and flipping scalding hot tortillas with her bare hands was practically second nature at that point in her life. "Turn that off, and let's eat."

David watched Sage assemble her breakfast tacos, copying how she sprinkled grated cheese and chopped cilantro on top. When he went to add the hot sauce, Sage grabbed his wrist, stopping his movement.

"This will kill you," she told him, taking the bottle away from him.

"It can't be that hot," David said disbelievingly, obviously not taking her warning seriously.

"I promise that it is," she replied, sliding the bottle down the counter away from them. "I eat it almost every morning and it still makes my eyes water and my nose run. It's brutal."

"So why do you eat it?"

Sage led the way to her small table, sitting down with her tea and plate. David sat across from her, his body looking bigger than usual folded into one of her chairs. "The flavor is unreal, and the burn is worth it," she said, shrugging before taking her first bite, humming at the perfect combination of flavors.

There was nothing in the world like breakfast tacos.

"This is the greatest thing I've ever eaten." David was looking down at his plate like his mind had just been blown. "Seriously, how did you make this?"

Sage felt the sides of her neck flush. "You literally just helped me cook. You put stuff in the pan and stir it. That's it."

David scoffed, arching a thick brow at her. "Sage, if I tried to make this by myself the entire complex would be on fire."

"You can't be that bad at cooking."

"No, I'm really that bad," David said after swallowing another bite. "My mom tried to teach me, but I'm worthless. I can bake chicken, boil pasta, make toast, and fry eggs. That's it."

"What a cliche," she teased, kicking out her foot under the table until she connected with his leg. "The young, successful bachelor who doesn't know how to cook for himself."

David laughed, a low, rich chuckle that reminded Sage of the night they met. There was an easy smile on his face, wrinkling the skin at the corners of his dark brown eyes. Then his gaze narrowed in on the vase of flowers that sat in the center of the table. The blue glass vase held a bouquet of orange, red, and pink dahlias she'd found at the farmer's market the previous week.

"Who got you the flowers?"

"I did."

David tilted his head. It obviously wasn't the answer he'd been expecting. "You buy yourself flowers?"

Sage let out a quiet sigh. She hated having to explain things like this, the little parts of her life where she took her own happiness out of the hands of the world. "I love flowers, so why would I wait around for someone else to buy them for me when I can get them for myself?"

She watched David, who looked at the bouquet with a thoughtful expression on his face. After a moment, he looked up at her with a smile. "Makes perfect sense to me," he said, and his voice was so kind that Sage felt the sudden burn of tears in her eyes.

She looked down, blinking furiously until she'd regained control over herself.

What the fuck, Sage?

David must have sensed not to press the topic, because he shifted the conversation to the team, asking Sage's opinion on one of their conference opponents.

It was too easy to forget who David was. As they ate breakfast tacos in her brightly lit kitchen, he was just a beautiful man who shared her passion for basketball and scratched absently at his beard as he listened attentively to every word she said.

When they finished eating, David cleared his throat, rising from the table and reaching over to gather up Sage's empty plate. "Dishwasher?" he asked as he carried the plates to the kitchen.

"Yeah, that's fine," she said, although she usually hand-washed when it was just her.

David busied himself tidying the kitchen, a focused frown on his face as he searched for where to put away the salt and pepper shakers.

"Those can stay on the counter," Sage offered, leaning against the counter and definitely not looking at his ass. *Definitely* not.

"I should head home." David wiped his hands on the colorful batik towel that hung from the handle of her oven. He whistled, and Daisy came prancing over from where she'd been curled up on a blanket that Sage had folded into a makeshift bed. Scooping up the wriggling dog, he gave her a kiss on the top of her head before turning to smile at Sage. "Breakfast was amazing, thank you." He opened his mouth like he was going to say something, but then closed it, shaking his head with a quiet chuckle. "I was going to offer to return the favor, but I'll spare you the pain of suffering through my cooking."

Sage snorted a soft laugh in response. "You're welcome anytime," she said, the offer completely sincere. She liked having David in her home. More accurately, she liked David.

"What you said earlier," she blurted out, not entirely sure what she was going to say even as her mouth was opening and forming the words. "You too. I mean, me too." She felt her cheeks flood with heat. "Fuck. I mean that I like being around you too. And your ass is perfect. Literally perfect."

David looked at her, wide eyed and blinking, like he wasn't sure what to say.

"So we should be friends," Sage continued. "Friends who

hang out and eat together. Who find the other attractive. People do that, right?" She took a breath. "What do you say?"

David nodded. "That...that would be good."

Sage sighed, surprised at the relief she felt hearing David's agreement.

"I'm going to head out," David said, nodding his head toward the front door. "Thanks again for breakfast."

"And thank you for everything with the car," Sage replied.

She followed him to the front of her apartment, standing aside as he opened the door.

"David?"

"Hm?" He turned back to look at her, Daisy's blonde head poking out above his shoulder.

"Give it time. The guys are going to get there."

She didn't need to explain that she was talking about the team. David shot her a sad smile, and then walked away.

CHAPTER 14
C U SOON WITH SOUP
DAVID

2 - 9.

A record of 2 and 9 going into their first conference game.

They'd scraped by two close wins, but the majority of the games had been won handily by their opponents, who beat them by an average margin of 15 points.

To their credit, the players were working their asses off. They ran hard in practice, challenged each other, and were starting to execute the plays correctly. But still, the team wasn't clicking. Their timing was still off — passes behind the guy cutting to the lane, two players scrambling for the same man in transition and leaving the basket unguarded.

David tried to figure out the social dynamics of the team. Some of the guys seemed really close, and he knew that a group of the juniors shared a house based on overheard conversations. Those older guys — Monty, Zephyr, Erik, and Horty — had taken the underclassmen under their wing, which David was relieved to see. Jordan, who was, objectively, their best player, seemed completely removed. Jenks was the only one who ever went out of his way to interact with his co-captain, and even then it was evident that Jordan would have preferred to be left alone.

David climbed out of his car, shooting a quick text to the pet sitter he'd found to feed Daisy on game days. He adjusted his tie, stashing his phone in the inside pocket of the navy blue blazer that he'd paired with chinos. He felt silly, but there was something about dressing nicely for games that made him feel more prepared, and even more qualified. Not that it was helping him, but still.

Tonight they were playing Harding University out of Maryland. They'd come in second in the conference the previous year, and based on scouting reports, were a physically and mentally tough team.

David had prepared the guys like he normally would: game tape of the other team, reviewing the plays their opponent would rely on, and practicing the offensive and defensive sets he thought would give them the best advantage going into the game.

He hoped it would be enough.

The guys needed a win. They were at the point in the season where it became almost impossible to fight against the momentum of repeated losses. Losing got easier, comfortable even, and it started to feel like there was no chance.

But David knew it would just take one win. One goddamned win and it would all change. He'd been on teams — hell, he'd coached teams — that had been in the same position, and he'd seen it all turn around.

They just needed to get it done.

After a brief stop in his office to collect the leather folio that held his game notes and lineups, David made his way down to the gym and locker room. Guys were starting to trickle in, and he gave a few fist bumps and nods to the players.

He walked into the gym just in time to hear a hacking cough from the supply closet tucked under one of the pull-out bleachers. He frowned. *Must be one of the interns.*

Then Sage walked out, pushing the ball rack that they used for warming up. Her face was buried into the crook of her arm as another cough wracked her whole body.

"Fogerty," David called out, walking across the court toward her.

Sage lowered her arm, and David couldn't keep the wince from his face.

Her nose was bright red, and there was a slightly glazed look to her eyes; the unmistakable look of someone who'd lost the fight with a cold.

"Coach." The word was rough and raspy, and immediately sent her into another round of coughing.

"What the hell are you doing here?" This maniac of a woman was out of her damn mind if she thought she belonged anywhere other than bundled up in a bed with hot tea and a bowl of chicken noodle soup.

Sage sniffled and shrugged. "Doing my job?"

He didn't think she meant for it to be a question.

"Sage," David started, shaking his head. "You need to go home."

Her posture shifted as she tried to draw herself up to her full height, undoubtedly about to make some *very* convincing argument as to why she was perfectly capable of doing her job. It reminded him of the way she'd responded to his offer of help the night when he'd found her car broken down on the side of the road.

Obviously, convincing her to look out for herself wasn't the way to get through to her.

"If you get the team sick, the season is done, Sage."

She glared at him, but he could see that that line of reasoning was actually getting him somewhere.

"I'll have one of the freshmen take stats," he added. "We'll take care of it. You need to go home and get better."

Sighing, she nodded. "Kaley got the jerseys and warmups in there for the guys," she said, her voice an absolute wreck. "The iPad is already on the bench. Make sure to tell the guys doing stats that sometimes the program glitches if you try to assign a rebound and turnover to the same player in the same possession. You just have to input them twice and it should work."

David noticed that even though she was obviously suffering, she'd still made the effort to dress nicely for the game. Tight trousers exposed her ankles and a flowing blouse was the color of the pink flowers she'd had on her table. Her hair was pulled up into a ponytail.

Why did she have to be so damn pretty?

"Text me when you get home," he said before he was aware that the words were leaving his mouth.

Sage opened and closed her mouth, confusion on her face. "Do I have your number?"

Shit. "Ah, I guess not. I've got yours from your staff paperwork." He scratched at the hair on his jaw, which he'd managed to trim into something that resembled a well-groomed beard. "I'll text you so you have mine."

What he didn't tell her was that he'd saved her number in his phone weeks ago, under the guise that maybe, someday, he might get the chance to use it.

Sage nodded. "That's fine." She started to leave, but turned back, looking at him with that earnest sincerity that was so *Sage*. "Good luck tonight."

He offered her a smile. "Thanks, Lefty." He let himself watch her walk away for a few seconds, trying to channel some of the confidence that seemed to be so natural for her.

But then someone called his name from across the gym, breaking him out of any temporary escape from the pressure of that night's game. As he crossed the bright, polished floor, his shining Oxfords clicking sharply on the hardwood, he pulled out his phone.

He found her contact quickly, and after a few fumbling taps of his thumbs, he pressed send.

> Take care, Lefty. It's David.

The locker room door shut behind him.

David took a few steps before slumping back against the stone, rolling his neck in an effort to release some of the tension that felt like a goddamned pinched nerve.

"Some things were better tonight."

David looked over at Tim, who stood leaning against the opposite wall of the hallway outside the locker room. He looked more thoughtful than pissed off, and for a moment David considered what the stoic man would do if he threw his play board at him.

Probably just frown.

"It sure as hell didn't feel better," David muttered, clearing his throat to try to get rid of the rasp of his voice. He always sounded like a wreck after a game.

Another twenty point loss. It wasn't how David had envisioned his first conference game as a head coach, back in the summer when he was packing up his Bronco to move back south. He'd been so optimistic then, hopeful, imagining things like championship banners and rings.

"The defense was better," Tim argued, looking intently at him. "The guys were covering the middle well, and they were able to adjust to the added screen in the second half."

He wasn't wrong. The defense had done some good work out there.

"And," Tim continued. "Monty was more vocal out there. Having younger guys step up and act like leaders is going to make a difference for the whole team."

David shook his head. Tim was right. There were things that were starting to turn around, and he knew it would take time to bounce back. But to lose their first conference game in their home gym stung. It hadn't helped that Harding's assistant coach had shot David a cocky smirk every time they'd scored. *Asshole.*

"What are we going to do about Jordan?"

The question had been heavy on his mind. With every game they played, it looked like the senior's game slipped farther and farther out of his grasp. Jordan looked lost out there, and yet it seemed like the worse he played the harder he tried to force his shot. In addition to his teammates losing faith in him, he was losing faith in himself.

Tim frowned. "You've got to get through to him, Coach. He's got to trust you, and he's probably going to need a hell of a lot of reassurance that you believe in him, especially after he's been struggling. We both know he's got it in there. He's just got to get out of his own way and show up and play ball."

"I'll set up a meeting with him this week."

David looked back as he heard the locker room door open behind him. Monty gave him a tight smile, dressed in team sweats and obviously fresh from the shower. He held something out to David, who held his hand out in reflex.

"Miss Fogerty asked me to give you one of these after the game." Monty dropped something small into his hand. With a lazy wave, he took off down the hall. "Later, coaches," he called.

David looked down. In the palm of his hand was the familiar green and yellow paper wrapper of a throat lozenge.

A breath huffed from his chest as he unwrapped and popped the lozenge into his mouth. He balled the wrapper up and stuffed it into his pocket.

When he looked up, Tim was watching him with a curious expression on his face.

"She's a damn good team manager," was all he could think of to say.

How r u feeling?

David typed out the text to Sage as he flopped down onto his couch. As soon as he'd gotten home, he'd taken off his suit and changed into sweats and a hoodie, and now that he was comfortable he flipped on the TV to watch something mindless. Daisy jumped up to join him, curling up on his lap like she knew he needed the affection.

There was a loud ping from his phone, and he picked it up to see Sage's response.

> Not great, but okay.

David frowned. She'd looked pretty rough earlier, and he wasn't sure he bought the casual brush off.

> Do u need anything?

> Nope.

> ...Is this u being stubborn?

> No.

> Also, use real words, Coach. You're a grown up.

A loud laugh burst from him, startling Daisy, who gave him a disgruntled growl before settling back in. He knew he was lazy over text, but what was a guy who grew up with AIM supposed to do?

He grinned as he typed out his response.

> K.

Her reply came immediately.

> Stop it.

He laughed again, but paused as he thought about her, sick and alone in her apartment. He wished he could...

Picking Daisy up with him, David ran over to the kitchen,

opening a couple of cabinets until he found what he was looking for. Grinning and feeling inexplicably better, he gathered his findings up in a plastic bag and ran back to the couch for his phone.

> C u soon with soup.

David was already out the door with Daisy under his arm when she replied.

> What? No.

> David.

> Don't you dare.

———

Sage answered the door as soon as he knocked.

Her nose was even redder than it had been earlier, matching her cheeks. Blonde hair stuck out from where it was piled on top of her head, and she was bundled up in a massive hoodie that almost reached her knees. Her mouth was pulled down into a frown as she glared at him.

"What are you doing here," she asked, obviously trying hard — and failing — to look like someone who was completely fine.

David held up the bag. "I brought soup." Then he held Daisy up with his other hand. "And cuddles."

Sage's face softened as she looked at the small dog. "Come here," she said, reaching both hands out toward him.

For a moment, David thought she meant him. *Did she want a hug?*

He loved hugs. Big hug guy. He'd love to give her a —

Daisy. Right. Of course she was talking about Daisy.

He held out his wriggling dog. Sage gathered Daisy against her chest, quietly cooing as the golden pup lathered her face in kisses.

"How are you feeling?"

Sage shrugged. "It could be worse."

Rolling his eyes, David looked past her into her apartment. "Can I come in?"

Again she shrugged, more occupied with snuggling his dog than listening to him. He couldn't blame her. Daisy was an exceptional cuddler. But she stepped aside in a silent invitation before turning and shuffling back inside.

Sage went right to the couch, curling up in one corner and pulling what looked like a handmade quilt up and over her long legs. Daisy settled in on her lap, and David felt overwhelmed with gratitude for the comfort his little dog could provide to Sage.

If he couldn't, at least Daisy could.

"So you brought soup."

David nodded, pulling out the can of Campbell's chicken noodle. "Pot?" he asked as he walked into her kitchen.

"To the left of the oven," she called, her voice hoarse and rasping.

He rifled through a few drawers before he found the can opener, and in no time at all the soup was warming on the stove. His eyes caught on the copper kettle that sat on the stovetop.

"What kind of tea do you want?" he asked, going straight to the drawer where he remembered her retrieving her tea from when she'd made them breakfast.

"Chamomile?" She sounded surprised.

David quickly found the teabag, drawing on his memories of fixing his mom a cup of tea after dinner when he was growing up as he added a spoonful of honey from the jar he'd found in a cabinet. By the time the tea was steeping the soup was bubbling. It only took him a moment to track down a bowl, and then he was carrying the soup and tea out into the living room.

He couldn't help but smile when he saw Sage, who, bundled in the hoodie and quilt, looked like a turtle barely peeking its head out of a shell.

Adorable. Absolutely *goddamn* adorable.

She watched him with a glare that looked like it was more for show than her seriously being annoyed that he was bringing her soup and tea.

"Eat," he said, setting down the bowl and mug on the low wooden table that sat in front of the couch.

He hesitated, suddenly aware of the fact that he'd barged into her home. *Should he leave? Shit, he should probably leave…*

"Tell me about the game." Sage reached for the bowl of soup, blowing on the spoon a few times before bringing the first bite up to her pink mouth. He watched as she sipped at the broth, and when her lips quirked up in her crooked smile he found he could finally breathe again.

"Right. The game." David circled around the table before lowering himself down on the opposite end of the couch from where Sage was curled up. He'd all but forgotten about the game since he'd walked into Sage's apartment, and thinking about it again made his skin crawl. "It wasn't good."

Sage watched him as she slowly ate the soup. When she didn't say anything, he continued.

"Some things were better," he conceded, thinking of Tim's words earlier. "The defense was pretty good, but offensively we just can't make the plays happen." He rubbed a hand over his face as he shook his head. "And Jordan is a mess out there."

"So what's your plan?"

David opened his mouth and then promptly shut it again. Honestly, he hadn't gotten to that part yet, still stuck in the disappointment of their most recent loss.

Rather than pretend, he went for the simple truth. "I don't know yet." A rough sigh escaped him. "I need to look at the tape and review the stats, and —"

"If you had a team meeting right now, what would you tell them?"

"I," David started, trying to imagine himself standing at the front of the windowless classroom where team meetings were held. He could see the guys in front of him, and could perfectly imagine their expressions in the locker room after that night's loss.

It wasn't the time for X's and O's. Players didn't need to hear about the plays they'd run incorrectly after a loss.

"I'd tell them that I believed in them." David leaned forward, bracing his elbows on his knees. "It sounds like a goddamn cliche, but that's what I'd say."

"I think they'd appreciate hearing that," Sage said before another coughing fit shook her body. David was reaching for the mug of tea before he was fully aware of what he was doing, and when he handed it to Sage, she reached for it eagerly. She took a long drink, just sitting there and watching him for a moment before she added, "I know that, as a player, I always did."

Daisy's collar jingled as she adjusted her position on Sage's lap. Sage, who must have sensed the dog's attempt to get more comfortable, extended a leg out along the couch.

Once again, David's body acted on auto-pilot as he reached over and tugged the quilt down to cover Sage's now-extended leg. Of course, doing that then moved the blanket away from where it was tucked up around her shoulders.

Sage reached out with her free hand and grabbed at the cloth. "Why are you stealing my blanket?" Her eyes narrowed into what he could now identify as a glare that was meant to convey amused annoyance.

David pointed down at her foot. "I'm trying to cover your feet."

"This blanket isn't big enough."

He stood up. "Do you have any more?"

Sage's eyes followed his movement. The green of her eyes was more golden than the vivid, bright greens of the plants that were scattered around the living room, and he noticed that while her lashes weren't especially dark, they matched the brown of her eyebrows.

"Seriously?"

David nodded.

"There's another one folded on my bed."

He found the other blanket in question, feeling extremely conscious of the fact that he was in her bedroom. He tried to avoid looking too closely at anything, although he did notice the old pair of Hyperdunks on the floor beside her bed.

When he walked back into the living room, Sage's eyes were closed. Her chest rose and fell in a slow, steady rhythm.

Carefully, he unfolded the blanket and set it down over her, making sure that it reached far enough to cover her outstretched foot. Daisy was still sound asleep where she was curled up in Sage's lap. He started to reach for his dog, but paused when he saw that one of Sage's hands was tucked under Daisy's belly.

He scrubbed his hands over his face, unsure of what to do.

Whatever his plan was, he didn't want to wake Sage.

Grabbing his phone, he typed out a quick text. He waited for Sage's phone to buzz where it sat on the table next to the empty bowl and mug.

> Lefty, I'm at my place, left Daisy with u. Text when ur up and I'll come get her.

He carried the dishes to the kitchen and washed them both, placing them to dry on the towel laid out on the counter top.

A part of him wanted to stay. Sage's apartment was homey and warm in a way that he hadn't figured out how to create in his own space yet, and he could easily picture himself leaning his head back against the couch and taking a nap. With how much he'd been working, he needed it.

But he'd run out of excuses to put off the stats and the game tape that waited for him. He had a job to do, and damn if he wasn't going to figure out what was wrong with his team.

Or with him. The problem could very well be him.

CHAPTER 15
KALE YEAH!
SAGE

By the time Monday rolled around, Sage was back to feeling normal. A few days of rest, sleep, and what felt like hundreds of mugs of tea delivered by a sheepishly smiling David seemed to have cured her. The snuggles with Daisy hadn't hurt at all either.

When she'd woken up in the middle of the night on Saturday with David's dog still curled up on her lap, she'd half expected to find the man somewhere in her apartment. But a quick glance at her phone revealed the text he'd left her — of course, with abbreviated words, because apparently being articulate was a lost art. The dog seemed happy enough, and so Sage had scooped Daisy up and taken her into her bedroom, where they both fell back to sleep almost immediately.

If she'd been disappointed that David hadn't stayed, she blamed it on the fever.

In the morning, she texted David about picking up Daisy. Of course, that meant he came back over armed once again with canned soup, only this time he also brought a carton of chicken bone broth. "I got an organic one," he'd mumbled as grabbed the pan from where he'd set it to dry the night before. "Seemed like something you'd be into."

He'd looked so big in her kitchen, his long arm reaching for

spices while the other stirred the broth on the stove. His wide
body took up space in a way that almost made her feel small. Safe,
even.

And he'd just stuck around.

No matter how many times she'd suggested he leave, or
mentioned that he probably had better things to do with his time
than watch her nap or cough or blow her nose for the millionth
time, David stayed.

When he wasn't actively doing something — making her tea
or heating up another pot of broth — he sat in the opposite corner
of her couch, one leg folded on the cushion while the other
stretched out in front of him, with a book in his hand. He pulled
out those fucking *delicious* glasses when he read, and Sage
couldn't find it in herself to complain about his presence.

She hated the fact that she needed help, but there was something about David that didn't leave her feeling unsettled in the
wake of his kindness. In the short time that she'd known him,
she'd seen little glimpses of a man who directed his attention and
efforts into caring for others. She'd seen the way he'd insisted on
making sure she was home safe on multiple occasions, like the
thought of something happening to her under his watch was
unbearable. The way he'd practically moved himself into her
apartment over the weekend, insisting on doing everything
for her.

She'd drawn the line when he'd tried to vacuum the carpets.

Maybe it was because she'd been so sick, but it had been easier
than she'd expected to just sink into the warmth of being taken
care of. Her roommates used to give her shit, saying that if her car
went off the road into the river, Sage was more likely to take up
residence with the frogs than call to ask for help.

⊏══⊐

After the third night that week of David showing up at her
apartment with takeout, Sage put her foot down.

"David," she said, looking down at the pizza box he'd placed on her counter. Daisy had already made herself comfortable on the large pillow that had unofficially become her dog bed. "If you want to hang out, then at least let me cook." She held a hand up when David opened his mouth to respond. "I'm better now, and if I eat any more pizza I'm going to get sick all over again."

David's shoulders sagged as he rubbed one of his big hands over his face. He still looked weighed down by exhaustion; she could see it in the purple smudged under his eyes and the deepened frown lines around his mouth. "Honestly, Lefty," he said, his voice rough and matching the lack of energy in the rest of his body. "I'll probably cry if you cook something right now. I've been surviving on frozen dinners and take out, so something homemade sounds like the greatest thing in the whole goddamn world."

Sage couldn't help but smile as she looked in the fridge. "How does spaghetti sound?"

David groaned — a low, rumbling sound that sent a rush of heat down her spine. "Sounds incredible."

It only took a minute to gather the ingredients from the fridge and put a pot of water on to boil. Sage fell easily into the rhythm of moving through her kitchen, smashing the broad side of her knife down on the cloves of garlic to make peeling them easier.

"Can I help?"

Sage glanced up, her fingers continuing to tackle the brittle skin that covered the garlic cloves. "Nope," she said. "Get something to drink, sit down, and tell me about your day."

David scowled at her, but rounded the counter to look in the fridge. "You have a bunch of weird stuff in here."

She snorted a laugh, scraping the now chopped garlic up with her knife and tossing it in with the ground beef that was browning in a skillet. "It's just sparkling water and kombucha," she said, moving on to chop the white onion.

"What's kombucha?"

"Think a tangy, fruity tea."

"Which one should I try?"

"Probably the blueberry." She turned around, ready to warn him about the —

"Jesus!" David shouted as bubbling kombucha exploded from the lid of the glass bottle, flooding over his hands and soaking the front of his t-shirt in the pale purple drink. He held the bottle away from his body as he rushed to stand over the sink. "What the hell was that?"

She tried not to laugh.

She really fucking tried.

But David looked at her with a mixture of horror and betrayal, like she'd set him up for this ultimate humiliation. Laughter burst from her chest, loud and without constraint.

"I," she gasped, trying to catch her breath. "I was trying to warn you, but you were too fast!"

His face glistened, and his exhaustion enhanced his appeal, deepening his features and making him appear rugged, and, somehow, even more handsome. She wished, with a sharp and almost painful yearning, that he was someone different.

She watched as his tongue swept over his bottom lip, catching a stray droplet of kombucha. His brows arched up, allowing the light to illuminate his dark eyes. "At least it tastes good," he admitted, his mouth curving into a reluctant smile. "It's really damn sticky, though."

Sage jumped into action, wetting a towel and tossing it to him. She looked down at his soaked shirt, grimacing.

"Let me go find you a shirt," she said as she ran to her room. She looked through her t-shirts, quickly finding the largest one she had.

When she returned to the kitchen, David had obviously tried to mop up the spilled kombucha. "Here." Sage handed him the green t-shirt.

David held the shirt up against his body. "This won't fit," he grumbled, frowning down at himself.

"Trust me. It will."

David gave her an exasperated look, but, with a sigh, reached back to pull his wet shirt over his head.

Sage's mouth dropped open.

Fucking *fuck*.

She knew he was big. She'd seen his back, shoulders, and biceps straining against his clothing. But to see the curve of his shoulders bare? To see the dark hair that swirled across his chest and continued down his broad stomach? The trail that disappeared below the waistband of the sweats that hung below his hips?

Her skin prickled, her cheeks heated, and *fuck* if she didn't want to lick him. Everywhere. Why, of all of the things she could do with him, *licking* came to mind, she had no fucking idea.

He was just so...big. And as a woman who'd spent the majority of her life towering over those around her, the thought of this man doing things to her body with his body made her...

She shuddered, trying to gather herself as he pulled the t-shirt down, tugging it over his torso. She'd been right. It fit him well, even offering a little extra wiggle room.

"What?"

She glanced up, finding him watching her with a guarded expression. There was even a hint of color on his cheeks.

"You're just..." She waved her hand at his upper body.

David's eyes dropped down. "It's rough, I know. I've got to be better about what I eat, and —"

"You're really, really fucking hot," Sage interrupted, unable to keep her thoughts to herself at the sight of this man — this powerful, attractive man — deluding himself to think that he was anything other than perfect. "When I read novels about hot cowboys they're always described as being big, hairy men, and I mean, I always imagine them in my head. But you're it. You're like a fantasy straight out of a book, and I'm having a very hard time keeping my shit together when you look like *that*."

David's gaze rose up to meet hers and his lips parted, still wet from where he'd licked the kombucha away. "Damnit,

Lefty," he said roughly, shaking his head. "You can't say things like that."

"I'll say whatever I want," Sage teased, crossing her arms over her chest.

His brow furrowed as he looked down at the shirt again. "Does this seriously say 'Kale Yeah!' on it?"

"It was a gift from my old roommate, Mary. Apparently the fact that I eat a lot of kale is one of my most noteworthy personality traits."

David chuckled. "Can't say I'm a big fan of kale."

Sage suddenly became aware of a sharp, acrid smell that accompanied a haze of smoke that hovered in the air around them. "Fuck!"

She ran to the stove, turning off the burner and grabbing the skillet. She tossed the pan into the sink, turning the water on to wash away the charred remains of what was supposed to be their dinner.

"Fuck," she repeated, slumping back against the counter.

"So, pizza?" she heard David ask from behind her.

Sage shook her head. "After that, I need tots."

⬭

"Why are these so fucking good?" She moaned around a hot tater tot that was crisped to perfection and topped with melted cheese, green onions, and bits of bacon.

Across the table, David chewed with a wide grin on his face.

The Grove was crowded, but their timing had been perfect, arriving right when a group was vacating one of the picnic tables close to the stage. A band was setting up, unloading a variety of guitars, a drum set, and banjo.

"So you read novels about hot cowboys?"

Her cheeks heated almost instantly. *Guess they weren't going to pretend she hadn't word-vomited all over her kitchen floor.*

She nodded. "Western, small-town romances."

David stabbed another tot from the heaping platter between them. "What do you like about them?" He sounded genuinely curious.

"In so many stories, it seems like characters just hop on the plot train and get carried along for the ride. Nothing against that, but as someone who's had a pretty unremarkable life, I don't find them relatable. But romance novels? The characters almost always have some sort of personal struggle they are working through that drives the book forward. Sometimes it's confronting their past." She paused to swallow against an unwanted lump in her throat. "Sometimes it's gaining the confidence to chase after what they want. Whatever it is, the characters in romance novels feel just a little bit closer to living life like the rest of us." A smirk curved on her lips. "As for the cowboys? I don't know, really. There's something beautiful about men who act all stoic and unaffected, but at the end of the day are brought to their knees by a woman."

David took a long pull from the Corona he'd ordered. Sage had felt a wave of deja vu as she watched one of his thick fingers push the lime down into the bottle. He set down the beer and locked eyes with her, his thick lashes somehow picking up the golden lights from the strings that hung above them. "That's a pretty damn convincing argument," he said, leaning forward to brace his forearms on the table. "Might have to pick up one of those."

Sage snorted into her jalapeño margarita. "Do you read many books with graphic sex scenes?"

"Uh," David coughed through a mouthful of food. The ambient hum of conversation that surrounded them seemed to grow louder for a few seconds as he chewed and swallowed. "Can't say that I do," he finally replied, scratching his beard.

"Don't knock it 'til you try it."

What. Sage immediately wished she could take the words back.

David's thick brows shot up his forehead. He reached a hand up to cover his mouth, but not before Sage saw his amused grin.

Dropping his hand, he leaned out across the table. "Graphic sex?" His voice had somehow gotten lower, even more rough than she was used to. "I've tried it a few times."

"Oh my god." Sage covered her face with her hands, willing her flaming face to cool down.

"If it ain't the beautiful man and my best friend!"

Sage opened a gap between her fingers, looking right up into Maggie's grinning face. The woman planted her hands on the edge of the table, glancing between the two of them. "Did he do somethin' to you, blondie? Do I need to hurt him?"

Sage shook her head, snorting a laugh. "You really are a balls to the wall kind of person, aren't you?"

"Sure am." Maggie looked over at David. "So you finally got over your 'oh no it's too complicated we work together' bullshit and asked her out? Nice." She held her hand up for a high five.

David ignored the offered hand, instead glaring at her, his expression incredulous. "Well, since you asked, Sage and I are *friends*, eating a meal together as *friends*, hanging out as *friends*."

Wincing, Maggie lowered her hand. "My bad." She glanced back over her shoulder at Sage. "For the record, I think it's stupid."

Sage had no idea what was happening. "What's stupid?"

"You two not bein' together out of some misguided sense of morality," Maggie said, waving her hand between them. "If there was someone who looked at me the way that you guys look at each other, you bet my momma's gravy I wouldn't waste a day without them." Without pausing, she reached into her back pocket, drawing out her phone. Her thumbs tapped for a moment, and then she tossed it down on the table in front of Sage. "Put your number in there and I'll text you."

Rather than respond to the rest of what Maggie had said, Sage picked up the phone, entering her name and number before handing it back. She could feel David watching her, but she wasn't quite ready to look at him.

Not yet.

Maggie flashed her a smile. "Well, you two enjoy your *friendly* dinner, then. Next drink is on me."

Sage watched her walk away, struck once again by what a whirlwind Maggie was. She had the kind of magnetic personality that drew people to her, like Brinley and Cori did. Whatever that magical thing was that they all possessed, Sage didn't have.

"I'm going to run to the bathroom," David said, bracing his hands on the table in front of him as he stood up. Sage couldn't help but stare at his forearms. "Need anything?"

Fucking forearms. She wet her lips. They looked like they were wrapped in rope, the skin there tan and dusted with dark hair. What would it feel like if he —

"Sage?" A big hand waved in front of her face. "You okay?"

"Fine," she squeaked. "Totally fine."

David didn't look like he believed her, but he gave her a small nod before turning and walking away.

Was she watching his butt? Yes.

"Hey."

Sage jumped in her seat, whirling around to look at whoever had interrupted her *very* subtle appreciation of David Hughes' ass.

An objectively good-looking man with a nice smile and a nice enough face lowered himself down onto the bench beside her. His business casual clothing was also...well, nice. It was all nice and he looked nice and Sage had never felt more indifferent about a man in her life.

When she didn't respond immediately, the man fussed with his short black hair. "Can I get you a drink?"

"No thank you," Sage said, already shaking her head. "I'm actually here with someone."

Something in her stomach did a backflip at the admission. Because they weren't here like that. He was David and she was Sage and they were *friends*. Friends who shared tots and breakfast and dinner and couches.

"Oh," the man offered her an apologetic smile. "That's my bad. I hope you have a good night."

As he stood up, Sage caught a glimpse of David walking back through the crowd toward their table. She watched his eyes dart over to the stranger, and saw the exact moment his eyebrows snapped together and his lips curved down into a scowl.

Maybe she was imagining it, but she thought he might have sped up as he walked back to her.

"Welcome back from your adventure," Sage said as David sat down.

The frown hadn't left his face. "Why did you do that?"

"Do what?"

David let out a heavy sigh. "I don't want to keep you from…" His voice trailed off.

Sage cocked her head to one side. "Keep me from…?"

"If you want to hang out with him I under —"

"I wasn't interested," Sage interrupted. Her cheeks heated, and she stabbed a tot and shoved it into her mouth.

"Oh." David watched her, his expression blank.

"Do you date?" Sage winced. They'd officially departed from *safe conversation topics to have with your very hot coworker* and her question didn't help them get back on track. Not even a little bit.

David at least seemed like he was taking the question seriously. "I haven't in a while," he admitted, his eyes trained down at the decimated tray of loaded tots between them. "My last girlfriend was up in Chicago." His gaze lifted to hers. "What about you?"

Sage almost choked on the bite she was currently chewing. "Date? Nope. Not my thing."

"Really?" He looked genuinely confused, if not a bit concerned. "Why not?"

She swallowed against the harsh tightening in her throat. How was she supposed to explain that in high school when everyone else was figuring out how to survive awkward dinners at Vinny's and making out in the back row of the movie theater, Sage had been lying to her mom about going to sleepovers and waiting by her phone in the off chance that the guy she'd been infatuated with *might* ask her to rendezvous in an abandoned parking lot?

She couldn't say that. Instead she shrugged. "Hook-ups work fine for me."

Sage watched his face carefully, like a part of her expected him to recoil. But instead he just nodded, his expression thoughtful. "I don't think I could do that," he admitted, his voice softening. "When I want a woman enough to hook-up, there's no way in hell I can just walk away." His eyes shut for a moment, and her attention was pulled to the way his long lashes cast shadows across his cheekbones. "Once I have her, I won't want to give her up."

Sage didn't know how to respond to that, or why his admission made her skin itch and her neck heat. Reaching for her drink, she took a long sip, trying to focus on the burn of the tequila against the back of her tongue.

"Want to dance?"

She blinked. "What?"

David nodded toward the band, who was now playing country covers only about ten feet from their table. How Sage hadn't noticed the loud, amplified music was beyond her.

"I asked you if you want to dance with me, Lefty."

Sage glanced over her shoulder at the wooden dance floor, where a few other couples were already two-stepping. Her gaze returned to David, who watched her with a patient, fond smile.

"Fine." She tried to sound like she was just doing it for him, like she was indulging *his* need to dance with her. But based on how David watched her as he reached for her hand and pulled them both to standing, he could see right through her.

She let him lead them to an open spot, the music swallowing the air around them as he turned and tugged her toward him. It was such a nonchalant move, but it sent her stumbling forward, forcing her hands up to brace herself against his broad chest.

Before she had a chance to enjoy the feeling of him under her fingertips, he firmly grabbed her right hand, pulling it out and away from their bodies, and, at the same time, she felt his other hand trail down her back before settling at the base of her spine.

With a gentle push of the hand on her back, they were moving. She couldn't do much beyond following David's movements. He moved almost lazily, guiding her with the firm, steady pressure of his hand. She knew the steps well enough — *short and short, long* — but she'd never danced with someone who took the entire weight of decision making off of her shoulders.

Their bodies were flush, her chest pressed to his and her face at the perfect height that, if she wanted to, she could turn and press her nose into the spot where his neck met the curved muscle of his shoulder.

She could catch a hint of his smell — a combination of that almost beachy scent and a soap that was common enough that she should recognize it. She could see the way his Adam's apple dipped as they moved and felt his slow, deep breaths against her. He was still in her ridiculous 'Kale Yeah!' t-shirt, but it didn't matter. Not when the warm glow of the lights hit his forearms like something out of a fantasy.

In pulling her against his body, one of David's legs had slipped between hers, leaving her practically straddling one of his thick thighs. The seam of her jeans rubbing against his leg was doing absolutely indecent things to her body.

Was this an elaborate sex dream?

It was a familiar scene: the brooding, quiet man asks the girl to dance. His effortlessly sexy dance moves make her come in her Levi's. He whispers naughty things in her ear in his low, throaty voice, and then they go outside to his truck and she rides him in the back seat.

Save a horse, ride a cowboy, or something like that.

But David was wearing soft joggers and Nike sneakers, not Wranglers and boots. And Sage, in her baggy jeans and single French braid, looked nothing like the protagonists from the novels she read.

Yep. Not a dream.

"What are your plans for Christmas?" David asked, his mouth close enough to her ear that she could feel the whisper of his breath against her skin.

Sage forced an exhale from her lips. She needed to get a hold of herself before she actually started grinding against his leg like a horny teenager. "Staying here," she said, rising on her toes so she could speak against his ear and be heard over the music. "Didn't think it was worth it to fly back to Cali for only five days."

She also wasn't entirely ready to subject herself to her mother, but that was another conversation.

"Hm." It was a low hum that felt like it vibrated her bones. She shivered. "What would you normally do for the holiday if you were home?"

Sage smiled, temporarily distracted as she thought of the traditions that had emerged in her family over the years. "On Christmas Eve, we always gift books to each other and read while we eat tomato soup and grilled cheese sandwiches. Then on Christmas, we do a 'make your favorites' feast rather than traditional holiday food. Everyone makes their favorite dish, and then we fill in the sides as needed to make sure it's a balanced meal."

She felt his chuckle rumble in his chest. "Sounds very much like you," he said.

Her cheeks warmed. "What about you? What are your plans?"

David didn't immediately respond. Sage's attention slipped back to their bodies, and she felt the moment when the thumb that rested against her lower back shifted, slipping up and under the hem of her t-shirt. When his skin brushed against hers, she felt her breath catch in her lungs.

There was an air of anticipation between them, like whatever happened next would set into motion a series of events that they were powerless to stop.

Sage tipped her head forward until her forehead met the cotton of the shirt that looked so different, so fucking *good*, on David's bigger body. She knew that she was dancing on the edge of the boundaries they'd drawn, but she couldn't bring herself to step away.

"Staying here too," David finally said, and she felt the scratch of his beard against her cheek as he shifted his head away. "It's getting late. We should probably head home."

"Right," Sage said, beginning to extract her body from his hold. "Good idea."

When she went to tug her hand away from his, she felt his grip tighten for just a moment. She stopped, looking up at him, but found his gaze focused on where their hands were still connected. He opened his mouth like he was going to say something, but then shook his head and pulled his hand away.

"I got the tab."

Sage opened her mouth to protest, but David was already walking to the bar. An odd emptiness settled in her stomach as she gathered her bag and moved toward the exit.

It was just dancing.

CHAPTER 16
FLUFFY CORGI BUTTS
DAVID

David paced the hallway outside of the locker room, fidgeting at the scratch of the sweater he'd decided to wear for the game.

The dark green knit crewneck was a bit out of his normal fashion wheelhouse, but his mom had bought it for him and it made him feel a tiny bit better about disappointing her with the news that he wouldn't be coming home for Christmas.

He wasn't sure what the hell he'd been thinking when he told Sage that he was planning to stay in Charleston for their short holiday. In the thirty-five years that he'd been alive, he'd never *not* gone back to Atlanta to celebrate with his family.

Christmas was very much their thing.

But his goddamn mouth had run away from him, and he'd found himself fumbling through the excuse that a few of his players were staying around and didn't have a place to go. Of course his wonderful mother had immediately understood, and promised to send a box of sweets in the mail for him to share.

He hated lying to her, but he hated the idea of Sage spending Christmas alone even more.

"We're ready, Coach." Jordan poked his head out of the locker room door.

David nodded, taking a moment to gather himself before following him inside.

The whole team sat on the benches, already dressed in their uniforms and warm ups even though it was still a few hours before the game. He'd called them in early, and there was a part of him that was still surprised to see that they'd actually listened to his request.

He could feel the heaviness in the air — their opponent tonight was Greenville University, a team who'd won almost all of their games so far this season. No matter how well they played, it was going to be a tough game.

David stood before them, shoving his hands into the pockets of his slacks and rocking back on his heels. He thought of the speech he'd planned, about playing hard and working together, about finishing their final game before Christmas on a strong note.

But the words wouldn't come.

He took a deep breath. "So, as you can probably tell, I need a haircut."

The room was silent. The players looked at him before looking at each other, obviously unsure of how to respond to him.

He reached a hand up and tugged on the hair that was undoubtedly tufting up around his head. "Come on, guys. It's nuts, isn't it?"

Monty was the first to break. His huffed laugh ignited the rest of them, and soon the whole team was doubled over with laughter as they looked up at David.

"Coach," Patrick Eno, one of the freshmen, managed to get out. "It's like one of those fluffy corgi butts."

"What?" Jenks elbowed him in the side as he shook his head. "Corgi butts are white, dude."

"But doesn't it kind of have that fluffy tufted thing going?" Patrick argued, waving his hands around his head.

Monty jumped in. "I think he looks like Doc Brown from *Back to the Future*."

"Hey!" David glared at the point guard as the rest of the team howled. "That man was balding up top! I've got this big floppy mess up front. That's at least one thing I've got going for me."

"So you gonna get a haircut?" Zephyr asked.

"Honestly, everytime I go, they screw it up so badly that I've been avoiding it." David shrugged. "But it's getting to the point where it can't get much worse than this, you know?"

"Jordan cuts hair," Jenks offered, glancing over at his co-captain.

"Seriously?" David turned to Jordan just in time to see him shoot a scowl down the bench toward Jenks.

"I mean," Jordan said, his voice barely above a mumble. "I'm alright at it."

"Got any scissors with you?"

Jordan's blonde eyebrows shot up his forehead. "Don't we have to warm up?"

David checked his phone. "We've got another twenty minutes before you need to get out there."

Jordan's brows furrowed as he looked at David, like he was trying to figure out what his angle was. Honestly, David wasn't entirely sure what he was trying to accomplish by letting one of his players cut his hair. All that he knew was that the second the team had started arguing about corgi butts, the feeling in the room shifted.

"Fine." Jordan reached into his locker, grabbing a leather dopp kit and looking up at David. "Where are we doing this?"

The team jumped into action, dragging a folding chair into the group shower. Someone produced a towel, and next thing he knew David had stripped out of his sweater, leaving him in an undershirt with a towel slung over his shoulders.

"Alright boys," Jordan said, looking around at the guys that had crammed into the shower to surround David. "What are we doing with this mop?"

David grinned as the guys laughed. It was the first glimmer of humor he'd seen from the senior, and something that felt a lot like pride warmed his chest. He didn't give a shit that he was the butt of the joke. He'd take it any day if it meant seeing these guys come together.

Ten minutes later, he was looking at himself in the mirror, shocked into silence as he turned his head back and forth.

"Damn," he said, unable to believe what Jordan had been able to do.

The sides were trimmed enough that the hair sat neatly, and he'd left the top long enough that it fell back from his face but wouldn't fall into his eyes. The back was also trimmed up from his neck, and already he felt more comfortable without the constant itch of hair on his skin.

He looked good. Objectively good. Like a man who had his shit together and who people would listen to. *Who knew the power of a goddamn haircut?*

"Coach, you're looking good for an old guy," one of the younger players called out. There was another ripple of laughter that ran through the room, and David chuckled as he pulled his sweater back on.

He walked over to Jordan, who was putting his things away in his locker. "I owe you lunch," he said, extending a hand. "Best haircut I've ever had."

Jordan blushed, but shook David's hand. "It's no problem, Coach."

David returned to the middle of the room, watching his guys settle back into their spots.

They weren't his in the sense that he hadn't chosen them. He hadn't watched their high school games or recruited them. He hadn't been the one to share the news that they'd get the chance to fulfill the dream of playing college basketball.

But they were his now. They were his team, and he was reminded of what an honor it was to get to be here in the room with them.

"I've been tough on you this year," he said, making sure to keep his eyes roving over the group as he spoke. "There's a lot of talent in this room, and it's hard to watch us not pull out wins when we have so much going for us. But that's not how this sport works. You can be the best shooter in the world, but if your confidence is shaken, you can't make a shot to save your life." He shook his head. "I'm sorry if I've taken that confidence from you. You were all chosen to be in this room because you're talented players who have earned your spot on a college roster."

David focused his gaze on Jordan, who was looking down at his tightly clasped hands in his lap. "This is our last game before you all go home to spend a few days with your families. I want you all to go into those days without the weight of past games on your shoulders."

Shifting back to the rest of the group, he realized that, for the first time that season, every single one of them was hanging on to every word he said.

"The only way I know how to do that is to go out there and share the weight. Share the responsibility of stopping the ball. Share the need to get every rebound and the determination to get the ball in the hoop. If you do that, then regardless of the outcome, all of us here in this room will leave tonight knowing that what happened out there was our best."

Every player was looking at him, and a few nodded along as he wrapped up his speech. He looked over at Jordan and then at Jenks, who both watched him with obvious determination on their faces. "Captains," he continued, speaking to the two seniors. "Come up with a game plan for tonight. You've seen the tape. You know who these guys are. Take ten to talk with the team, and then bring the plan to me."

With one last nod at the group, David turned and walked out of the room.

"What the hell did you say to them?" Tim asked, leaning over into David's space as the home crowd cheered when Jordan hit another three.

"All I did was let them give me a haircut," David replied, unable to keep the huge smile from his face. He looked up at the scoreboard. They were only down 35 - 30 coming up to the end of the half.

They were playing their asses off, making Greenville fight to earn every point. At Jordan and Jenks' suggestions, they'd dropped any attempt at half-court pressure and focused instead on protecting the basket and getting their bigger guys into position to rebound.

And then there was the fact that Jordan couldn't miss a shot. He didn't celebrate his makes; his face remained stoic and almost expressionless as his teammates celebrated around him, but he returned their high fives and even shouted an occasional "Let's go, boys."

It was the shift that the guys needed.

As the clock counted down to the half, Monty and Matty scoring brought them within a point of Greenville, who couldn't get a shot off before the buzzer.

The team couldn't help but celebrate as they ran into the locker room. A part of David wanted to remind them that they were still losing, but he couldn't bring himself to say anything. The fact that they were so close with a team like this was worth celebrating.

As had become customary, David, Tim, and Sage hung back in the hallway outside the locker room to give the players a minute and to give the coaches a chance to talk over their game plan.

"Must have been a hell of a haircut," Tim said, a grin on his face as he leaned against the wall opposite of where David stood. "I don't think I've ever seen Jordan play like that."

David glanced over at Sage, who'd had that crooked smile on her face for the entire first half. Even as her fingers had tapped away on the tablet, the smile never wavered.

She looked incredible in the blue blazer and pants that she frequently wore to games. Combined with the ponytail and heels, she looked like she should be the one sitting at the head of the bench.

"He's 5 for 6 from the three," she said, looking down at the tablet she held in her hands. Her eyes jumped up, meeting his gaze head on as she addressed him. "They're playing out of their minds tonight, Coach."

For some reason, hearing those words from her meant more than he could quantify.

"I don't think I'm going to say much," David said, looking over at Tim. "Just to keep doing what they're doing."

"Sounds good." He gave a nod to David before going into the locker room.

David stood there frozen. Had Tim just given him a nod of approval? He rubbed a hand over his beard, a combination of embarrassment and pride warring in him as he berated himself for being so affected by the older man's praise.

"Nice work," he heard her say, and he blinked to see Sage standing in front of him with her fist extended.

He bumped his hand against hers. "Thanks, Lefty," he said, remembering what it had been like to dance with her.

Dancing with her had been a mistake. Up until then, so much about her had been a product of his imagination. Was her skin soft? How would her body fit against his? How would she respond to his touch?

Now he knew too much.

He knew that her skin was soft like silk and yet cool to the touch. He knew that her body tucked perfectly against his, her height bringing her close enough that it was easy to whisper against her ear. He knew that she softened like butter in his arms.

He should have known better. Everyone knew that dancing with someone was the only foolproof way to suss out chemistry. If you moved together well on the dance floor, well, then chances were you'd be fucking electric in bed.

And *damn* if they hadn't moved like they'd been dancing together for years.

Shaking his head, he realized he was alone in the hallway. He had a team to coach, and a goddamn game to win.

The sound in the locker room was deafening. Sweaty bodies leapt up and down, shouts and cheers filling the humid, sweat-stenched air.

They'd won.

It had been down to the wire, but in the final seconds, they'd managed to pull ahead, earning a 58 - 57 win. His post-game speech had only lasted about three seconds: "I'm incredibly proud of what you guys did out there together," followed by a few more words from Tim calling out the players who'd had a stand-out game.

Now, in the wake of it all the guys were celebrating, bouncing around like puppies, and David watched, not even trying to keep the wide, relieved smile from his face.

"You staying around here for the break?"

He glanced over at Tim, who stood beside him. "Yeah, I'll be sticking around."

"The wife and I would love to have you over for dinner," Tim said, keeping his gaze trained on the antics of the players. "Just let me know what night would work for you."

David cleared his throat. *Damn the old man throwing curve balls tonight.* "Sure," he managed to choke out, feeling a bit over-whelmed by whatever emotion was causing his chest to tighten. "That'd be great, Tim. Thank you."

Tim nodded, clasping him on the shoulder with one of his weathered hands. "See you soon then," he said, before shouting one last 'Good work' to the boys and heading out the door.

David's eyes caught on Sage, who was weaving her way through the guys, snatching up the discarded warm up shirts and tossing them into the laundry cart in the corner. "Make sure all your stuff goes in the cart," she shouted over the noise. "Just because you're winners now doesn't mean you get to be all sloppy."

"Come on, Sage!" Monty called. "You know we'll keep the young ones in line for you."

Zephyr balled up a towel and tossed it at Monty's head. "Stop talking like you're one of the old guys, kid."

Monty caught it and threw it right back. "I'm only five months younger than you, ass-"

"Language!" David called out, his voice croaking and broken like it always was after a game.

"Asshole can't be a bad word, Coach," Patrick said, scratching at his blonde hair. "It's anatomical."

Sage snorted, shaking her head as she walked over to join David. One hand reached into her pocket and produced the paper wrapped throat lozenge that he'd come to expect after every game. She threw it to him and he caught it easily, unpeeling the wrapper and then popping it into his mouth.

"Thank you," he said, offering her a smile.

She returned his look with a grin of her own. He noticed her gaze lingered on his hair.

"What do you think?" he asked, pointing to his head.

Sage took a moment, her bright green eyes darting from side to side as she took him in. Her cheeks flushed as she looked him in the eye. "You look good," she said, keeping her voice quiet enough that her words were very clearly intended just for the two of them. "Way too good."

He wished they were alone. He wished that he could draw her into his arms and tell her just how relieved he was that they'd won, how his eyes kept seeking her out during the game, how just seeing her at the end of the bench made him feel stronger.

"You're going to do Christmas with me," he heard himself saying. *He probably should have phrased that like a question.*

Sage blinked, her lips parting. "Uh, okay."

"Good."

"I get to cook though," she added, raising a brow at him.

"Sure. Whatever you want." David smiled down at her, feeling so damn lucky that he'd stumbled into an existence that included Sage Fogerty.

So goddamn lucky.

———

"What are we cooking for Christmas?"

Sage braced her elbows against the handle of the shopping cart, and it took monumental effort for David to ignore the way her black leggings stretched over her ass and thighs.

He shook himself. "We're going to do the thing you talked about, where everyone cooks their favorite thing."

Sage stood up, turning to face him. "Really?" Her expression tightened as she looked at him. "Are you sure you don't want to do whatever your family does?"

"No," David said, shoving his hands into the pockets of his hoodie to keep from reaching for her. "I don't like cranberry sauce, so it's all good."

Snorting, Sage turned back to the cart, starting to walk slowly down the aisle. "So what are you going to make?"

"Loaded tots." It was an easy decision. David was a simple man, really. Tater tots, Daisy and a woman in leggings were all he needed to be happy.

"Nice. I'm going to make burgers." She paused, as though thinking. "And something green. You need to eat more green stuff."

David scoffed. "There was lettuce *and* onions on the sandwich I ate yesterday."

"That barely counts," Sage replied. "You said your friend was coming too, right?"

Right. He'd invited Chuck, who had the same shortened break due to the swimming team's schedule. His friend had teased him ruthlessly at the fact that they were going to be spending Christmas at his intern's apartment, but David brushed it off. He and Sage were friends, and he stood by the fact that it wasn't weird for them to be spending the holiday together.

Not weird at all.

"Chuck will make something good," David said, grabbing a bag of marshmallows and tossing it into the cart. "He's a good cook like you."

Sage looked between him and the bag.

"What? I like my hot chocolate with marshmallows." He scratched at his beard. "And sometimes I eat them plain when I'm feeling especially festive." He waggled his eyebrows at her and grinned.

Sage laughed another one of her snorting laughs, shaking her head as she steered them up another aisle.

"I was also thinking," David started, "that, depending on what you have going on, maybe we could hang out on Christmas Eve and do the book exchange thing you were talking about."

The cart stopped, and David turned, trying to gauge Sage's reaction by the expression on her face. She looked carefully blank in that moment, her lips parting as she stared at him.

Immediately, he tried to backpedal. "Sorry, that's probably too much. We're already doing Christmas, and I shouldn't assume that you want to spend more time with me than you already are, I...shit, I'm sorry, and —"

"David." Sage reached out and grabbed his wrist. Her skin was so cold against his, and he had the irrational urge to take her hand in his until some of his warmth transferred to her. "Spending time with you is honestly the best part of my week." She smiled, and David's chest ached. "Trust me, if I don't want to hang out, I'll tell you."

David swallowed. "Okay."

"So that's a yes to Christmas Eve. We can do it at my place, and then Christmas at yours?"

"Deal."

"What should I wear?" David shouted from his closet. It was midmorning on Christmas, and he was still wearing the sweats and t-shirt he'd slept in the night before.

He'd gone to Sage's place, where they'd exchanged books — a new mystery by a British author he'd never heard of for him, and a Western romance set in Canada his mom had sworn was amazing for Sage. She'd made tomato soup and grilled cheese sandwiches, just like she'd said, and they'd posted up on opposite ends of the couch to eat and read.

It was probably the best Christmas Eve he'd ever had.

"Wear that sweater your mom got you!" Chuck called out. He'd shown up early with coffee and doughnuts, and they'd spent the morning watching Sports Center and taking Daisy for a long walk.

"And pants?"

"Jeans, or those brown corduroys you never wear would be good."

David grabbed the corduroys. "Seriously, what would I do without you?"

"Dress like a seventeen year old gym-rat," Chuck shouted.

Chuckling, David finished pulling on his clothes before joining Chuck in the living room.

"You look good, man," his friend said from the kitchen. Chuck was making some sort of baked mac and cheese casserole, and had already started cooking.

"Are the decorations okay?"

David had spent a day or two trying to make his apartment look somewhat festive and seasonal. He'd bought the tiniest live tree they'd had at the store, along with some red and gold balls and lights. He'd also bought a few candles that were supposed to smell like a pine forest, and had Christmas music going on his phone.

It wasn't much, but it was something.

"The place looks great," Chuck reassured him, before letting out a low laugh. "You need to chill out."

"I am chill!" Of course David shouted in the least-chill way possible right as someone knocked on the door.

Chuck's laughs rang out from the kitchen as he walked to the front door.

"Jesus," David muttered, running a hand through his hair. He still wasn't used to the fact that he could wake up in the morning and not fight a losing battle to tame his hair into submission. "Get your shit together."

He opened the door.

"Merry — holy shit."

Sage stood on his doorstep, looking like something out of a personalized David Hughes Christmas fantasy.

Her hair was pulled back from her face in one of those braids that started on the top of her head and then went all the way down her back. Something sparkly was brushed onto her eyelids, making the green of her eyes shine like the color was something living.

She wore a silky red dress that left most of her bare legs exposed, and when he glanced down, he almost choked. There was no missing the two tight buds of her nipples pressed against the red fabric, and he felt the heat of arousal flare low in his belly. A red and orange flannel shirt hung open on her shoulders, and *of course* she was wearing her Nikes.

Of course she was.

"Hi," she said, almost hesitantly.

"You look beautiful." The words spilled from him before he could remember that those were the thoughts he was supposed to keep to himself.

She held his gaze even as her cheeks flushed and she smiled. "You look pretty beautiful yourself, Coach."

David realized he was still posted up in the middle of the doorway like some sort of hulking bouncer, and shuffled to the side to let Sage in. "Please come in."

Sage carried at least two of those cloth reusable grocery bags, and she paused only to toe off her shoes before carrying them to the kitchen.

"Hey," Chuck said, waving from where he stood behind the counter. "You must be Sage."

"And you must be Chuck," she replied, going to join him in the kitchen. "Swimming coach, right?"

"Yeah. It's nice to meet you," Chuck said. "I should thank you, you know."

Sage had already started unloading her bags and making herself at home. David hovered just outside the kitchen, unsure of how he was supposed to help. "And why's that," she asked.

"Thanks to you, this idiot has stopped showing up at my house every other day with groceries."

"Hey!" David protested. "You like it when I bring you groceries."

Chuck rolled his eyes as he tossed his head to get his hair out of his eyes. "I like it when you come to hang out, Hughes. I just don't know how to handle it when you bring a year's supply of toilet paper."

"That was once! You'd mentioned you were almost out."

"Dude, we're over thirty. I can mention that I need something without you jumping onto your white horse to save me from potential bathroom disasters."

"So you're saying you want me to stop bringing you olives?"

Chuck's eyes snapped up. "No. You can keep bringing the olives."

"I like this guy," Sage commented, obviously amused, as she rummaged through the cabinets.

"Me or him?" Chuck asked.

"Both," she replied, but she smiled at David in a way that made him hope that, just maybe, her words meant something different when it came to him.

Conversation and banter flowed easily as they finished cooking, and soon enough they were sitting down to the best combination of foods David had ever consumed in a single sitting. There were burgers, tater tots loaded with cheese and bacon, a mac and cheese casserole, roasted broccoli, a salad with goat cheese and fruit on it that was surprisingly delicious, and then a huge variety of holiday cookies that his mom had sent. Chuck had brought some dark beers, and Sage had brought a bottle of peach wine.

Afterwards, they sat sprawled around the living room. David had tried to offer Sage the couch, but she'd insisted on sitting on the floor. Of course, Daisy immediately curled up with her head on Sage's thigh, and David smiled as he watched her scratch absently at Daisy's ears.

"So what do you guys have planned for the team when they get back?" Chuck asked from the other end of the couch.

David shrugged. "Practices. Maybe some community service."

"Dude," Chuck said, giving David a look like he was missing something obvious.

"What?"

"You've got to make it fun," Chuck explained, shifting his beer from one hand to the other. "They're leaving their families to come back to school early, and you can only practice so much in a day. I always make them do team bonding stuff, like cooking meals at the older swimmers' houses, or doing silly scavenger hunts around the city. Honestly, it doesn't matter what they're doing as long as they're doing it together and it leaves them too exhausted to get into trouble at the end of the day."

David glanced over at Sage, who was nodding along with what Chuck was saying. "What do you think?"

"It's a good idea. The team doesn't have that tight-knit vibe yet."

"Will you help me plan some stuff?"

Sage smiled at him. "For sure."

Chuck pushed up to standing. "Hughes, Sage, refill?"

David shook his head. "Nah, I'm good."

Sage nodded, handing her glass off to Chuck before turning back to David. "I got you something."

"Me?"

She exhaled a soft laugh. "Yeah, you." She got up from the couch, and he couldn't help but watch her long legs as she went over to her stuff and pulled out a brown paper bag with a piece of red ribbon tied around the handles.

She handed the bag to him before returning to her spot on the floor.

David looked down at the bag and then back up at her, sudden regret curdling his stomach. "I didn't get you anything," he admitted. *Why the hell hadn't he gotten her anything?*

Sage looked up at him with an indulgent smile. "David. You gave me a book last night and now you're hosting me for Christmas. That's more than enough."

It wasn't. It wasn't even close to enough.

"Open it," Sage prompted.

Still stuck on the fact that he'd failed to get Sage a Christmas present, David tugged the ribbon free and took out the green tissue paper that covered whatever the bag contained. Reaching a hand in, his fingers met a hard, smooth surface. *A mug?* He pulled it out.

It was a little ceramic pot that was shaped like a dachshund. It was small enough to fit into the palm of his hand, and set into the top was a plant with two glossy, green leaves.

He exhaled a soft, low laugh. "It's adorable," he said, looking up and catching Sage's pleased smile. "I can't promise I'll keep it alive, but I'll sure as hell try."

"Oh, David's for sure going to kill that," Chuck said, walking back in with Sage's wine and another beer for himself.

Sage crossed her legs under herself. "It's really not that complicated. You already keep a dog alive!"

Chuck laughed loudly. "You'd be amazed at how tragically inept he is at taking care of green things."

"Thank you," David said loudly to Sage, pointedly ignoring Chuck. "I really do love it."

"You're welcome," Sage replied as her cheeks turned the prettiest shade of pink, and David wondered if maybe she'd come over every day, just so he could feel the way that the tightness in his chest loosened whenever she was around.

Chuck cleared his throat. "So are we watching *Elf* or *Bad Santa* first?"

David jumped up, grabbing the cookies and a few extra blankets as Chuck and Sage bickered about the merits of watching one movie first or the other. He settled back on the couch as the — correct — decision was made to start with *Elf.*

Chuck got the movie queued up while Sage moved from her spot on the floor so that she could see the TV. She looked up at David before glancing down at the open spot of carpet in front of his spot on the couch.

Wordlessly, he nodded, spreading his legs so that there was space for her.

He caught her floral scent as she settled in front of him, leaning her back against the couch between his legs. Her shoulders were pressed to the inside of his calves.

David closed his eyes. *Settle down,* he tried to command his traitorous body, but she was just so *goddamn* close. He wanted to reach out and grab her braid, tugging her head back until her lips were tilted up like an offering.

It would be so easy.

But then there was Chuck, looking over at him with absolute delight in his eyes as he muffled a laugh.

He took back everything he'd ever said about Chuck being a good friend.

As the opening credits began, David tried to relax as much as he could while resigning himself to battling the overwhelming sense that he was supposed to be touching the woman in front of him.

CHAPTER 17
BECAUSE OF THE RULES
SAGE

Sage sat on the bleachers, grateful for the Southeastern team hoodie and sweatpants she'd thrown on that morning. The practice gym was fucking freezing, and while the players obviously appreciated it, as someone who wasn't running around, she was pretty miserable.

David and Coach Dixon stood together, heads bent over a game board as the guys finished up a drill, and Sage felt her skin heat as her eyes dropped to David's stupidly sculpted ass.

Men in sweatpants. *Fuck.*

She'd spent the two days after Christmas trying to focus on planning team bonding activities, but beautiful David Hughes with his new haircut and his fucking sweaters that were so nerdy and perfect on him had basically taken up residence in her apartment.

He'd showed up every morning armed with Daisy, coffee, and a backpack, and then promptly made himself at home on her couch. He'd work on his laptop while she cooked breakfast, and after they ate together, they'd take Daisy for a long walk before going back to the apartment.

His presence in her life was annoyingly distracting, but still, there was something about him being in her space with his big body and whatever body wash he used that left her feeling settled. Grounded, maybe. Even when he left in the evening, the scent of him lingered, clinging to her couch cushions like a memory she wasn't allowed to forget.

Attraction wasn't new to her. She'd even experienced the kind of attraction that overtook rationality and left her without any sense of where she ended and the other began.

Whatever she felt for David Hughes, it wasn't that.

Even though her body wanted him — *fuck, did her body want him* — and she may or may not have gotten herself off a few times to the image of his big hands digging into her thighs as she rode him, Sage recognized that whatever she felt for him was different.

He was a friend. Maybe one of the best she'd ever had. Honestly, that was enough for her.

But maybe, when the season ended, they'd give into the physical attraction between them that refused to go away and surrender to the hook-up of a lifetime. There was no way it could be more than that. By that point in the year, Sage would be halfway out the door and off to wherever her still-unknown career took her.

If the idea of never seeing David again made her feel nauseous, she pretended not to notice.

But she'd noticed other things about him.

David was generally quiet, lost in his work or whatever book he was reading until he occasionally broke the silence to ask Sage a question. He had a tendency to lose track of time, and without Sage's reminders to drink water and eat he would probably go all day without moving.

In the evenings, they'd part ways for an hour or two, during which Sage did the necessary things like showering and laundry, before they'd meet up again at The Grove for dinner.

And now that the team was back, their winter break schedule of two-a-day practices and a combination of team meals and other activities — planned by Sage — commenced.

They were wrapping up a two-hour practice, when David started getting them set up for four on four King of the Court.

"We're two short, Coach," Zephyr called out as they distributed colored jerseys.

David glanced over at the bleachers. When his eyes caught on Sage, a slow smile spread across his face. "You're in, Lefty," he said, nodding toward the court.

Her gut turned to ice, but she veiled her reaction with a cocked brow. "Only if you play," she responded, trying to ignore the muffled pounding in her ears.

"That's the plan."

She watched as David tossed his game board down on the sideline and removed the long whistle he wore around his neck. He, like her, was dressed in a hoodie and sweats, and as the players realized what was happening, they started to whoop and shout.

"Let's go, Coach!" Monty jumped up and down, a wide grin on his face as his braids bounced where they were tied up on the back of his head.

Fuck. She wasn't going to be able to get out of this. And maybe, just maybe, she didn't want to. She couldn't deny that there was a spark of something in her chest that had her itching to test herself, to put herself up against these guys and see what she still had.

Standing up, she pulled off her hoodie and bent down to tighten the laces of her shoes. They weren't what she would normally wear to play, but they were functional, at least.

"Alright," David called out, looking around the assembled team. "Sage is on Black and I'm on Green."

She put on the practice jersey that was tossed her way, assessing her team. Damian and Patrick were both freshmen guards, and then Jenks, at almost seven feet, was a true center.

"First basket wins, and winner stays," David called, ushering his team out to start.

Sage bent her knees, trying to speed through warming up her legs as her team lined up under the basket.

She watched the first match-up, taking note of the different players, but her gaze kept snagging on David. He moved with the grace and efficiency of someone who felt as at home on the court as he did in his own bedroom.

He took up space in the high post, dishing the ball out to a guard whenever it touched his hands. And when he shot the ball — *fuck*, it was effortless, his form perfect, and Sage thought she'd never seen anything so beautiful in her entire life.

Sage felt her lips curve up into a smile.

"I've got Coach," she said to her team.

Jenks shook his head and laughed. "Bold move, Lefty."

Scowling, she reached over and flicked the big center's bare shoulder. "You don't get to call me that."

"But he does?" He looked pointedly at David, whose team was still trying to get a basket up.

She felt her cheeks warm, but she shrugged. "He lives in my apartment complex. Sometimes I see him walking his dog."

"He has a dog?" Patrick leaned in closer.

Sage decided right at that moment that she was going to force David to bring Daisy to practice tomorrow.

"Yeah, a huge, intimidating dog," she said. "Really scary."

David's team scored, and the next group ran out as the losing team rotated off the court.

Sage's attention returned to the teams in front of her, and she bounced on the balls of her feet. Energy coursed through her. Her hands flexed, already imagining the feeling of the smooth leather against her skin.

Five seconds later, David made a pass through the middle to Foley, who made a quick lay-up.

The losing team grumbled, but Sage tuned them out as she ran out onto the court. David stood off to one wing, bent over with his hands braced on his knees. His chest heaved, and sweat already gathered on his hairline and upper lip.

COURTSIDE   181

"How you hanging, old man?"

David shook his head as a low chuckle vibrated from his chest. "Where I come from, it's bad luck to talk shit before you're winning," he said, his voice rough.

Sage grinned, lowering down into a defensive stance as she saw Patrick checking the ball in.

As soon as the ball was in play, David moved forward, ducking his shoulder as he tried to get past her. But Sage anticipated the move, leaning her chest heavily into him and forcing him to adjust his path to go behind her.

She pulled back from him enough to see the ball, which was currently on the opposite wing, but she kept one hand planted on David's chest.

He wouldn't be able to go anywhere without her knowing.

"Handsy," he muttered, hooking his arm around her back to try to get the angle to move closer to the ball.

Whatever hesitation Sage had felt before stepping on the court was gone, replaced by instincts and muscle memories that were so much a part of her that she'd almost forgotten they were there.

She hung back for a second, just enough time for Horty, David's teammate, to think the pass was there. But as soon as the ball left his hands, Sage darted into the path of the pass, stealing the ball.

Immediately her head was on a swivel, and she caught the flash of black out of the corner of her eye. She hesitated for a second, already hearing the shout of disapproval if she made a risky pass.

But there was no one watching her, right? This practice wasn't about her. None of the coaches gave a shit how she played. Fuck, they weren't even *her* coaches.

Her hesitation had cost her the first opening, but already another idea had taken form.

She could feel David's body pressed against hers, a position that, in any other context, would have been inherently sexual. But that was the last thing on her mind as she turned to face the basket, keeping the ball tucked against her hip.

She ignored David's face that hovered inches from hers, instead watching the rise and fall of his chest. Her eyes darted up to the basket over his shoulder, and she saw the exact second his weight shifted forward.

She faked the shot, selling it with a deep knee bend and a tilt of her chin.

David lunged forward, and easily, like she'd never spent a day away from the game, Sage ducked under him and took a hard dribble toward the basket. And when Zephyr's man came to stop her, she made the easy dish pass across the lane to her teammate, who finished with an open lay-up.

"Let's go!" Zephyr shouted, coming toward Sage with both hands raised.

She was probably smiling like a fool as she returned the high fives, but she was so overwhelmingly happy at that moment that she forgot to hold herself back.

No one in the gym could possibly know how monumental what had just happened was. She felt a wave of relief that her return to basketball, a moment that had been building in her imagination for the past five years, had gone unnoticed. Anticlimactic, even.

And the game went on. Her team was beaten a few plays later, and so they went back and forth, with no team showing any particular dominance over the others. It was competitive, sure, but there was laughter and teasing and everything Sage associated with a team who genuinely enjoyed spending time together.

And by the time they wrapped up and the guys headed to shower off before their team dinner, Sage was drenched in sweat, exhausted, and happier than she'd been in a long time.

⊏⊐

After five days of practices, team dinners, a failed attempt to get the guys to do a gingerbread house decorating competition, Daisy making a few appearances at team gatherings, a yoga class that had completely kicked her in the ass, and way too many hours spent in the company of men, Sage bowed out of that night's team dinner, which Monty and his roommates were hosting at their house. She'd made sure they were all stocked with groceries on the team card, and then escaped to The Grove to see Maggie.

"Sage!" Maggie called out as soon as she sat at one of the stools. Luckily, on a Monday evening, the bar was pretty quiet. "The usual?"

"Please," Sage replied, tugging at the floral print blouse she'd pulled out of her closet. For some reason she'd gotten it into her head that she wanted to wear something other than sweats and a t-shirt.

Sage accepted the margarita the bartender slid across the wood toward her. "How have you been?"

Maggie looked surprised at the question, but the surprise quickly faded into a grateful smile. "Really good, honestly. Men are still idiots, but other than that I'm great."

Sage laughed. "How so?"

"There's a guy I've been with off and on for a while, and while I'd like for it to be a bit more on, he keeps pullin' away." Maggie frowned down at the bar, picking at a spot on the wood with one of her red painted nails. "I'm too old to put up with someone who isn't willin' to share their life with me. If I'm puttin' myself out there, then the least he can do is meet me halfway. And since he's proven to be an asshole who wants to hide me away like a dirty secret, I'm going to break it off." She wrinkled her nose at Sage. "And I hate breakin' up with people."

Sage took a long drink of her margarita, grateful for the burn of the jalapeño infused tequila. "So what would it look like if you were going to stay?" She winced, afraid that her voice betrayed the dull pain that tightened in her chest.

Maggie considered her question for a moment, like maybe she

was trying to piece together the odd phrasing or understand what it was that Sage wanted to know.

"Keep in mind that I am in no way an authority on relationships of any kind," Maggie started. "But the way that I see it, we've only got so many hours to be alive on this earth. Regardless of what happens after, at some point we're all going to die."

Sage's expression must have reflected her confusion, because Maggie waved a hand at her. "I promise I'm goin' somewhere with this," she said, before picking up where she left off. "So if I'm going to spend time with someone, their company needs to make my life better. They need to bring me somethin' that improves my life, not only physically, but actually makes my days better."

"I'm pretty content on my own," Maggie continued. "I don't *need* to have a boyfriend to feel happy or to get off. I can do those things for myself." She shot a smirk at Sage. "That means that if I'm going to let someone in, then it's because they're fuckin' awesome and I want to spend more time with them. Not because I'm not happy or complete without them."

Sage blinked. "Wow."

"Did that make any sense?" Maggie bent down, pulling out a tub of limes, which she began chopping into wedges on the counter behind the bar. "Sometimes I get ramblin' and lose track of what I'm sayin'."

"No, it made a lot of sense," Sage replied, her brain churning at a million miles a minute. "Too much sense, actually."

Maggie gave an understanding nod. "Any luck in figurin' out your future?"

"Fuck no," Sage said with a snorted laugh.

"Well, cheers to that," Maggie said, joining in her laughter. "Now give me an update on your beautiful boyfriend."

"Still not my boyfriend." But Sage grinned, relaxing into the ease of teasing banter with a girlfriend, something she didn't realize she'd missed.

Sage was still smiling as her apartment door shut behind her.

Her skin buzzed with the kind of energy she'd only ever felt after a win, and as she kicked off her heels and tossed her jacket onto the back of her couch, she felt like she could run a marathon.

It was the last Friday of the break, and Southeastern had pulled off another win.

Tonight, it had been a good win, the kind of win where the momentum was in their hands the entire game. It was the kind of win that could change the trajectory of a season.

Sage had done her job, tracking stats and double checking that water bottles were kept full. But she hadn't been able to keep her eyes from David, who, in black slacks and a blazer, looked every bit a confident head coach. He'd paced, focused and engaged with every moment that was happening out on the court, his heavy brows pulled down over his dark eyes. Every time they'd scored, he'd clenched his hand into a fist and given a single pump, allowing himself that one small moment of celebration.

Her phone buzzed in her back pocket. She pulled it out and looked at the screen. It was a text from David.

Come over.

The buzzing under her skin intensified. She glanced at her front door and then back to her phone, anticipation sending her heart rate into overdrive.

She was being ridiculous. They hung out all the time. David practically lived in her apartment. But normally he'd just show up when he wanted to see her. He'd knock on the door and she'd answer.

For him to text her like this? It was different. *Something* was different.

He was giving her the choice. The ball was in her court; if she wanted to come over, the invitation was clearly stated. And if she didn't? She had an easy out.

Her thumbs were tapping on the screen before she'd concluded her thought.

Two minutes later, she was knocking on the door of David's apartment. She shifted from foot to foot, goosebumps on her skin in spite of the heavy, warm air.

The door was wrenched open.

"Hi," David breathed, smiling down at her.

He'd also lost his blazer, leaving him in a pale blue Oxford that he'd unbuttoned enough to show a flash of the dark hair that she knew covered his chest. One side of the shirt was untucked, leaving him looking rumpled and disheveled in the best way possible.

Fuck, he was hot.

"I'm so goddamn happy right now," David said, and he opened his arms to her.

Sage surged forward, wrapping her arms around his strong middle. When she felt his arms envelop her, she relaxed, letting her cheek rest against his chest as her hands pressed into the firm muscle that covered his back.

Time slowed as they stood there wrapped together in David's open doorway. Sage breathed deeply, inhaling the familiar scent of him that never failed to draw her in. Above her, she could feel David's breath against her scalp, sending a wave of goosebumps down her spine.

In that moment, months of wanting came to a head, and waiting and holding herself back felt like the silliest idea in the world.

So she drew back from his grip just enough that she could look up at him. When she saw the same wanting reflected in his eyes, she let her hands slide around to his front before running them up his chest and curling them around the back of his neck.

Fuck waiting. She was going to do it.

Sage pulled his head down. The first brush of her lips against his was tentative, contrary to the confidence she'd summoned when she pulled him to her. All of her awareness narrowed to the nerve endings where their lips met, and as soon as she registered the warmth and softness of his mouth she fell head-first into him.

A tortured moan tore from David's throat as he responded to her. His lips parted and she tasted him — honey and herbs from the lozenge she'd given him after the game. He licked into her mouth, slowly, decadently, like she was something sweet. Something worth tasting again and again.

Suddenly they were moving. David's hands had come up at some point to cradle her face, keeping them connected as he pressed her back against a wall. She refused to break the kiss, pouring every bit of pent-up desire into this connection between their bodies. But then he pushed his hips into hers, and there was no ignoring the hard length of him that met her lower stomach.

David swallowed her whimper, nipping at her lower lip before tearing his mouth away.

Sage stood there, panting as she tried to catch her breath. David lowered his forehead to rest against hers, his breathing equally ragged.

"Damnit, Lefty," he growled.

Her body fucking *ached* for him. Arousal curled in her stomach, tightened her nipples, and her movements were frantic as her hands went to the front of his shirt.

She managed to undo three buttons before his hands covered hers, gripping her with enough strength to halt her progress. "Just once," she pleaded, the throbbing between her legs driving her to roll her hips against him. "Please, David."

David's breath somehow grew harsher, like each exhale was punched from his chest. "No," he rasped, his hold on her hands unrelenting. His head shook. "Fuck, I want to, but no."

Her eyes closed. She swallowed. "Because of the rules," she whispered.

"No, Sage." His hands returned to cup her jaw, and he lowered himself so that his face was the only thing she could see. "Not the rules." His thumbs brushed over her cheeks, his eyes leaving hers for a moment to trace the movement. His mouth, swollen and red from kissing, curved up into a soft smile. "If we do this, it won't just be once. It won't just be some hook-up you can walk away from. It sure as fuck won't be *mediocre*. If we do this it'll be real. I'm talking dating, Lefty. You and me together, okay?"

Sage thought about Maggie, about not needing anyone, but still choosing someone if they made life a little better. She thought about David in her apartment, David on the court, David with his perfect shot and big hands and the way that kindness poured from him like a spring.

Life with him could be good. So fucking good.

"Okay."

David looked as surprised as she felt. "After the season?" he asked tentatively.

Sage nodded. *Yes.* Whatever this attraction was between them, Sage had no doubt that they were in it together. That there *had* to be a future where they got to work through whatever seemed to be alive between their bodies.

After the season, she repeated to herself silently.

And, as she hugged him one last time and left him standing there, wild eyed and tenting his slacks, she turned back to give him one last glance, adding, "See you in the morning for breakfast, Hughes."

It wasn't a question.

CHAPTER 18
UNBOTHERED
DAVID

Sage had kissed him.

Even weeks later, he still burned with the memory of her commanding him with soft hands wrapped around his neck. The way she'd taken what she wanted, confident and beautiful and *goddamnit* he was hard again. His body didn't give a shit that they'd agreed that while there was no shortage of want between them, they wouldn't do it again. At least, they wouldn't do anything until after the season. After the season they would... well, they would try.

All he knew was that the next morning he'd gone over to her place and she'd greeted him with her lopsided smile and made him breakfast, just like she'd done every day since the break began. Almost like nothing had happened.

It was just a minor inconvenience that every time he was around her he had to shove aside the almost crippling urge to push her up against the closest surface and peel away every stitch of clothing that she wore. The fact that he was almost constantly battling more and more elaborate fantasies about Sage Fogerty — her long body stretched out under him, her nipples hot against his tongue — meant that he was spending a concerning amount of time with his hard-on straining against his briefs.

Damn blondes who never wore bras at home.

But the break came to an end and then they were back to the grind. Days spent in the office, traveling at least once a week, and evenings spent pacing on the court.

He still saw Sage almost every day, even outside of practices and time spent with the team.

Given his complete lack of culinary skills, he was the takeout guy. A few times a week he'd text her and see what she was craving, and then bring over food and his laptop. They normally worked while they ate — her on homework and him watching game tape.

David didn't want to jinx it, but the team was playing unexpectedly well. Even with all of his blind optimism going into the season, he hadn't imagined that they would actually have a fighting chance at the conference tournament.

But whatever they'd done over the break seemed to have paid off. They'd only had one loss in the past three weeks, and there was a tangible excitement in the locker room every day. David felt it, and he could tell that the guys felt it too.

They'd just wrapped up their last practice before heading out to an away game. They were playing Harding again, and David could already imagine their assistant coach's face when they lost.

If they lost.

"Coach."

David glanced behind him, slowing down as Tim caught up to him.

"Hey Coach," David replied.

Over the break he'd spent a quiet evening with Tim and his wife, Dana, who was quite possibly the nicest woman he'd ever met — other than his own mother, of course. She'd made homemade chicken pot pie, and they'd talked about the kinds of things that coworkers who don't know each other very well talked about: weather, work, and family. He learned that Tim was an avid golfer and that he had two grown children who lived out of state.

Tim looked up at him, pushing his glasses up his nose with the back of his hand. "I just want to make sure that you're doing alright," he said, looking at him with sincere concern. "This is the time of year where it can get to be too much, and it won't do anyone any good if you're burned out."

"Right," David replied, at a loss for words. "The winning feels pretty good."

"Sure, but when you do this job, you've got to make sure that there's more than the win."

David frowned. "What do you mean?"

"If any day that doesn't end in a win up there on the scoreboard constitutes a loss in your book, then you won't last very long." Tim put a hand on David's shoulder, pulling him to a stop in the empty hallway. "You're a good coach, David. Maybe even a great one. But you have to figure out how to make this job sustainable over a lifetime, and putting the weight of every single mistake those kids make out there on your shoulders is going to break you down."

"I know that," David admitted.

"Do you? Because from where I'm sitting you walked around here looking like your puppy had been kicked until they started pulling out wins. Now you're all bouncy and happy, and if I've noticed, then the team has noticed too. And do you know what that says to them?" Tim paused, staring unflinchingly at David. "That tells them that winning is the only thing that matters. The only thing that matters to you. And you know that isn't actually what life is about, Hughes. Just make sure they know that too."

David let Tim's words sink in, months of memories flashing as he thought back on how he'd conducted himself throughout the season.

Now that they were winning, he felt unburdened, like he could finally breathe. Because that was his job. It was his job to turn a group of college athletes into a winning organism.

But what about when they lost? Because of course they'd lose. They'd spent the whole first half of the season losing, and they were going to lose again. Did his players trust that he'd still value them after a loss? Based on his attitude early in the season, probably not.

Goddamn it.

David released a long exhale. "Thank you," he said, looking Tim in the eye.

There was nothing but kindness and genuine concern in Tim's eyes as the older man nodded in response. "Have a good night, Coach," he said, giving David's shoulder a firm squeeze before walking away.

> Hey u home?

No, I'm out playing pool with Maggie.

She says hi, by the way.

> Nice. Thrs something on ur door 4 u.

What is "thrs?"

Thursday?

> Lol

> "There's"

Ha.

> Wut.

Just wanted to see if you knew how to spell it. And you do, so points for Hughes.

> **You're mean.

Yes.

David Hughes.

Lefty.

Why are there flowers by my door?

I wouldn't know about that.

David.

Yes?

...

Do u like them?

Of course I do, you turd.

Did u just...call me a turd? After I got u flowers?

Thank you.

Ur welcome

The team shuffled onto the plane, a long line of team-branded black sweats and hoodies, with the exception of David, Tim, Sage, and their trainer for the trip, Jake. He was new on the staff, and seemed nice enough.

Sage certainly seemed to think so. The two of them had been locked in conversation since they'd arrived at the airport, and David was slowly losing his goddamn mind. He didn't care that she was talking to some scrawny kid around her age. David was fine. Perfectly calm and fine.

Sage moved into an empty row and settled down in the

window seat. When Jake followed, taking the seat next to her, David had to bite his tongue to keep from telling the entitled little shit to move from *his* spot.

But they were at work, and there was no reason for him to sit next to the team manager. Maybe if he could get Tim and Sage to share a row with him they could be having a conversation about stats, but…

Nope.

He kept his eyes down as he walked past her. Even though he wasn't looking at her, he could perfectly picture her: high pony-tail, dark eyebrows arching over her green eyes, her mouth probably twisted into that little smirk that made the dimple appear in her cheek.

He ended up sitting a few rows back with Tim, and nodded politely when a businessman in a suit joined them.

Ah, the joys of flying commercially.

The flight passed uneventfully, and as soon as they deplaned Sage pulled out her phone and confirmed the bus that would take them to the hotel. As they walked to the baggage claim, her long legs made the rounds as she went to each player and confirmed their food order from the sub shop that was going to deliver their pre-game meal.

She was really damn good at her job.

Things continued to go smoothly at the hotel. As the head coach, David got his own room, while Tim and Jake shared and Sage, as the only woman on the trip, got her own room. The rest of the players were mixed between upper-classmen and younger players. It served to facilitate team bonding, and kept the younger guys from doing anything too stupid.

A few hours later, they were climbing back on the bus and going to the gym for their game. Harding's campus was just outside of Baltimore, and they had a beautiful, newer gym that David couldn't help but envy.

The bus dropped them off at the players' entrance, and they all made their way to the visiting locker room. The guys that needed the trainer peeled off with Jake, while the rest started to get changed and settled.

Sage only lingered in the locker room long enough to make sure everyone had their equipment set up. She wore another one of those pantsuits with the slacks that cut off just above her ankles. It was purple, like the color of a ripe plum, and with the gray blouse she wore underneath she projected confidence, at ease in her authority as she bantered with the guys. The fact that she wore her Nikes rather than dressy heels just made her even more attractive in his eyes.

This woman in a pantsuit was going to kill him.

As they moved through warm up, Tim's words from the day before echoed in his head. Rather than standing back while the guys went through their dynamic stretching routine, David went to the baseline, offering encouragement and reassurances.

He got a few odd looks, but the guys seemed to adjust to him being there fairly quickly. When they started chirping him about letting Jordan trim his beard, he gave them a teasing scoff and returned to the bench, where Tim stood watching. The assistant coach gave him a sharp nod, and David felt himself smile in return.

Immediately his eyes searched for Sage, out of a combination of habit and an actual need to confirm that they were good with the book going into the game.

Rather than her usual spot on the bench, she stood off to the side of the bleachers, her body turned away from them. Without thinking, David walked over to her, moving as quickly as he could without breaking into a run.

"Sage," he said as he approached her.

She jumped, turning around to face him.

Immediately, he stilled.

It was like she'd shrunk before his eyes. Her expression was haunted and her posture had slumped, her shoulders curving forward as she gripped the tablet against her chest. Her mouth made the shape of a smile, but it looked like it had been painted onto her face by an amateur artist.

"Coach," she said.

There was something off about her voice. "Are you okay?" he asked, concerned.

"Totally fine. Great. Good." She tucked a wisp of hair behind her ear, refusing to look directly at him. "Just making sure we're all good on the Wifi."

David frowned. "Sage," he began.

"I need to finish up the book." She moved past him, her shoulder brushing against his chest.

He wanted to grab her and pull her against him. He wanted to hold her until she told him what the hell had her so spooked. He glanced up at the clock. *Goddamnit.* It was time to head back into the locker room.

He'd have to talk to her after the game.

CHAPTER 19
WHAT A GIFT LIKE THAT MEANT
SAGE

No.

He couldn't be there. How the fuck was he there?

Sage tried to keep track of the game. Her eyes bounced from the glowing screen of the tablet to the streaking splotches that she knew were bodies running up and down the court, but it was all blurring together. The colors, the lights, all of it swam before her eyes like paint smeared on glass.

Everything was fuzzy — the sounds muffled, her breathing shallow — but through it all she felt him.

At first, she'd thought it was just an uncanny resemblance. The world was full of tall men with skin the color of rich ochre and pale eyes. But then he'd looked at her from the opposing team's bench, and there was no denying the fact that Evan White was there.

The second she became aware of him, it was like every single layer of warmth and self-assuredness she'd built up around herself was stripped away in an instant, leaving her naked and bare.

She'd gained weight since he'd last seen her, and she felt the extra mass on her body like it was strangling her, painfully aware of how her thighs strained against the fabric of her slacks and

how broad her shoulders were. Her hair was up in a ponytail —
he'd always hated it like that.

The rational part of her brain was there, screaming for her to
stop and think and *just fucking ignore him,* but she couldn't. She
couldn't seem to remember how to be the person she'd become
when confronted with the man who'd shaped how she used to be.

And, of course, David was watching her. Watching her more
than he should. But she couldn't handle him right now, not when
she was barely handling herself. She'd missed plays. Missed
assists and turnovers as she tried — and failed — to focus.

When halftime came around, she was surprised to see that
they were ahead by five. She'd been so lost in her head that she'd
barely noticed the court in front of her.

Trailing after the team as they walked to the locker room, she
felt the looming presence of David walking silently beside her.
Something about him being there reassured her. Made her feel
stronger than she actually was.

But then she heard the click of dress shoes against the stone
floors approaching, and she felt her muscles seize, tension filling
her entire body as an unmistakable scent hit her.

She'd bought him a bottle of Hugo Boss cologne before she
understood what a gift like that meant. Especially a gift like that
from a fifteen-year-old to her coach.

He approached on her left, pacing himself so that he could
walk alongside her.

She hated how familiar he was. She even recognized the jacket
he wore — a heathered charcoal gray with silver buttons. He'd
worn it when they qualified for Nationals her sophomore year. He
was still barely taller than her, and his eyes were still just as blue
as they'd always been.

"Sage," he said softly, under his breath.

Sweat gathered on her back and all that she could do was keep
walking. Maybe if she ignored him he would —

"Please. Let's talk after the game."

She felt him move away, only then realizing she'd been

holding her breath. She let out a shaking exhale, shaking her head like maybe it was all a nightmare that she could escape.

But it wasn't a dream.

Halftime passed in a haze as she avoided the concerned glances David kept shooting at her, and then she was back on the bench doing it all again.

***

They won.

She should be excited and celebrating with the team. This win clenched their spot in the conference tournament, defying the expectations everyone had after seeing them play at the beginning of the season.

But she felt nothing, while simultaneously holding back a tidal wave of every feeling she'd shoved down and walked away from in the past five years that threatened to drown her at any moment.

Sage forced herself through the motions: retrieving the book, cleaning up the bench, gathering their balls, making sure the guys packed their uniforms and warm ups before heading out to the bus.

She was carrying the ball bag down the hall when Evan found her.

"Sage," he said again, and she felt her sanity fraying, splintering, the hours of being locked in a heightened state of anxiety finally catching up with her. She was minutes away from collapsing.

"Talk to me," Evan pressed. His voice was too sweet, too gentle, and as he continued, she felt herself speeding up, trying to put more space between them. "It's been forever, sweetheart. Just hear me out." He reached out and curled a hand around the back of her neck, his fingers pressing against her pulse point, just like he used to. "I've missed you."

Her skin was cold. She jerked away from him, even though

there was a sliver of herself that urged her to stay. "Evan, please," she said, hating how small her voice had become.

"Sage."

Relief warred with humiliation at the sound of David's voice. She kept herself still as he walked up, coming to a stop beside her.

"Coach," David said, his voice cold as he addressed Evan. Turning to Sage, his expression softened. "Everything okay?"

Evan laughed, his wide, bright smile so charming that Sage had to forgive her younger self for seeing what she thought she did in him. "We're all good," Evan said, all nonchalance and ease. "Sage and I know each other from California." His eyes turned to look at her, and she forgot how to breathe. "She was such a promising player. One of the best I've ever coached."

She was going to pass out. Her eyes burned, but even now she couldn't pretend like a compliment from Evan didn't feel like oxygen after hours trapped underwater. His praise was *everything*.

In that moment, she hated herself even more than she hated him.

David shifted beside her. "Right. Well, we've got to get back to the hotel."

"Think about it, Sage," Evan said, looking right at her like it was only the two of them in the room. "It'd be great to catch up."

Sage forced her feet into motion.

She could feel David following as she walked out the doors, shoved the balls under the bus and climbed on board. She felt him behind her as she slid into the first open row of seats, but was still surprised when he sat down beside her.

He turned his body toward hers as the bus began to move, his knees pressing against her thigh. "Are you okay?"

"Yeah. Fine."

His brows pulled down over his eyes. "I don't believe you," he whispered, his voice sandpaper in the darkness of the bus.

"That's not my fucking problem," she hissed back at him, losing a bit of the stranglehold of control she'd had over herself.

Immediately, she wished she could take the words back.

Everything around her was falling apart except for the man beside her who refused to accept her lie. Shame curled in her stomach, and she turned, pressing her forehead against the cool window.

She heard the rustling of fabric as David got up, obviously moving to another seat. Obviously moving away from her. And when she pulled out her phone and found his number, the shame that burned hot and violent inside of her raged unchecked.

Courtyard Marriott.

The text from Evan came a moment later.

See you soon.

The elevator doors slid open with a ding, and Sage walked out into the lobby.

She wore jeans that were too loose and a thin camisole she'd packed to sleep in. She knew he wouldn't like it, but when she'd packed for this trip, Evan White was the last person on her mind.

As she'd stood in front of the floor length mirror in her room, she'd felt like a battle was waging inside of herself. The Sage Fogerty who went to Southeastern, bought herself flowers, and had a best friend who read books with her and brought her soup wanted to tell Evan White to fuck all the way off to a dark sewer somewhere in Europe where human excrement had been piling up for centuries.

But equally as loud was the Sage from five years ago who wanted nothing more than the approval of the blue-eyed man who was so much more than her coach. It was all she'd ever wanted.

So, in spite of herself, Sage was going to see him.

Stepping into the lobby she stopped, her breath catching in her throat.

David sat perched on the edge of one of the couches, his long fingers fiddling with the brim of his hat. His hair was mussed, his mouth drawn into a frown. He still wore the sweater and slacks he'd worn to the game.

She took a few steps toward him.

His head jerked up. Something like pain flashed across his face as he looked her up and down.

He cleared his throat. "Are you going to see him?"

Sage found that she couldn't form words, so she nodded.

He rubbed his palms over his face as he exhaled roughly. "I don't like it, Sage," he said, his voice muffled by his hands. He dropped them down into his lap, picking up the hat again and resuming his fidgeting. "There's obviously something going on..." He trailed off, clearly hoping that she'd jump in and clarify the situation.

But she couldn't. Not when she had no fucking idea what she was doing. She didn't know how to explain to this man who was so *good* why she was about to walk out into the cold Baltimore night to see another man. A man who was decidedly *less* good in every way that mattered.

It was one of those moments where she felt like her life was living her. Like at some point she'd given up the reins and now she was barely holding on and just trying to stay alive.

Sage shook her head, pushing her loose hair back over her shoulder. "I just...I have to go," she finally said.

"Come on, Lefty," he pleaded, leaning forward like he was going to get up from the couch. Like maybe he was going to reach for her. "You're upset, and I hate that I don't know what's hurting you."

Her phone buzzed in her back pocket.

She gave David one last look, and the obvious devastation in his eyes almost brought her to her knees.

It would be so easy to stay. Most of her *wanted* to stay. But then her feet were moving and the automatic door slid open, the cold air immediately sending shivers up her bare arms.

She walked right up to the black SUV that was parked on the other side of the brightly lit unloading area, pulling open the passenger door and climbing in.

She glanced over at Evan, who sat in the driver's seat, reclined to the point where she had no idea how he was able to drive safely. He sent an easy smile her way, and then put the car into gear.

Neither of them said anything. Music played, softly enough that she wasn't sure if it was a song that she recognized or not. The seat warmer was turned on, and she shifted as heat seeped through her jeans.

She wanted to make a joke about how she felt like she'd pissed herself, but she didn't.

That wasn't who she was with him.

They drove for a few more minutes before Evan pulled into an empty retail parking lot, easing his car into a spot in a back corner tucked under a tree. Yet another thing that felt familiar.

With the car in park, Evan shifted, turning toward her and leaning over the console. Again, one of his hands found the back of her neck, and he pulled her toward him. "I've missed you, sweetheart," he murmured, his breath hot against her mouth. *Cinnamon.* He still chewed cinnamon gum. His lips brushed hers once. "It hasn't been the same without you."

And then he was kissing her.

She hated herself.

She hated the feeling of his mouth, and the wrongness of him touching her made her eyes well up with tears. She tried to pull away from him but he chased her, his tongue pressing against her lips even as she kept her mouth tightly closed.

Evan's phone buzzing in the cup-holder between them finally interrupted his onslaught. Sage twisted her face away, glancing down at the phone.

Her entire body went cold. There, illuminated on the screen, was a photo of Evan and a beautiful woman.

A beautiful woman in a strapless wedding dress with her arms

wrapped around Evan, who was wearing a tux. The same woman ·
who Evan had been dating eight years ago when she first met
him. The same woman who Evan had told Sage repeatedly meant
nothing to him. The woman he'd promised to leave as soon as
Sage turned eighteen.

"Are you fucking kidding me?"

Sage's voice echoed in the car, too loud and too strong. But
whatever lingering part of her that had wanted to climb into the
car with Evan White was gone. Crushed. Obliterated.

"What is wrong with you?" A harsh laugh combined with a
sob burst from her. "Why, when you have her —" she pointed
down at the image still illuminated on the phone — "are you
here? What did I ever do to you? Fuck, what did *she* ever do to
you?"

Evan watched her, his mouth tight.

"You knew how much power you had over me back then,
didn't you?" Rage filled her, burning away any other emotion that
tried to gain traction. "You knew that you'd never choose me. You
fucking *knew* and yet you still picked me, stringing me along and
molding me into something I never wanted to be."

There was so much that she wanted to say to him. Years of
lingering doubts that she hadn't faced head-on, insecurities that
all went back to *him*. But, as she tried to catch her breath, her
cheeks wet with the tears that just wouldn't stop, she realized that
he didn't deserve it.

He didn't deserve to know how he'd shaped her. He had no
right to hear how he'd haunted her life, even years after he
walked away. How he'd taken up residence in her head until it
was his voice that whispered uncertainties every time she'd taken
a step forward.

He wasn't worth any more of her breath.

How had it taken her so long to realize that she was whole and
complete as she was? That the person that she was outside of this
car, the woman she'd become in the years since this man had left
her behind was stronger than she'd ever been able to imagine?

"What the fuck am I doing here," she whispered, her voice hoarse. "Take me back."

Evan inhaled sharply. "Come on, Sage."

"Now, Evan."

She looked right at him. She straightened her shoulders, gathering the pieces of herself that he'd torn through so easily. Silently, she began to put herself back together.

And when he pulled up in front of the hotel and she climbed out of the car, she didn't look back.

CHAPTER 20
ANYTHING, LEFTY
DAVID

David couldn't sit still.

From the second Sage had walked out of the hotel he'd started pacing. Nervous, frantic energy coursed through him, preventing him from even a second of peace. Not when she was gone. Not when she was gone with *him*.

Whatever he'd seen between Sage — *his* Sage — and Evan White had landed in his gut and curdled like spoiled milk.

It was obvious that there was some kind of history between them, and, based on what he'd just seen, it was probably a history that went way beyond what should have transpired between a high school player and her coach.

Bile rose in his throat.

It didn't help that there were a million unsaid things between him and Sage. That he felt — no, he *knew* — that she was his, in some way. But there had been nothing between them except promises and exchanges of friendship. And then she'd kissed him, and they'd parted as friends?

He couldn't figure out a goddamn thing, and until she was back and he'd seen for himself that not a single blonde hair on her head had been harmed, he was going to stay right where he was.

"Coach?"

He whirled around, not giving a shit that he probably looked maniacal since he'd lost the sweater after anxiety had driven him to sweat like he was playing in the fourth quarter.

"Tim?"

The older man approached him, dressed down in simple black sweats and tennis shoes. His eyes searched the rest of the lobby before he turned his concerned expression to David. "Is she still gone?"

David opened and closed his mouth. "What?" His voice was wrecked from the game, and he realized in that moment that Sage hadn't given him a lozenge like she usually did.

"Fogerty. Is she still gone with that Coach White?"

"How do you —"

Tim waved off the question. "I saw him harassing her earlier. In the hallway." He shook his head as his frown deepened. "That man is bad news."

David felt his stomach drop. "What do you mean?"

Again, Tim shook his head. "I knew him back when I coached in Nashville at a junior college for a while. It was about five years ago, and he was fresh out of coaching club ball in California." He scratched at his collar. "He got in some hot water for pursuing younger girls, and ended up leaving rather than making a scene. After the school let him walk away without facing any consequences I got the hell out of there. Couldn't stand being a part of a program that let someone get away with that."

David couldn't suppress the shudder that went through him. "Damnit, Tim. She's out there with him now, what should we —"

"We wait. Or, I should say, *you* wait, because it's obvious that the two of you have something going on."

"We, no, we don't," David stammered, panicking at the thought of now trying to explain away the closeness between him and Sage: the friendship, the maybe something more.

"Stop it." Tim leveled David a look over the rim of his glasses that had him shutting his mouth. "I'm not here to give you a hard time. Do I think it's wise? No. But she's a grad student, an adult, and if I thought that you were the kind of man who would put the two of you into a compromising position while working together then we would have had this conversation months ago." Tim's face softened into a small smile. "But aside from all of that, it's obvious that you are *friends*, and that's why I think that when she walks through those doors after whatever the hell is happening right now, you should be the one waiting for her."

David could do nothing but nod. Tim returned the gesture before walking back to the elevator. As soon as he was out of sight, David resumed his pacing, never taking his eyes away from the door.

He had no idea how much time had passed when the doors opened.

Sage stood there with her head held high, her expression defiant, and silent tears streaming down her red cheeks.

Immediately he was running. *Help her, help her, help her* pounded in his head and he reached for her, gently gripping her shoulders as he lowered down to look her in the eye. "What happened," he breathed, trying to control the maelstrom of emotions warring within him.

She sniffed once, shifting her gaze so she looked over his shoulder. "I don't want to talk about it."

"Sage," he started, fighting the need to pull her close to him and hold her tight until all of the pain was erased from her eyes.

She shook her head, and her loose blonde hair shifted where it was draped over her shoulders, shining like honey in the lobby lights. "Please," she said, quiet and resigned. "I just want to go to bed."

With a nod, David stepped back from her, and something broke in his chest as he watched her posture slump, her long, strong arms wrapping around her stomach as she started toward the elevator bay.

The elevator ride up was silent.

He fought the urge to hold her, knowing deep down that if he touched her it would be for the selfish desire to satisfy something within himself and not for her benefit. There were a million things he still had to learn about Sage. He wasn't naive enough to think that she'd shared all of the pieces of herself with him in the few short months they'd been friends.

But he had learned that she was the kind of person who needed to stand confidently on her own before accepting the company of someone standing beside her. And he had the feeling that tonight, in the wake of whatever had happened, Sage needed to stand alone.

When the doors opened, Sage turned to the right, and David followed, silent, even though his room was the opposite direction.

He stood back while she unlocked the door. When she pulled it open, she glanced back over her shoulder, hesitating as her red-rimmed eyes met his.

"Let me know if you need anything," David said softly, mindful of the quiet rooms around them. "Anything, Lefty."

She nodded and then slipped inside, the door clicking shut softly behind her.

⊂══⊃

David had showered and was laying in bed with his book when his phone buzzed on his nightstand. He'd texted Tim that Sage had made it back safely, and thought it was most likely a response from him.

When he picked it up, he barely glanced at the screen before he was out of bed and pulling on sweats and a t-shirt, not even bothering with shoes.

Phone in hand, he walked as quickly as he could down the carpeted hallway. As he knocked softly on the door, he glanced back at the message on the screen.

Please come over.

The door opened, and Sage stood there, hair pulled back in a braid that hung over one shoulder. She still wore the same thin shirt she'd been wearing earlier, only she'd changed into sleep shorts.

But David couldn't think about how beautiful she was, not when her face crumpled and another wave of tears streamed down her face.

A choked whimper shattered the quiet between them. "You shouldn't be here," she said, wiping at her tears with both of her hands.

Pain constricted his chest. "You asked me to come, Lefty," he said, softly. "I'll always come when you ask."

She didn't respond, only pushed the door open wide enough to let him in. David walked past her, catching a whiff of her floral scent before stopping in the open space next to the single queen bed. "What happened, Sage?"

Her bare feet padded over, and she dropped down on the edge of the mattress, leaning forward to bury her face in her hands. "I," her muffled voice began. "Do I have to say?"

David decided that listening to his instinct to go to her was the greatest idea he'd ever had. He moved to the bed, kneeling on the ground in front of her and bringing his hands up to encircle her wrists.

"You don't have to say anything. But you're crying, and I've never seen you sad like this." His thumb brushed across her skin. "Do I need to hurt someone?"

Sage shook her head. "No."

"Then what do you need?"

Another sob shook her body, and David settled for tightening his grip just slightly. Only enough to let her know that she wasn't alone.

"I think right now I just need you to be here with me," she whispered, still hiding her face in her hands.

"Done." David stood, and then climbed onto the bed. He settled himself against the headboard, patting the open mattress next to him. "Come here."

He was honestly surprised when Sage complied, crawling up and taking the spot next to him. Her posture was stiff, and her eyes looked down at where her hands were clasped in her lap.

It was so obvious that she was in pain.

He let one of his hands come to rest on the mattress between them. He kept his fingers open, relaxed, on the off-chance that she might need him. Letting out a careful breath, he tilted his head to look at her. "Please tell me what happened so that I can fix it."

Sage let out a harsh, wet laugh. "You can't fix it. It's already done."

"But it has something to do with Evan White." He didn't phrase it as a question.

Somehow her posture stiffened even further. "Do you know him?"

"No," David quickly replied. "I've just heard rumors that he's an asshole who chases after younger girls."

She shook her head with a pained smile, her gaze fixed on the door.

"Sage. Look at me." She turned back to him, eyes squeezed shut. David tried to slow his breathing, to keep his voice calm and controlled. "What did he do to you?"

She opened her mouth to respond, but all that came out was a broken cry.

David was officially over being a gentleman.

He reached for her, gathering her in his arms and tugging her towards him. She barely needed the encouragement, burrowing her head into his chest as her hands grabbed at his shirt, gripping him like he was a lifeline in a storm.

His heart hammered as he held her, and on a whim, he brought a hand up to brush back a piece of hair that was stuck to her tear-streaked cheek. He couldn't bring himself to take his hand away, instead finding a steady rhythm stroking his fingers over the soft skin of her temple.

"Sage," he whispered. "Please talk to me. I've got you."

A minute passed, where the only sounds were her ragged

sighs against his chest. He felt the rise and fall of her breathing slow.

"I...we...we used to have a thing."

"A thing." David tried to keep his touch soft. Steady.

She nodded.

"When?"

He could see her hesitation. "When, Sage?" He couldn't keep the command from his voice.

He felt her exhale. "It started when I saw a sophomore."

"At Southeastern?" In his effort to wish away the unthinkable, he willed himself to forget that *she'd never played college ball.*

"No." Her voice was barely a whisper.

Goddamnit.

David was going to kill that man. He'd never been even remotely violent, but the cold, calculating rage that filled him was quite possibly the most real and potent emotion he'd ever experienced in his life.

But he shoved that down — as much as he could — knowing that Sage didn't need that from him. She didn't need his rage on her behalf. He forced himself to take a painfully slow deep breath. "Was he your high school coach?"

"My club coach," she confirmed.

His stomach turned. "So you guys had a thing?" He was proud of how nonchalant he sounded. Like he wasn't about to track down the bastard who had preyed on this incredible woman, likely *assaulted* her, when she was just a kid.

A fucking *kid.*

"Yeah." Her admission was quiet. "Looking back, it's such an obvious cliche." Her voice was starting to regain some of her usual strength. "He told me he was going to leave his girlfriend when I turned eighteen, and I was stupid enough to believe him."

He hated hearing the harshness that she directed toward herself. How could she think that anything about that situation had been her fault? He opened his mouth to respond, but Sage kept talking.

"Honestly, it wasn't even the hooking up and all of that that hurt the most." There was a hitch in her voice. "He...he took basketball away from me. I couldn't see it at the time. He always said he was trying to make me better. He had me on a diet that sapped all of my strength, saying it would help me get faster. He told me that my high school coach was trying to sabotage me, so I stopped trusting her. I trusted him when he told me that he was reaching out to college coaches, and when no one came to watch me play, I believed him when he told me that I just needed to work harder to get their attention. I don't know what he was telling them, or if he was even talking to them at all. Whatever he did, it kept them all away." Another sob shook her body. "Fuck, I was just watching my life-long dream fall to pieces around me and he was there, ready to comfort me, when the whole time he was the one tearing me down."

David was speechless, his insides a complete wreckage in the aftermath of Sage's admission. "Goddamnit, Sage," he said, his voice grating from his chest.

Her head tilted back, giving him the first glimpse of her face. Her eyes were brutally green and red-rimmed, her expression soft and sad, but somehow more settled than before.

She offered him a small smile. "It's really fine. It's all turned out okay."

David shook his head. "I'm so sorry. I'm so, so sorry."

"I think I needed to go see him tonight to prove to myself that it was all a lie, you know?" She leaned absently into him, her eyes drifting shut for a second before she looked back up at him. "The second that I saw him tonight it was like I went right back to being that girl again. Everything that I've made of myself just disappeared the moment he said my name, and I *hated* that, David. I hated that he could do that to me after all this time."

There was so much to say. A million things he wanted to say to her, reassurances and condolences and, more than anything, the need to convince her that she burned so brightly that no one — *no one* — could take it away from her.

Instead, he settled for simply being there. She'd asked for him, and he was going to do exactly that: be there with her. "I'm glad you're safe now," David said, letting out one small bit of truth.

"Me too," she said, settling her head back into the crook of his arm. "I'm just glad I'm here with you."

David took a deep breath. "Me too, Lefty. Me too."

They settled into silence. One minute bled into the next, and his fingers kept trailing over her skin, brushing through her hair. He couldn't imagine being anywhere else.

Eventually Sage's breathing slowed, her body softening against his. He craned his neck to catch a glimpse of her face — she was sound asleep, her lips parted and her features finally relaxed.

He shifted carefully, pulling his phone from his pocket with his free hand. He set an alarm for early enough in the morning that he'd be able to get back to his room before the rest of the team was up. Tossing his phone down, he settled back and let his eyes drift shut.

Before exhaustion pulled him under, he let himself, for just a moment, indulge the hurt. There were questions he hadn't asked, and *damn it* he wanted to trust her more than anything in the world. But had something happened between Sage and Evan in that car?

And if it had, what did that mean for him?

CHAPTER 21
KIND AND GOOD
SAGE

Sage settled into her seat on the plane. She'd kept her headphones in on their walk through the airport, sending the silent signal that she wanted to be left alone. She'd grabbed a seat between two strangers, sacrificing the loss of personal space for what was hopefully going to be a blissfully quiet trip home.

She needed a fucking break.

Ideally, she needed at least twenty-four hours alone. She couldn't even begin to sift through the events of the previous night, not until she had the time and space to fully process and parse through it all.

She'd barely woken up when David's alarm had gone off. She'd felt him carefully disentangle her hands, which had clung to his t-shirt like she was afraid he was going to leave her. She'd ignored the numerous texts from him throughout the morning, needing to put herself back together before she could return to the comfortable friendship that had existed between them.

Embarrassment heated her skin. She'd shown him too much. It was a moment of excruciating weakness that had brought her to text him, but in that moment she'd needed... Well, she'd needed *him*, and she knew that he'd show up at her door. She never planned to tell him everything. But it had been so nice, even for just a little bit, to settle against his warm, strong body. To pretend like his comfort was hers to take.

The flight passed quickly, her audiobook of one of her favorite Westerns serving to block out the rest of the world.

Once they got back to the Humphrey Center, she had a bit of work to do to make sure that all of the equipment was put away. She could feel David watching her as she went through the familiar motions, but avoided eye contact by keeping busy.

As she drove home, her phone rang. She glanced at her screen, sighing. She debated ignoring the call, but decided at the last minute to answer.

"Hi Mom."

"Sagey!" Her mom's voice filled the car, and for a second her eyes burned with emotion at the familiar warmth that only her mom could summon.

"What are you up to?"

"Oh, I just finished changing the chickens' bedding. School starts back up tomorrow, so I'm trying to finish up all of my chores before going back to work."

"Nice." Sage could picture the robin's egg blue painted chicken coop nestled in the top corner of their sloped backyard.

"How are you doing?"

"Fine," Sage answered as she rolled down her window to enter the gate code for the apartment complex. "Staying busy with the team and classes."

"Any news on the job hunt?"

Sage grimaced. She knew that it was irrational; her mom's questions about her post-graduation plans were completely reasonable. It was totally warranted for her to be curious and concerned about her kid having a concrete plan. But Sage couldn't help the way her skin crawled when her mom brought up the topic.

"Nothing yet," Sage admitted reluctantly. "I honestly haven't had time. We've been traveling almost every week. My advisor has some ideas, so my plan is to hit the ground running when the season wraps up."

"Hm." Sage could perfectly imagine the pursed-lip expression that probably pinched her mother's laugh-lined face.

"What, Mom," she asked, rather than waiting for the lecture that was inevitably coming.

"I just want you to make sure you don't miss out on a perfect opportunity because you're waiting," she said. "Did you get a chance to look at the postings I sent you? The one with the baseball team looked really good. Starting at sixty-thousand, Sage. Can you imagine?"

Sage sat in her parked car, her head tilted back against the headrest. "Yeah, Mom. I'll give them another look though."

"Good." In the background, she heard the click of the back door opening. "You know I love you, right?"

Sage closed her eyes. "I know. Love you too. And I've got to go."

"Okay, well call me when you have more time to catch up."

"Sure, Mom."

"Bye, Sagey."

"Bye."

Sage hung up the phone, exhaustion making her whole body feel impossibly heavy. She dragged herself and her luggage out of her car and up the stairs to her apartment, barely making it to her bed before she collapsed into a heap, powered off her phone, and fell asleep.

⌐⌐

After an indulgent three hour nap, Sage dragged herself to the couch and grabbed her laptop.

Her stats from last night's game were absolute garbage, so she logged onto the team drive and queued up the tape that they'd already uploaded.

The idea that she hadn't done her job well because of something as trivial as being faced by someone from her past grated on her, and she was determined to redo the stat sheet before practice the next morning.

With a cup of tea in one hand, she focused on the game playing on her laptop in front of her.

The team looked good. Really fucking good.

She tapped out the stats on the tablet, tracking the plays with the attention she'd been missing the night before. A few times she paused to watch a play again, not because she'd missed something, but because an idea or an adjustment crossed her mind.

Finally, she paused the tape and ran into her bedroom, tracking down a barely-filled notebook on the bookshelf where she kept her school books and textbooks. Grabbing a pencil from her bag, she went back to the couch and flipped to a blank page.

Before she could second guess herself, she started writing. Sketches of plays surrounded by words as she tapped into a well of thoughts and ideas she hadn't even realized were there.

She knew basketball. She'd lived and breathed basketball. She shouldn't be surprised that she had a lot to say on the subject, but still, when she flipped the third page and hadn't yet reached a stopping point, she couldn't quite believe it.

An hour later she'd finished correcting the game stats and had somehow filled ten pages with various notes and ideas.

It was getting dark, so she packed up her stuff and changed to go shoot on campus, needing to expend some of the nervous energy that filled her body.

Twenty minutes later she was alone under the buzzing lights, her muscles warming up as she moved around the basket. She felt the beginning of sweat on her forehead, and lifted the hem of the old t-shirt with cut off sleeves that she'd thrown on to wipe it away.

Already, she was coming back together.

But even though she felt the pieces of herself returning to their previous equilibrium, there was something different. Seeing Evan had opened up something that she'd previously ignored, something that she'd had to walk away from in order to survive.

That final year of basketball — her senior year — was supposed to be the culmination of something. It was supposed to be the crowning achievement of a career that had started when she was just seven years old, as well as what opened the door to playing at the next level — playing in college.

Evan had been her coach for four years at that point. He'd been young, charismatic, and passionate, and had her entire team hanging on to every word he said.

Sage had set herself apart with her skill and her work ethic, willingly devoting all of herself to basketball, spending every minute of her spare time at the gym. It helped that she'd been tall from a young age — hitting her full height in eighth grade.

Of course she'd developed a crush on Evan. All of them had. The boys around them had acne and hadn't hit their growth spurts yet. Evan was tall and handsome and drove a new car. What she hadn't expected was for him to take an interest in her. And when he had, it was a teenage fantasy come to life.

She'd been a sophomore in high school when he first started asking her to stay after practice. Extra drills turned into long, heart-felt conversations and offers of a ride home. He complimented her, while still challenging her to get better. He continuously raised the bar, and Sage chased his praise with a rabid need to earn his approval.

She would have done anything he asked.

The first time he leaned over the center console and kissed her in the darkness, she thought she'd died and gone to heaven. This man wanted *her*. He was choosing her.

It escalated from there. She bailed on friends and teammates to meet him in his car. Sometimes he'd take them to a motel, and on those nights she felt even more special. She kept playing, getting better and better. Coming out of her sophomore year, the dream of a college scholarship didn't seem like too far of a reach. Her high school coach, who she'd always respected, encouraged her to keep working and focus on staying healthy.

And then that summer, the diet had started. Evan convinced her that it would give her an edge over the other girls her age. That was combined with cardio workouts on the track, running and running until she had to limp back to her car, weak with exhaustion.

She lost weight. Years of hard-earned muscle practically melted away. All the while, Evan reassured her: *You're getting faster. You'll be able to be more dynamic. You can become a guard and you can score more.*

Sage never thought to doubt him. Why would she? He'd chosen her, and had believed in her from the beginning.

And then they'd gone to tournaments in the summer, and everyone expected college coaches to come watch her. She'd tried to be humble about it, but she'd expected it too.

But they didn't come.

She worked harder, pushed herself beyond what was healthy, because that *had* to be the reason. She must not have been good enough.

The pattern carried on. The summer season passed, and she'd played well enough, but not nearly as well as had been expected. Her high school coach began to express concern about her weight loss, and when Sage reported that to Evan, he'd brushed off the comments as a lack of understanding. He was training her to be an elite athlete, something her other coach could never understand.

Fast forward to her senior season. No college coaches had called. Her relationship with her high school coach had fractured, driven by distrust and Sage's disregard for her input. Basketball, which for years had been the greatest love of her life, had become something she dreaded.

Her eighteenth birthday was at the end of January. Evan had told her repeatedly that as soon as she turned eighteen, they'd be together. They'd stop hiding away in his car and sneaking into motel rooms. He'd told her that the girlfriend who he lived with was just a placeholder while he waited for her.

Fuck, she'd been naive. Her birthday had come and gone, and nothing changed. Evan withdrew, claiming to be busy or otherwise occupied, and Sage was left with the ruins of a final basketball season, playing a sport she hated, surrounded by teammates she'd alienated years ago, faced with an empty future.

Choosing Southeastern had been a welcome relief. She couldn't stand to stay in Santa Barbara, where her failures haunted her wherever she went.

She missed her tenth shot in a row.

Letting out a sharp, frustrated exhale, Sage chased after the ball and then paused, looking up at the basket. She stared at the vivid orange rim until the image began to blur.

She inhaled. Held it in until the pressure in her lungs ached. Exhaled.

The next shot went in. She chased down the ball, dribbling out to the wing before setting up again, her palms sliding easily over the leather before her finger found one of the seams.

That shot went in, and then the next. All of her focus was on the net in front of her, her body reacting to the exact bounce and roll of the ball each time it dropped through the net. She settled into an almost meditative state, quiet except for the squeak of her shoes on the hardwood and her heavy breathing as she moved around the court.

The gym around her was silent, and her mind quieted.

Sage had no idea how much time had passed before she brought the endless cycle of shoot, dribble out, shoot, dribble out, to a stop. She had to catch her breath; her shirt was wet with sweat and her face was hot, flushed from exertion.

There was a distinct calm that always settled over her when she walked away from the court, unlacing her shoes and peeling off her sweaty socks. And today, with that calm came the feeling that she'd picked up the broken pieces and put herself back together. Maybe, she was whole again.

⊏⊐

"Sage!"

She jumped up from where she was slumped over the front of her shopping cart in front of the tortilla chips.

David Hughes, looking like a bear emerging from hibernation with his unkempt hair and deep purple circles under his heavy-lidded eyes, pushed his cart toward her.

"Hi," she said, offering him a hesitant smile.

"You didn't respond to my texts," he said, his voice grating from his chest like rusted metal dragged across gravel.

Sage winced. "Sorry, I just needed to regroup after..." She trailed off, unable to put words to the colossal shit show that had been her run in with Evan. It was even harder to explain what had happened after.

Sage wasn't a big sharer. Never had been outside of her relationship with her sister. But she'd sat there wrapped up like a koala bear in David's strong arms and spilled out all of the things she'd kept hidden.

His eyes searched hers. "Are you okay?"

She nodded. "Better now."

David mirrored her nod, and she glanced down to see his hands gripping the handle of the shopping cart. He cleared his throat. "I wish you'd called," he said, his voice quiet. "I wish you'd asked me for help."

If it had been anyone else, Sage would have brushed them off. But this wasn't just anyone. This was David, who was kind and good, who kept showing up selflessly. Who she was going to try to do something new and terrifying with after the season.

"I don't talk about Evan," she admitted, forcing herself to maintain eye contact, to look directly into his deep brown eyes. She could try to give him a little bit more of herself. "My sister's the only one who knows what actually happened between us. Seeing him again," she swallowed against the emotion that burned her throat. "I never thought I'd see him again. And like I said, it was like suddenly I was the same kid who idolized him all over again, even though I know I'm not that girl anymore. I've worked really fucking hard to outgrow that experience, David. I don't just let people into my life or let them tell me what to do. So to have you see me like that…it was humiliating." Her voice had quieted to a whisper. "I never wanted you to see that part of me."

David watched her for a moment with an anguished expression on his face. Then he slowly pushed his cart forward, coming up beside her.

"And David?"

"Hm?"

She steeled herself with a breath. "You should know that Evan kissed me. When we were in the car."

David's expression was carefully blank. She watched his Adam's Apple bob as he swallowed. "How did you feel about him kissing you?"

"I hated it," she said, the truth of her words hitting her like a blow to the chest. "I fucking hated it, but I didn't stop right away, and I don't want you to think —"

David stepped up to her, one of his big hands coming up to cradle her jaw. "Hey," he said, his voice a whisper. "I believe you, Lefty. And in case you need the reminder, no one should *ever* do that without your permission. No one."

She nodded, unable to find the words.

David's thumb swept across her cheek before he released his hold on her. "Can I shop with you?"

She stared at him for a full breath before finding her voice. "Sure," she replied.

David smiled at her. "Right then," he said, looking over into her basket. "What else do you need?"

Sage looked between him and her cart. "Eggs?"

"Come on. Let's go get you some eggs."

For a moment neither of them spoke, the only sound between them the whine and click of the carts as they reached the end of the aisle.

"You know you don't have to have it all together with me, right?"

Sage stopped. She looked at him, *really* looked at him, and saw nothing there but trust and care and all of the things she'd never let herself need from another person.

This man had held her through the most painful moment in her recent life, a moment when her past had dropped suddenly into the middle of her world without warning. He'd held her and offered nothing but compassion. Not only that, but he still looked at her like she was someone worthy of knowing. Even after seeing her broken, he looked at her like she was whole.

She still wasn't entirely sure how she'd come to have David Hughes in her life, but found that it was suddenly hard to imagine day to day life without him.

There was the kissing, sure. She'd spent too many nights in bed thinking about the kissing that was waiting for her at the end of the season. But what about this? About the friendship he gave her so easily and the moments when he seemed to know just what she needed?

At some point those things had started to matter just as much. Maybe even more.

The next morning, Sage showed up at David's apartment after her workout armed with coffee and a blueberry muffin. She knew that he had a weakness for the streusel topping.

The gesture was enough to bring them right back into their pattern of companionship — spending time together in the evenings after practice, sharing meals, and, occasionally, taking Daisy for walks through their neighborhood.

And the team kept winning. They'd more than earned their spot in the conference tournament at that point, and Sage worked with the athletic office to book flights and hotel rooms for the team to go to Tampa, where the tournament would take place.

When she'd texted Brinley the news that they'd advanced, her sister had replied with an email confirmation for two plane tickets to Tampa for her and their mom. Sage couldn't tell if she was more excited or nervous that they were coming. She wasn't even playing, but it still felt like she was right there with the team as they approached the end of the season.

The notebook she'd started scribbling in was now almost completely full, and she kept it on hand in her bag in case ideas struck. She'd started categorizing her notes to include player development for each of the guys on the team and drill recommendations based on position.

They closed out the regular season with a record of 15-12. In their conference, they were 13-3, a record that no one had expected. They were the dark horse going into the tournament, and while Sage knew that they were lucky to be there at all, there was still that tiny glimmer of hope that, maybe, they could pull off a few miraculous wins and go to nationals.

The night before flying out for the conference tournament, David was over at her apartment. He sat on one end of her couch, long legs stretched out in front of him. Daisy was curled up between his thighs, watching Sage where she lay sprawled out on the carpet, double checking the travel itinerary for the next day.

"Sage."

"Hm?" She scrolled down her screen, triple checking they'd gotten all of the player names spelled correctly on their tickets.

"This is incredible."

She glanced up to find David thumbing through the pages of her notebook. She'd forgotten that she'd left it open on her couch.

David's eyes stayed focused on the paper in front of him as a slow smile spread on his face.

It really was a fucking *lovely* smile.

"What you've done here," David said, finally looking up at her. "It's incredible, Sage."

She felt her cheeks warm. "You already said that," she said, unsure of how to respond.

"So I take it that you're thinking about coaching?"

"I," she began, but trailed off as she looked over at the pages and pages of notes that David held in his hands. She thought about how, in the past few months, she'd started to see the game from the outside looking in. She'd started to see it like a coach.

"David," she said, looking wide-eyed up at him. "Coaching is a job."

David laughed, shaking his head. "Believe it or not, one of us in this room is actually *employed* as a coach."

Sage rolled her eyes, but then flopped onto her back, staring up at the stark white of the ceiling as all of her thoughts of what came next shifted, clicking into place in a new pattern that she hadn't fully considered was a possibility.

She could be a coach.

She could coach *basketball*.

CHAPTER 22
TONIGHT IS FOR YOU
DAVID

They won their first game on Thursday night against College of Conway handily — 70 to 52. Friday morning they were up in the stands watching other teams play, and knew by noon that their next opponent would be Harding University. Evan White's team.

David kept a close eye on Sage throughout the day, but saw nothing but easy smiles from her, even when Evan stood on the sidelines below them.

His stomach still heaved when he thought about what Sage had told him. The fact that her athletic career had been ruined by a coach made him see red. A coach was supposed to protect, nurture, and inspire. They were in a position to have an incredible impact on the lives of their players. It was a pressure that David felt on an almost daily basis, and he never stopped trying to figure out how to be better. How to be better for *them*.

But this man had exploited her. Had assaulted a minor and, if his current position as an assistant coach for a college team was any indication, had faced next to no consequences for his actions.

A part of David felt a responsibility to report him.

Now that he knew what he'd done, how could he not? This man was still coaching, still working in close contact with young people even after, if Tim was to be believed, another institution was made aware of his misbehavior. Of his *illegal* and goddamn reprehensible behavior.

But he knew that it wasn't his story to tell. If Sage decided to say something, that was her choice to make. As much as it pained him, that course of action was Sage's and Sage's alone.

Swooping in and taking that choice away from her would crush whatever trust he'd managed to build between them so far. David could recognize that trust from Sage Fogerty was a precious and rare thing. Their connection was one of the greatest gifts he'd ever been given, and he planned to protect it. To cherish it.

Later that night, the boys suited up for their second game — the conference tournament semi-finals. There was a nervous energy in the air, but David could see in their bodies that they were ready.

David tugged on his blazer before clearing his throat. Immediately, the room went silent. Every pair of eyes focused on him.

"Tonight is for you," he began, projecting his voice to fill the room. "You're here tonight because of what every single one of you has contributed over the past few months. Your time, your focus, your effort, and your commitment to your teammates is what has landed us here today." He felt a smile curve his lips. "I cannot express how proud I am of all of you." He took a moment to meet the gazes of each player. "You proved everyone wrong. Hell, you proved *me* wrong, and I'm a better man and a better coach because of the impact each of you has had on my life.

"So go out there tonight and give it your best. This is a team we've beat before, so you know they're going to come out with something to prove. Lean on each other, work together, and play your damn hearts out."

With that, David looked over at Jordan and Jenks, who sat side by side in the middle of the bench, surrounded by their teammates. "I'm going to leave you guys with your captains. Listen to them and decide on a plan. You know each other and you know your opponents, and I trust whatever you come up with."

David beckoned to Tim and Sage, who stood off to the side. He met her gaze for just a moment, and the obvious pride and affection in her eyes almost made his knees buckle.

Were they hiding their feelings from anyone? Because even if they won tonight and won the conference championship, the days of the season were numbered. It was only a matter of time before a loss ended their run, and then suddenly, the reason that had kept them apart would fall away.

There would be nothing stopping them from...what? From being together?

David could already see it. Hell, he'd already spent way too much time imagining it. They already spent time together. They already shared each other's spaces easily and comfortably. Add touching and kissing and exploring her body — the thought was goddamn *intoxicating*.

"Good work in there," Tim said, interrupting his thoughts. "They're as ready as they'll ever be."

David laughed, rubbing his hand over the beard he'd trimmed that morning, leaving only a thin layer of stubble on his cheeks and jaw. "We've done all we could, and however tonight ends, it'll still be a successful season."

Tim clasped a hand on his shoulder. "Couldn't agree more, Hughes. You've done great work with them."

Damn this old man for making his throat close with unwanted emotion. Damn him.

"Thanks, Coach," David managed to choke out, blinking a bit too fast to appear natural. Straightening his shoulders, he led them out onto the court. He and Tim took their places at the top of the bench, while Sage settled in at the end.

Even though David's gaze was focused out on the court, taking in the monumental moment that he was lucky enough to be a part of, he could feel the presence of the tall blonde at the end of the bench.

As soon as the season was done, he was going to ask her out. David was going to take Sage Fogerty on a proper date, complete with flowers and dinner at a place that wasn't too fancy for jeans and one of those thin little shirts that she never wore a bra with.

And then he'd kiss her, *really* kiss her, and it would be amazing.

So goddamn amazing.

They lost.

It was the kind of loss that left David gutted, but so incredibly proud.

The entire game had been close, within five points, with the lead passing back and forth in waves. Even at the end it had been in their grasp, with Harding pulling ahead by four in the last minute, and, in spite of every single one of the Southeastern players leaving everything out on the court, they couldn't close the lead.

David felt like he'd been out there with them. He'd started sweating in the first five minutes of the game and had never stopped, shedding his blazer and even rolling up his shirt sleeves to his elbows. Even then, he was pretty sure everyone in the crowd could see that sweat had soaked through the back of his blue shirt.

But he hadn't given a damn, because every single part of him was out there with those kids as they fought together. He was with them as their muscles strained and as their voices grew hoarse from communicating with each other on defense.

He'd coached harder than he'd ever coached before. He'd leaned on Tim, getting his assistant's input as much as he could while he paced up and down the sideline.

He was exhausted.

All he wanted was sweatpants, a beer, and a tall blonde and his dog cuddled up on his couch.

He walked down the hallway, his brown Oxfords slapping

against the stone. Tim walked beside him, and David consciously slowed down his steps to match the pace of his shorter assistant.

"Hell of a season, Coach." Tim knew better than to smile and laugh and brush aside the loss as a thing of the past, but still, his words meant something. His acknowledgement meant more to David than he could ever express.

"Couldn't have done it without you," David answered honestly. At first, he'd seen Tim as a threat to his authority, as proof that the institution hadn't believed in him. But they had slowly warmed to each other, and, by the end, Tim had become more than a mentor. He was someone David trusted. Someone he hoped to work with again.

They reached the locker room and pushed inside.

Jordan stood in the middle of the room, his green jersey soaked and his skin flushed pink. "Keep your heads up, boys," he was saying, his voice louder and betraying more emotion than David had ever heard from him. "Think about the team we were at the beginning of the year. Think about how little we trusted each other. And look at who we were tonight. Out there, we were a family. We fought hard for each other, and we were so dang close." He turned to the other seniors, who all sat beside each other at one end of the bench. None of them had dry eyes as they listened to their teammate, and David felt his own eyes burn as he watched them. He remembered being in their shoes like it was yesterday. "For some of us, this is our last chance to ever wear these jerseys. Me, Zephyr, Chris, and Jenks will never get another shot at this. We're going to pack up at the end of the year and go off to do whatever comes next. Coach," Jordan turned to David, obviously trying to keep his expression steady as he looked him in the eye. "We couldn't have done this without you. You were exactly what we needed, and I'll never forget the lessons you've taught me. Never."

Well. David was definitely crying.

Jordan continued. "But for the rest of you, look around this room. These are your brothers, and if you want to end up back here next year, if you want to go further than we did, you all need to come together and decide to go after it. Stay in touch over the summer. Stay local and play and lift and challenge each other to continue to get better." He paused, wiping awkwardly at his face as he sniffed. "Right. Well. Love you guys." And with that, he sat back down on the bench.

David and the rest of the team immediately broke out in applause, and Jordan's face got even redder.

"There's not much to say after that," David said above the noise, and the guys quickly quieted. "This loss hurt, and we all know that we could have won, but the reality is that we didn't. That's the way this sport works. You work and plan and spend hours of your life preparing, and then it comes down to one single game. And that's why I agree with Jordan. Keep your heads up. You defied expectations this year. No one thought you'd be able to do what you all did to get here. And as I said before the game, I am so proud of every single one of you. Nothing about tonight's game changes that."

There was more to say. There was *always* more to say.

But at that moment there were parents and relatives who'd flown across the country to see these guys play, and he wanted to give them as much time with their families as possible before they had to go back to the hotel. Because they lost, they'd fly out early the next morning.

"Alright. Let's call it, and then go out and thank the family who came in to see you guys." David motioned to Jenks, who got up and put his hand out in the empty space in the middle of the room. Immediately, the rest of the guys got up, piling their hands on top until they were all one smushed together group of sweaty, exhausted men.

And Sage. He couldn't forget Sage, who still smelled like flowers. He beckoned her toward the huddle, and she didn't hesitate to put her hand in alongside the rest of them.

"Eagles on three!" Zephyr's voice filled the room. "One, two, three…"

"Eagles!"

Their voices combined, the volume almost uncomfortable as they had one last moment together in the wake of a game.

David watched them disperse, heading to the showers as they fell into comfortable teasing and banter. Most of them would be back the next year, and, if he was lucky, he would get the chance to coach them again.

He lost track of time a bit once he reached the lobby, pulled into conversations with each of the players and then exchanging greetings and introductions with the families that had made the trip to watch them play.

Sage stood off to one side with a woman he recognized as her older sister, Brinley, and an older woman dressed in overalls and a flowing floral blouse.

He wanted to go to Sage. This was her moment too; her steadfast reassurance had constantly reminded him that he'd earned his place on the bench. She'd helped him learn to let go enough to breathe. She'd made him a better coach, and, arguably, a better man.

There was also the fact that he could still taste the honey from the lozenge she'd pressed into his hand after the game.

It tasted like her.

But he didn't want to interrupt her time with her family, knowing they'd traveled all the way from California to be there. He didn't want to presume and go up to them.

David was only able to watch her unnoticed for a moment. She must have felt him, because she looked up and their gazes collided with a heat and warmth that had him inhaling a sharp breath. Her green eyes blinked, and she offered him a quick smile before she turned back to her family.

He pushed the heel of his hand into his sternum as he cleared his throat, shifting so that he was no longer staring so obviously. *Get your shit together, David.*

He felt a sharp elbow in his side and looked over to see Monty grinning at him.

David cocked a brow at him. "What," he said cautiously.

Monty's grin widened. "Just wondering when you're gonna get your shit together and ask her out."

David's mouth dropped open. "Excuse me?"

"Come on, Coach. Everyone knows. Everyone ships it."

"Ships it?" *What in the hell was happening?* ·

Monty let out a bright laugh. "We're rooting for you, Coach." With a wink that also scrunched up his other eye, he took off to join a group of the guys that hovered near the entrance.

"Watch it, Monty!" David called after him, feeling a mixture of amused and embarrassed at the idea that at least one of the players had picked up on his feelings for Sage.

Shaking his head, he scratched his jaw. Just then Jenks' dad came up and introduced himself, and David was pulled into another conversation.

Finally, he wrangled the team onto the bus, urging them through goodbyes as he ushered the stragglers outside.

He'd just climbed on the bus when his phone buzzed in his pocket. It was a text from Sage.

> I'm going to stay with my family tonight. Hope that's okay.

David shoved aside the misplaced disappointment as he typed out his reply.

> Of course. Thx for everything this year.

> You too, Coach. Congrats on a great season.

> Couldn't have done it without u.

> You*

His mouth curved into a smile as he leaned his head back on the headrest.

He couldn't wait to get home.

CHAPTER 23
DON'T FALL FOR IT
SAGE

Sage slowed to a walk as she muttered an apology to the frowning flight attendant at the front of the plane.

Half of her hair was falling out of the braid she'd slept in, and her eyes were gritty with sleep — or the lack thereof. She walked down the empty aisle, painfully aware that every fucking passenger was watching her find her seat.

Of course she immediately saw David, sitting about halfway back with a frown pulling down his lips as he watched her. She couldn't hold his gaze.

When she passed him on her way to the single empty seat toward the back of the plane, she muttered a quick "Sorry," but didn't look at him.

She couldn't.

Finally she settled into her seat between two of the freshmen players, offering them both what had to be a strained smile before putting her earbuds in and closing her eyes.

Her head was a fucking mess.

She'd been on such a high after the game. Even though it had ended in a loss, there had been such a tangible sense of togetherness in that locker room that even Sage had felt the heady belonging of being a part of the team. They'd left everything out there on the court, and it was the perfect culmination to a season that, while it had started rough, had ended in greater accomplishments than anyone had expected.

And then there had been David, who at the beginning had looked so uncomfortable in his position. In those early games, she'd watched him like she was trying to learn him. To understand him. He'd fidgeted with the sleeves of his blazers. He'd second-guessed himself when the players asked him questions. His uncertainty and lack of confidence had been right there on the surface, where anyone could see it.

But he'd changed. Somewhere along the line he'd found something inside of himself to draw on. Something that lent him strength, calm, and the self-assuredness of someone who knew that they were right where they belonged.

Somehow he'd become more beautiful too.

He'd always been nice — so *fucking* nice — to look at, but now Sage got the sense that maybe he felt like he was worthy of it all. His posture had straightened. His wide, uninhibited smile was almost constantly on his face. He moved decisively, spoke with certainty, and where Sage had been drawn to him before, now her body had convinced her that she belonged permanently cuddled up on his lap with her face nuzzled into the stubble on the underside of his jaw.

It was a ridiculous, almost silly feeling, but rather than laughing it off as a moment of hormone-fueled insanity, Sage found herself actually entertaining the idea. He'd said *"After the season"* when she'd kissed him, and she'd nodded. And now, finally, they'd arrived at that moment that had seemed so far into the future that Sage hadn't totally believed that it would actually come to pass.

In the moments after the game, Sage had wanted, more than *anything*, to blow off her family and drag David Hughes to the airport and onto the next flight back to Charleston. Back to the world they'd created, together, between their two apartments. There was nothing stopping them from — *what* exactly she didn't know, but she hoped like hell that it involved seeing David Hughes naked and getting beard-burn from how much time she planned to spend kissing his jawline.

Another more hesitant, fragile part of herself hoped that it also included reading on the couch together and taking Daisy for walks. Sharing tots at The Grove. Grocery shopping. More dancing in David's arms. A continuation of the things that made up the landscape of their friendship.

But her mom and Brinley had rushed toward her with open arms, and all thoughts of running away fled as she burrowed into the familiar warmth of her family.

"Tough loss," Brinley said, tucking a piece of Sage's hair behind her ear with a proud smile on her face. "But you looked like a badass up there."

Sage leaned heavily into her mom's arms, inhaling the familiar patchouli scent that she'd watched her mom dab onto her neck every morning throughout her childhood.

"Hey, Mom," she said, feeling a wave of emotion that only a reunion with a mother could bring up. "I've missed you."

"I've missed you too, Sagey." She planted a soft kiss on her cheek and then drew back so that she could look her in the eye. "You are beautiful. You know that, right?"

Sage rolled her eyes as she felt her cheeks heat. "Stop it."

Brinley let out a musical laugh. "She's right, you know. You look hot as hell right now."

"Did I see Coach White on the other team's bench?" Her mom looked genuinely curious, like she was inquiring after an old friend.

Sage waited for her body to respond, waited for muscles to cramp and her gut to hollow with the dread that talking about Evan summoned in her. But there was nothing besides a little sliver of pain, like prodding a bruise that had faded to yellow.

"Yep," Sage replied. "It's him."

Her mom beamed, her face carving into the deep lines of

someone who had managed to find plenty of laughter throughout their life. "Did you say hello to him?"

"Yeah, Mom. Sure did."

She caught Brinley staring at her from behind their mom's shoulder, her eyes wide with the unspoken expression of a sister who'd been left in the dark. Sage shook her head, silently promising *Later.*

"How's your hotel?" Sage tried to listen to her mom and Brinley argue about the conventional air freshener the cleaners had used in their room, but her eyes had found David, who was standing among the players and their families on the other side of the lobby.

He was already watching her. She could feel his gaze on her in the way that two people who are somehow attuned to each other notice such things.

David looked at her without any hesitation, like he knew that they would go home together at the end of it all. And then his smile spread across his face, and Sage felt warm. Warm and good and *right*, like she was right and he was right and they were right together.

"Why is he looking at you like that, Sage?"

Sage snapped her eyes over to her mom, who watched her with that sharp, almost bird-like pointedness that had always signaled trouble.

Brinley let out a huffed exhale. "Mom, leave her alone."

That only seemed to fuel the ire of Cheryl Fogerty, who rounded on her older daughter with a pointed finger. "What? I know about men like that." She glanced back over at Sage, who was trying to use telepathy to tell the stupidly handsome man across the room to *stop fucking looking at her.* Her mom went on. "They come in all big and good-looking and powerful with their age and wisdom and convince you that you can't live without them." She shook her head. "Don't fall for it, Sagey."

It wasn't her mom's fault that she didn't know what had happened between Sage and Evan White. In the eyes of Cheryl,

Coach White had been an inspiring mentor who took a special interest in Sage's future. The truth was that the situation her mom was warning her about had already happened. It had happened when she was young and naive and so jaded about love that an older man giving her attention *had* felt life-saving at the time.

That wasn't what she felt about David. That wasn't who David Hughes was.

"Mom, he's not like that," she argued, keeping her voice low to avoid being overheard by the people around them.

Her mom gave her a wry, almost pitying smile. "That's what they all want you to think. They see a strong and beautiful young woman like you and try to capture your shine all for themselves. Don't do it! Don't give up your freedom for anyone!"

Sage felt a throbbing bloom behind one of her ears.

Brinley stepped closer and put a hand on their mom's shoulder. "Mom, stop it," she hissed.

"I won't see her hurt, Brinley." Cheryl was wild-eyed as she looked between her daughters. "I won't see her make the same mistakes I did. Your father was just like that, Sage. He was handsome and older and seemed to have it all figured out." She wiped at her nose with the back of one hand, the various beaded bracelets she wore rattling against one another. "It started small, with me giving up little things to make our lives work together. First it was going dancing with my friends, and next thing I knew it was my career! My financial independence. And then when he left us, I had nothing. There was nothing of myself left."

"Jesus, Mom," Brinley snapped. "Can you please stop putting your own baggage on her? Sage is perfectly capable of making her own choices."

"Fine, fine." Their mom waved her hands in surrender, her eyes once again kind and so recognizably maternal. "Just be careful, okay?"

Sage could do nothing but nod. Her body, which had just been so full of warmth and confidence and certainty, was cold.

Cold, hollow, and numb.

But still she'd gone with them to dinner at a local spot Brinley had found, and they fell into familiar conversations and jokes and laughter. She'd shared Brinley's bed in their hotel, claiming it was easier to crash with them than to go back with the team.

And once their mom had fallen asleep, the two Fogerty daughters shared a whispered conversation that lasted late into the night. Sage told her sister about seeing Evan again. About going to him after the game and the pain and closure she'd come away from the situation with. She told her about kissing David, and about what she hoped was going to happen when they got home.

Brinley told Sage about her boyfriend, Rohan, who was so deeply devoted to her. She talked about how he cooked for her, confessed his fear of disappointing his father, and loved her in a way that was so shockingly selfless that neither of them could believe that he was real.

At some point they'd both fallen asleep.

When she'd given her rushed goodbyes that morning after oversleeping, Brinley had held Sage tightly against her, holding her in place long enough to whisper:

"Live your own life, Sage."

Her sister's words still echoed in her head as the roar of the engines pulled her into sleep.

⊏⊐

When they got back to Southeastern, Sage exchanged farewells with the players, making numerous promises to meet in the gym to shoot and play pick up. If any of them noticed that her smile was forced or her mind was elsewhere, they didn't comment. Her bullshit was her own, and she didn't want to take away from what these guys had just accomplished. She remembered what it had been like in the hours following the ending of the season.

Her mom's words had thrown her off of her axis. Rants like those from Cheryl Fogerty were nothing new, but there was something different about hearing it directed at her. To realize that there were perceptions about any situation where an older man was pursuing a younger woman.

Sage honestly hadn't taken that into consideration.

Of course she was aware of his age. She had the internet — she'd looked at what years he'd been in college. But beyond that fact, his age hadn't come up in their lives in any meaningful way. Sage took pride in being herself, in owning her body and her actions and moving through the world with confidence.

But she did give a shit about people thinking she was weak or unable to take care of herself. Is that what people would think if she and David were together as a couple? Would they think that Sage saw David as an easy ticket to a comfortable life?

Fuck.

Somehow she managed to dodge a frowning and determined David and finally, Sage was safe in her car, driving home. She didn't turn on music, needing the silence to try to tease through the tangle in her head.

As soon as she was home she got in the shower, turning the water hot enough that it smarted the surface of her skin. Once she was out and dry she sought out her comfiest clothes: old sweatpants, a hoodie, and thick wool socks.

She grabbed her phone from her bag. Guilt curdled her stomach as she bypassed the ten text messages from David, but she wasn't ready yet. She just needed a little bit of time.

Maggie answered on the second ring. "Hey, what's up?"

"Can I come over?"

There was a moment of quiet. "Are you okay?"

"Not really."

"Come on then."

⸺

Maggie's place was about 15 minutes northwest of town, in a second floor apartment in a building that looked like it hadn't been painted in the past twenty years.

"You made it," Maggie said, holding the door wide open.

Sage gave her friend a grateful smile. "Thanks for having me."

The apartment was cozy and reflected a level of interior design that Sage could only dream of possessing. Between the colorful rugs, bright paintings, silver-framed mirrors and at least seven different-colored orchids all in full bloom, it was easy to ignore the out-of-date appliances and the cracked formica floors.

"I love your place," Sage said.

Maggie, who was dressed down in cotton shorts and a white men's undershirt, shrugged, adjusting the ponytail on the top of her head that looked like a fountain. "It's not much, but it's mine and the rent's good." She pointed to the long futon couch, covered in a floral patterned blanket. "Go. Sit. I'll get snacks."

Any doubt that Sage had felt about calling on her relatively new friend evaporated at the mention of snacks.

Minutes later, they were both bent over a plate of carrots, bell peppers, and potato chips, along with a tub of some sort of creamy dip that Maggie had made.

Sage swallowed a bite, licking a drop of stray dip from the corner of her mouth. "How've you been?"

Maggie's face softened. "Good. Really good." She stretched out one of her legs, wiggling her painted toes. "Work at the bar is good, school is good —"

"School?" Sage looked at Maggie, incredulous. "You're in school?"

"Beauty school," Maggie said, obviously trying to downplay it.

Sage threw a pepper at the other woman, who shrieked when it fell down the front of her shirt.

"Beauty school is badass, Maggie. How long have you been going?"

"About six months now."

Sage shook her head. "Seriously, that's so cool. I'm unfortunately underskilled in the beauty department."

"Shut up." Maggie rolled her eyes. "You're a natural blonde and you're hot. Now tell me what's goin' on with you?"

Sage's smile faded. "My mom said some things that got under my skin and now I'm ignoring David."

"Do you want to talk about it?"

"Not really."

Maggie hummed. "Want to watch *Grey's Anatomy* and forget about the world?"

A relieved laugh burst from Sage's chest. "Fuck yes."

CHAPTER 24
I THOUGHT WE DID
DAVID

"The mailbox is full and cannot accept any new messages at this time. Goodbye."

"Goddamnit," David muttered, staring down at his phone.

He pulled up his messages, frowning at the twelve unanswered texts he'd sent in the three and a half hours since they'd gotten home from their conference loss.

David turned back to his living room, barely registering the takeout containers from their Italian place that were laid out on his coffee table or the flickering candles he'd bought months ago with this exact moment in mind. He tapped his phone against his leg, trying to calm his breathing. It grew more and more shallow with every passing second that his phone didn't ring. *Just fucking ring,* he silently implored, willing the device to do something. Anything.

Anything to know that Sage was safe.

He tried her number again. "Come on, Lefty," he pleaded, his hand trembling from gripping the phone so tightly.

Nothing.

David jumped into action, like maybe if he moved quickly enough he could outrun the panic that clawed its way up his throat. He blew out the candles, and giving Daisy a quick pat on the head, headed out the door.

Less than five minutes later he stood outside of Sage's apartment. He'd taken the long way, walking through the manicured grass behind her building so that he could look up at her balcony and see if her lights were on. Dread tightened his stomach when they weren't.

But still he pounded on her door.

"Sage," he called, certain that he was loud enough for her to hear him through the door. "Sage!"

The silence that met him was deafening, drowned out by the roaring in his ears that had reached a volume that had his head pounding.

Now he was afraid. He knocked one more time, even though he knew there would be no answer. As he forced himself to breathe, he pulled out his phone.

"Chuck," he said as soon as his friend answered. "I...it's Sage. I can't find her and —"

"I'm on my way."

David hung up, dragging himself step by step away from the place where he knew Sage would be safe. Except she wasn't there and she wasn't responding, which meant that she could be anywhere, and there was no guarantee of her safety.

Fuck.

Chuck found him sitting woodenly on his couch, phone in one hand and a crushed water bottle in the other.

"Breathe, David," Chuck said, dropping to his knees in front of him and gripping his shoulder with a firmness that David needed to remind himself that he was alive. David forced his lunges to empty, his exhale harsh. Chuck squeezed him tighter. "I'm sure that she's fine."

David's head was shaking before Chuck finished speaking. "You can't know that. Don't say shit like that when I have no idea where she is, and she isn't answering my calls or my texts."

"It's late afternoon," Chuck said, his voice infuriatingly calm, just like it'd always been when David lost control. "Could she be with friends right now?"

The panic in his throat flared. "Friends," he started, thinking about Sage, about the evenings they spent together, trying to remember if she mentioned hanging out with other people, if there was —

"Maggie." David shot to his feet. "We've got to find Maggie."

Chuck frowned. "Maggie?"

David was already shoving his feet into his shoes and grabbing his keys. "The bartender from The Grove. She and Sage are tight."

"Got it." David heard Chuck heave out a heavy sigh. "Oh, David," he said, his voice quiet.

David glanced back at Chuck, who stood looking down at the take-out and the candles and the flowers he'd picked out because the blue matched the suit she'd worn to so many games. The one she looked breathtakingly beautiful in.

Swallowing against the knot in his throat, David rubbed the back of his neck.

"Did you guys have plans?"

David looked up at Chuck, letting out a strained laugh. "I thought we did," he admitted, before turning to the door. "Let's go find Maggie."

━━━

David wove his way through the packed crowd at The Grove, his heart sinking when he realized that none of the three bartenders were Maggie.

"She's not here," David said, trying to keep his voice even as he spoke to Chuck.

"Let's ask him." Chuck nodded toward a short, wiry man with a shaved head who was currently filling a tray full of pint glasses from one of the taps along the wall behind the bar.

David didn't think twice about using his body to his advantage, wedging his way forward until his chest rested against the bar.

"Hey," he called out. The bartender looked up. "We're looking for Maggie. Any chance you could help us get in touch with her?"

The man looked briefly amused. "Hell no," he said with a laugh.

"Come on." The shred of control David had over himself in that moment wavered. He forced himself to exhale slowly through his nose. "We wouldn't be here if it wasn't important."

"You think you two are the first assholes who've come around here trying to score her number?"

"Listen, man," David growled, leaning his upper body over the edge of the bar and using every bit of his size to tower over the piece of shit who was standing between him and the reassurance that Sage was okay. A reassurance that was becoming more and more urgent with every passing minute. "Maggie is friends with my girlfriend who's missing, and I'm trying to find her."

The man was unimpressed, looking David up and down like he was nothing more than a fly who'd had the audacity to land on his bar. "Get out of here," he said, dismissing them with a wave of his hand.

David's control snapped. "If something happened to her," he started, his hands already clenching into fists.

A warm hand closed around his arm, pulling him back. "Dude," Chuck said, his voice low. "Calm the fuck down."

Chuck didn't loosen his grip, tugging David along with him as he wound his way back through the picnic tables. David was barely there, the lights passing overhead in a yellow blur and the sounds of conversation and laughter blending into a grating buzz that threatened to break him.

Maybe he was already broken.

Chuck gave him a final push that sent him through the entrance and out onto the brightly-lit sidewalk. Another tug on his arm had him following Chuck down the block, one step following another until they turned onto a side street. Steady pressure on his shoulder left David no choice but to drop down to the curb.

David's chest was ripping in two, fear that he hadn't tasted in twelve years crushing his lungs until breathing felt impossible. His head dropped down between his knees and his hands knit together behind his neck, his body collapsing inward like that would somehow make it all feel like less.

He'd been there before.

The floor under his feet had been linoleum rather than cracked cement, and the antiseptic in the air had burned his nose when he'd remembered to breathe. Now the warmth of the air was only barely tainted by exhaust from the traffic a few blocks over. The rhythmic beeping of machines was replaced by the hum of air-conditioning units and the occasional honking of a horn.

Then, he'd known without a doubt that Johnny was in one of those rooms fighting for his life. He'd sat there at the edge of the waiting room, crumpled under the crippling weight of his irresponsibility.

Now, as he sat on the curb, a voice that was mostly buried under the roar of the panic that filled him reminded him that he didn't know if Sage was hurt. She could be fine; that there was no reason to assume the worst.

But what if? What if something had happened and he hadn't been there for her, hadn't done the one thing he'd promised himself to always do for the people he loved?

"She's going to be okay," Chuck's voice filtered through the darkness. "I know you're scared, man. If it were me, I'd be terrified. But there's nothing we can do right now other than trust that Sage has a good reason for not getting back to you. If nothing else, trust in her." David's eyes fell shut as he felt Chuck's hand on his back. "Let's go get Daisy and you can stay with me tonight. We'll wait for her together. You shouldn't be alone right now."

An hour later David lay sprawled out as much as he could on Chuck's couch, an afghan thrown over his legs and Daisy snoring softly where she lay curled up between his knees. The kind of exhaustion that came from hours and hours trapped in a state of panic weighed on him, but the idea of sleep felt laughable.

Not when Sage could be out there. Not when she might need him.

━━

David woke up in the morning with a stiff neck, a throbbing lower back, and Daisy enthusiastically licking his cheek. He must have nodded off at some point. He lifted Daisy from his chest gently, always careful with her little body. She squirmed as he pushed himself up to sitting, placing her on the floor beside his bare feet.

Any hope that he'd wake up to a different world was immediately shot as he looked down at his phone. No new messages.

The dread was right there, souring his mouth as he stood up. He was going to find her. He'd start at the places she frequented — the gym, the coffee shop, the grocery store — and then? Then he was going to start calling hospitals.

He found Chuck in the kitchen, already pouring coffee into a to-go mug.

"So what's the plan?"

David looked at the serious expression on his friend's face. There was no mocking. No reminders that his fear was irrational. There was nothing but care and concern.

Emotion clogged his throat. "I'm going to look on campus," David finally managed to choke out. "The gym, the library."

Chuck nodded. "Give me your keys and I'll go back to your apartment with Daisy. Text me her apartment number and I'll make sure to knock."

"Thanks," David said, even though that single word barely scratched the surface of the gratitude he felt for his friend. "You're the best."

Chuck gave him a small smile. "I've got you, man."

When David saw the beat up silver sedan in the Humphrey Center parking lot, he was overwhelmed with the need to both punch a wall and burst into tears. Probably at the same time.

He ran toward the practice gym. With every step, hurt and fear twisted into anger, and by the time David flung open the double doors, he was *livid*. Fucking livid and raw around the edges, like his whole body was a fresh bruise that had spent the past day being repeatedly poked and prodded.

But no matter how hot his rage burned, seeing Sage Fogerty whole and healthy threatened to bring him to his knees. Everything from the flush of her bare arms to the swing of her ponytail was a reminder that she was beautiful and she was okay.

Thank God, Lefty. Thank fucking God she was okay.

Now that he'd confirmed that her heart was still beating and all of her limbs were intact, David marched over to where she was shooting. He went straight to the basket, perfectly timing his arrival so that he could snatch the ball out of the net.

He knew she was going to make it.

For a brief second he considered the ball in his hands. It felt light — a women's ball, he realized — and the leather was worn and soft against his fingertips.

Using all of his strength, David cocked back his arm and threw the ball as far as he could across the gym. He watched as it bounced once, twice, three times, before rolling and coming to a stop in the distant corner.

Well. That felt pretty damn good.

Letting out a heavy breath, he turned back to Sage, who stood at the top of the key with her hands braced on her hips and her mouth gaping as she stared at him.

"When are you going to get it through your stubborn, beautiful head that you can't just disappear on me?" His voice came out in a low growl, raw and unrestrained.

Sage's dark brows knit together, and he could see a response on the tip of her tongue.

"You can't do that," he went on, his head shaking as he tried to catch his breath. "I didn't know where you were, and when you didn't respond…" His hand tore through his hair, the sharp pain as he caught on a knot bringing a flare of focus with it. "I thought you were *dead*, Sage. I called and called and got nothing."

He could see her expression shift, defiance melting into pained regret. "I just needed to be alone for a bit," Sage said softly.

David let out a laugh that sounded more like a canine whine in his ears. "You…I…Sage?"

Breathing wasn't supposed to be this hard, was it?

"David."

Sage's face hovered in front of him. She looked panicked, her green eyes — so goddamn green — darted back and forth. He thought he felt her hands on his arms, and he wondered why someone who's cheeks were so pink and full of life had hands as cold as ice.

"David," she pleaded. "Fuck, David. Please, what do you need?"

Someone was wheezing, and David wanted to tell them to shut the hell up with the racket, but he couldn't seem to get enough air. Firm hands gripped his shoulders and he crumpled, legs folding under him regardless of his furious command for them to *work, stay up, don't let her see you like this.*

But then his ass hit the floor and the air was too cold against his cheeks, and he reached for her. Hands stretched out and grasping, because even through the fog he knew that there was someone there who could make it better.

The skin of her neck was still sticky with sweat when he buried his face there, arms wrapping her up and holding her tightly against him. He felt her weight, heavy on his lap, holding him in place, and her body stayed strong, steady, even when he curled in on her.

"I've got you," Sage said softly, her finger-tips tracing up and down his back. "I'm here, and I've got you."

At some point he remembered how to breathe. He identified the natural light streaming in from the high windows and the expanse of hardwood floor beneath him. He tried to match his breaths to the steady rise and fall of the chest that was pressed against his, but quickly gave up. The woman breathed like oxygen was optional — slow, unhurried, and patient.

When he inhaled, his lungs filled to their full capacity. *That was good.* The exhale that followed was just as complete.

David drew back. "I'm sorry," he said, clearing his throat against the rasp in his voice. "This isn't...I don't do this."

Sage sat back on her heels, still straddling his lap. "Talk to me, David." The look in her eyes was so concerned, so careful, and he hated that. Hated that she looked at him like he was broken.

And while a part of him wanted to offer some sort of reassurance that he was fine, a louder voice demanded honesty. If he was really going to try to do this with Sage Fogerty, he needed her to understand this — to understand *him.*

"When I was a senior I was named captain of the team," he started, looking around at the gym that hadn't changed beyond repainted lines and fresh nets. "I was so goddamn proud. I'm sure I was annoying as shit. Just ask Chuck."

Sage's lips twitched into a tentative smile. "I can only imagine."

Some of the ache in his chest eased. "I tried to be good at it. Checking in with all the guys, coordinating rides, finding a tutor if someone was struggling. It was just my thing." David tightened his jaw. "Anyway. One night we were all going out to a house party after a big win. We didn't have to practice the next day, so we decided to cut loose. I'd had a big game, so I drank more than I normally did. At some point I lost my phone, and spent the night dancing before going home with a girl. I didn't track down my phone until noon the next day. One of the freshmen, Johnny, had called me. He'd called and called and messaged. I guess he was drunk and trying to get a ride back to campus." He closed his eyes for a moment before continuing. "When he couldn't find me, he decided to drive himself. He drove his car head-on into another vehicle, killing the older couple in the other vehicle on impact."

Sage looked at him, horrified. "David, I'm so sorry."

"It took a while to track him down. We looked everywhere. Finally his mom called our coach after being contacted by the hospital. He didn't make it through the night."

"Oh my god," Sage breathed, the heartbreak on her face a shadow of the pain he'd felt in the weeks after Johnny's death.

David leaned back, resting his weight on his hands. "So I never drink much, just in case. And I'm...I'm weird about knowing where people are." He shook his head. "Ask my friends. They all text me when they get home after we've all been out together. I know it's crazy. Ex-girlfriends called me controlling and paranoid. Maybe they were right." He looked Sage directly in the eye. "But it's a part of me that I don't know how to turn off."

Sage blinked, watching him like she was seeing him for the first time. Reaching out one of her slender hands, she traced the large white letters on his shirt. *Her* shirt, he corrected himself.

"I didn't know," Sage said softly. "I turned my phone off and then was with Maggie, and I...I wouldn't have left you in the dark if I'd known, David. I hope you know that."

He shifted his weight, freeing one of his hands so he could grab hers, threading their fingers together. "I know, Lefty," he sighed. "Are you alright?"

Her mouth curved into a small smile. "Yeah. I was thrown off by some things my mom said after the game and I just needed a little bit of time to get my head straightened out."

"And now?"

"Now what?"

David looked down at their intertwined hands. "How are you feeling about...this?"

Her dark brows arched. "About holding hands in the middle of the gym floor?"

Always with the goddamn jokes, he thought, even as his lips twitched up into a smile. "About being with me."

"I'm not always going to answer, David."

It took him a moment to catch up with the abrupt turn of the conversation. "Oh. Right." A little bit of that nervousness flared up in his throat.

"Hey." Her fingers gripped at his chin, commanding him to look her directly in the eye. *As if he'd ever look away from her.* "I want this with you. I don't know about you, but the person I am when we're watching game tape in your apartment or making breakfast at mine is more me than I've felt in a long time. And I want more with you. All of it, maybe." A flush of pink spread across her cheeks. "But I'm an independent person. Sometimes I need to be alone."

David swallowed. He would work on letting go. On trusting. He'd do all of that and so much more for her. "Okay, Lefty." He pressed his mouth to the soft palm of her hand. He kissed her skin, slowly, indulgently, like he had nothing to do but be exactly where he was.

"Can we go get some food?" Sage asked as her fingers curled into the short hair of his beard, scratching over his cheek and jaw.

"Yeah." Neither of them moved. "You've got to get up first, though."

Sage made a quiet growl of protest. "But you're very comfy."

"Comfy and hungry, Sage. Get up." He slapped a hand against her ass.

"David Hughes," Sage said, rearing back with an expression of mock horror. "Did you just spank a woman in your place of work?"

David rolled his eyes. "Why are you like this?"

"Because you get all flustered and seeing you sputtering makes me happy." Sage climbed off of his lap, pushing herself up to standing before extending a hand down to help him up.

Somehow he managed not to groan as he stood up. "That's not very nice," he muttered, brushing off the back of his sweats. "Come on," he said, starting to walk toward the door. "I want to feed my girlfriend."

"Wait!" Sage called out. When he turned, there was a delighted smirk on her face. "Some asshole threw my ball all the way over there."

She pointed to where her ball sat in the far corner of the gym.

David let out a resigned sigh, realizing that this was life with Sage Fogerty. A life where the only thing that could possibly interfere with eating was basketball, the thing that brought them together in the first place.

He shifted his weight. "Race you," he taunted, breaking out into a sprint, blowing right past Sage just in time to hear her shouted "Fuck!"

And then he heard the squeak of footsteps behind him, and he started to laugh. Even as his lungs burned and his muscles protested, still stiff from a night spent on Chuck's couch.

He didn't even care when Sage passed him, snatching the ball up and immediately launching into a series of taunts that all revolved around him being old and slow.

He didn't care because Sage was smiling so wide that her mouth was open, and each of her exhales came out as a laugh.

He'd done that. And there was nothing in the world that David Hughes loved more than seeing the people he cared about safe and happy.

CHAPTER 25
SO FUCKING POLITE
DAVID

David Hughes stood on Sage Fogerty's doormat, bouquet of flowers in hand.

After returning from the gym they'd parted ways, agreeing to meet at Sage's place after they'd both cleaned up. It *was* their first date, after all.

David had taken the time to shower and change into jeans and a soft orange button up that he normally only pulled out for the birthday parties of his friends' wives, which always were somewhere too fancy that didn't serve enough food.

Sage answered the door in faded jeans and a little tank top that exposed the softness of her belly. And her nipples — *goddamnit* this woman was going to kill him with her hard little nipples pressed against the almost transparent white fabric. Her hair was still wet, pulled back into a braid that curved over her shoulder.

He was so fucking done for her.

"Hey," she breathed, lips quirking up into that crooked smile.

"Hi." David was probably smiling like an idiot, but he couldn't find it in himself to care.

She stepped aside and pointed over her shoulder. "I have steaks."

David slipped out of his shoes before walking into the living room. "I got you these," David said, holding out the flowers and feeling suddenly shy standing there in front of her.

Sage took the bouquet from him, burying her nose between the blooms and taking a slow inhale. Her eyes fluttered shut and her cheeks flushed pink. "They smell amazing," she breathed, opening her eyes and smiling up at him. "Thank you."

"I'll get you more," he blurted. "Flowers. I know it's your thing, but can it be my thing too? Or would that be too many flowers?"

Sage's expression was so fond and her cheeks so pink, like maybe she was a little bit embarrassed on his behalf. "You're ridiculous," she said as she exhaled a soft snort. "There's no such thing as too many flowers."

She moved to the kitchen, and David followed, watching as she put the flowers into a large glass jar. Then she opened the fridge and took out a plate with two thick ribeyes stacked on it.

Jesus, this woman.

Sage wasn't facing him; her hands were busy in a way that only someone who is able to multitask in the kitchen can achieve. She chopped, sliced, stirred, and David watched the golden light in the room catch on the dips and swells of her shoulders and her strong upper back.

He knew that he should offer to help, but in that moment he couldn't tear himself away from the simple joy of watching her.

"I want to tell you something about me," Sage said suddenly, her hands never faltering from their sure movements. "I think it might help. You told me about what happened with Johnny, and I feel like I understand you better now. I get you in a way that I didn't before." She glanced back over her shoulder at him. "I've never had a boyfriend, but unless all of the books I've ever read are based on complete bullshit, I'm pretty sure that being honest is a good place to start a relationship."

David smiled as he leaned his elbows on the bar. "I don't think your books were lying," he agreed.

"My dad left when I was little," Sage continued, turning back to her cooking. "He was a successful man who had one of those jobs in upper management with a corner office. One day he came home with divorce papers and told my mom that he'd fallen in love with his secretary, and he left us with nothing to start another family." A sharp sizzle filled the air as she laid the steaks carefully down in a cast iron. "I don't really remember him, but it fucked my mom up. Like *really* fucked her up. She hadn't worked since she'd had Brinley, and all of a sudden she was a single mom who had to support two kids. She'd never finished her degree, and it was like all of the choices she'd made over the years to make her relationship with my dad work came back to haunt her at once." Sage opened the oven, using a kitchen towel to protect her hand as she pulled out a pan of roasted asparagus.

"So I grew up with a single, hard-working mother who, like a broken record, constantly reminded us of the dangers of older, successful men. I understood where she was coming from, but I think it maybe hurt us — Brinley and me — more than it helped." She flipped the steaks one by one. "I think it maybe led me to crave that forbidden thing she talked about. Maybe it led me to Evan." She shrugged, and David noticed that the mention of him seemed easier, like maybe the grip that experience had held on her had loosened.

"Last night at the game my mom saw you looking at me." Sage turned around, leaning her body back against the counter in a way that somehow accentuated the bare skin of her stomach leading down to her jeans. "And then she saw how I was looking at you, and then she knew, because she's my mom and just *knows* things. Of course then that led to another lecture about older men and inevitable hurt and relinquishing freedom." Sage looked at him, *really* looked at him with all of her attention, leaving no doubt that she was there with him. That they were together in this.

"After that I just needed some time to, I don't know, recalibrate, maybe?" She shook her head, like that wasn't the right word for what she was trying to express. "But it wasn't about you. It wasn't about how I feel about you or how you are with me, because you've never been anything but respectful, David." Her lips curved up into a smirk. "Sometimes too respectful, if I'm honest."

"I wish I'd asked what was going on," he said, hating that she'd been struggling and he'd missed it.

Sage's smile softened. "It's not on you. I shouldn't have disappeared without telling you. Now that I know what that was like for you, I'm not going to do it again. We've got to figure each other out, right? Sometimes I need a little room to breathe when I'm sad, just like you need to know that the people you care about are safe. It's just who we are."

Sage turned back to pull the steaks from the pan. David watched her, considering how to say what he wanted to. Words were such clumsy things when compared to the acute truth of what he felt in his chest. "I just...Sage, I want to do this right. I already know that I like spending time with you, and I know that I'm attracted to you, but now that this is *real* I don't want to mess it up."

Steaks set out on a plate, Sage turned back to face him. "All we can do is show up and try, right?"

"Right," David agreed, feeling light and almost giddy, like he could tip over into laughter at the smallest thing.

God. She was his. After months of wanting and imagining, he was here and she was his.

Two minutes later they sat at Sage's small round table with plates piled high with ribeyes, mashed potatoes, and grilled asparagus. She'd pushed the vase of blue flowers to the side so that they could see all of each other while they ate, and she lit a short, golden-colored candle on the table between them.

They'd shared countless meals together, mostly while sprawled out on the couch watching game tape or hunched over whatever novels they were reading. Sometimes they'd talk, catching up on menial things like the team or Sage's classes or whether or not Daisy liked the organic treats more than the non-organic ones.

But tonight, as they sat across from each other at the table, their silverware scraping against Sage's colorful ceramic plates, David was painfully aware of how little he knew about her. He knew her in the way that friends know what it feels like to share a space together, but what about *her*?

"What's your favorite color?"

Oh god, David.

"Green." Sage paused to chew before pointing her fork at him. "You?"

"Blue." *Like shallow water or pantsuits or the flowers right there on the table between them.*

Sage's smile grew. "Favorite movie?"

"*Goodfellas.*"

"Seriously?" Sage laughed, her face transforming into surprised delight. "I *so* didn't expect that."

"What'd you expect?"

She shrugged, her smile turning teasing and playful. "You seem more like a *Wayne's World* kind of guy."

David laughed, leaning back in his chair and stretching one of his legs out. He glanced down, noticing how close his foot was to hers. Black Costco cotton next to colorful knit wool.

"So what about you," he asked, right as his foot nudged hers.

For a moment she was still against him. But then, in a move that was more tentative than he would have expected from someone like Sage, she shifted so that her foot rested on top of his.

He watched her lips part, her lower lip so plump and enticing that he wanted to bite it. Lick it. Hold it between his teeth with just enough pressure to make her breath hitch.

Her voice was noticeably breathy when she responded. "*Love and Basketball,*" she said, her eyes darting down to where her foot rested on top of his.

David felt his smile spread. "Of course it is."

Sage rolled her eyes, but her cheeks were pink and she couldn't contain her smile.

Somehow they got from favorite movies to sports movies which then led to an in depth discussion about the best coaches in professional basketball. The food — which was *delicious* — disappeared from their plates as they talked, and somehow it was the same as it had always been with Sage while also feeling completely different. There was a newness and excitement hovering just under the surface, like his heartbeat couldn't quite settle into a slow, easy rhythm.

Conversation continued as they carried their dishes to the sink. It continued as David washed and Sage dried, and as Sage tracked down glass tupperware to pack away the leftover potatoes, David washed the pots and pans.

He listened carefully as Sage told him *exactly* how one should and shouldn't wash a cast iron pan. "No soap. *Never* soap," she'd practically growled, stopping him before he could touch the soapy sponge to the surface of the pan.

She grabbed a beer for David — Corona, he noticed fondly — and a glass of peach wine for herself.

"It's probably the most embarrassing thing about me," she said as she folded her legs under herself. "I know it's disgustingly sweet, but I love it and life is too short to waste time drinking things I don't like."

"Fair enough," David said, lowering himself down to the opposite side of the couch.

He took a long pull from his beer, watching how Sage's eyes dropped to his throat as he swallowed.

He lowered the beer to rest on his thigh, unable to take his eyes from her.

He noticed her shifting her weight where she sat, how the movement pulled at the bare skin of her stomach. The flush from her cheeks trailed down her neck and onto her chest, the skin pink and practically glowing in the golden light.

His heartbeat seemed to grow louder, the thumping sensation spreading from his chest up into his throat and down into his abdomen. Anticipation, the culmination of months of denying the way his body demanded the woman in front of him, had his cock twitching against his thigh.

He was so tired of waiting.

Sage cleared her throat. "Um," she began, and while her voice had the slightest tremble, her eyes held his gaze, green and bright and burning. "Is there a reason that we're not...you know..." She trailed off, waving her hand back and forth between them.

He immediately knew what she was asking.

Relief was instantaneously replaced by a raging, torrential need to touch her. He could finally loosen the hold on himself, let his body do what it had wanted to do for months now.

"Thank god," he said with a ragged laugh, setting down his beer and reaching for her. "Come here."

There was a sudden flurry of movement, legs and arms and the cushions dipping and then suddenly Sage Forgety was in his lap again. Her strong thighs bracketed his hips, her weight settling on him, and then her mouth was on his.

Sage kissed him like she knew exactly what she wanted. Their lips slotted together, her plump bottom lip trapped between his, and *fuck*, somehow it was even better than he'd remembered. Even better than the kiss in his doorway that had played over and over in his head.

Her body softened against his as he hardened beneath her. She tasted like peaches, and beeswax and mint from the chapstick she wore, and he pressed his tongue forward, groaning as she opened for him.

But her tongue was there and ready, immediately tangling with his. He tried to slow down, to let their bodies move slowly together as they eased over this final barrier between them. He wanted to savor this moment, when Sage became his in a way that he'd only imagined.

"Is this okay," he asked, resting his hands on her ass.

Sage hummed in response, and then they were kissing again, only this time David used his grip on her to pull her hips toward him, fitting her snuggly over the front of his jeans where his cock strained against the fabric.

David drank down her moan as her center met him, and he felt her long fingers reach up and tangle in his hair, tugging and pulling, using her hold on him to find a rhythm, rolling her hips against him.

His body was on fire. Energy hummed through him, his muscles straining with everything he wanted to do with her — *to* her. Every brush of her core against him — even through their clothing — had him closer to detonating, to coming in his pants like a goddamn teenager.

One of his hands slipped up her back, meeting nothing but soft, bare skin. "Is this okay," he whispered, dropping his mouth to her jaw, where he kissed and licked and, carefully, nipped with his teeth.

Suddenly he was wrenched away. Sage gripped his face between her hands, and she glared at him with a combination of heat and annoyance. He noticed, with satisfaction, that her lips were already swollen and red from his attention. "Remember when I told you to treat me however you want?"

David swallowed. "Yeah, Lefty. I remember."

"Then stop being so fucking polite," she commanded, bringing their faces together so that their foreheads barely touched. "I want you."

Maybe it was what David had been waiting for — confirmation that she was as ravenous for him as he was for her. Her body communicated the same thing: flushed skin, shallow, panting breaths, green eyes taking on the dazed look of someone driven by insatiable want.

And so he stopped holding back. He let go completely, a low sound rumbling from his chest as his thumbs brushed over her nipples. He decided then that he lived for the little hitches of her breath when he touched her.

Her hips continued to work against him, but he could tell that it wasn't enough. That even though her body and his cock were meeting, she needed more.

And it was his goddamn job to give it to her.

In one move, he shifted Sage so that she was straddling one of his thighs. Immediately she responded with a gasped "Fuck," and a shiver went through her entire body as her center met his broad leg. Maintaining his tight grip on her hips, he guided her to resume the rolling rhythm of forward and down, then back. Forward and down, then back.

Each roll forward elicited a desperate whimper. She tossed her head back, revealing her long neck and closed eyes as she took from him. He'd never been so happy to provide, fucking euphoric at the idea that she was using his body however she pleased.

"Oh, fuck, David," she gasped.

Leaning forward, he drew one of her tight nipples into his mouth, sucking at her through the thin fabric of her shirt. He felt her shudder against him, and David doubled his effort, sucking and licking, alternating between breasts as he felt her rhythm begin to falter.

"You're going to come, aren't you, Lefty?" He almost didn't recognize the rough voice as his own, but once the words started, he couldn't stop them. "Fuck, you beautiful girl. Look at you." He scraped her nipple with his teeth, never taking his eyes from her flushed face. "Never seen something so good. You're going to come on my leg and it'll be the prettiest thing I've ever fucking seen."

He felt the exact moment when she tipped over the edge.

Her body tensed, went suddenly still, and then tremors wracked her entire body, starting from between her legs and radiating outward. Her mouth opened and *damnit* he'd been right, unable to hold back his own choked shout as she came with a silent scream.

"Take it," he panted, hands steady on her hips as she rode out the orgasm, feeling the throbbing demand of his own body that begged to follow her. "Take what you need from me."

Her movements slowed, the sound of her labored breaths filling the thick air between them.

He needed to come. *Fuck,* he needed it. He glanced down at where his hard cock stood lewdly at attention behind his fly. Looking back up at Sage, he found her glazed eyes were on him.

"Can I," he began, removing a hand from her hip and moving to the button at his waist.

Sage inhaled sharply. "Fuck yes," she breathed. "Show me."

As David brought both hands up to free himself from his jeans, Sage shifted back to straddle his thighs, leaving enough room between them for them both to have a perfect view.

A groan rumbled in his throat as he took himself in hand, shoving his briefs down and out of the way.

This wasn't the time for slow and indulgent, even though with Sage's gaze fixed on his fist a part of him wanted to put on a show. To make it good for her.

But he couldn't hold back. He began to stroke himself, rough and quick, gripping tightly enough that it hurt a little bit. Just the way he liked it.

He wasn't going to last, so he watched Sage, letting her fuel the pleasure that already burned through him. He took in the dark, damp circles over her nipples where his mouth had been on her. He took in the pink flush of her bare skin. He took in the way she watched his fist like she was committing his movements to memory. Like she wanted to learn what pleased him as much as he wanted to know how to please her.

David came with a strangled moan, sharp heat searing down his spine as his release coated his fist. Pulse after pulse of pleasure leaving him stuck in that timeless place just after orgasm for what felt like entire minutes.

He hadn't realized that he'd closed his eyes until he opened them and found Sage staring at him with rapt attention, her tongue licking across her lower lip as she glanced between his face and the absolute mess he'd made of himself.

David watched, frozen, still trying to convince his lungs to work properly, as Sage reached down and grabbed his wrist where he still gripped his softening cock. He let her lift his hand up, not fully comprehending what was happening until she drew two of his fingers into her lush mouth.

She held eye contact with him as she licked his hand clean — finger by finger.

If he was a younger man, he'd be hard and ready to go again, but as it was his cock barely mustered a half-hearted twitch as her tongue worked against his skin.

When she was done, she pressed a tender kiss to his palm.

"You're fucking incredible," David breathed, slumping back against the couch to enjoy the view of her above him.

Her swollen mouth curved up in a smile that was almost shy. "You're not so bad yourself," she said, and then immediately was overtaken by a yawn.

David squeezed her thighs. "You tired?"

"Mmhm." She tilted toward him, laying her head on his shoulder and nosing against his throat. "Want to stay?"

Of course he wanted to stay. But he had plans with this woman.

"Yes," he said, kissing her mussed hair. "But not tonight."

"Why not?"

"Because I want to take you on a real date first."

She huffed. "Lame."

David pinched her thigh, grinning when she squeaked in protest. "Shut up, Lefty."

Sage climbed off of him, obviously reluctant to separate them. Standing between his thighs, she leaned forward and braced herself on his knees. Her lips brushed his in a soft kiss. "I'm pretty fucking happy right now," she whispered.

Before she could move away from him, David wrapped his

arms around the back of her thighs. He wasn't ready to end the closeness between them.

"Me too," he replied, resting his chin against her stomach. "So we're doing this?"

"Dating?"

"Mmhm."

One of her hands came up to comb through his hair. "Yeah, David. We're doing this."

David smiled. Somehow his chest grew even warmer, even more full and content. He pressed a quick kiss to her exposed hip before looking back up at her. "Every year my buddies from college make a trip out to Lake Murray over spring break. We rent a big house and grill out and swim and a few of us make fools of ourselves trying to fish. Will you come with me?"

Sage blinked down at him. "Are you sure?"

"I'm sure," David didn't hesitate to reply. "Please?"

She looked at him like she couldn't quite believe that he was serious, as if asking her was something unexpected. "Okay." She paused, seeming to consider her question before she spoke. "Do you think it would be alright if I invited Maggie?"

"Of course," David said, confident that his friends would welcome both Sage and the fiery bartender with open arms. "She'll drive Keaton nuts," he added, already imagining his tightly buttoned friend clashing with Maggie's brash and unrestrained sense of humor. "It'll be perfect."

Sage smiled. "I'll ask her tomorrow," she said.

David pressed another kiss to the skin of her belly, already imagining Sage stretched out on the hot wood of the dock with miles of bare skin for him to explore. How her blonde hair would look catching the pinks and oranges of the sunsets.

"Breakfast tomorrow?" David asked as he got up, tangling his fingers with Sage's just because he could.

"Deal." She went up on her toes, silently asking for another kiss.

David smiled even as he kissed her, their tongues meeting for a brief moment before he pulled away again.

"Goodnight, Lefty," he said, still not quite able to believe that this was real, that he was kissing Sage Fogerty after she'd come so beautifully on his leg and cleaned up his mess with that perfect mouth of hers.

He was still smiling when he walked into his apartment and was greeted by Daisy, whose tail wagged hard enough that her entire body wriggled. Leaning down to scratch at her ears, David whispered, "We did it, Daisy. We got the girl."

CHAPTER 26
A BASEMENT DATE
SAGE

Sage had her backpack slung over one shoulder and her duffel in hand as she approached David's Bronco idling in front of her apartment.

"Hi." David flashed his wide smile at her through the open passenger window.

Dark sunglasses rested on the ridge of his nose, and a black baseball cap was pulled down over his head. He wore a white t-shirt that stretched over the muscles of his chest.

This man was *hers*. Hers to touch and kiss and climb like a tree.

It was all a bit hard to believe, even as she tossed her stuff in the back seat and climbed into the front. Even as she leaned across the center console and pressed her lips to his. Even as their tongues tangled, caressing with growing urgency until she felt the warmth of pleasure ignite in her lower abdomen.

Pulling away, David reached out a big hand and squeezed her thigh. "Ready?"

Sage nodded, looking into the back where Daisy was curled up on a blanket, fast asleep.

The drive to Lake Murray would take about two and a half hours. The rest of the group had left earlier that Friday, but Sage had had an afternoon meeting with her advisor about a project for his class. David had been entirely unbothered when she'd told him about the delay to their departure, claiming it gave him extra time to "shop for road snacks."

Maggie had immediately agreed to come when Sage asked, claiming that she was due a holiday from the bar and that she was "really good at lakes," whatever that meant. She would be driving her own car up the next morning.

"I made you a tea," he said, gesturing to the to-go mug in the cup holder. "I also brought chips, sliced apples, three different kinds of chocolate, those weird mustard pretzels you like, and cheese sticks."

This ridiculous, beautiful man.

"That should probably cover us," she teased, slipping out of her flip flops and resting her feet on the dash in front of her.

David swatted at her leg. "Feet down."

"Why?"

He huffed. "If we're in an accident, you're going to crush both of your legs, Lefty."

"Fine. But I get to DJ." She grabbed her phone and plugged it into the audio cable that went in through the tape deck.

Soon, she was singing along with Kacey Musgraves, watching as the blur of suburbia faded into big swaths of green only interrupted by the seemingly endless waterways that wound through that part of the state.

She knew that she wasn't the *best* singer, but she couldn't find it in herself to give a fuck, not when she caught David's occasional glances, and the way a fond smile curved his lips every time he looked at her. He looked at her in a way that made her feel inexplicably good and whole, like his affection wasn't conditional on her being a certain way, looking a certain way, or behaving a certain way.

They made one stop for gas and a bathroom break, and it was dusk when they pulled off of the two-lane highway, following a winding road through the dense forest that surrounded Lake Murray.

Long driveways curved away from the road, leading to houses that were hidden by the trees. They drove for a few minutes before they reached a quiet stretch of road with a cul-de-sac up ahead. David slowed and turned down a driveway that was marked with a stone mailbox.

The narrow drive was lined with flowering pink camellias and neatly trimmed oaks, and took two or three turns before it opened up to a large, brightly lit home. Two cars were already parked in the driveway, and Daivd pulled up behind them, cutting the engine.

He glanced over at Sage. "Ready?"

She reached into the back seat and scooped up a wriggling Daisy. "Let's do it."

The instant the large wooden front door opened, Sage was swept through a series of loud and very overwhelming introductions. She barely had time to put Daisy down on the floor before she was pulled into the social frenzy.

"Sup, team manager," Chuck shouted from where he sprawled on one of the long leather sectionals.

"I'm Rebecca," called out a stunningly beautiful woman wearing a white sundress. Thick braids were coiled up in a bun on the top of her head, and her lips were painted a fuchsia pink that glowed against her warm mahogany skin. Her smile was wide and warm. "We've heard so much about you."

She pulled on the arm of a well-dressed man who was about as tall as David. Sage vaguely recognized him from the first night she met David at the bar — shaved head, kind eyes, and a small gap between his two front teeth. "This is my husband, Darius."

"And I think I owe you an apology for cock blocking you," another man said, awkwardly waving from where he sat next to Chuck.

Chuck reached over and punched him in the shoulder. "Seriously, Tommy?"

"What?" Tommy had mousy brown hair and an unremarkable haircut, and his t-shirt and board shorts showed off the kind of muscles that came from hours spent in the gym trying to look a certain way.

"You're an idiot," Chuck added, before turning back to Sage. "This is Tommy. If he hadn't been on the team with Hughes and Darius we would've dropped him years ago."

Sage hadn't caught Tommy's response, because another man was introducing himself.

"Keaton Redd," he said as he offered his hand, his Southern accent more pronounced than the others. "Pleasure to meet you."

"Nice to meet you," Sage replied, appreciatively looking the man up and down.

Where David was dark-eyed, dark-haired and always a bit disheveled, Keaton was green-eyed, blonde, and meticulously put together. His skin was a warm beige, like he spent just enough time in the sun to seem like an outdoorsman. His hair was long enough that it curled down below his ears, and he wore it combed back like an old-money heir. Honestly, based on how he dressed — some sort of linen shorts and a chambray button up with the sleeves rolled to his elbows — he probably did come from wealth.

Sage felt a warm hand wrap around her waist. One tug and she stumbled back, stilling when she felt David's firm body against her.

She craned her neck to look back at him, unable to keep the grin from her face when she saw him glowering at her. "What?" she teased, keeping her voice quiet, just for him. "You've been hiding your hot friends from me."

David's scowl deepened. "So what if I have?" He glared over her head, like he was considering challenging Keaton to some ridiculous contest of strength in order to prove his own worth.

Sage snorted a laugh. "You are a fucking silly, beautiful man," she murmured, pressing a kiss to the underside of his jaw. The stubble there tickled her lips, and she felt a shiver of wanting travel down her spine.

David made a low growling sound that only made Sage laugh harder.

"I see it," Sage heard Keaton comment from behind them.

"I told you they were adorable," Chuck's voice chimed in.

"Alright, leave them alone." Sage turned around to see Rebecca walking toward them, shaking her head at the rest of the group. "David, we put you guys in the corner room with the lake view."

David nodded, obviously understanding her.

"Why don't you take the bags up and I'll take Sage out back." Rebecca shot Sage a conspiratorial smile. "Ever since the steak disaster of 2011, I've been the designated grill mistress."

"It's not my fault I saw a Curlew sandpiper!" Darius protested from where he had started chopping a head of cauliflower in the kitchen. "They're incredibly rare."

"*Thought* you saw," David added, his hand squeezing her hip before he withdrew and reached for their bags, which they'd placed on the bench by the front door. He smiled fondly at her, watching her with a kind of intensity that made Sage's skin heat. "Go," he encouraged, nodding toward Rebecca. "And don't believe anything she tells you about me."

Sage grinned. "Of course not," she said, turning and following Rebecca out a back door.

Even in the growing darkness, Sage could see what a beautiful place they were in. The wide wooden deck was lit with string lights, and a long, driftwood table surrounded by chairs stretched across one side. An outdoor seating area was tucked in the other corner, oriented to look out at the view of the lake. Close to the door there was a large grill, trailing gray smoke up into the darkness.

Sage walked to look out over the railing.

The house was built on a hill; while they'd walking in the front door on the ground floor, the back balcony was raised above ground. Below, Sage could see a flagstone patio with a firepit encircled by Adirondack chairs. From there, she could barely make out a stone path that led down to a long dock that stretched out into quiet, black water.

"This place is incredible," she said.

Rebecca came up beside her, crossing her arms and leaning on the railing. "Isn't it? Keaton's family knows the homeowner. They started coming here for spring break when they were seniors, and they've been coming every year since."

"When did you join?"

Rebecca laughed. The sound was rich, and matched her voice, which was low and musical. "Darius and I met eight years ago, but he waited a year before he invited me along. Do you want a drink?"

"Sure. What do you have?"

"Everything, honestly," Rebecca said with that low laugh again. "Beer, wine, a pitcher of margaritas in the fridge. Someone brought a handle of Southern Comfort, and of course Keaton brought some sort of scotch that comes in a hand carved wooden box. Rich prick," she added, but Sage could hear the fondness in her voice.

"A margarita would be great." Sage replied, feeling something inside of her relax at how genuinely *nice* this stranger was being to her.

"Good choice," Rebecca said as she slipped back inside.

Sage let out a slow breath. She'd been nervous about coming here with David's friends. It was still so new between them, and they'd both been busy to the point that it felt like they barely had time to do anything other than share meals and fool around on the couch.

It was silly, really, but Sage had somehow reached twenty-three years old without ever actually dating someone. Well, technically she'd gone on a closely supervised date to the bowling alley with Brock Harlow when they were 6th graders, but that didn't count.

Her first experience of anything that resembled a relationship was whatever she was supposed to call what she had with Evan.

She'd been obsessed with him all while trying to feign unaffectedness; the only thing worse than having a secret high school hook-up was a high school hook-up who couldn't keep her emotions in check.

Standing there on the deck right on the edge of the darkness, it was easy to look back on that time in her life from a distance. To see Evan White for what he'd been: a predator. But it was still just as easy for her to remember what it had been like to be the girl who'd received his advances like they might save her. Like if she could craft herself into the person and player he saw in her, then maybe she could have it all.

But of course that had ended, and, as a college student, she had found the transactional nature of the hook-up scene suited her. Meet someone, go back to their place, romp around and hopefully get off, and never stay the night.

It had worked well for her.

Actually dating? Actually deciding that she wanted more with a man than a physical exchange of *you come/I come*? The thought was still terrifying.

But she couldn't imagine *not* doing it with David. The idea of giving up his company was inconceivable. And his friendship *and* his body and orgasms?

Sign her the fuck up.

So she'd dove into dating David Hughes with no idea what to expect. And so far, it was shockingly similar to how things had already been between them.

They already hung out. They already shared meals. They already texted each other throughout the day.

Of course, now there were other things.

There was the fact that David was a toucher. He had his hands on her body at all times, either holding her hand, touching her lower back, or, when they sprawled out to read on his couch, he hauled her feet up onto his lap and dug his big thumbs into her arches. She was now, officially, a foot rub person.

There were also kisses — quick kisses in greeting, prolonged goodnight kisses where his big hands cradled her face with a tenderness that threatened to melt her.

And then there were the kisses that led to more, typically involving him pressing her against the closest solid surface, their tongues curling together in a way that made her core throb.

Those were her favorite.

A part of her was surprised that in the three weeks that had passed since the season concluded they hadn't progressed beyond their hands. Her hand wrapped around him, tugging and twisting until he came with one of those choked groans that lit her skin on fire, and his fingers — long, thick, and so much rougher than hers — circling her clit with perfect, steady pressure before pressing inside of her, ultimately causing her complete obliteration.

David approached touching her like a scientist, watching her face and body, gauging each and every reaction. When she grew too still he adjusted, whereas when she trembled and jerked he remained steady and consistent. When she whispered "Harder" because she couldn't wait another second, he obliged.

And she *came*.

Every single fucking time, Sage came with a silent, twisting shudder, like her body still couldn't quite believe that this man had done that again. That *any* man had the patience and attention to get her off consistently.

"Here you go." Rebecca walked up beside her and handed her a glass.

"Thanks." Sage took a sip, humming as soon as the tang of lime hit her taste buds. "Fuck, that's good."

Rebecca grinned. "Darius may be worthless with a grill, but he makes a damn good margarita." She nodded toward the grill, where a tray of steaks sat waiting. "Want to help?"

Soon, she and Rebecca were deep into a discussion of steak cooking techniques. Rebecca swore by the grill, whereas Sage had only ever used a cast iron. They both agreed that butter was necessary, but disagreed about whether or not rosemary was too overpowering.

Before long the rest of the group joined them. The guys carried out bowls of food and place settings for the long table, talking over each other and effortlessly oscillating between teasing and sincerity in the way that only people who have spent many years together could do. More drinks were poured, the steaks were served, and then they were all sitting together, passing around the various dishes and making last minute runs to the kitchen for whatever they'd forgotten.

It was all delicious. The steaks were accompanied by roasted cauliflower and sweet potatoes, steamed green beans, a spinach salad, and a loaf of bread that had come from a Charleston bakery Sage had never heard of.

She mostly listened, piecing together who each of them were from how the conversation flowed.

Rebecca owned a successful hair salon in Cannonborough, and she'd recently expanded her business to include other cosmetic services as well. Darius was a science teacher at a small local high school, and seemed to truly love the work that he did.

Tommy was the manager of a rental car office. It was one of those companies that taught business and managerial skills, and he was currently in the chase for a promotion to a regional manager position. His ex-wife, Courtney, had apparently taken their dog, which Tommy was still salty about, but couldn't justify racking up more court fees to get him back.

Sage also learned that Tommy spent a lot of time at Chuck's house, either raiding his fridge or napping on his couch. She couldn't figure out if Chuck was actually annoyed with Tommy — the fond, almost soft looks the red-headed man kept sending him didn't exactly scream *'pain in my ass.'*

Keaton was a stereotype of Southern wealth plucked right from the pages of *Charleston Magazine*. He was a lawyer at his father's firm, Redd and Whitaker, and was one of those men who was deeply committed to his weekly visit to the golf club. He'd been on the swim team with Chuck, which was how he'd gotten in with the group back in college.

Sage also learned that another couple, Ford and Louisa, usually came along for the trip, but they'd just had a baby in November and decided to sit out the year.

They included Sage in the conversation too, asking about her degree and how she'd liked her time at Southeastern. There were also plenty of questions about what it was like having David as a boss, no matter how many times they tried to clarify that he hadn't *technically* been in charge of her. Throughout it all, David kept a steady, firm hand on her thigh, his thumb absently brushing the bare skin revealed by her cut-off jean shorts.

They were a good group of people, Sage thought, as the meal wound to a close. She stepped right in as plates were stacked and empty glasses gathered. She and Chuck loaded the dishwasher while Keaton hand-washed the larger dishes, Darius dried them, and David returned them to their proper places in the tall, hard-wood cabinets that filled the open kitchen. Tommy and Rebecca dished up the leftovers, arguing about which movie they should watch that night.

Drinks were refilled and the group started moving toward the living room, where two leather sectionals made a large U shape around an absurdly large TV. Sage was following along, going with the flow of the group, when someone tugged at her hand.

She turned, looking up at David's face as he pulled her in the opposite direction. His smile was almost bashful, maybe a little bit embarrassed as he led her back behind the kitchen, through a door, and down a sparsely-lit narrow stairwell.

When they reached the bottom David flicked on a light, revealing a basement that had been converted into a combination man-cave and arcade room. A polished wooden bar was built into one corner, and a pool table and foosball table took up most of the open space in the middle of the room. A few old arcade games stood against one wall, and the whole mood was set by the old pool lights that hung down from the ceiling.

Sage turned to David. "What are we doing?"

He scratched his beard. "Ah, we're going on a date."

"In the basement?"

David looked around them, rocking back on his heels as his cheeks puffed out with a loud exhale. "Yeah. That's the plan."

"Not that I don't love a good game of pool," Sage began, taking a step toward him. "But why exactly are we calling this a date?"

David groaned, scrubbing at his face with his hands. "Because I'm an idiot and I made some comment about taking you on a real date before spending the night with you. And we've both been so busy that it hasn't happened yet. And now here we are, about to share a bed for the first time, and I haven't had the chance to do the thing that I said I was going to do." He let out a harsh exhale, wincing. "So now I'm improvising and I know it's lame, but —"

Sage cut him off with a kiss. One of the slow ones that felt indulgent, like they had all of the time in the world.

After they broke apart, their breathing heavy, Sage walked over to the cue rack, picking one at random. "A basement date it is then," she said, and honestly, she couldn't imagine anything better than getting her ass kicked in pool by a man like David Hughes.

Especially if the night ended with them in bed together.

They were both terrible at pool.

David was marginally better, but even he occasionally missed entirely.

They kept getting distracted — first with a heated discussion about who was most likely to step into the captaincy on the team next season, then a debate about what music they should play, which David won when he put on The Eagles.

Sage teased David's lack of skill, only to scratch immediately after. David decided that leaning coyly against the table with his ass popped out was the best way to distract her, and, well, he wasn't wrong; the man had an incredible ass.

There was a lightness to David there in that basement, a playfulness that Sage had never seen in him. Like he was in a place where he could fully relax and let go of whatever worries usually weighed on him. He was quick to laugh, and his smile never faded.

Sage had four balls left and David had two when she trailed her fingers up his back as he bent over to shoot. She had three left when he crowded her against the table's edge, dropping kisses on the sensitive skin where her shoulder met her neck.

David was on his last shot when Sage leaned out over the table across from him, fully aware of the fact that the low neckline of her tank-top likely meant that he was getting an eye full of her tits.

When he missed, Sage threw her head back in a delighted laugh.

When David circled the table and picked her up before depositing her on the edge of the pool table, her body flared to life. He stepped between her thighs, and her breath caught in her throat as his hands cupped her breasts, thumbs brushing back and forth over the tips of her nipples.

Sage arched into his touch, finding a glimmer of relief, and yet craving more and needing more to the point where she felt like she might explode if he stopped.

"David," she gasped, her voice coming out in a desperate whine. "Where's our room?"

Rather than answering, David pulled her to her feet, and, linking their hands together, dragged her from the room.

They ran together up the basement staircase, through the kitchen and past the living room, ignoring the catcalls and whistles from the group watching the movie. Then David was pulling her up another flight of stairs. When he reached the top he turned to the right, running down a long hallway until they reached the final closed door.

David flung the door open, tugged Sage through, and then slammed it shut behind them.

They were on each other immediately.

It only took seconds for them to wrestle each other out of their clothes, leaving Sage in nothing but her underwear and David in black briefs. His skin was hot, his hair coarse under her touch as she ran her palms up his chest.

Again, David kissed her. The kiss was frenzied, their lips pulling and tongues battling, like they were still figuring out their rhythm together. David's hands, which rested on her hips, guided her forward, even as their mouths remained fused together. Without warning, David tipped backwards onto the large bed, pulling her down on top of him.

The kiss broke as David shifted beneath her, scooting up the bed until he lay flat against the white comforter that glowed in the dim light from the lamp on the bedside table.

For a moment, she simply ogled him.

For someone with such a strong body, David was capable of incredible softness. His body was sprawled out, the curves and swells of his muscular legs soft and lax against the white duvet.

She needed to touch him, so she climbed up his long body, trailing her fingertips up his thighs and skirting over the fabric of his briefs. For the moment, she intentionally ignored the thick press of his erection straining against the dark cotton.

She straddled his thighs, the width of him spreading her open, and she watched as his dark eyes dropped down to where her cotton thong barely covered her. Her fingers continued their journey, dragging over the softness of his stomach and over his hairy chest, and she relished the way that his breath hitched and stuttered under her touch.

She looked up at his face. His gaze was burning, eyes almost black, and there was no mistaking the unfiltered want in the way that he looked at her. His face, already a specimen of masculine beauty, was somehow more striking in that moment than she'd ever seen. Her eyes dipped down to his mouth, at his soft, barely parted lips.

In a sudden change of direction, her fingers trailed down his torso until she reached the waistband of his briefs.

"I want to suck your cock."

A choked groan fell from David's mouth, and she felt his muscles strain and flex under her hands. "Fuck. Okay. Yes, please." The words were rushed and his voice rasped as he added, "only if you want…"

Sage wasted no time pulling the briefs down, her breath catching in her throat when her movement freed the hard length of him. He was so fucking beautiful — his spread thighs covered in a smattering of dark hair, and his cock thick and leaking against his lower belly.

She couldn't believe that she'd spent hours of her life with this man without doing *this*. Not when he looked so good and watched her like she was something precious. Like she was a gift.

Letting her eyes fall shut, she lowered her mouth to him.

The moment her tongue brushed the impossibly soft skin, a broken "Sage" fell from his mouth. She'd never loved the sound of her name as much as she did at that moment. She explored him, starting at the tip and then trailing down to the base that was nestled in thick dark hair. His scent was intoxicating, a mixture of heady, masculine musk and a barely noticeable hint of his soap. Breathing him in as her mouth explored his heavy sac, she relished how every touch elicited a hitch in his heavy, panting breaths. She took him fully into her mouth, swirling her tongue around him before swallowing him down. Her hands on his thighs struggled to hold him in place as his hips bucked up, thrusting him all the way to the back of her throat.

She tried to breathe through her nose, but refused to stop him, not when he was so obviously undone under her attention. She found a rhythm bobbing her head up and down, spending extra seconds in the places that caused his stomach to jump and his thighs to tremble.

"Stop," David growled, pulling her off of him before hauling her up his body. He cradled her face in his huge hands and pulled her mouth to his in a claiming kiss.

Their bodies met, his length jutting up against her core and perfectly brushing the apex of her thighs. A whine escaped her throat as their mouths collided, the kiss perfectly hot and filthy — a promise of what he wanted to do to her.

Sage rolled her hips against him, the building need in her body crossing over into desperation. His cock felt good against her — *so fucking good* — but she was ready for more. Ready to lose the scrap of fabric that still separated them and finally feel him inside of her.

She tore her mouth away from his. "I need it," she panted, the pounding between her thighs like a heartbeat, making her frantic.

She felt David's fingers curl around her braid, tugging her up so that her chest lifted from his.

"I want to taste you," he ground out, and even in dim light she could see the way his eyes raked down her body.

"Not tonight," she said, her voice breathy and strained. "I need you inside me now."

Something that looked a lot like disappointment flashed across David's face, but the expression faded quickly as he nodded up at her.

"Condom?" Sage asked, even as she shifted above him to strip off her underwear.

"Nightstand."

Sage crawled over to the small table, immediately locating the square wrapper. Tearing it open with her teeth, she walked on her knees back over to David.

"You came prepared," she said, her voice rough with want.

David hissed as she rolled the rubber down the length of him. Once he was covered to the base, Sage resumed her position straddling his hips, gripping him in one hand as she hovered over him.

"I didn't want to presume," David began, his strong hands brushing up her sides before wrapping around and settling on her ass. "I can't believe we're here," he said, his whisper full of reverence, like maybe he hadn't meant to say the words out loud.

Rather than responding, Sage began to lower herself onto him. Her head fell back, her breathing shallow, as she accepted him into her body inch by excruciating inch.

It was a stretch, but in an exquisite way that sent spikes of sharp pleasure from her nerves straight to her brain, sending her arousal into a frenzied overdrive. She felt her body adjusting to him, and when he was fully seated inside of her, a whimper fell from her lips.

"You..." David's voice rumbled beneath her. "I knew it was going to be like this. I fucking *knew*."

She hadn't realized that her eyes had drifted shut. Maybe it was her body's way of telling her that the overwhelming satisfaction inside of her warranted the full attention of her senses. Like maybe the sight of him in addition to the feeling of him filling her would have been too much.

She gave her hips an experimental roll forward.

Oh, fuck. *That*. She did it again, only this time David thrust up to meet her.

She couldn't stand the thought of not seeing him, and she forced her eyes open. Immediately, she was hit by the full force of his gaze, and the look in his eye sent a shudder of pleasure down her spine. And as their bodies found movement together, she stared down at him.

So much of what she saw was familiar. There was none of the thrill of discovering someone for the first time, of learning their features and body through intimacy. No, she knew David, and David knew her.

She knew that he was self-conscious of his body, which was incomprehensible because to her, he was a wet dream. She knew that even though dark hair shadowed his jaw and neck he'd only shaved two days ago. She knew the weight and certainty of his touch against her skin. She knew that there was a sweetness to David Hughes that she was only just beginning to see.

"God, Sage. Do you have any idea how many times I've imagined this? You, riding me like you were made for me?" David's voice was low, almost a growl, with his accent slipping out more than she was used to. The sound of stretched vowels and the smoky rasp had her body clenching around him.

His hands gripped her hips and she felt his legs repositioning behind her. His hips thrust up, bucking into her, and the sudden movement had her falling forward, bracing herself against his chest.

"Fuck," she cried, as the new angle had him thrusting directly against that spot inside of her. She shifted, adjusting her body so that in addition to the internal stimulation she could grind her clit against the base of him.

"That's it. Take what you need." Sweat dotted David's forehead, and a piece of his dark hair had flopped forward onto his forehead. "Yours, Sage. This cock is yours. These hands are yours. Tell me what you need and it's done, beautiful."

It built, the pressure between her legs that started like a vibration under the skin of her inner thighs and curled up her spine, tightening her muscles until she couldn't stop the trembling in her arms and legs.

"You," she said, struggling to find enough breath to form words. "You on top. Now."

David moved her like a wrestler, leveraging his strength and size to hold Sage against him as he flipped them. Somehow he was able to execute the entire move without withdrawing from her.

Draping himself over her, his breath was harsh against her chest as he slung one of her legs up and over his arm, spreading her open for him. He rolled his hips forward and her vision blurred. She wrapped her hands behind his neck and tangled her fingers into his hair, hanging on like she wasn't already hurtling toward the edge.

David's head hung down between his shoulders as he moved

above her, and she could feel the harshness of his breath against her breasts every time he thrust inside of her.

"What do you need," he asked between heavy breaths.

Sage untangled one of her hands and reached down between their bodies, finding the wetness of her slit.

"That's it," David praised. "You know exactly what that little clit needs, don't you?"

A moan fell from her mouth as she began rubbing tight, frantic circles, her inner muscles tensing and clenching around him.

"Fuck, Sage," David breathed, and his movements slowed as he dragged his cock in and out of her. It was unhurried, like he was savoring every moment of being inside of her. She felt his lips brush against the sensitive skin on her neck. "It's never been like this. Ever." Another painfully slow thrust that left them both shaking. "I know you won't believe me, but," *thrust*, "this? With you? It's so much, Sage." He sunk his teeth into the place where her neck and shoulder met, biting with unexpected strength before drawing back and running his tongue over the place where his teeth had undoubtedly marked her. "It's so much more than anything else has ever been."

Sage had transcended beyond words, so she kissed him, pulling his face to hers and pouring out all of the feelings and thoughts that she couldn't articulate into each brush and curl of her tongue. Her fingers still worked between her legs, sending her closer and closer to the edge.

With a harsh groan, David sped up, his movements becoming frenzied. Sage felt the shaking in his body, and knew that he was close.

So was she. "I'm almost there," she managed to whisper, knowing that David would be waiting for her. He wouldn't let himself go before she'd found her release. He was just that kind of man.

He groaned. "Get there, please." There was a desperation in his voice that mirrored the way his hips stuttered.

One, two, three more circles and *there*. She was fucking there.

Launched off of a cliff, her entire body tightening and throbbing while her mind went harshly, blissfully blank. Waves and waves of pleasure ripped through her, and there was no choice but to ride it out, wrapped up in the heavy warmth of David's body.

She barely heard the "Yes, Sage. Fuck, yes," that tore from his chest before he followed her, chasing his own release. Even through the overwhelming pull of her own pleasure, she could feel the pulse of him inside of her.

"So good," he breathed, burying his face into the crook of her neck even as his hips continued to thrust almost lazily against her. "So goddamn good."

Sage struggled to find her own breath, her body limp and relaxed, relishing the weight of David on top of her. Her fingers tracked up and down the sweat-slicked skin of his broad back, her chest so full that she thought it might overflow the confines of her skin.

She thought she wouldn't mind staying just like that forever. But after a few more seconds with nothing but the sound of their breaths filling the room, David slowly withdrew from her body, carefully holding the condom in place as he climbed off the bed.

Sage rolled to her side, unabashedly watching his ass as he walked to the door in the corner that she assumed led to a bathroom. He disappeared for a moment before he emerged, still stunningly naked, his sweat-slicked skin practically glowing.

"What," he asked when he noticed her watching him. There was still that softness about him that made something in her chest ache.

"Just admiring your body," she answered honestly.

In a sudden burst of movement, David dove back onto the bed, launching himself at her. She shrieked, but quickly surrendered to the onslaught of kisses.

David pulled the covers over both of them, laying on his side and pulling Sage into his chest. While she loved the tickle of his chest hairs against her nose and the weight of his arms wrapped around her back, Sage knew she wouldn't be able to fall asleep like that.

She pulled away and looked up at him. "I can't do face to face smushed snuggling."

David opened his mouth, and, based on the pained expression on his face, was about to apologize.

Quickly, Sage turned over, scooting herself back until she was perfectly spooned against him, her back nestled against his front. "This I can do," she said.

David's low chuckle ruffled the hairs on the back of her neck. "I can work with this."

CHAPTER 27
CREEPY, BEADY-EYED DEMONS

DAVID

There was nothing in the world that compared to the peace that David felt when he was at the house on Lake Murray.

He and the guys had made their first trip to the lake only a few weeks after Johnny's death, at a time when they'd all been shells of themselves — devastated and unsure how to move forward.

It was Chuck who'd brought up the idea of them all going somewhere quiet together. David, Ford, Darius, and Tommy, the seniors on the basketball team, had automatically agreed, and it was a given that Chuck and Keaton, who spent most of their time with them anyway, would come along as well.

They'd spent hours and hours on the deck that first year. Most of the time they were silent, lost in their own heads, but occasionally one of them would have a moment of courage and speak up, trying to put their feelings into words.

None of them were any good at cooking yet, so they'd grilled hot dogs and made boxed mac and cheese, but it had been exactly what David had needed. And by the end of it there'd been a shift, like the tentative vulnerability they'd found together established a certain level of trust and safety that hadn't existed before.

Even now, years later, David sat out on the dock in board shorts and a t-shirt with a mug of coffee in one hand as his feet splashed in the cool water, and felt blissfully content. The sun had just crested over the tops of the tall trees that circled the lake, turning the water from deep black to vibrant blue. Darius and Rebecca, both still in pajamas, sat next to him, and all of them watched as Sage, Chuck, and Keaton did some sort of body-weight workout on the mowed grass at the edge of the lake.

"Twenty more burpees and that's it," Chuck panted, pushing his curls back from his forehead.

"You're not very nice," Sage grumbled, but obediently jumped in the air before dropping to the ground into a pushup.

David took advantage of the moment to watch her. In only a sports bra and some tiny running shorts, she looked every inch an athlete. Her skin glowed in the morning light, with the shine of sweat that only made the long, lean lines of her body all the more pronounced.

She was a goddamn vision.

They'd woken up that morning sprawled out on opposite sides of the bed, but had quickly closed the distance between them. David had ignored her protest about morning breath and proceeded to kiss her thoroughly while his hand went to work between her legs, bringing her to a silent, shaking orgasm that left him right on the edge of his own release. And when Sage had crawled under the covers and wrapped those pink lips around him, well, he'd lasted about half a second before coming down her throat.

For the first time, they stood together at the sink, watching each other in the wide mirror as they brushed their teeth and got ready for the day. There had been a brief moment of discomfort when he'd looked at his body in the mirror, but then he'd noticed the way Sage's cheeks flushed when he scratched at the hair on his belly.

If she liked the way he looked, who was he to argue with her taste?

Sage did things quite simply: brushed her teeth, washed her

face with a bar of soap she'd packed in a plastic bag, and put on sunscreen that smelled like coconut.

"If I don't put on sunscreen my face turns into one giant freckle," she'd grumbled, which made him smile.

He'd held her hand as they walked down the stairs, and then sent her outside with the others while he made her tea. By the time he'd walked down the back steps with their drinks, she'd already been roped into the workout.

"They're animals," Darius was saying from where his head reclined on Rebecca's thigh.

His wife shook her head. "Better they get it out this way. You know how Chuck gets when he's been cooped up for too long."

David looked around. "Where's Tommy?"

"Sleeping still."

He looked at Darius in disbelief. "Seriously? It's after nine."

"Your point being?"

"I haven't slept in past nine in years."

"You also never drink more than one mixed drink or two beers," Darius retorted.

He wasn't wrong.

Rebecca reached over with her bare foot and nudged David's thigh. "I like her."

"Sage?"

She smiled. "Mhm. She's everything you need: confident, vibrant, and independent."

"You think so?"

Darius chuckled. "She's got this thing about her. Like she's not afraid of the world, or maybe even like she's daring the world to mess with her. You could use a little bit of that in your life."

David frowned, thinking of Sage's confidence. Her strength. Thinking of how much he'd come to count on her proximity; even when she was at the far end of the bench, it was enough for him to know that she was there. Something about her inspired him to trust his gut. To stand up a little taller.

There was no question that she made him better.

"Fuck," Chuck groaned, flopping down on the deck next to them. "That felt good."

Sage followed, dropping down right next to David. He pressed a quick kiss to her temple, tasting the salt on her skin. "Here." He handed her the mug of tea, grateful it was still warm.

Her lips curved into that crooked smile. "You made me tea."

"Of course I made you tea."

She shook her head. "You're too much."

"So Sage," Keaton asked, settling down in an old fashioned folding lawn chair, completing the lounging group on the wide dock. "What are your plans after graduation?"

David stilled.

It wasn't that he'd been avoiding asking Sage that exact question. He'd wanted to, but he hadn't wanted her to feel pressured to answer before she was ready. Because *what if* she was planning on moving away? He wasn't sure that he was ready to hear her response.

Sage leaned back, tilting her face up toward the sun that now shone directly down on them. He watched the way the light hit the hairs that had escaped her ponytail, glowing the color of honey.

"I'm thinking about coaching," she said, and David could hear the little bit of hesitation in her voice. "Ideally at the high school level."

David opened his mouth to respond, but Chuck jumped in. "That'll be great, Sage."

"Well," she continued. "Even if I find a coaching job, it probably won't be enough to live off of. So I'll need to do something else while I get my feet under me."

"There's pretty good money in private coaching," Keaton added. "I did some training the summer after college before starting law school. If you get the serious athletes it's decent enough."

"Would you ever go back to California?"

What the fuck, Chuck? David fought an overwhelming urge to drop kick his best friend into the lake.

Sage shrugged. "Probably not. But if I don't find something, I'll at least have to think about it."

A relieved exhale punched through him. *She wasn't leaving, she wasn't leaving, she wasn't leaving.*

Or, she wasn't leaving as long as she found a job.

David reached over and gently squeezed the warm skin of her thigh. "You're going to be an incredible coach, Lefty. Not a doubt in my mind about that."

Sage leaned down, nudging his shoulder with her forehead. He knew her well enough to recognize the gesture for what it was. Silent gratitude.

A sudden shadow passed over his head.

Before he could second-guess his reaction, David had dropped his coffee, leapt to his feet and, without hesitating, dove headfirst into the lake.

The water was still chilled from the night, and as soon as he surfaced he was sucking in lung-fulls of air as he tried to shake the water from his hair. He heard the familiar laughter of his friends, but his eyes went straight to Sage, who was staring at him with an expression of shocked confusion.

"I," she started, glancing between David and the others, who were all doubled over and hollering. *Assholes.* "What the fuck was that?"

David glanced up, catching the curve of the black wings as the grackle swooped over the roof of the house and disappeared from sight. *Creepy, beady-eyed demons,* he thought, scanning the sky in case more of them were around.

"David is afraid of birds," Chuck managed to gasp out between laughs.

David paddled back toward the dock, managing to shoot his best friend the middle finger as he scowled up at him. "Not all birds, you asshole," he grumbled. He reached up to grab the edge of the platform, and, gathering his strength, pushed himself up out of the water. "Just the skinny black ones."

Sage's eyebrows shot up her forehead as a grin pulled at her lips. "Grackles?"

David shuddered as he stretched his legs out on the warm wood of the dock.

"David," Sage continued. "You're huge. They're small. Make this make sense to me."

Behind him, Rebecca giggled.

He let out a groan. "They're unpredictable!"

Now Sage's laugh joined in with the others. With a resigned sigh, he flopped back onto his back, crossing his arms over his face just in case the goddamn terror of a bird decided to show back up.

⊏⊐

As soon as Maggie arrived and was settled into her room, the whole group — including Tommy, who'd finally dragged himself out of bed — went out on the pontoon boat that came with the house.

David was content to sit on one of the bench seats in the front with Sage's bare skin pressed against his. He had a hat pulled down over his forehead and sunglasses on to battle the bright glare of the sun on the still water.

Sage looked too good to be real in an orange bikini that left miles and miles of her skin exposed, and she wore a green trucker hat to shade her face. Her hair was in two braids, which curved down her chest and rested on her pert breasts.

His brain was reduced to a refrain of *lovely, lovely, so goddamn lovely.*

Maggie and Rebecca sat together on the facing bench, and the three women had fallen into a conversation that bounced from topic to topic amid laughter and loud proclamations of "What" and "No fucking way!"

Keaton drove the boat, and Darius, Tommy, and Chuck sat in the back, quietly conversing over beers.

It was good. So good to be there, and any lingering fear in the back of his mind that Sage might not fit in with them was completely washed away as he watched the relaxed smile on her face.

He couldn't lose her.

The thought crashed into the forefront of his mind, loud and demanding. He knew it wasn't his choice to make. It was hers, all hers. Sage was at a point in her life where endless opportunities were open to her. She could go anywhere and do anything, and *goddammit* he wanted that for her. He wanted to watch her take on the world.

But was it wrong that he wanted to be there for it all? He wanted to be up close, to see her first thing in the morning when she was all soft and cuddly, to make her tea in a to-go mug, and then to see her at the end of the day, to walk through the park with Daisy together, to eat together, and then to lay her out in their bed and *worship* her.

He wanted that so badly that his chest ached.

And if she was coaching? He could already imagine them debating the merits of zone versus man defense and sharing play ideas. She'd poke through his self-doubt the way she always did, and he'd encourage her to trust her gut. They'd take on the world together, working from the courtside to build up the next generation of players.

He had an idea, one that could make it all work out. One that would keep Sage there in Charleston. Keep her close to him. Keep her *with* him.

He just had to convince her to accept his help.

═══

The week passed in a blur of diving into the cool water, applying aloe lotion to sunburned shoulders, grilling out on the deck, pool tournaments, and almost constant banter between Maggie and Keaton, who'd decided that they disagreed on anything and everything.

It had started with an argument about what actually distinguished a top shelf liquor, and quickly devolved into a shouting match about classism and taste and Southern wealth. The rest of them had briefly considered intervening, but honestly the two of them seemed to be enjoying themselves.

Every night, David took Sage to bed, where they continued to figure out new and creative ways to get each other off. Nothing compared to those moments when their bodies were moving together with nothing between them but sweat and hunger and a growing realization on David's part that he never wanted to let her go.

It was a perfect break after the grind of the winter months, but by the end of the week David was ready to go home.

This would be his first year going through recruitment, and he was excited to travel around the country to scout the next class of Southeastern players. Players he would bring to the program.

And, for the next three years at least, it was *his* program. He'd gotten the email midweek from Connie with confirmation that they were offering him not only a contract extension, but a raise to go along with it. It was more than he could have imagined during those long, sleepless nights early in the season.

He'd shared his news with the group, and everyone had been predictably excited for him. But nothing compared to the pride and happiness in Sage's green eyes when she'd held his face in her hands and whispered, "Fuck yes, Coach," before kissing him senseless in the middle of the kitchen.

They'd celebrated privately — and very nakedly — later that night.

It was everything he'd wanted, what he'd dreamed about since he'd hung up his green and gold jersey, and yet there was a little feeling of dread that he couldn't quite shake.

Now, it was the Sunday afternoon before the end of the break, and they were all packing up to make the drive back to Charleston.

Goodbyes and hugs were exchanged, along with promises to plan dinners and an evening at The Grove in the next few weeks.

David leaned against his car as he watched Sage and Rebecca exchange numbers. Sage's skin had turned a golden tan, and her blonde hair had lightened in the sun. He could easily imagine her on a beach in California, with her cut off jeans and thin-strapped tank top.

Finally they were on the road, with Daisy curled up in Sage's lap. They were quiet, but it was the good kind of quiet that came after days of constant social interaction and late nights. David was content, perfectly at peace with the way things felt between them. Well, except for the question of the following year.

"So I've been thinking about what you said. About coaching."

Sage glanced over at him. "Okay."

"I've got a buddy who coaches at one of the bigger high schools in Charleston. Their program is good — they've been to state almost every year since he started. I'd be happy to call him and -"

"No." Her face was expressionless, impossible to read as she shifted in her seat to face him.

David took a slow breath, momentarily tightening his knuckles on the steering wheel. "Can I ask why not?"

"I want to earn my spot, David. Wherever I end up, I want to go somewhere that wants me for who I am."

"What about references?" He couldn't figure out why she was being so fucking *stubborn* about this. "There's nothing wrong with using the network that you have. Everyone does."

"I said no," she repeated, and a wry, sad smile crossed her face as she shook her head.

David remembered his first year coaching, when he'd been unsteady on his feet, confident in the basketball but totally clueless as to how to relate to the young men who'd barely reached puberty. And in those moments they'd looked at him like he couldn't possibly relate to their lives. Like he couldn't possibly understand.

That was how Sage looked at him across the console. Like he was missing something obvious that was right there in front of him.

He let out a long huff of air. His hand found her thigh, resting against her skin in a way that had become comfortable and familiar. He gave her a firm squeeze. "Okay, Lefty. Just let me know if you change your mind."

"I will."

They'd gotten home and after grocery shopping and Italian takeout, Sage went back to her place to get some sleep.

Out of curiosity, David pulled up the local job postings for high school basketball coaching positions.

The results were abysmal. Only two postings for varsity women's programs, and the JV programs paid so poorly that he couldn't imagine Sage going for it. All of them cited a need for previous coaching experience, which, technically, she didn't have.

David tossed his laptop onto the couch next to him, burying his face in his hands and letting out a frustrated groan.

The job prospects for her in Charleston weren't good. There were only two professional sports teams — a soccer team and a minor league hockey team, both small enough that they likely didn't have many jobs. He'd checked their websites, and they were only hiring janitorial staff.

The thought of Sage Fogerty doing anything other than what she dreamed of doing made him nauseous. Shouldn't she get the chance to do what she wanted?

And if that chance wasn't in Charleston, she'd have to leave.

He wouldn't — *couldn't* — be the one to make her stay. Not for him. Not where her entire life and future were waiting ahead of her. It would be selfish.

"Fuck," he muttered, grabbing his phone from the table. His thumbs moved over the screen, composing a message.

He hit send before he could talk himself out of it.

Flopping back on the couch, he glanced over at Daisy, who let out a forlorn whimper from where she was cuddled up on top of one of the cushions.

He grabbed his most recent novel and his glasses, settling back onto the couch. He forced his eyes to focus on the words on the page, in spite of the sinking feeling that he'd just done something irreparably stupid.

CHAPTER 28
ON MY OWN MERIT
SAGE

The weeks after spring break turned into the kind of academic sludge that reminded Sage of the week before finals. However, apparently the last two months of school for the Sports Management students were an actual nightmare.

She was exaggerating a bit. But there were projects and papers and presentations and meetings that filled up her days, leaving her feeling like she was working a 9 to 5. She'd gotten in the habit of packing a lunch of dinner leftovers to take with her to campus, because she had neither the time nor money to afford eating at the cafe on campus every day.

Even her laptop had started whining whenever she powered it on, like it was as exhausted as she was.

She'd still managed to get her workouts in before driving to class, but she hadn't had the time or energy to go to the gym at night to shoot. After months spent courtside, even though she'd been at the end of the bench, she found that she missed basketball. She missed it in a way that she hadn't allowed herself to in the years since her career as a player had ended.

She also missed David.

He'd been traveling almost every week, actively scouting their potential recruits for the following year. When he was gone, they exchanged occasional texts, which was more than enough for her. She didn't need constant communication to know that he cared about her.

Sage had started taking care of Daisy when David was gone, which she loved. Even though her schedule was bonkers, walking the dog a few times a day got her outside and in the sun. She may or may not have even smuggled her into the library in her bag a few times.

And, on the days when David was home, things were good. Really fucking good.

They shared most of their lives with each other. They shared meals. They shared reading, each of them with their own books, lost in separate stories but together with their legs tangled on the couch. They both loved to exercise; when David was in town, they'd go to the gym together and then move through different routines, occasionally passing the other with a fond pinch or slap to the butt.

David had tried to rope her into the yoga flow that he did after he worked out, but Sage had her limits.

And of course they shared basketball, both as a passion and — hopefully for Sage — a vocation.

The search for coaching jobs wasn't going well. She'd posted her resume on four or five different hiring sites, and hadn't heard from anyone other than the typical outside sales positions that targeted recent college graduates. She was at the point of considering a 9 to 5 office job and then trying to find a JV or assistant coaching job that she could do in the afternoons and evenings. It wasn't that she minded working her way up. In an ideal world, she'd learn the ropes from a more experienced coach before taking on the responsibility of a team of her own.

It all came down to the money. She couldn't afford to dive head-on into coaching without having sustainable income from somewhere else. The money she'd saved would last through the end of the semester, and then she had to get a job if she wanted to keep paying rent and eating vegetables.

She *really* wasn't ready to give up vegetables.

But she also wasn't ready to give up her life in Charleston.

Beyond David, there was Maggie, who'd been over to her apartment a few times for late dinners and way too much wine. There was also Rebecca, who'd taken to sending her recipes, and Chuck, who shouted his greetings at her whenever they passed in the Humphrey Center.

She had a life in Charleston. One with friendships and routine and community.

David had a rare Saturday morning at home, so they took Daisy downtown to the farmers market. They strolled down the cobbled brick walk, checking out the booths of seasonal produce, flowers, and locally made products. The pink-stoned steeple of Citadel Square Church towered up above Marion Square, and somewhere a band was playing an acoustic cover of The Beatles' "Eight Days A Week."

David wore khaki pants that made his ass and thighs look indecent and a dark blue short-sleeved button-up. Sage's sundress was a soft cotton jersey, green, with a scooped neckline and capped sleeves. It was probably the most comfortable article of clothing that she owned.

They walked hand in hand, winding their way through the throngs of people. Daisy trotted ahead of them, greeting everyone with a jingle of her collar and a smile. They had to stop every few minutes so that someone could pet her and coo over how cute she was.

"Graduation is a month away. How are you feeling?"

Sage glanced up at him. His grip on her hand tightened.

"Ready to be done," she answered honestly. "This semester has been brutal."

His smile was reassuring. "You're almost there," he said, rubbing his thumb over the back of her hand. "Should we, ah, well, should we have a conversation about next year?"

"Sure." She forced herself to swallow against the nervousness that burned in her throat like acid. "What about it?"

A few moments lapsed before David spoke. "Are you planning on leaving?"

"No." She watched David's shoulders drop as his head tilted back and his eyes shut. "Unless you don't want me to stay?" Sage dropped her gaze down to the brick in front of them. "I don't want to assume, but I'm going to stay in Charleston. Even if you told me you wanted to be done with this — with us — I'd still want to stay."

"No!" David pulled them to a stop. "I'd love it if you stayed." He flashed her a soft smile. "I'm nowhere near done with this."

Sage searched his brown eyes for a moment. She remembered that first night in the bar, searching his eyes then and finding nothing but warmth and sincerity there. Now she could easily identify affection, and maybe, if she wasn't imagining it, something more.

David had one of her canvas bags over one shoulder, overflowing with the produce she'd picked out. In his free hand he held a full bouquet of yellow tulips. He'd insisted on picking the one with the most buds so that she'd get the chance to enjoy them longer.

Yeah. There was no fucking way she was leaving him any time soon.

"That's good," Sage finally said, only to be interrupted by Daisy tugging at her leash, obviously annoyed that they'd paused. She heard David let out one of those low, warm chuckles that sounded like real maple syrup, and she leaned into him.

It felt good, for just a second, to lean on him.

———

Sage slipped into her blue blazer as she walked into the Summit High School athletic building. The facility was obviously new, built with blue-gray stone and steel details, impressive enough to make the Humphrey Center look like an ancient relic.

She had an interview for a *fucking* coaching job.

She'd gotten the call on a Monday afternoon just as she was leaving a group project meeting in the library. It was the head coach of Summit High School's girl's basketball team, and he was looking for an assistant who would also coach the JV team. He also mentioned that the school was hiring English tutors, if that would be something she was interested in.

As soon as he hung up she'd jumped in the air like a little kid on Christmas morning. If she got the job, she'd have enough work to make a living, and, after only a minute of research, she learned that the team was good. Like *really* good. Two appearances in the state final in the last five years kind of good.

She'd immediately called David, who was recruiting in D.C.. He'd congratulated her, even though he'd seemed a bit less enthusiastic than she thought he'd be. He was probably just tired from all of the travel, she rationalized.

She'd taken extra time getting ready for her interview — going for the full suit, low heels, and pulling her hair back into a high ponytail. As David called it, the "power pony."

She really, really wanted the job.

She wanted it so badly that she'd already caught herself looking up blazers in the team colors — navy and white. She'd already started combing through her notebook from the season, imagining crafting a speech for her first team meeting.

She wasn't trying to get ahead of herself, but after years of not knowing what the next thing was, having the clarity of purpose put a new fire in her veins. After all of the emails from her mom and meetings with her advisor, after floundering anytime someone asked about her future, she finally knew what she was going to do.

Coach Michael Atkinson was a lean man around Sage's height, with a soft smile and a strong handshake. He walked her through the gym, showing off the state of the art facility on the way to his office. He was dynamic and charismatic, and his commitment to the girls in his program was obvious based on how he talked about them. All of his varsity players were playing year round on club teams, and many of them were on their way to being college players. It was an elite program with all of the resources a high school team could ever ask for.

Once they reached his office, Sage sat in the leather-backed chair in front of the desk while Michael settled in. "I've got to be honest with you," he said, leaning back in his chair with his hands clasped behind his head. "When David texted me about you, I wasn't sure what to think about taking on someone so green."

It felt like her organs had dropped right out of her body plummeting into the earth. Sage forced herself to speak. "I'm sorry, did you say that David spoke with you?"

Michael smiled. "Yeah, he told me that you were looking to get into coaching after completing your masters. He's an old friend and a great coach, and I trust his judgment. After he vouched for you and talked about what you'd done for them over at Southeastern, I knew I wanted to bring you in."

She said something in response, but the part of her brain that was conscious of events in the immediate moment was completely offline. She must have continued to form words that made some sort of sense, because she sat in that chair for another half an hour before she registered Michael offering her . the job. The tutoring would be a conversation with another department, but he'd take care of it all. According to him, she was a shoo-in.

"May I think about it?" Those words she was aware of forming.

Michael looked surprised, but quickly recovered. "Of course. Get back to us in the next week."

"Thank you." Sage tried to smile as she stood up and extended her hand.

"We'd love to have you," Michael replied.

She was sure that her expression was faltering. "It's a really amazing opportunity," she said, her voice sounding hollow even to her own ears. "Thank you so much for considering me."

The walk out of the building was a blur. It was oppressively hot outside; the heavy, humid air immediately brought sweat beading on the surface of her skin.

When she got to her car, she peeled off her jacket and threw it into the back seat.

She couldn't go home. Not yet.

She drove to the Humphrey Center. It was mid-afternoon on a Tuesday, and rather than make the familiar trek to the practice gym, she walked into the main gymnasium. She took in the golden wood of the floors as she kicked off her heels and unbuttoned the cuffs of the blouse she'd put so much thought into. She rolled up her sleeves as she walked over to the supply closet tucked beneath the bleachers. Punching in the familiar code, she grabbed a ball and slowly padded on bare feet out to the main basket.

She started to shoot. Within a minute she was lost in the familiar movements, and with her body occupied and in motion everything that boiled inside of her began to rise to the surface. Anger, frustration, and betrayal all channeled into the bend of her knees and the flick of the ball off of her fingertips.

She didn't name her thoughts. She didn't try to understand what raged inside of her. She wasn't ready to put words to the disappointment that threatened to carve out her insides and leave her empty.

When her bare feet began to ache, she stopped. She put the ball into the closet and grabbed her things, sliding her feet back into the heels that had seemed like a good idea earlier.

Her phone buzzed inside of her bag. She ignored it.

She wasn't surprised to see David pacing in front of her apartment with Daisy tucked under one arm and his phone gripped tightly in his hand. She remembered that his flight was due to get in early that afternoon and they'd made plans to hang out as soon as he was back.

He rushed toward her the second he saw her. "Where have you been?" He did that ridiculous thing where he looked her body over like he was going to find some sort of injury on her.

When he didn't find anything, he looked her directly in the eye, his brow furrowed with concern. "I was worried."

Sage unlocked the door to her apartment. "I went to shoot."

She pushed the door open, walking inside and flicking on the light. David followed her.

"Did the interview go okay?"

Dropping her stuff onto the couch, Sage turned around to face him. "I don't know, David. Has Michael given you an update yet?"

She watched his expression shift. Watched the pained twist to his mouth as his chin dropped down. Watched his eyes fall shut, his dark lashes curling against his skin as he shook his head. "Sage, I —"

"I told you no." There was no point in pretending. She let all of it pour into her voice, refusing to hold anything back from him. "I told you no and *still* you went behind my back and did what you thought was best for me."

David opened his eyes and looked directly at her. "I wanted to help."

"But you didn't listen! I've told you over and over again that I'm the kind of person who wants — no, *needs* — to figure things out on my own, but you just had to butt in, didn't you?"

"Sage," he ground her name out like it was painful. "You deserve to get a chance to do the thing you love in the place where you want to do it, and sure, I'm a selfish bastard who doesn't want you to move halfway across the country. But you're it for me." He took a step toward her. "You're my person, and I don't want to imagine what it would be like to not have you here."

Tears burned her eyes. "You asshole. You absolute fucking asshole." She had to turn away from him, looking instead at the philodendron that had grown long enough that she'd had to pin it up against the wall. Now it made a green chain that extended up and over the arched opening between the living room and little dining area. Before she'd moved in, it had barely been a foot long.

"If you actually cared about me, like really and truly cared about me, you never would've done this." She didn't fight the way her voice broke. "I thought you knew me better than that, David. I thought you were my person too, but if you can't see that what you did was completely fucked up and out of line, then I guess I was wrong."

"What are you talking about? I know you, Sage."

She looked up at him, at the panic that widened his eyes and how his hair stuck up on one side. It was only then that she noticed his t-shirt. Neon green with large letters proclaiming *Kale Yeah!* Her shirt.

Another something inside of her crumpled.

"You know, that's what Evan used to say."

Devastation crumpled his face. "Sage," he started, shaking his head.

"What? That's what he used to tell me. 'Trust me, Sage. I'm looking out for you. I wouldn't lead you astray. I know you, Sage.' That's what he would tell me when he gave me a meal plan that left me weak and underweight. The same thing he'd say when I asked him if he was inviting college coaches to my games. And guess what? He quietly sabotaged my career, all while assuring me that he knew best, until I'd burned every bridge except for the one that connected me to him." She wiped at her wet cheeks. "So excuse me if I have no tolerance for men I'm fucking who think they know what's best for me."

She watched the words hit. She watched David cover his mouth with one hand as he blinked against the moisture that gathered in the inner corners of his dark eyes.

Let them out, she wanted to tell him. *It'll feel so much better if you let them out.*

But she didn't.

"I didn't think of how," he started. "Sage, I'm so sorry, I —"

"This thing between us? It's built on mutual respect. I come to you already whole — flawed maybe, but still complete, and you come to me the same. That's why it works, David. My life has been so much better with you in it, but don't think for a second that I *need* you. And now that you've done this, what do you think it tells me about what you think of me? Do you really think I'm so incapable that I can't start my career on my own merit? Because if that's what you think, I honestly don't want you around right now."

Tears streaked over his cheeks and disappeared into the shadows of his stubbled cheeks. "Please, Sage."

A sob tore from her chest. "I think you should go."

David nodded, turning toward the door.

"Wait," Sage called, willing her body into motion.

David stilled.

She went to Daisy, still tucked under David's muscled arm, and lowered to give the dog a kiss on the nose. "Love you, Daisy girl," she whispered.

Daisy let out a whimper and licked Sage right across the mouth.

Sage turned away and listened to the door click shut behind her.

CHAPTER 29
NOT A CHOCOLATE KIND OF PROBLEM

DAVID

"You fucked up."

David sat on Chuck's couch, his face buried in his hands. "I know, but —"

"I'm an asshole and even I know you fucked up," Tommy added from where he sat in one of the arm chairs that framed the large picture window on one side of Chuck's living room. Chuck sat in the other.

"I'm not arguing with the fact that I fucked up," David said, shooting a glare at Tommy. "All that I'm saying is that *all* of us got help along the way." He pointed at Chuck. "You got hired by the same coach who'd just spent four years seeing what a good leader you were. Your character and skill was what ultimately got you the job, but the *connection* was what got you in the door in the first place."

Chuck shook his head. "Of course *we* know that, David. But does Sage? We're all on the other side of it looking back on those years. That was *ten years ago*, man. We can acknowledge the calls our mentors made and the help we got because we've ultimately found success down the line that we earned with our own merit."

David frowned, pressing the heel of his hand into his sternum where a steady ache had taken up residence ever since Sage had compared him to that absolute piece of shit who'd hurt her.

He honestly hadn't thought it would be a big deal.

But goddamnit, he'd been wrong. He thought she'd be upset, sure — he wasn't a complete idiot — but he'd counted on her understanding. That she'd be able to see where he was coming from. David knew that Sage was going to be a good coach. He knew it so deeply in his bones that he didn't think twice about calling a friend on her behalf.

The truth was that he wouldn't have called if he hadn't believed in her. He didn't have a single doubt that once she had the opportunity in front of her, Sage would prove herself a million times over. But now? His actions had hurt her more deeply than he'd ever considered.

"Have you talked to her?" Chuck asked, his expression kind.

David shook his head. "She told me that she didn't want me around."

"So then give her some space to cool down," Tommy shrugged. "Then you go and bring her chocolate and talk it out and then you're all good."

"I don't think this is a chocolate kind of problem."

Tommy tousled his hair with one hand, making the whole front poof up in a way that looked completely ridiculous. "So how are you going to fix it?"

"I don't know," David admitted.

Chuck looked thoughtful. "I'd start by apologizing."

"If she told you she needed space, then I'd start by giving it to her. Based on experience, I'd listen to what she says." Tommy shrugged.

"Since when are you the expert on communicating with women?" David snapped. Everything hurt and he was so fucking tired.

"Come on, man," Chuck admonished, sending a disappointed look David's way.

Tommy cocked a brow at him. "Since I *didn't* listen and my wife fucking left me, asshole."

"Sorry," David muttered. "That was shitty of me."

"Yeah it was, but you're sad and I love you, so we're good." Tommy got up and walked into the kitchen.

"I hate not doing anything to fix it," David admitted to Chuck.

His friend gave him a sad smile. "You picked her, Hughes. If Sage is the kind of person who needs to take on things like this alone, then you've got to respect that if you want to be with her."

"I know." He let out a frustrated sigh. "She's so capable, Chuck. She's capable and beautiful and tough, and every minute of my life this year has been better because she's been in it. So how am I supposed to sit back and do *nothing* when I know what it takes to get a good coaching opportunity?"

"I think you're supposed to support her and trust her, as painful as that may be."

"And what about the part of me that needs to take care of her? I don't think you get it; I feel like I'm being stabbed in the chest when I think about her taking on the world by herself. Not because I don't think that she can, but because there's nothing that compares to the feeling of taking care of her."

"You should probably talk to her about that," Chuck said, shifting in his chair to tuck his long legs up under himself. "And regardless of how either of us see it, it's obvious that the job was taking it too far."

David nodded. The way that Sage had looked at him after he'd sent what he thought was an innocuous text had left him absolutely fucking gutted. Hollow. Because Chuck was right: it didn't matter how David had intended the gesture. To her, it had meant something completely different. Whether intentional or not, he'd hurt her. He'd damaged the life that they were building together. He'd stomped on the thing between them that was still tender and new.

And the thought of intentionally hurting Sage made him feel like he was going to vomit.

"There's no right or wrong way for people to be together." Tommy had wandered back into the room, beer in one hand and a bag of baby carrots in the other. "The way I see it, all that matters is that the people in the relationship understand the expectations and what needs the other is hoping to get met. And it's up to each person to say what those needs are."

David blinked, turning to stare at Chuck. "What the hell happened to Tommy?"

Chuck reached out and grabbed a carrot from the bag, crunching it between his teeth. After several loud chews, he responded. "Divorce has made him wise." His blue eyes narrowed on David's chest. "Also what the fuck is that shirt?"

David looked down at the t-shirt he'd borrowed from Sage and never returned. He spent a slightly embarrassing amount of time wearing the green shirt, but it was soft and fit him well and always made him smile.

"It's Sage's," he said softly, rubbing a hand over his chest. Like maybe the motion would soothe the ache that had settled there.

"You look ridiculous," Chuck said with a laugh, before his expression sobered. "Get out of here and go for a walk, or something. There's no rush to figure it all out."

David took a slow, ragged breath. "Fine. You're right."

"Come back for dinner," Chuck called out as David walked toward the door, keys jangling in his pocket with every step, trying to ignore the mounting dread in his chest.

CHAPTER 30
THE BRAVEST THING
SAGE

"Will you judge me if I pop the button on my shorts?"

Maggie arched a dark eyebrow at her from where she was wiping out glasses with a towel. "You'll get no judgment from me."

Sage reached down below the bar and slipped open the button of her jean shorts. "Fuck," she sighed, feeling her stomach relax into the extra few inches of breathing room. "That feels good."

"You're drunk."

Sage waved a hand in the general direction of her friend. "I know this."

Maggie looked at her like she was a vaguely disappointing sandwich. "Are we gonna talk about it?"

"Why?" Sage frowned down at her almost empty margarita. She threw the rest of it back and slid the glass down the bar, watching the way the condensation smeared across the shiny wood.

Maggie looked at the glass, obviously unimpressed. "Because talkin' is better. Thoughts get all twisted and fuzzy, and sometimes you don't actually know what you feel until you say it out loud." She filled a glass of water from the tap and slid it down the bar toward Sage. "And you're my friend and I'm supposed to help when shit like this happens. It's how the friend thing works."

Sage took a long drink of water. She was drunk enough that she felt the tequila in her mouth, in the way that her lips and tongue lagged just a little behind her brain when she tried to speak.

"David did a shitty thing."

"What'd he do?"

"I told him not to do something and he did it."

Maggie blinked at her. "Sage. Come on. You're givin' me nothin' to work with here."

Sighing, Sage slumped back into her seat.

It had been six days since she'd told David to get out of her apartment.

The first three days she'd been pissed. So pissed that she'd snapped at the perfectly nice cashier at the grocery store when he didn't give her the two-for-one discount on her wine. She'd needed the space to breathe and recalibrate, to move through the hurt and disappointment until what was left was herself.

The next two days she'd genuinely been so busy with school that she'd barely had time to feed herself or go to the bathroom.

But now? Now she really fucking missed him. She'd had a taste of life without David Hughes in it and she didn't want that. Not when she could make the choice to be with him again.

"He offered to call a friend and hook me up with a coaching job here in Charleston, and I told him no. Then he went behind my back and did it without telling me. I didn't realize it was David's friend until I was at the interview. It was my dream job, Maggie. It was everything I'd ever wanted, and they even offered me the position at the end." She winced, remembering the sharp sting of humiliation she'd felt in that moment, like everyone was in on the joke except for her. "I thought they picked me because they wanted Sage Fogerty, but they only picked me because of stupid David Hughes and his stupid beautiful face that everyone seems to love."

Maggie tapped her nails against the polished wood of the bar. "Okay."

"Okay?"

Maggie seemed to be wrestling with what to say next. "So he made a mistake."

"Yes!" Sage slapped a hand down on the bar, wincing when the surface of her skin smarted. "I told him not to and he did!"

Maggie nodded. "But you got an interview for your dream job."

"Yes."

Maggie gave her a look that Sage didn't like. Not at all.

Sage narrowed her eyes at her. "What."

"So we're mad at David," she started. "I get that. But don't you maybe want to consider sayin' yes?"

Hurt flared in Sage's chest. "You don't get it," she said, leaning forward until her chest rested on the bar in front of her. "I can't just forget that the only reason I got the job was because of him."

"Hey," Maggie said, bracing herself on her elbows and looking Sage intently in the eye. "I'm on your side here. All I'm sayin' is to think about it."

Sage let herself imagine, just for a moment, that she was the kind of person who would consider saying yes to the job. That she could rewrite the pieces of herself that reacted to help like an unwanted touch. Because it was a good job. An *incredible* chance to start a career in coaching.

But she was who she was, and in spite of all of the ways that she'd grown and changed, Sage Fogerty couldn't forget where she came from. She'd never completely outrun the fact that she was Cheryl Fogerty's daughter, or the girl that Evan White chose out of a random lineup of her peers.

Those pieces of her didn't define her, but they were there to stay.

"Even the really good ones make mistakes sometimes," Maggie mused, tucking a piece of her now-blue hair behind her ear. The color suited her. "So is it over?"

"Over?"

"Are you breaking up with him?"

"Fuck no!" Sage realized how loud she was and felt her cheeks flush. "No. I don't want it to be over."

"So then what are you gonna do?"

"I don't know," Sage admitted. "I'm afraid, I think."

"Of what?"

Sage let out a pained laugh. "Of everything! Of choosing him and him not choosing me back. Of forgiving him."

"Why?"

"What if I'm wrong and he hurts me again?"

"You know," Maggie said, walking back over to brace her forearms on the bar in front of Sage. "People don't talk about how hard it is to offer forgiveness. Not just sayin' the words, but actually believin' in it. I think it's one of the bravest things a person can do."

Sage hummed. "He's so tall."

Maggie cackled. "That he is."

"And he wants to go down on me." Sage plucked a piece of ice from her water, squeezing it between her fingers until it popped out one side and skittered across the surface of the bar. She frowned at it.

"I was *so* not expectin' that," she heard Maggie mutter. "Isn't that a good thing?"

Sage shrugged, thinking back to the one time she'd let Evan put his face between her thighs. "Dunno. Tried it once and the guy gave me shit for taking too long. Never done it since."

She looked up and caught Maggie's horrified expression. "What the fuck is wrong with men," Maggie said, shaking her head. "So are you thinkin' about lettin' David, you know, celebrate lady-taco Tuesday?"

Sage cracked up, snorting loudly before getting control over herself. A little glimmer of vulnerability snuck through the tequila haze. "I don't let anybody see me like that," she said quietly.

Maggie, to her credit, leaned in closer. "Like what?"

Sage fumbled for the right word. "Vulnerable."

Maggie gave her a sympathetic look. "Guess you're just gonna have to decide if David is just 'anybody' or if he's somethin' else."

Sage didn't know what to say to that, so she refocused her energy on trying to talk Maggie into making her another margarita. Unfortunately she failed, in spite of her whining and complaining about the terrible service. She even threatened to leave a one star online review.

"You'll thank me tomorrow," Maggie had said as she ushered Sage out the door and into the passenger seat of her small SUV.

"Why am I in your car?" Sage asked much too late. They were already driving.

"I'm takin' you home."

Sage scoffed. "I can walk just fine."

"You're irrationally stubborn and very silly," Maggie commented as she turned into the apartment complex. "Think you can make it from here?" she asked, coming to a stop next to the curb.

"Chya." Sage paused to lean on the door. "I'm glad you're my friend."

Maggie's eyes softened. "Right back atcha."

Sage shut the door and started walking toward the gate, pleasantly surprised that her feet and legs were cooperating.

"Sage!"

She turned back to see that Maggie had rolled down the passenger window. "Miss me already?"

Maggie laughed and shook her head. "Don't even think about goin' to see him tonight!"

How did she know…

"But I miss him! And he's tall!"

"And you're gonna make a fool of yourself." Maggie started to pull forward. "Go get your ass in bed, and then you can go see him in the mornin'. Don't you want to brush your teeth before all the make-up sex the two of you will be havin'?"

"You're a terrible wing-woman!" Sage shouted after the car.

Sage resumed her walk to the gate. It only took her three tries to get the code right.

Luckily for Sage, she wasn't great at doing what people told her to do.

She'd make a quick stop at her apartment to brush her teeth and then she'd go see him.

It was the perfect plan.

She pushed her front door open with her shoulder and fumbled with her phone, narrowly avoiding accidentally calling Danny with the Flip-Flops, a guy she'd hooked up with in California a few summers back. Once she'd pulled up David's contact, her thumbs tapped out a message that had become familiar. One she'd sent every night, even when she wasn't quite ready to forgive him.

Home and safe.

It was too bright when Sage blinked her eyes open.

Immediately she squeezed them shut again, not ready to face the sun and the headache and the roiling in her stomach and *stupid fucking hangovers can go fuck themselves.*

After a minute of trying to will herself back to sleep, Sage relented, flinging back her covers and dragging herself out of bed. Her first stop was the kitchen, where she threw back two glasses of water and then shuffled to the bathroom to brush her teeth, feeling herself relax a miniscule amount when no longer confronted with brutal, fuzzy cottonmouth. She groaned audibly as she dragged on clothes and stuffed her feet into her running shoes.

The walk to the gym only added to her misery, which was compounded by the realization that she hadn't made it to David's apartment the night before. And if she hadn't made it over there, that meant that things were still unresolved between them. He probably thought she wasn't going to forgive him.

But she couldn't go over there like this. Workout first, then food. Then go get David Hughes back.

She suffered through her workout, only making it through a half an hour of moving before the demand for something in her stomach had her limping back to her apartment.

Ten minutes later she sat on the floor with a plate piled high with bacon, and nothing else. It was exactly what she needed.

By the time she'd finished the plate, exhaustion was weighing down her eyelids. *Maybe just a quick nap and then she'd go over there.* Mind made up, Sage fiddled with her phone alarm and then crawled over to the couch. With her face buried in the pillows and her legs draped off the edge of the cushions, she fell fast asleep.

⸻

"Fuck fuck fuck fuck."

Sage ran down the stairs from her apartment, her hair flapping around her shoulders.

Some quick nap, she thought as she tried to button her jean shorts while sprinting down the sidewalk. Now it was dark, and she'd wasted an entire Saturday sleeping.

Objectively, there wasn't a rush. There was no reason for her to be running like a raging bull was hot on her heels.

But now that her mind was made up, she didn't want to wait a second longer.

She was barefoot, and felt a wave of gratitude for smooth cement sidewalks. She also hadn't showered after her workout, which wasn't at all ideal. But at least she'd managed to grab shorts from the hamper of clean laundry that sat in her dining room to go with her t-shirt.

She was too old to pull off running through an apartment complex without pants on.

As soon as she got to David's apartment, her fists banged on the door. Over and over and over and —

"Sage?"

David stood in his doorway, dark eyes blinking at her like he couldn't quite believe what he was seeing. He was shirtless, leaving his broad, hairy chest on display. Her gaze fixed on the dip between his pecs, where she knew her cheek fit perfectly when he held her.

"Hi." She held her hand up in a wave and then immediately regretted it, lowering it and instead shoving it into the way-too-small pocket of her shorts.

His wide mouth pulled up into a hesitant smile that was so hopeful it made her chest ache. "Hey."

"I'm so tired of missing you."

A breath left David's mouth in an audible *whoosh*. "Come here, Lefty."

She closed the distance between them, burying her face into his solid, warm body and wrapping her arms around his middle. She inhaled deeply, unashamed to be drinking in the scent of him. Taking in his comfort.

She felt his arms encircle her, holding her tightly against him. She felt the low, contented hum vibrate in his chest and the press of his face into her hair.

This. This was exactly where she wanted to be.

"I'm so sorry, Sage. I need you to know how sorry I am." His voice was gentle against her scalp.

"I know," she replied, and she *did* know. She knew because she knew David and trusted him more than was logical. And she knew that they needed to talk, to clear the air between them so that they could move forward together. But first, she let herself simply enjoy him. Sage nuzzled her face into his chest, wrinkling her nose and grinning at the tickle of his chest hair.

"I was about to hop in the shower," David said, like he was offering an explanation for his lack of a shirt.

Not like he needed one.

She tilted her head up, eyes grazing the underside of his strong jaw before meeting the maple brown of his gaze. "Great," she said, her smile spreading across her face. "I need a shower too." Extracting herself from his arms, Sage walked around him and into the apartment, heading straight for David's bedroom.

"Fuck," she heard him mutter behind her, but she was distracted by the unmistakable tinkle of Daisy's collar as the golden dog ran out of David's office. Her long ears flapped with every bounding step, and Sage dropped to her knees.

"Hey pretty girl," she sang, burying her face into the soft hair on Daisy's back. "I missed you so much."

Daisy licked her face in response, and Sage told herself it was because the dog missed her too, and not because she tasted of salt and sweat. She felt the weight of a hand on her upper back and she looked up, finding David staring down at her with unmistakable intention.

"Should I get the guest shower set up for you?" His voice was low and rough, textured in a way that she swore she could feel against her skin.

"Nah," she said, climbing to her feet. "Yours should be fine."

His nostrils flared as his eyes darkened. "Well come on then, Lefty."

Sage followed him through his neatly tidied bedroom and into the bathroom, which, in all the time they'd spent together, she'd never been in. "Holy shit," she said, taking in the white, stone counter, raised sink bowl, and, most impressively, the walk-in shower tucked into one corner. "Do you pay extra for this?"

David let out a low laugh. "Oh yeah."

Sage started undressing, tugging off her shirt and wrestling her way out of the still-damp sports bra that seemed determined to stick to her body.

She noticed David staring at her bare skin, and she threw her discarded t-shirt at him, catching him right in the face.

"You're a mess," he grumbled, shaking her shirt from his face and looping his thumbs into the waistband of his sweats.

Luckily she didn't need her eyes to remove the rest of her clothing, freeing her up to take in her fill of David's naked body. His thighs flexed as he stepped out of his pants, and she stared unabashedly at the thick length of him, already bobbing, half-hard between his legs.

He moved to the shower, reaching in and fiddling with the knobs until the hiss of good water pressure hitting the tile filled the room.

"I got some stuff for you," he said, kneeling down to open the cabinet under the sink. "There are a few shampoos for you to choose from. I tried to get organic ones, but I didn't really know what I was looking for. I noticed that you smell like flowers, so I got a jasmine one — I hope that's alright. And I've got clean towels, and a scrubby thing if you like that, and —"

"David."

He pulled back and looked up at her. "Hm?"

"Get in the fucking shower."

His expression softened, his smile curving into the same one he gave her when she did something especially ridiculous, or when she woke up in the morning to find him already awake and watching her. It was one of those expressions that reminded her that what she had with David Hughes was uniquely good.

She loved it when he looked at her like that.

He pushed up to his feet, and her mouth watered as she watched the flex of his quads as he straightened. Steam already filtered out from the gap above the shower door. David reached out and pulled the door open.

Sage climbed in, stepping under the wide spray. The water was hot enough that it smarted perfectly against her skin. She felt David's body behind her, the barely-there brush of him as he circled around her.

They stood there with the water falling between them, their naked skin speckled with droplets. David's dark hair was plastered down on his forehead, and a few pieces curved around his ears.

"Can I wash your hair?"

Sage looked up at him, more than a little bit perplexed by the offering. "You don't have to," she said, hoping to reassure him.

His mouth twitched up into a smile. "I want to."

Shrugging, Sage nodded. She couldn't imagine the appeal of doing something so mundane for someone else.

And then his strong hands pulled her directly under the stream of hot water, and a steady finger on her chin tilted her head back. His fingers threaded through her long hair, and *ohhhh shit*. That felt really fucking good.

Her eyes must have fallen shut at some point, because she heard the click of a bottle cap and then the sweet smell of jasmine filled the shower. David's fingers were just rough enough against her scalp, scratching and applying the perfect amount of pressure.

"I'm never washing my own hair again," she said with a sigh.

David's chuckle was low. "I think I can work with that," he murmured. He rinsed her hair with the same attentiveness before applying conditioner.

He pulled her away from the direct flow of the water, and when his hands brushed over her shoulders, they were slicked with soap. "Sage," he began, his voice graveled. "When I texted Michael, I never thought —" He cut himself off, and she opened her eyes to see him shaking his head. He ran his soapy hands over her stomach, caressing her skin like it was his job to cherish her. "I was thinking about the help that I got along the way. How my college coach made a call to get me my first coaching gig in Atlanta. And I just thought I could do that for you — help get you in the door. Because you're going to be incredible, Sage. You're going to be an amazing coach, and I never would have sent that text if I didn't believe that."

"I appreciate you saying that," Sage said softly, "and I hear where you were coming from with the job, but I'm not going to take it. I know that I'm being stubborn about it, but I said no, David. I said no and you did it anyway."

David's eyes closed and he shook his head. "I'm so sorry," he whispered, the words heavy with emotion. After a moment he seemed to collect himself and he knelt down in front of her, hands kneading into her thighs. "I'm so fucking sorry."

Her hands found their way into his wet hair. "Look at me," she asked, tugging gently on the dark locks. When his face tilted up, a smile spread across her face unbidden, an involuntary reaction to seeing David Hughes on his knees before her. "You screwed up. Just like I screwed up months ago when I disappeared on you. We're still getting to know each other; of course shit like this is going to happen. And I forgive you. I forgive you because there have been a million little moments that have shown me the man that you are. And not being with you?" Sage shook her head, smiling so fondly at this incredible man. This kind, caring man who made a mistake. "Not being with you fucking sucks, David."

His laugh was ragged. He stood up, and Sage glanced down at the bottle of body wash he held in one large hand.

Her mouth dropped open, her gaze darting between the green bottle and David's confused expression.

"No way."

"What?"

"No fucking way do you use Irish Spring."

David held up the bottle. "Yes? Is there something wrong with it?" His mouth pulled down into a frown as he turned the bottle around to look at the back. "I mean, I guess it's not organic, but I've never —"

Loud laughter burst from Sage's chest, so consuming that she threw her head back even as she wrapped her arms around his naked torso.

"Why is my soap so goddamn funny?"

"I just," Sage gasped, struggling to draw in air. *Was she actually crying?* Yep. She was laughing so hard that she was crying like a madwoman. "I had this whole thing about only hooking up with men because they used grown-up soap," she said, and then another wave of laughter overtook her. Once she regained her composure, she pointed at the bottle. "Unlike the college boys, who all used Irish Spring."

David looked incredulous. "What? Everyone uses Irish Spring."

Sage grinned at him. "They really don't."

"My dad uses Irish Spring," David protested, but she could see amusement crinkling the corners of his eyes. "I'm calling the guys as soon as we're out of the shower."

"You're going to have to wait," Sage said, pressing her wet body against his.

He looked down at her. "Oh yeah?"

She drew courage from his blatant attraction. The way his feelings for her were right there, tossed out into the open for anyone to see. No hiding. No hesitation.

"I want you to go down on me."

CHAPTER 31
ECHO OF IRISH SPRING
SAGE

His maple-syrup eyes darkened, pupils blown wide. She watched as his tongue wet his upper lip, like he was thinking about tasting her. "Now?"

"I mean, I was thinking a bed might be better than the shower, but whatever you think is —"

Suddenly the water shut off, leaving nothing but the echo of drips against the tile and lingering steam in the air.

David held the door open, his eyes fixed on the place where her thighs met. "Get on the bed, Sage."

Sage snatched a towel from the rack as she ran into David's room, taking only a moment to run the soft towel over her skin before tossing it aside and climbing up onto the bed. Flopping onto her back, she watched David walk slowly through the bathroom door.

She didn't understand it, but there was something profoundly erotic about watching a man absently rubbing a towel across his chest and stomach. Maybe it was the dark hair that covered his torso, or the way the vee of his hips sloped down to his already hardening cock.

He threw his towel aside and approached the foot of the bed. His eyes trailed up and down her body, lingering on her nipples and mouth. Sage fought the urge to squirm, urgent for some kind of touch against her skin.

"Be patient," David commanded, his voice dropping into an even lower register.

She watched, transfixed, as he climbed up, crawling until he hovered above her body, close enough that she could feel the warmth of his skin. She wanted it, longed for it, and tilted her hips up toward him. A shiver started at the base of her spine and traveled through the rest of her body, leaving gooseflesh on the surface of her skin.

"David," she whispered, needing him to do something, anything, to relieve the way that her body yearned for him.

He skipped her mouth entirely, dropping his lips to the base of her throat and trailing soft kisses down the valley between her breasts. The coarse hair around his mouth brushed against her, and she shuddered at the pleasure of his touch.

"I've been thinking about doing this since that first night." He sucked one of her nipples into his hot, wet mouth and her body bowed up, craving more, more, more. "Your fucking thighs, Sage. I've imagined you squeezing these perfect thighs around my head while I taste you."

A keening whine fell from her mouth, intensifying when he grazed his teeth over her sensitive bud. He moved between both breasts, repeating the torturous attention and winding her up and up until she felt her grip on reality begin to fracture.

Gripping his hair with both of her hands, she yanked him away from her. "Your mouth," she panted, her heartbeat already pounding between her thighs. "I need your mouth now."

David planted a quick kiss to her lips, and before she had the chance to respond, he was moving down her body with the grace of a predator. The muscles in his shoulders flexed as he dipped down and nipped at the tender skin of her belly.

When he reached the apex of her thighs, he looked up at her. "I'm going to take such good care of you," he rasped. "And you're going to tell me what you like. Tell me when it's good and I'll do it over and over until you come on my tongue."

And then his focus returned to her body. He licked and sucked like he was trying to devour her. It was like nothing else, there was no comparing it, and the build of pleasure within her reached a new, precarious height that had her almost afraid of what lay on the other side. She teetered on the edge of something that felt new and – terrifyingly — out of her control.

But David's firm grip on her thighs reminded her that with him, she was safe. He would be there to pick up the pieces when she inevitably fell apart.

And when she lurched over the edge and reality dimmed all around her, leaving nothing behind but pleasure unlike anything her body had ever experienced, even when her bones dissolved and overwhelmed tremors wracked her body, she knew that David Hughes had her.

That he would take care of her, and she would let him.

⊏⊐

"I think I'm going to look for a house," David said, leaning back against the wooden headboard. "With my contract extension, I think it's time."

Sage rolled onto her side, propping her head up on one elbow to look at him. "What are you looking for?"

"A big yard for Daisy, close to campus, big windows, and wood floors."

Sage smiled at how relaxed David was, his hair mussed from being grabbed and his lips soft and swollen. He'd insisted on getting her off twice with his mouth before he'd bent her over the edge of the bed and had his way with her. And when he came he'd gasped her name, a chorus of *Sage, Sage, Sage* against the back of her neck.

Now they lay boneless in David's bed, passing Sage's water bottle back and forth as they caught their breath.

"Sounds amazing," Sage said, nudging his calf with her foot as she worried at her bottom lip. "I got a job."

David sat up. "What?"

She couldn't hold back her smile. "Yeah. I got a call from a local private school a few days ago. It's small, but they needed a head coach for their high school boys program. I heard back from them yesterday, and I got the job."

"Sage," David breathed, his expression transforming as he beamed over at her. "I'm so goddamn proud of you." His gaze dipped down to her mouth for a second before returning to her eyes. "Is it enough?"

Affection warmed her entire body. "No," she conceded. "But I'm going to pick up some shifts at The Grove until I find something more permanent."

"Is that what you want?"

"Yeah. Because it's all mine." She didn't hesitate before sharing an idea that had started to take root in the past few days. "I'm thinking about getting a teaching certificate. I could do it part time, and, I don't know, I think it could be something."

"If you think it's something, then I'm all for you," David said, his voice earnest and full of promise. "For what it's worth, I think you'll be an amazing teacher."

A warmth filled her stomach and she felt her cheeks heat. "Thanks, I guess," she muttered.

"Take a damn compliment, Sage," David teased, but the happiness and pride in his eyes felt like a silent declaration. He took her hand in his, threading their long fingers together.

Sage snorted. For a moment she just looked down at their joined hands. She could barely see her skin peeking out between his fingers. "Did you really think that I'd leave?" She looked up at him. "That I'd leave you?"

David's expression was all the confirmation she needed.

"David," she said, clambering up to straddle his thighs so that she could look directly into his eyes. "I've never wanted anything as much as I want to be in the same place as you. The same town, the same apartment complex — fuck, maybe even the same house. Because I'm not done with this. With you."

"You're staying in Charleston," David's voice was soft as he reached a hand up to brush a piece of hair from her face. "I can't believe you're staying."

Tipping forward, her lips met his in a slow, lazy kiss. As she drew back, something caught her eye.

"David," she whispered, looking wide-eyed at his night stand.

He followed her gaze to the ceramic dachshund pot that she'd gifted him for Christmas. The spider plant, which was only a few inches tall at the time, had almost tripled in size and added multiple leaves.

She could see the hint of a nervous smile. "I've tried to take good care of it," he said. "I didn't really know what I was doing, so I looked some stuff up online. It seems happy enough."

Sage shook her head. "You're the best," she murmured, before tucking her face into the hollow under his jaw just like she used to imagine doing. She inhaled slowly, smiling to herself at the echo of Irish Spring that lingered on his skin.

CHAPTER 32
TO SEE HER HAPPY
DAVID

David Hughes woke up to the unmistakable feeling of long hair tickling his skin. On instinct, he opened his arms, a lazy, sleepy smile spreading across his face as he felt a warm body wriggling closer to him.

He cracked one eye and looked down at Sage, who had her face buried in his armpit.

"That can't be pleasant," David murmured, his voice rough from sleep.

Sage let out a muffled snort before lifting her head up to look at him. "It's actually quite nice in here."

He couldn't contain the sunk-down-into-his-bones happiness he felt when he looked at her. All soft from sleep and relaxed, with her own happiness wide open for him to see.

"You graduate today," he said, bringing a hand up to thread his fingers through her soft hair. "How are you feeling?"

"More excited about being done than about wearing the silly hood and hat."

David shook his head. "Don't undersell it." The sun filtering through Sage's curtains shone golden on the bare skin of her shoulders, revealing a few freckles that had crept up as spring moved into summer. "You just accomplished something incredible and today we're going to celebrate that."

Daisy chose that moment to bound up from where she'd been curled up asleep at the foot of Sage's bed. She stuck her wet nose right under David's chin before twisting to lick Sage's face. Within seconds they were all a giggling, wrestling mess as they tried to escape the tiny dog's enthusiastic onslaught of affection.

"Okay, okay," Sage shrieked, leaping up out of the bed in all of her naked glory. A grimace crossed her face, as she bent over with her hands on her knees. "Fuck, my quads are killing me."

"You could stretch after we work out," David commented mildly. "Or you could keep complaining about it."

Sage muttered something under her breath even as she bent one knee and tilted her hips to the side, her nose wrinkling as she half-heartedly stretched.

David stared at her, letting his eyes trail all over her golden skin. He loved the bikini tan lines that cut across her chest, and the little triangles of pale skin over her breasts. He loved the soft curves of her hips and the strength of her thighs. He loved the triangle of curls between her legs that matched the brown of her eyebrows.

"Stop it." Sage's hands were braced on her hips as she glared at him. "We both know there's no time for funny business today, and yet you're laying over there looking all hot and hard and ready to eat me for breakfast."

David glanced down, and *yep*. Her assessment was accurate.

He pressed his palm against himself and groaned. "What if I'm *really* fast?"

Sage's eyes narrowed, but he could see the smirk curving the corner of her mouth. "Don't go too fast, now. We're supposed to be celebrating, for fuck's sake." And with that she launched herself at him.

Twenty-seven minutes later, David held Daisy's leash in one hand and Sage's hand in the other. It was one of those mild

Charleston mornings that reminded David why he'd moved back. Why he'd always known he'd end up here.

They followed the sidewalk toward the coffee shop they'd taken to frequenting on weekend mornings. David wanted to treat them to pastries before Sage went off and started graduation prep. Apparently her sister was good at doing hair, whatever that meant.

He cleared his throat, squeezing Sage's hand in what he hoped was a gesture of reassurance. "I heard some news yesterday."

"Hm?" She looked up at him.

"I got an email that Harding is looking for an assistant coach." He watched her face carefully. "Apparently Coach White was fired."

If he hadn't known Sage's face like it was his own, he would have missed the fleeting flinch that tightened her expression. Her eyes darted down for a second before lifting to meet his gaze. "Figured that was coming," she said, her voice softer than he was used to hearing.

Again, he squeezed her hand. "And how are you?"

She shrugged, tipping her head against his shoulder for a brief moment. "Okay, honestly. I think a part of me wanted to let the universe take care of it, you know? Hoped that eventually it would all catch up with him."

"So what changed?"

"I thought about some kid like me. I thought about him doing it all again, and I hated knowing that I could've stopped it."

David let out a harsh exhale. Something in him loosened, knowing that the man who'd hurt her was finally beginning to face the consequences of his actions.

It had taken every ounce of his self control to step back and trust Sage when it came to Evan White. So much of him wanted to drag that goddamn horrible excuse of a man through the mud until there was no remote possibility of him ever working or coaching again.

But he knew Sage. As excruciating as it was to do nothing, he knew that it wasn't his choice to make. So he'd cared for her and supported her in the ways that he could, trusting that she would do whatever she needed to.

And, *damn it*, she had.

"You're incredible, Lefty."

Her expression softened and then she squeezed his hand, returning the reassurance that he'd offered to her. "I'm just trying to do the right thing."

David shook his head, voicing something that he hadn't realized had been bothering him. "It shouldn't have been up to you." He quickly added. "Not that you aren't more than capable of handling someone like him. But it's a goddamn tragedy that things like this fall on the shoulders of the people who survive them."

Her fingers tightened again. "You're a good one, David Hughes."

═══

David stood in the shade of one of the many magnolia trees that grew outside of the auditorium in the northwest corner of Southeastern's campus. It was only noon and he already regretted wearing a jacket with his shirt and linen slacks.

Sage had left him twenty minutes earlier to go get ready for the ceremony, leaving David with nothing but a vague description of her mother and sister — who had brought her boyfriend along — and instructions to find the four of them seats together.

Did he feel like he was too old to be going through the stress of meeting someone's mom for the first time? Yes. Was it also completely worth it because it was for Sage Fogerty? Also yes.

He shifted his weight, frowning at the constant stream of people walking past. *There had to be a rule somewhere that said that girlfriends weren't allowed to leave their conspicuously older boyfriends alone to meet their mom.*

"Coach!"

David looked over, smiling at the sight of Jordan walking toward him. He looked as neat and put-together as ever, wearing a black suit that was just a little too baggy on him. His face was bright, brighter than David was used to seeing.

The two men shook hands. "Congrats, Jordan," David said, giving what he hoped was a supportive squeeze before letting go of Jordan's hand.

"Thanks, Coach." His blue eyes darted around, a sign that David had learned meant that he was nervous. "I, uh," Jordan swallowed. "I actually wanted to ask you something."

"Of course."

"Well," Jordan began, rubbing his palms together. "I want to say thank you, you know, for everything this year. I know I wasn't doing good at the beginning of the season, and you helped me. You made me a better player. And, I don't know if you knew, but I've been studying business, and I really don't want to do that. I don't think I could sit at a desk and look at a computer all day." It looked like he was steeling himself, gathering courage for whatever he was going to say next. "So I was wondering, only if it works for you, if you'd ever be interested in having a graduate assistant, because I think I might want to be like you. I mean, I might want to coach."

David's throat bobbed, overcome with admiration for this young man who'd battled and grown and changed so much in the past year. He thought David had made him a better player? No, Jordan had made David a better coach and a better man.

"I'd be honored to have you on the bench with me, Jordan," David said, and it was the truth. He'd love to give Jordan the opportunity to learn about coaching, and it was an incredible honor that he was asking *him*. That David had been the kind of coach worthy of learning from.

Over his shoulder, David caught a flash of color and a group of three people — two women and a man — walking toward the entrance to the auditorium.

David turned to Jordan. "I've got to run," he said, already

starting toward the group. "But text me and we'll sit down and talk it through, okay?"

"Okay," Jordan replied, looking curiously at David. His eyes darted over to the group, who'd caught sight of David and were now very obviously moving toward them. His pale brows shot up. "Is that Sage's —"

"Yep."

A rare smile split Jordan's face in two. "Can I tell the guys? They're going to lose it."

David let out a sigh, rubbing a hand across his already sweaty forehead. "Fine. Now get out of here."

He could have sworn he heard a laugh as his ex-player walked away, but his attention was immediately pulled to the group who approached him.

"David," a woman around his age said, extending a manicured hand for him to shake. "It's great to meet you."

Brinley. Sage's older sister. She looked like she belonged in Charleston with her curled hair and bright dress. She also looked at David like she thought it was, actually, great to meet him. *That was a good start.*

"Brinley," he replied. "It's lovely to meet you too."

Her pink painted lips quirked into a grin. "And this is my mom, Cheryl."

David turned to the willowy woman who stood beside Brinley. He recognized her from the conference tournament. Bracelets covered her thin wrists, and her silver-blonde hair was pulled back in a braid. Her dress reminded David of butterfly wings, fluttering around her slender body.

"It's a real pleasure to meet you, Ms. Fogerty." David offered his sweaty hand.

Her eyes narrowed, but she returned the handshake. "Mr. Hughes."

He saw so much of Sage in the roundness of her cheeks and the stubborn glint in her green eyes.

"And," Brinley said loudly, obviously trying to interrupt whatever silent weighing was taking place between David and her mother, "This is my boyfriend, Rohan."

The two men exchanged a quick handshake, and David immediately liked him. He was tall, handsome, and had a bright smile that practically shone against his warm brown skin.

"Well, I've got us all seats," David said, itching under the continued hostile looks coming from Cheryl Fogerty. "Should we head inside?"

Cheryl turned to her daughter. "Brinley, why don't you and Rohan head inside. I'd like to have a quick conversation with Mr. Hughes."

David caught the moment Brinley's eyes widened. "Mom, I don't think —"

"We'll be fine," Cheryl interrupted.

David gave Brinley quick directions to their seats, and then he was left alone with his girlfriend's terrifying mother.

"I can't say that I'm happy to meet you, Mr. Hughes."

David forced himself to take a deep breath. "Ma'am, I —"

"I know all about men like you. Men who see someone beautiful like Sage and think that they can take advantage of her."

A wave of frustration rose in him. "Ms. Fogerty." He forced his voice to remain even. "Respectfully, I care about your daughter. I've been lucky enough to count her as a friend this past year, and you should know that there is nothing, *nothing*, I wouldn't do to see her happy." He made sure that Cheryl was looking him in the eye before he continued. "And that includes walking away. If she ever asked me to leave I'd go, if what waited on the other side was her happiness."

Something shifted in Cheryl's expression and she looked down. David waited. After a long breath of silence Cheryl looked up, a look on her face that reminded David of his own mother. "All that I want is what's best for her."

David nodded. "Me too. Sage is incredibly capable and stronger than I'll ever be, and there's not a doubt in my mind that she'll succeed in whatever she decides to do. I plan to stand by her side as she figures it all out, and if at any point she needs me, I'm going to be there for her. I'll be there, ready to reassure her that accepting my help is not a sign of weakness but of strength."

He thought about Sage, about the fact that she had a job and a path forward, one that she'd found all on her own. About the pride and excitement in her eyes when she talked about what was coming in the future. He thought about all of the times she said "we" when she talked about what came next, like there wasn't even a glimmer of doubt in her mind that David was a part of it. A part of her life.

There was one other thing he wanted to tell the mother of the woman who'd carved a place into his life and into the spot behind his ribs that sometimes felt like it might burst when they sat together on the couch lost in their own books. Or when they went to the Humphrey Center in the late hours before the building closed, just the two of them and a basketball, the sound of their teasing and laughter shattering the silence.

"Do you think I don't realize how lucky I am that she's decided that I'm worth it? That I'm worth the lectures and disapproval she's going to have to put up with because she's with me? An older man?" David shook his head. "I won't ever forget that."

Bells pealed out, signaling the top of the hour. David held Cheryl's gaze. Her mouth tightened for a moment and then relaxed. Her expression almost looked like resignation.

"We should go inside," David said, nodding toward the rush of people crowding the doors.

Cheryl nodded.

As he led the older woman through the crowd, he felt something in him loosen before clicking into place.

―――

It seemed fitting that they celebrate Sage at The Grove.

It had been Maggie's idea to congregate there. Probably

because she hadn't been able to get out of her shift, but hey, none of them were complaining.

David watched fondly as Sage threw her head back in laughter as she talked with her sister and Rebecca. She wore a dress that was green just like her name. It was flowy from her waist down and reached right above her knees. The top was tight against her skin, cut low enough in the front that it left the tan curve of the top of her breasts exposed. She looked beautiful, her outfit doing nothing to help his increasingly urgent need to get his girlfriend home and into bed as quickly as possible.

The gathered crowd was a mixture of his friends — well, *their* friends, now — and Maggie, Ms. Fogerty, Brinley, and Rohan, her boyfriend, representing Sage's side. David's mom had tried to come down for the party, but David had put the brakes on that idea. No matter how much his mom was begging to meet his girlfriend, he wouldn't take away from this moment in Sage's life.

"It all worked out for you in the end, didn't it?"

David cocked a brow at Chuck, who came to stand beside him. "I'd sure as hell say so."

"She's pretty fucking great," Chuck said, pointing his beer at Sage, who was now gesticulating wildly as she told a story.

David wasn't used to seeing her with painted nails, but found he was rather fond of the blue that Brinley had picked out. He couldn't wait to see her long fingers wrapped around his —

Chuck elbowed him in the side. "Get your head out of the gutter."

David opened his mouth to protest, but his friend rolled his eyes.

"Don't even try, man."

Relenting, David shrugged. "Wouldn't you if you had a woman like her?"

Chuck seemed to consider his question for a moment before shrugging. "Well, she's not exactly my type."

"Who's not your type?" Tommy sauntered up to the group, looking like an absolute tool in a pink button down and pressed khaki pants. He'd done something new to his hair, which was swooped over to one side of his head.

Chuck cast a quick glance over at him. "The comb over isn't working for you," he said, reaching out a hand and dislodging the hair from the tight hold of whatever product was holding it in place. "Stop trying to look like Keaton. You look just fine the way you are."

"Fuck off," Tommy muttered, trying to flatten his hair back down.

Sighing, Chuck grabbed Tommy by the shoulder. "Alright. Let's go to the bathroom and get that shit out of your hair. I promise I'll fix it."

David shook his head as he watched the two of them walk away.

A soft hand curled around his wrist. "Hi."

He turned to see Sage grinning up at him. Her eyes seemed greener than usual, maybe due to the sparkling copper on her eyelids or the glow of the string lights that hung from the oak trees above them.

"God, you look stunning." David leaned forward to press a quick kiss to her forehead, but was redirected by Sage, who used the tight grip of her fist on the front of his shirt to guide his mouth to hers.

His low groan was swallowed as her tongue pressed into his mouth. He met her in kind, and the crowd around them faded into the background as he kissed her. Her lips were perfectly cool against his and her tongue was hot and quick like she was trying to win.

It was the kind of kiss that left him ravenous for her.

When they broke apart, David let out a laugh.

She tilted her head to one side. "What?"

"I just keep thinking about that first night," David admitted, wrapping his arms around her lower back and pulling her body flush against his. "You were supposed to be my *'hop back on the bandwagon again'* hookup. A way to get out of a dry spell." He

shook his head, feeling a piece of hair flop forward onto his forehead. *Time to call Jordan about another haircut.* "I'd say that in the
end it worked out alright."

Sage's smirk widened. "And there I was just trying to find a
big man to take me for a ride on his big —"

David's eyes widened as he smacked a palm over her mouth.
"You are a goddamn menace," he whispered, pulling his hand
away just as her tongue darted out to lick him.

He knew her tricks.

"Come say hi to my mom," Sage said, ducking under his arm
and cuddling up against him.

David's fingers brushed the soft skin of her bare shoulder as
he took a long drink from his Corona. "She still scares me," he
admitted, even as Sage started pulling them both over to where
Keaton and Ms. Fogerty were locked in what looked like a very
intense conversation.

Sage rolled her eyes at him. "Man up, Hughes. She's a hippy;
she doesn't believe in violence."

Grumbling, David followed her, steeling himself for another
conversation with the mother of the woman he was uncondition-
ally obsessed with.

━━━

At midnight, David Hughes was regretting wearing the
formalwear that he'd thought was appropriate for attending his
girlfriend's graduation.

He was sweating in a way that was beyond socially acceptable,
a situation that wasn't at all helped by his girlfriend's body, which
was pressed flush against his as they danced to some alternative
song from the nineties that they somehow knew all of the
words to.

He tossed his head, fighting a losing battle against his hair. He
could reach a hand up to more effectively push it back, but he
didn't want to let go of his grip on Sage's hips.

He'd stopped after two beers, but he still felt drunk off of her and the music and the sweaty bodies of their friends surrounding them. Other bar patrons also occupied the small dancefloor, but their group had staked claim to the center.

It was the kind of night that left his face sore from laughter and his feet sore from dancing. He'd not only survived his conversation with Cheryl Fogerty, but had even gotten her telling stories about how Sage, as a four year old, had been determined to climb up onto their roof. While he wasn't sure he'd completely won her over yet, he no longer feared that his life was at risk. Not that he'd blamed her. Sage was a goddamn gift and deserved all of the love and protection in the world.

If he had to jump through hoops to prove that he was worthy of her then he would. No questions asked.

She was worth that and so much more.

CHAPTER 33
A REASON TO STAY
SAGE

The morning after graduating, after sleeping in, working out, and somehow fitting both of their tall bodies into Sage's shower, Sage and David walked hand-in-hand into the lobby of The Magnolia, the boutique hotel where Brinley, Rohan, and her mom were staying.

Passing through the brightly lit lobby that was painted a variety of greens with a few pink accents, they walked into the back patio restaurant. Wrought-iron tables with white tablecloths were arranged under a wooden pergola that was covered in blooming jasmine.

Brinley waved them over, looking put together as always in a floral dress and perfectly curled hair. Beside her, Rohan looked relaxed and at home in some sort of linen shirt that matched the orange in the flowers on her sister's dress.

It was disgustingly cute.

Her mom was also in a dress, with her graying blonde hair braided and twirled around her head and her tan skin more lined than Sage remembered. It was a rather harsh reminder that as she grew and moved forward with her life, her mother did too.

Sage exchanged hugs and greetings with her small, imperfect family — including Rohan, who had earned the honorary brother title simply by making her sister so fucking happy — and then sat down, watching with overwhelming fondness as David bent down to give her mom a warm hug.

"Wonderful party last night," her mom said as they all settled in. Her smile deepened the lines around her mouth. "Your friends are lovely, David."

David nodded, smiling easily. "I certainly think so, Ms. Fogerty."

Her mom scoffed. "Please call me Cheryl," she said, leaning over and patting David's hand. "My students call me Ms. Fogerty all day, and that's more than enough for me."

"I'll try," David replied, casting a quick smile over at Sage. She felt the firm grip of his hand on her thigh and she smiled back.

Their waiter arrived, and soon they were bouncing from topic to topic as they ate. Sage stole bacon from David's plate, and he ordered her another tea every time her mug got low.

It struck her just how much their lives were in rhythm. How months and months of friendship and proximity had built these little connections between them. When all of the small things added up, there was something solid and more real than she ever could have imagined. Something they had created together.

At some point David and Rohan excused themselves, probably to do something silly like argue over who was going to pick up the bill.

"Girls," her mom said, folding her hands onto the table in front of her and looking between her two daughters. "I just want to say how proud I am of both of you."

Neither of them responded. For Sage's part, she honestly didn't quite know what to say.

"After everything the two of you went through," her mom continued. "To see you both here, standing strong and steady with plans for your futures," she paused to wipe at one of her eyes. "It's all that a mother could ever want for her daughters."

Sage glanced over at Brinley, who was blinking furiously. She could already see the moisture gathered around her sister's eyes.

"Stop it, Mom," Brinley said, but there was no heat behind her words. Her mom reached out and poked Brinley on the nose, just like she'd done when they were little. Her sister's lower lip trembled, and she reached for a napkin, dabbing at her lower lash line.

"I know I was tough on you after your dad left. I didn't know how to handle my heartbreak, and I know that I gave both of you too much of my pain. I'm so, so sorry for that." A soft smile spread across her face. "But look at you two! After all of that, you both found men who care for, respect, and so obviously love you."

Sage let out a snort. "I'm not so sure about that."

The other two Fogerty women at the table shot her almost identical incredulous expressions.

"Of course he loves you," Brinley said, like it was an indisputable truth.

Her mom nodded. "That man is in love with you."

Sage looked between them and waved her hands, hoping to dismiss the topic entirely.

"What'd we miss?"

The three women looked up as David and Rohan approached the table. Both men were handsome in their own right, and Sage felt a wave of amusement at how well she and Brinley had done.

"We're all set," Rohan said, extending a hand to Brinley and helping her to her feet. He looked at her like she was the sun and the moon and maybe even the earth itself. Like she was *everything*.

Oh yeah. That man definitely *loved her.*

Sage stood up, watching as David circled around the table and offered her mom a hand. Her mom accepted his assistance before shooting a meaningful, eyebrow-raised glance at Sage.

She couldn't keep the smile from her face as she walked toward the front door of the hotel. They had a few hours before her mom, Brinley, and Rohan were heading to the airport, and they were planning on all going for a walk around King Street.

Sage hung back, slinging an arm over her mom's bony shoulder and taking a deep breath of her patchouli scent.

Her mom looked up at her with a sad smile. "You're not coming home, are you?"

"No, Mom." Sage let out a slow exhale, looking ahead to where David walked beside Brinley and Rohan. "But I promise I'll visit."

Her mom's smile brightened, and it seemed that all she needed was a small moment of sadness to mourn Sage's moving on. "You're happy here," she said, nodding at their surroundings, like somehow the brightly painted pink exterior wall and white trim around the windows encapsulated Charleston as a whole. "I can see it in your eyes. And that's all that I ever wanted for you, Sagey."

"Love you, Mom," Sage whispered, pressing a kiss to her mom's sun-warmed hair.

When they reached the street and started down the sidewalk, Sage found herself threading her fingers through David's, the skin of her palm meeting the skin of his. He leaned down and kissed her temple, the coarse hair of his beard tickling her skin.

Beside them, Brinley and Rohan walked hand in hand. "So what are your plans for the summer?" Brinley asked.

Sage squinted against the bright sun. "Bartending. Reading whatever the fuck I want." She bumped her shoulder against David's. "Hopefully dragging this one out to California for a visit."

She glanced up at him, catching the pleased smile on his face.

Brinley squealed. "Ooo yes! You guys have to come out. I'll get us a house on the beach."

"I always forget how rich you are," Sage said, kicking out a leg to knock against her sister's knee.

Snorting, Brinley nodded her chin toward Rohan. "You should see how much he makes."

"Most of it goes to student loans," her boyfriend protested.

"Meanwhile, I'll be here melting away in the humidity and working on my tan," Sage said. "Ah, I love to see my college degree hard at work."

"Don't forget about working on your teaching certificate," David added, squeezing her hand. "And running a few basketball camps."

Sage felt her cheeks flush. She should have been immune to David's compliments by now, but apparently her blush response was still as enthusiastic as ever. Glancing over at her sister, she saw Brinley smiling at her in that knowing, older sister '*I know better than you*' way that drove her crazy.

"What," Sage asked.

Brinley just shrugged, her expression almost smug. "I just never would have guessed that you'd be the one to stay in Charleston."

Sage subconsciously leaned into the solid body of the man who stood by her side. She thought of all of the things that Charleston had: Maggie and all of David's friends who at some point had become her own.

She thought about nachos and tots at The Grove and about the Southeastern gym. About magnolia trees and the long drive to Lake Murray.

And she thought about David. About mornings with him in the gym, about the flowers she found waiting on her table, about the apartment keys they'd exchanged a few weeks ago. She thought about Irish Spring and navy sheets and the fact that he refused to give back her t-shirt.

She thought about the way he had come to know her and she'd come to know him. And how that knowing had sunk in deep, leaving a warmth and contentment so full that sometimes it felt like her heart was going to beat out of her chest.

Sage inhaled deeply, the heat of the air gentle in her throat. "I never thought I'd have a reason to stay."

EPILOGUE
DAVID

"Alright guys. Wrap up with free-throws and then we're done."

The guys split up between the baskets, talking among themselves as they finished out practice. Jordan, now standing on the sideline with a whistle around his neck, walked with Monty, talking with him about an adjustment to his shot. To his credit, Monty listened as attentively to his old teammate and captain as he would have if it were David or Tim coaching him.

David took a deep breath, shoving his hands deep into his pockets, relishing the return to the gym after a long summer off from practicing and playing.

Beside him, Tim adjusted his glasses. "Today's the day?"

David swallowed against the lump in his throat. "Yep."

"Nervous?"

"Not at all," David said, letting out a laugh that definitely was pitched higher than normal. *Shit.*

Tim chuckled. "Don't be. You know she's crazy about you."

David grunted. "I wouldn't say that. It's more like I'm the lucky guy whose presence she tolerates."

"You're smarter than that, Hughes."

David shrugged, but he hoped Tim was right.

Once practice was wrapped up, David climbed into his car,

flipping on his music as he drove from campus over the river. He rolled the windows down, letting the slight cooling of the air as summer faded to autumn blow against his face.

He navigated the crowded streets until he came to Wagener Terrace, pulling out his phone and following the directions to Classical Academy of Charleston.

The school was nestled under tall trees, surrounded by groomed green fields. David followed a sidewalk toward the metal-sided gymnasium that was around the back of the main building. Even as he approached the door, he could hear the bright shriek of a whistle and the hollow bouncing of basketballs.

He pushed open the heavy metal door. The gymnasium was about as bare-bones as a space could be and still technically be considered a regulation court. The floor was vinyl tile that had seen better days, and the nets that hung from the two baskets were frayed and hanging on by a thread.

Wooden bleachers were pushed back against one of the walls, and a few folding metal chairs along the sideline were covered in discarded hoodies and gym bags.

And there, standing at center court with her hands on her hips and a whistle tucked into the corner of her mouth, was Sage Fogerty.

Her hair was pulled back into a ponytail — one much shorter than it had been just yesterday when he'd last seen her — and something pleasant thrummed in his chest when he saw that she was wearing one of his old crew neck sweatshirts.

"Hey," she called out, her voice commanding and loud enough to fill the entire room. "We're doing that again. I know that all of you want to be shooting threes out there like Steph Curry, but until you can make fifty lay-ups in a minute, you've got no business doing anything else."

The players — a scraggly bunch of high school boys who looked tiny in comparison to the college players he'd just left behind — hung onto her every word like she was the general of their army.

As soon as she blew her whistle they jumped into action, dividing into two groups and attacking the drill with a clumsy but earnest enthusiasm that made David smile.

He hung back until they finished, watching with absolute awe and affection as Sage coached, as she balanced encouragement with gentle criticism of their technique. How she commended effort and grit, while ignoring the teenage show-boating.

Her competence was breathtaking.

They wrapped up with a huddle, and then the kids dispersed to the sideline. David started walking out across the court, unwilling to wait any longer to hold his woman in his arms.

"Who's that guy?" David glanced over at one of the players, a tiny kid with a buzz cut and sticks for legs.

"Coach," another boy called out. "This guy your boyfriend or somethin'?"

Sage glanced up, that perfect twist to her mouth revealing the dimple in her pink cheeks as her eyes met his. Her green eyes danced with a giddy kind of happiness that felt like an achievement every time he saw it.

"Or something," she said, moving in David's direction. As she approached him, her smile grew. "What are you doing here?"

David opened his mouth to respond, but one of the kids shouted before he had a chance to speak.

"Does he know what a baller you are, Coach?"

David couldn't hold back his low chuckle as Sage cocked a brow at him. "I should probably remind him," she said, her voice soft enough that the players couldn't hear. Looking over David's shoulder, her eyes narrowed. "You boys get out of here. I don't want any emails from teachers about late homework. And eat your veggies tonight!"

Her command was met with a chorus of 'Yes ma'am's and 'Later, Coach's. David watched the fond smile teasing her mouth as she shook her head at them. "A bunch of children," she murmured, but he could hear the softness in her voice. Looking back at David, she poked him in the chest. "Not that I'm not happy to see you, but what are you doing here?"

David felt the nervousness that had churned in his gut for the past week rear its head again. But he forced himself to breathe, looking Sage in the eye and finding reassurance there that her presence never failed to provide. "I want to show you something," he said, reaching out and taking one of her hands in his. "If you're okay with that."

Curiosity sparked in her eyes, but she offered him an easy smile. "Of course," she replied.

His free hand reached up curled around the back of her neck, gently tugging on her ponytail. "You got a haircut."

Sage's cheeks flushed, a sight that still made David feel like the most powerful man in the world. "Rebecca did it this morning," she said, tugging the hair tie free and shaking it loose. It barely reached her shoulders.

"I love it." David smiled down at her. "It suits you."

They waited for a few minutes until the players were all picked up, and then David helped Sage pack away the team balls and close up the old gymnasium.

Soon enough they were in his car, driving south through downtown before heading back toward campus across the river. But they bypassed campus, instead driving slowly down the tree-lined residential streets.

Sage looked at their surroundings. "Are we going to Chuck's house?"

David smiled but shook his head. "Rebecca and Darius want to do dinner tomorrow."

"Mine or yours?"

"Yours," he said without hesitation. "Since we both know I'll be hovering and pouring your wine while you do the real work."

Sage snorted. "You really aren't that bad at cooking," she said, reaching across the console to rest a hand on his thigh. "That chicken you made last week was amazing."

"That doesn't count," David protested as he slowed down to turn onto another street. "I used a pre-made spice blend."

"Shut up," Sage teased. "It was delicious and you made it."

David gave a vague grunt in response before pulling into an empty driveway.

Shifting into park, David unfastened his seatbelt and looked over at Sage, who was looking at the home in front of them with a furrowed brow.

Suddenly her eyes widened and she whipped around to stare at him. "David," she breathed. "Is this…?"

David grinned. "Yeah, Lefty. It sure is."

Sage let out an excited squeal unlike any sound he'd ever heard her make and opened the door. "Can we go in?"

David fished into his pocket and pulled out the silver keyring.

Snatching the keys from his hand, Sage ran out into the front yard, laying a hand on the tall magnolia tree ringed with gray stones that matched the exterior walls of the old rambler.

David climbed out of the Bronco slowly, a wide, uncontrollable smile on his face as he watched her run up the front steps to the blue painted front door. He joined her just as she unlocked the door and walked inside.

She turned to him, rushing into his arms. A pleased hum vibrated his chest as he embraced her, pressing a kiss to the crown of her head. She looked up at him, and he felt the full weight of her beauty hit him right in the sternum. For a second, he forgot how to breathe. "Tell me everything," she said.

And so, with Sage tucked against his side, he did.

He showed her the original hardwood floors and the recently updated kitchen with a wide window over the sink that looked out to the backyard. He showed her the master bedroom and the bathroom that had been remodeled to have a deep tub and walk-in shower. He showed her the other two bedrooms, trying to be casual as he mentioned the possibilities for the space: offices, a library, maybe — *someday* — space for kids.

He made sure that they lingered in the back sunroom, a huge, brick-floored space with floor to ceiling windows. He might have mentioned how good the light would be for indoor plants more than once.

And then they went out into the backyard, where Sage gawked at the grand oaks that lined the yard with strands of moss hanging from the limbs, looking straight out of an advertisement for local tourism. David told her how maybe, just maybe, someone could put a vegetable garden in the back corner where there was plenty of sun.

"David," Sage said, after she'd pulled off her shoes and socks so that she could sink her bare toes into the grass. "You got your house, and it's perfect. So fucking perfect."

She went up on her tip-toes and kissed him, and David thought that nothing in the world could ever compare to kissing this woman in the backyard of his new home. A home that, hopefully, someday, he would share.

When they parted, David reached down and grabbed both of her hands, rubbing his thumbs over her smooth skin. He cleared his throat. "Someday," he began, willing his voice to be steady. "When — and if — you're ready, I'd love it if you lived here with me." He ran his tongue along his upper lip, suddenly aware of how dry his mouth was. "When I picked this place I was thinking about you. It's as much yours as it is mine. And if you want a room to be all yours, so that when I drive you nuts or say something stupid you can get some space from me, then it's done. I just," he inhaled slowly, trying to collect himself. "I love you, Sage. And every second since you walked into my life has been more than I ever dreamed life could be."

Sage looked up at him, and he saw so much in her eyes that he thought he might crumble if it wasn't for her hands wrapped up in his. "And what would that look like? Us living together?"

"How would *you* want it to look?" He didn't want to come on too strong. He wanted to give her the space to say no if it felt too soon.

Her expression softened. "I'd put up at least five bird feeders out here just to watch you scowl," she began.

David couldn't help the indignant scoff that burst from him. "Hey!"

But Sage wasn't finished. "We'd put a couch that was long enough for both of us in the sunroom, and we'd read there together every night. And I'd put a garden over there, and even though you'd be clueless you'd offer to help, because that's just who you are. And we'd put a nice hoop up in the driveway. We'd soak up as much of the summer as we could together because we'll always be crazy busy during the season. But we'd have this," she said, looking at their surroundings. "And, no matter what happens on the court, win or lose, we'd always come home to each other." Her expression grew serious, the green of her eyes somehow more potent when surrounded by the vibrance of the grass and the myrtles along the fence. "I always assumed that there was a cost to letting someone share my life. That I'd have to carve out more and more of myself until there was nothing left. But right now? Right now I feel whole, like I could take on the entire fucking world, David. I'm not scared of building a life with you. I'm here and I'm ready to choose this, with you, because it's the life that I want."

David felt his throat tighten with emotion. "Sounds good to me, Lefty."

"Do you feel ready?"

David blinked. "To live with you?"

She nodded, drawing her lower lip between her teeth.

"Yeah, Sage. I've never been more ready."

A smile spread over her face, and David felt his body catch flame. "Let's fucking do it," she said, rocking forward onto the balls of her feet and nudging his chest with her head. Untangling their hands, she wrapped her arms around him. He felt the rise and fall of her chest and the soft puffs of breath through the thin material of his t-shirt.

She was there and he was hers.

"David?"

"Hm?"

"Love you too." Her voice was muffled and soft, the words whispered into his chest, where they melted straight through his skin and into his heart.

He tilted her head up and kissed her, pouring the weight of every moment they'd shared into the pull of his lips against hers.

She broke away first, her panting breaths soft and warm. "And David," she whispered against the stubble on his chin.

"Yeah, Lefty?"

"I'm paying you rent."

David let out a low laugh. "Fine."

"And we're going to need more plants."

"Done."

"And -"

David interrupted her, pressing another kiss to her mouth. "Whatever you need, Lefty." He kissed the tip of her nose, her skin cool and soft against his lips. "How about we celebrate at The Grove?"

Sage smiled. "Nachos?"

"And tots," David said softly. "Don't forget about the tots."

Sage's eyes dropped to his mouth. "And after the tots?"

David chuckled. "Want to come home with me and start packing...among other things?"

Her smile was bright and lit up her entire face. "Yeah, David. I want that."

ACKNOWLEDGMENTS

Throwing words onto paper is just the beginning of writing a book. In my case, the words were supported by two dear friends, Allison Bugbee and Zac Caputo, who sacrificed their time and attention to answering my phone calls and letting me talk through the in's and out's of David and Sage's story.

Editing support also falls on the shoulders of Allison and Zac, with the additional expertise of Bailey Olderog, who was quick to come in with writing conventions and general hyping of my madness. Without these people volunteering their eyes, this story truly wouldn't be here. Thank you, you three, for showing up for me.

To Cecelia and Tia — thank you for your early thoughts on the story! Your encouragement fueled the push to get the draft out there, and I thank you from the bottom of my heart.

To Ashlyn, Laura, and miiisterbear — you're the reason I had the courage to do this.

I wouldn't be here without the HP fanfic community, especially the Dramione fandom (even though I've only given you one Dramione fic — sorry). Thank you all for showing up and cheering me on.

And to my John Dear, who doesn't get it but is the first to brag about my writing. Thank you, love. Your support means everything to me.

Lastly, to the people who stuck around this far — THANK YOU! My heart overflows with gratitude for you.

ABOUT THE AUTHOR

Taylor E Weston is an emerging author of contemporary romance novels that follow real, flawed people navigating their way through love and the world. Her stories are people-centric, and include a realistic amount of eating and making out.

She lives in Santa Fe, NM with her husband, son, and fifteen chickens. When she isn't writing or reading, you can find her traipsing around her garden in rubber boots, cooking with bacon, or playing trucks with her son.

Connect with Taylor at www.tayloreweston.com.

Made in the USA
Middletown, DE
04 February 2025

70323375R10220